D0245699

The Wartime Midwives

DAISY STYLES

PENGUIN BOOKS

PENGUIN BOOKS

UK | USA | Canada | Ireland | Australia
India | New Zealand | South Africa

Penguin Books is part of the Penguin Random House group of companies
whose addresses can be found at global.penguinrandomhouse.com.

First published 2019
003

Copyright © Daisy Styles, 2019

The moral right of the author has been asserted

Set in 12.5/14.75 pt Garamond MT Std
Typeset by Jouve (UK), Milton Keynes
Printed and bound in Great Britain by Clays Ltd, Elcograf S.p.A.

A CIP catalogue record for this book is available from the British Library

ISBN: 978–1–405–93619–4

www.greenpenguin.co.uk

MIX
Paper from
responsible sources
FSC® C018179

Penguin Random House is committed to a
sustainable future for our business, our readers
and our planet. This book is made from Forest
Stewardship Council® certified paper.

For my son, Gabriel

1. Mary Vale

On a blustery May morning, with the wind rattling the windows of the nurses' boarding house of Mary Vale Hall, Ada Dale struggled as always to confine her long golden-auburn curls under her starched white cap. Knowing she'd get a ticking off from Matron if she didn't present herself without a hair out of place, she stopped in the hall to check her appearance in an unsatisfactory small mirror. Throwing her navy-blue cape around her shoulders, Ada hurried along the long, echoing corridor that connected Mary Vale Mother and Baby Home to the convent of the Sisters of the Holy Mother, where she boarded in the wing specifically set aside for staff accommodation. Passing the beautiful golden-and-blue statue of Our Lady of the Sea, Ada automatically crossed herself. Though brought up a Protestant in her home town of Sheffield, Ada had grown to respect the customs and practices of the Catholic Church during her stay at Mary Vale; if you spent as much time with nuns as Ada did, one inevitably picked up certain customs, and this was just one of them.

Ada checked her fob watch and saw that she had a few minutes to spare, and, having always been drawn to the outdoors, she pushed open the heavy front door and walked out into the large garden that wrapped itself around the big old, multi-gabled, redbrick house. Mary Vale had originally been built by the parish as a place for the destitute and insane but was now used as a refuge for unmarried pregnant women and their babies.

Standing in the garden, Ada's roving gaze landed on Mary Vale's attic windows; she always spared a thought for the poor, sad souls who'd been confined to those high, dark rooms so long ago – locked away after conceiving a child out of wedlock. She'd read in Mary Vale's old records of rejected spouses, women who'd been committed to the asylum, condemned on some trumped-up charge to a brutal and unjust internment so that their husbands could claim their inheritance. Thinking of the women presently occupying the Home, Ada was sure that Mary Vale was a far happier place these days.

'Though,' she thought as she breathed in and filled her lungs with fresh air, 'the place regularly echoes with the cries of heartbroken mothers unable to keep their babies.'

Ada again checked the time and quickly followed the garden path that led across a railway track and on to the beach. Standing buffeted by the stiff spring breeze, she admired the breath-taking, sweeping view of Morecambe Bay before her, while behind her ranged the soft, swelling hills that steadily rose to meet the lower fells of the Lake District. Ada marvelled that the view was never the same, though the landscape remained constant: the ever-changing light and shifting tides coloured it differently every day. On one such as this, a passionate fell-walker like Ada itched to stride out and ascend to the mountaintops.

'Wait until you're next off-duty,' she firmly told herself.

Clutching on to her nurse's cap, which was in serious danger of being blown into the Irish Sea, she retraced her steps into Mary Vale.

As she hurried through the maternity ward, Ada passed several girls who were busy about their morning chores. When she'd arrived at the Home, just over a year ago, Ada had been shocked to see heavily pregnant women mopping, scrubbing, polishing and lugging heavy buckets of coal and laundry. She'd been brave – or foolish – enough to query this with Matron, who had coldly pointed out that the expectant mothers were obliged to help with the upkeep of the Home. Matron had added that cleanliness was of the utmost priority in an environment where infection could quickly result in death. But Ada sensed it was more a case of Matron wanting to see these 'fallen women' atone for their sins.

Passing a sweating girl straining to clean the high windows that ran the length of the maternity ward, Ada called out, 'Be careful! Shall I fetch you a ladder before you do yourself a serious injury?'

'No, thanks, Sister Ada – I can't stand heights,' the grinning girl called back.

Ada shook her head; she didn't know who was the more stubborn: Matron or the girls themselves. Ada washed her hands, then knotted a long apron around her waist and entered the delivery room, where she heard a young girl's screams; she knew these would alarm the other girls nervously awaiting the birth of their own babies, so she closed the door firmly behind her to reduce the noise. Ada turned to the midwife in charge.

'Morning, Sister Ann,' she said with a warm smile, eager to do what she could to help.

Sister Ann, Ada's closest friend and colleague, smiled warmly back before quickly saying, 'Good to see you,

Ada – could you open the window? I think Shirley here would appreciate some fresh air.'

Ada opened the window as wide as it would go, grateful for the salty sea breeze that replaced the hot, foetid air in the room. Sister Ann continued bathing her patient's clammy forehead as she prepared her for her next contraction.

The small, skinny girl lying on the bed looked more like twelve than her actual age of fifteen. Her dull, brown, shoulder-length hair was presently matted with sweat and her brown eyes, large in her thin, pinched face, were full of fear and dread. Panicking, she cried out, 'Sister Ann, help me, there's another one coming!'

'Relax, Shirley, dear, you're doing fine,' Sister Ann said gently. 'Let's remember all those breathing exercises we did in the fitness classes.'

'I can't remember owt!' the frightened girl shouted. 'It hurts too bloody much.'

Seeing the girl's tender, pale belly rising and tightening, the nun gripped her sweaty hand. 'Let me talk you through it,' Sister Ann said patiently. 'Come on, Shirley, breathe with it . . .'

'It 'urts, Sister!' the grunting girl shouted again. 'It 'urts like 'ell!'

'I know,' Sister Ann soothed. 'Try not to tense, lovie, breathe in.' Eased by the softness of the nun's voice and trusting in her implicitly, Shirley calmed her breathing and exhaled slowly and steadily. 'Good girl!' Sister Ann exclaimed. 'That's much better – now relax and get ready for the next one,' she advised.

Confident there was no better midwife in the whole of the North-West than Sister Ann, Ada busied herself replenishing the water jug so Sister Ann could offer Shirley regular small sips of water. As her colleague continued to help Shirley with her breathing, Ada checked the baby's foetal heart with her stethoscope; then she quickly monitored the girl's blood pressure and heart rate, both of which had risen alarmingly, she noted, as she examined the patient's chart clipped to the end of the bed.

'Her blood pressure's a bit raised, which can't be good for baby,' Ada whispered to Sister Ann.

Sister Ann nodded in agreement before she whispered back, 'I was holding off on the gas and air.'

'Are you sure?' Ada muttered. 'It looks like she needs it.'

Sister Ann relented, and the two women did their best to relieve Shirley's pain, which was lessened by the gas and air, but it was nevertheless a long, gruelling morning for both patient and staff.

'Poor lamb,' Sister Ann murmured to Ada as Shirley moaned and writhed on the bed.

'She's barely more than a child herself,' Ada murmured back, as again she checked the foetal heartbeat. 'The baby's fine, thank God.'

'I only wish I could say the same for Shirley,' Sister Ann said as she reapplied a cold, damp flannel to her patient's forehead.

'There, there, it'll soon be over with,' Ada soothed as Shirley flinched and another contraction started.

It turned out to be a tough delivery for the nervous fifteen-year-old, who ripped badly during the birth and lost a lot of blood too. Groggy from the drug she'd inhaled, the new mother hardly seemed aware of the scrawny little girl she'd at long last brought into the world. After gently cleaning the baby and wrapping her in a warm shawl, Sister Ann handed her to Shirley.

'She's perfect,' the nun assured her.

Shirley drowsily managed to summon the energy to touch her daughter's tiny pink fingers. 'She looks like a little dolly,' she murmured.

Ada, who was sterilizing instruments in order to stitch Shirley's wound, added softly, 'She's lovely.'

She couldn't fail to notice the lack of response from the fretful patient, who suddenly thrust the child back at Sister Ann.

'I don't want her, Sister!' she wailed, her face racked with distress. 'I told you before – I don't want her!'

Aware that Shirley had opted for an adoption – after all, what choice did she really have? – Ada and Sister Ann didn't push the matter. Instead the nun gently settled the child in a small bassinet while Ada got on with stitching Shirley, who made things ten times worse for herself by screaming and wriggling throughout the procedure. Ada, who wished the relaxing effects of gas and air hadn't worn off quite so quickly, looked at the girl and frowned.

'Shirley, dear, it would be far less painful if you could just lie still till I've finished – only two more stitches to go,' she added reassuringly.

'TWO!' Shirley loudly protested.

Afraid that she might have to spend the next half-hour inserting two stitches, Ada spoke firmly. 'Grip the bed-head tightly and slowly count to twenty.'

Mercifully, the touch of cold metal and the steady, rhythmic chanting of numbers had a calming effect on

Shirley; though she continued to scream the place down, she nevertheless lay still enough for Ada to finish her task.

'Well done, sweetheart,' Ada said, as she laid the stainless-steel kidney bowl on the bedside table. 'Now how about a nice hot cup of tea?' she asked briskly, and turned to her patient, who, exhausted by her ordeal, was already slumped against her pillows fast asleep.

In the nursery Sister Ann introduced the new arrival to the girls on the bottle-feeding rota.

'Shirley's daughter,' she announced as she laid the sleeping child in a small, empty, white canvas cot at the end of a long row of cots all containing mewling infants awaiting their turn to be fed.

'Heavens above, she's tiny!' a girl changing a howling baby's nappy exclaimed.

'She can't weigh more than two bags of sugar!' another gasped. 'How's Shirley?' she quickly added.

Not wishing to go into graphic detail, Sister Ann simply said, 'Exhausted, and relieved it's all over with.'

'Poor kid,' one of the girls murmured sympathetically.

Leaving Shirley peacefully sleeping with screens around her, Ada got on with the job of tidying up the delivery room. After sterilizing all the instruments, she swabbed down the delivery table with a mixture of hot water and disinfectant, then loaded the stained and bloody sheets into a laundry bag. As she worked, Ada wondered (for possibly the hundredth time) how many of the girls who arrived at Mary Vale didn't even know how they'd got pregnant. It seemed ridiculous that in 1939 a young woman could be ignorant of the facts of life. What were the girls' mothers thinking? It was their moral responsibility to educate their daughters. Judging from the stories she'd been told, most of the mothers shirked their duty because it was too embarrassing to go into the messy physical details.

'At least when they leave Mary Vale, they know for sure where babies come from,' Ada thought sadly.

Poor little Shirley, who had been repeatedly raped by her stepfather, certainly knew the brutal facts of life. 'What on earth would the poor kid do when she left the Hall?' Ada fretted. She couldn't go home and risk being raped again; she needed protecting, not abandoning. But where was the money to come from if Shirley stayed on longer than was usual?

Ada was familiar with the workings of the Home and how it stayed financially afloat, providing privacy and shelter for rich and poor women alike. The richer girls with adequate funds to pay for their stay were charged according to their family's income or savings, while the poorer girls, who made up the majority of the Home's residents, were dependent on the convent's charitable trust to provide the shortfall, offering them places at a reduced rate or, in exceptional circumstances, like poor Shirley's, an entirely free place.

In most cases the pregnant women arrived when they began to show, so their stay might begin approximately four to five months before their due date; however, there were exceptions. Nancy Wheelan, a recent arrival, was a case in point. Though her baby wasn't due until the autumn, her outraged father, desperate to hide his sinful daughter away from decent, upright folk, had spent most of his savings on securing Nancy a place at Mary Vale until she'd given birth.

Once their babies were born, the mothers were expected to leave within a month to six weeks after their delivery. Some bolted as soon as they'd been signed off by the Home's resident obstetrician, Dr Jones. But others clung on, dreading the moment when they would be forced to hand their child over for adoption. A few fortunate women left with their child in their arms; Shirley certainly wouldn't be one of them, Ada thought, as she recalled how adamant Shirley had been about having her baby adopted, which everybody agreed was probably for the best for both mother and daughter.

The days when mothers had to say a final goodbye to their babies were always difficult, but Sister Ann, a saint in many respects, had a gift from God when it came to comforting the babies who would remain at Mary Vale until they were adopted. Some of them may have known a brief spell of intense maternal love as they were nursed by their birth mother; others may not. In the end, they all shared the same loss: their mothers had gone. The girls working in the nursery (most of them awaiting their own delivery) tried everything in their power to comfort the babies they felt sorry for, but it was Sister Ann, walking up and down the ward, rocking the babies in her arms until they finally slept, who truly soothed them best.

'Sleep heals and memories recede,' the nun told Ada, whose bright eyes filled with tears.

'How do you know that, Sister?' she asked.

'From their eyes,' the nun replied. 'Babies are no different from puppies,' she explained with a smile. 'They know when they're loved.'

Between them, Ward Sister Ada and Sister Ann handled the practical issues of caring for the babies in the nursery and their patients on the post- and ante-natal wards. One of the conditions of acceptance into Mary Vale was that all the women awaiting their delivery helped with the duty rotas, which went virtually around the clock and were drawn up every week by Sister Ann and Matron. The hospital was a permanent hub of activity and could function efficiently and hygienically only with the assistance of the residents. While a team of girls bottle-fed the babies in the nursery every four hours, another team in the prep room would be busy preparing the dried-milk mixture for the next feeds and sterilizing all the bottles and teats in boiling water. In the sluice room dirty terry-towelling nappies soaking in buckets of a bleach solution had to be hand-rinsed before they could be taken to the laundry.

Though only twenty-six, Ada had worked in busy hospitals in Leeds, Sheffield and Manchester after she'd qualified as a state-registered nurse. An ambitious and dedicated nurse, Ada had had little time for romance during her training; she always seemed to be working long, gruelling shifts or preparing for yet another nursing qualification. However, a girl with Ada's natural beauty couldn't go unrecognized for long. Stunned by her bright, sparkling blue eyes and abundance of luxuriously long, flame-coloured hair that forever escaped her nurse's cap, trainee doctors would make detours along the winding hospital corridors to track Ada down. Though she enjoyed their company and laughed easily at their flirtatious jokes, Ada had never been interested enough to accept any of their invitations to the cinema or the local dancehall. Not that Ada didn't like dancing – she simply adored it! But she preferred dancing the jitterbug and the jive with her girl-friends to being clasped in a stranger's arms throughout the length of a steamy foxtrot.

It was at the local palais that Ada had first met Brian, a handsome young musician who toured the country play-ing with a swing band. Catching sight of him on stage, swinging his hips as he played the trumpet with the glit-tering dancehall lights accentuating his sharp, high cheek-bones and the swoop of silky black hair that fell over his high forehead, Ada's pulse quickened. He certainly didn't miss the long-legged, shapely girl in a clinging red crêpe dress dancing to the strains of 'Little Brown Jug' the band were playing out. During one of the group's breaks Brian sought out Ada and politely asked if he could buy her a drink. Enchanted by her wide smile and perfect, even white teeth, Brian could barely drag his eyes away from her, and he begged to see her the next time he was in town. It was an ideal arrangement as far as Ada was concerned; she could continue concentrating on her career while still enjoying the company of broad-chested, handsome Brian whenever he showed up in Manchester. Unfortunately she never discovered the true depths of her affection for him, as shortly after their fifth meeting Ada was told (from another member of the band, jealous of Brian's suc-cess with the best-looking girl in the ballroom) that Brian was, in fact, engaged to be married.

Ada's immediate reaction had been deep embarrassment: to think she'd been drinking and chatting with an engaged man in front of the band members, who probably knew his fiancée. How duplicitous of him! To flirt and kiss her in public when he had a girl waiting for him at home. Ada didn't stoop so low as to have a row with two-faced Brian, or even to demand an apology; men like him weren't worth it, she decided. Instead she simply turned her back on red-faced Brian, walked out of the dancehall and made sure she never went back there again if his swing band was booked to play.

The experience of being duped and shamed left Ada cautious; realizing that, unlike most of her friends, she was in no rush to start courting, Ada threw all her time and energy into her work even more than before, and she loved it with an increasing passion. Competent, cool and compassionate, she'd worked her way up the career ladder, gaining an extra qualification in midwifery. It was her interest in obstetrics that had driven Ada – by then a respected and popular ward sister at Manchester Royal Infirmary – to apply for a senior nursing post at the Mary Vale Mother and Baby Home. When interviewed by Matron, Sister Ann, the convent's Reverend Mother and Sir Percival, the chairman of the Home's Board of Governors, Ada had shown such passion and commitment to her work that she'd been offered the job right there and then.

Ada had been sad to leave Manchester and the nurses' home where she'd made so many good friends; she knew she'd miss the buzz of the busy city dominated by cotton mills, whose belching factory chimneys regularly turned the air black and sooty. Nevertheless, through all the tearful farewells, Ada had no doubt about her move to Grange: something drew her to Mary Vale, where she knew she could provide needy women with expert nursing care. During her working life Ada had come across many so-called 'shamed' young women whom she'd seen dragged into hospital to give birth and then abandoned by their families. It had shocked and saddened her when later some of the same unfortunate women, who'd been working the streets of the city as prostitutes in order to survive, had returned to the hospital for treatment for syphilis or gonorrhoea. There had to be a better way to treat pregnant women who'd got into trouble, brave-hearted Ada had decided, and that was now her mission.

When Ada had arrived at Mary Vale, she found to her joy and relief that she would be working alongside similar, like-minded women: Sister Ann and the Reverend Mother had given their lives over to helping girls outcast by society. Ada guessed that Sister Ann was a good ten years her senior, though it was difficult to judge the nun's age, not just because she wore a wimple that covered her hair, but because of her completely clear complexion and serene smile that lent a sweet innocence to her face.

As their friendship developed, Ada learnt that Sister Ann had studied midwifery in Bradford, after which she had followed her vocation and joined the Sisters of the Holy Mother in the convent attached to Mary Vale Home. Initially daunted at the thought of working with a nun, Ada soon discovered what a fine professional Sister Ann was; they complemented each other with their different skills and their vastly different life experiences. Ada had more advanced technical skills, while Sister Ann was more nurturing and intuitive; she was also, as Ada grew to find out, hilariously funny and a great mimic. Her take-offs of bumbling Dr Jones and bossy Matron had Ada in stitches, and, after a flying visit from grandiose Sir Percival, Ann stuck out her chest and strode about the sluice room in exactly the same pompous manner as Sir Percival.

'Stop! Please stop before I die of laughter,' Ada implored, with tears streaming down her face.

After they'd both got their breath back, Ada managed to speak.

'You're an amazing impersonator – where did you learn to do that, Sister?'

'Mi dad worked down the pit but at the weekend he'd earn a bit of extra cash by doing stand-up acts in Oldham's working men's clubs; he was a bit of a local legend,' she added with a proud smile. 'Sadly, he died when I was a teenager.'

'But he passed on to you his gift of making people laugh,' Ada said fondly.

'Indeed,' Sister Ann agreed. 'You know, it was a serious dilemma for me when it came to deciding between a vocation in the Church or a life of entertaining working-class folk in pubs!' she joked.

'I'm glad you decided on God,' Ada replied.

'Me too,' the nun agreed. 'I don't know where I'd be without Him.'

After finishing her chores in the sluice room, Ada went to check on the girls feeding in the noisy nursery, where babies were waking up from their naps eager for their bottle. Ada immediately picked up Shirley's mewling baby, and, after settling her comfortably in the crook of her arm, sat down and tried to feed her. When the fretful child resisted the bottle, Ada put it aside and gently rocked her back and forth, softly singing until she drifted off to sleep. The peace of the moment was disturbed by the distinctly recognizable sharp click-click of Matron's approaching feet.

Everybody stiffened. Matron Maud Harding, a tall, whip-cord thin woman with dark, greying hair and an imperious expression, was a proud woman who had trained on the Western Front in the First World War; the toughness she'd developed there continued to this day. Where Sister Ann was a ministering angel and Ada a wonderful nurse, Matron was a vengeful tyrant who made sure her patients were regularly reminded of their sins of the flesh.

'Here she comes,' a girl close by muttered under her breath. 'And, from the look on her face, she's on the war path.'

Matron peered at the sleeping baby cradled in Ada's arms, wrinkling her nose as if she were staring at something unpleasant.

'Shirley's?'

'Yes,' Ada replied, as she laid a protective hand on the slumbering child.

'Good, that'll free up a bed in the pre-natal ward,' Matron said shortly.

Lowering her voice so that she wouldn't be overheard by the girls around her, Ada spoke firmly. 'Shirley will need rest in the post-natal ward; she's lost a great deal of blood.'

Ignoring Ada, Matron continued to stare disapprovingly at Shirley's small, frail daughter. 'It will be difficult to place such a feeble-looking specimen,' she sniffed.

Though bristling with indignation, Ada maintained the same low voice. 'The child had some difficulty breathing to start with, but she's fine now,' she said defensively, before adding, 'I'm sure Father Benedict will have no trouble finding a home for her; he has a natural gift for matching babies with the right families.'

Yet again Matron ignored her comment, brusquely turning to the girls. 'Who was responsible for polishing the staircase in the entrance hall this morning?'

'Nancy Wheelan,' one of the girls informed her.

Matron shook her head. 'I should have known,' she said. 'Where is the hopeless child?'

'She went for a lie-down after we had our dinner,' another girl volunteered.

'What does she think this is?' Matron scoffed. 'A five-star hotel?'

With her black brogues click-clacking on the highly polished wooden floor, Matron walked away, leaving the girls sighing with relief at her departure.

'If it was one of the posh girls who was having a lie-down, Matron wouldn't be complaining,' a bold girl whispered behind Matron's ram-rod-straight back.

Her neighbour snorted as she winded the child she'd just finished feeding. 'Snobby old bitch! She always prefers the ones with the money!' Rolling her eyes melodramatically, she added, 'God help poor Nancy when the old bat tracks her down.'

2. The Prettiest Nippy in Manchester!

Carrying a loaded tray of soup of the day, grilled kidneys and green beans, Emily Todd made her way across the Lyons Corner House café in Manchester city centre, where just about every person present noted the sexy sway of her shapely bottom and the swell of her chest, emphasized by her trim waist. Radiating a charming smile, Emily transfixed almost every male in the room.

'There you are, Mr Carter,' she said as she set the food before one of her many devoted customers. 'Piping hot, just as you like it.'

Cleverly circumnavigating Mr Carter's big outstretched hands, which had more than once landed where they shouldn't, Emily placed the contents of her tray on the table, squirming with the knowledge that Mr Carter would be ogling the edges of her lacy brassiere as she bent forwards.

'Thank you, thank you so much,' Mr Carter jabbered like a grateful chimpanzee.

'I'll be back for your pudding order,' Emily promised. 'And my tip too,' she thought to herself. 'I'll be needing every extra penny I can get hold of from now on.

Tearing his mesmerized eyes from Emily, Mr Carter gave a yearning sigh before dipping a spoon into his vegetable soup. Emily took orders from two middle-aged women in dowdy hats, who stared disapprovingly at her thick, mahogany-brown hair, which always escaped from the confines of her lacy nippy's cap. A noisy family flagged her down for tea and toast, while Mr Carter ate his food and waited expectantly for her return, an eager smile on his face.

Nobody could have guessed that Emily, with a welcoming word for all her customers and a bright smile plastered on her face, was hiding inner turmoil. For the news she had been fearing had been confirmed that very morning by her doctor: she was pregnant. As she waltzed in and out of the kitchen trying her best to ignore her rising panic, the only thoughts in Emily's head were: 'What on earth am I going to do; and where in God's name is George?' Tall, handsome, brave, bold Squadron Leader Holden, her George whom she'd been in love with since he'd first walked into her café and ordered lunch. Smiling softly, she allowed herself a moment to remember. She'd all but swooned at the sight of him, sitting on a spindly chair wearing his smart new blue RAF uniform, casually smoking a Senior Service cigarette while being dazed by Emily's deep blue eyes and pouting red lips. Unable to take her eyes off him, Emily had blushed as she remembered she was supposed to take his order.

'What can I get you, Sir?'

'What do you suggest?' he had said, grinning flirtatiously.

Trying to keep her face straight, Emily had suggested the dish of the day,

'Rissoles!' she'd exclaimed, which had caused both of them to collapse with laughter.

That had been a year ago; and since then Emily and George had met up whenever they had a free moment and George could get away from RAF Padgate in Warrington, where he was stationed. They'd both struggled to control their growing passion, but eventually there had come a point when their need for each other licked through them like a red-hot flame, consuming sense and reason. Lying in George's arms, Emily had had no regrets; their love-making had felt as natural as breathing. Now she was entirely his and one day soon they planned to get married. They'd continued to have sex regularly, always taking care to use precautions – although Emily recalled shakily the one night when George had discovered that the condom he'd used had split.

Emily had tried to ease her concerns, but there was no avoiding the fact that she'd missed a period, as luck would have it during a time that George's squadron had been ordered to stay on their base and therefore he couldn't see her. He'd written an urgent letter to Emily a few months ago, telling her that they couldn't meet until restrictions were lifted.

'With all the news coming from Europe, Hitler's latest antics with the Czechs, and us trying to keep the Poles happy, we're on high alert. I'm so sorry, my darling, you're constantly in my thoughts, I miss your lovely face so much. I hope you are missing me as much as I'm missing you?'

And that was the last Emily had heard from her beloved. Now, her condition confirmed, she desperately needed to talk to George; they must marry. She knew he loved her – of that she had no doubt – but how would he take the news of a child? As time passed, Emily had begun to seriously worry about George. She'd immediately replied to his letter telling her of their orders to remain on the base, but she'd not heard anything back since. WHY hadn't he got in touch? Was he all right? Was he even still at Padgate? For all she knew, he could already have been moved. The forces were famously tight-lipped about imparting any information; government propaganda posters everywhere declared LOOSE LIPS SINK SHIPS! BE LIKE DAD — KEEP MUM! But now she was more than worried; she was in trouble. Desperate for advice and comfort, and having to face the fact that, for now, George was out of reach, Emily decided to confide in her closest friend at work: Ivy. When she finally had a break, she found the older woman chain-smoking in the staff canteen.

'Have you got five minutes?' Emily asked, as she settled down on the chair beside Ivy, who offered Emily a Woodbine. 'You look in need of a fag.'

Formerly a heavy smoker, Emily shook her head: since she'd fallen pregnant, she couldn't abide the smell of tobacco. 'I'm pregnant,' she said.

Ivy listened attentively to Emily's outpourings before she asked, 'When did you find out for sure?'

'The doctor confirmed it this morning,' Emily whispered, her face sheet-white.

Ivy pursed her lips. 'Have you had a chance to think what you're going to do, lovie?'

'I've been thinking of nothing else,' Emily blurted out. 'I'm going round and round in circles,' she tearfully confessed.

'Do you need to get rid of it?' Ivy asked bluntly.

The idea of an abortion hadn't even crossed Emily's mind, but instinctively she knew this wasn't for her. She and George loved each other, and the plans they'd made for a future life together always involved having children of their own. Emily was certain George would want her to keep his child as much as she now knew for sure she did. It would all be all right, once she had got hold of him.

'I know George would want me to keep it,' she answered with absolute conviction.

'Has he told you that?' Ivy asked.

Feeling like a fool, Emily muttered a feeble, 'No, he doesn't know yet.'

Ivy looked directly at her. 'You haven't told him?' she gasped.

Emily's shoulders drooped as she shook her head, and, mumbling self-consciously, she quickly added, 'Like I said, I only found out for sure this morning.'

'Then you somehow need to break the news soon,' Ivy said sharply. 'If you want to keep it, he needs to know.'

With fear building up inside her, Emily confessed that she hadn't heard from George in weeks. 'He hasn't had any leave at all or been allowed off the base,' she explained. 'He might not even be in the country for all I know,' she added despairingly.

Looking concerned, Ivy said urgently, 'You *must* write to him immediately, God help you if he's been posted abroad: with all the trouble brewing in Europe, his squadron could have been sent anywhere. But if he's still in the country, he'll get your letter and he'll find a way to contact you if he loves you as much as you say he does.'

Emily's lovely blue eyes overflowed with tears. 'Oh, Ivy! I *know* George would make contact if he could – he loves me, he'd never let me down,' she cried.

Ivy, a hard-headed realist, stubbed out her cigarette in the ashtray before she replied, 'He might well love you, Em, but that's not necessarily going to help you if he's not even in the country to get your message.' Looking Emily straight in the eye, she asked, 'You just have to hope he's still on the base.'

A tearful Emily frantically nodded her head in agreement with Ivy.

'And if not,' Ivy continued, 'would your family support you through a pregnancy?'

A flush of embarrassment suffused Emily's distressed face. 'Never!' she exclaimed. 'They'll more than likely disown me.'

'How about his family?' Ivy continued.

'They're very nice,' Emily told her. 'Though I've only met them once.'

Emily's mind flashed back to the winter, when she'd briefly met Mr and Mrs Holden in a pub in Piccadilly. Though Emily had been shy about being introduced to his parents, George was determined.

'I want them to know what a wonderful girlfriend I have,' he announced proudly. 'Em, I'm their only child; they hate being excluded from my life. I know they'll love you to bits.'

And it had been a very pleasant meeting – they'd all got on like a house on fire – but that had been before she was pregnant and before George had disappeared off the radar.

'Do you know where they live?' Ivy inquired.

'In Chester,' Emily answered feebly.

'Nothing more than that? No address, phone number?'

Emily blushed. 'I never asked,' she blurted out. Seeing Ivy's incredulous expression, Emily tried to defend herself. 'I didn't think it was important at the time!' she cried.

The older woman gave a heavy sigh. 'And you've been going out with George for how long?'

'Just over a year,' Emily replied hesitantly.

Emily realized for the first time how pathetic her story must sound: she hadn't laid eyes on George or even heard from him in all the weeks she'd suspected she might be pregnant, and she didn't have a clue where his parents lived. In a matter of a few hours her world – formerly so happy and secure, with George at its centre – was suddenly tilting on a quite different axis now that this morning's news had forced her to face reality.

'If you're going to keep the kid, you'd better come up with something fast; otherwise you could end up giving birth in the workhouse.'

Seeing Emily's shocked face, Ivy took hold of her trembling hands. 'I wish I could do something, lovie . . .' she murmured, her voice trailing helplessly away.

'There's nothing anybody can do,' Emily said, as she wiped away her tears and straightened her shoulders. 'I've got money put away that George gave me; I'll use it to keep my baby. I'll manage somehow. I will write to him tonight,' she assured Ivy. 'You never know,' she added with a hopeful smile, 'I might have heard back from him by the end of the week.'

Determined not to waste any more time, Emily immediately wrote to George, telling him of her condition and how much she needed to see him. Knowing she'd never get a minute's privacy at home, Emily stayed on after she'd finished work and wrote the letter in the smoky staff canteen. After she'd stamped and addressed the letter to Squadron Leader George Holden, C/O RAF Padgate, Emily made her weary journey home, wondering how long she'd have to wait till she had the reply she was so counting on.

Sixty miles away, Matron was on the prowl for Nancy, whom she found fast asleep on her narrow bed in one of the larger bedrooms on the second floor. Oblivious to the exhaustion of the girl curled up in a tight foetal position, Matron yanked the blanket off Nancy and dragged her to her feet.

'Do you call that polishing the stairs, madam?' she snapped at bleary Nancy, who didn't know whether she was awake or dreaming.

Bustling the barefoot, trembling girl out of the room, Matron marched her down the stairs to the hall, where she announced, 'They're a disgrace! Do them again.'

Nancy gazed up at the ascending steps and banisters that seemed to go on forever, recalling how earlier, when she'd been on her hands and knees laboriously polishing the staircase, she'd really thought she might faint with fatigue. Thrusting a tin of polish and several rags into Nancy's hands, Matron stalked off.

'No supper for you until you complete your chores.'

Shaking, Nancy slumped in relief as Matron disappeared, then feebly started her task; but she was soon startled by the sound of approaching footsteps. She looked up and was relieved to see it was only Sister Ada.

'Sister, oh, Sister Dale,' she cried weakly. 'Matron's really angry with me.'

Knowing too well how vindictive Matron could be, Ada tried to hide the rage that flared up in her eyes; no matter what she personally felt, it was important as Mary Vale's ward sister that she maintained her professional distance.

'Let me help,' she said kindly, as she reached out to remove the tin of polish from Nancy's hand.

'No,' the girl gasped, clutching the tin close to her chest. 'Matron will kill me if she finds out you helped me!'

'Matron won't know a thing about it,' Ada replied with a smile. 'She's got a meeting with Sir Percival at Crow Thorn Grange – now, for goodness' sake, give me that polish.'

Overwhelmed with gratitude, Nancy handed over the rags and polish. 'Thank you, Sister,' she mumbled, then added guiltily, 'I know it sounds like I'm skiving, but really I feel weak and dizzy most of the time. All I want to do is sleep,' she confessed wearily.

Ada peered closely into Nancy's eyes. 'I suspect you might be suffering from anaemia. I'll run some checks on you tomorrow morning. Now go and get a cup of hot, sweet tea from the kitchen and leave me to get on with the job of polishing these wretched stairs.'

Smiling gratefully, Nancy did as Ada instructed and made her way into the kitchen, where she was greeted by vastly pregnant Irish Maggie, who cried out, 'Jesus, Mary and Joseph! You're as white as a ghost!'

The cook and housekeeper of Mary Vale, Sister Mary Paul, looked up from the big range from which she was removing several large loaves of bread. 'Less of the blaspheming,' she chided, as she placed the bread on the worktop to cool.

'Sorry, Sister,' Maggie apologized. 'But you have to admit the poor kid looks a right fecking mess!' Suddenly realizing she'd sworn again, Maggie stopped short and blushed. 'I can't say anything right for bloody trying,' she tittered.

Smiling at Maggie, who rolled her eyes in mock despair, Nancy marvelled at her resilience. Though Maggie constantly put her foot in it, nothing ever seemed to get her down; she was like a huge rubber ball: she bounced back from everything, unlike Nancy, who barely had the strength to get through a day at Mary Vale.

'Sit yourself down, child,' Sister Mary Paul said gently, pulling out a wooden chair for Nancy to sit on and giving her a mug of hot tea.

'Aren't I in the way?' Nancy asked self-consciously.

Sister Mary Paul nodded to a big pile of sandwiches on the kitchen table. 'No, we've nearly finished making the sandwiches for supper,' the nun said. 'You're fine where you are.'

As Nancy obediently sipped her tea, she felt her body relax in the presence of the kind, good women working around her; with allies like Sister Ada and Sister Mary Paul, she realized with a sudden rush of love that she was not alone.

Knowing full well that when Matron returned the first thing she'd do would be to check Nancy's work, Ada rubbed and dusted the stairs and banisters until they gleamed.

'All done,' she announced, as she joined Nancy in the kitchen.

'I know I didn't do a great job this morning, Sister,'

Nancy admitted with a blush. 'I just hoped Matron wouldn't notice and I'd get away with it.'

Maggie, who'd overheard her comment, gave a loud, derisive hoot. 'Don't kid yourself,' she scoffed. 'The owd witch doesn't miss a trick.'

Frightened that Sister Mary Paul might be offended by Maggie's rudeness, Nancy hastily laid a warning finger on her lips, but irrepressible Maggie babbled on. 'You know, we should give the old bat a broomstick!' she announced. 'Then she could fly away, right out over the Irish Sea!'

Ada hid a secret smile. Like Maggie, she wouldn't have minded a bit if Matron Maud Harding flew out of their lives and never came back, but that was never going to happen. Matron was a fixture at the Home and they all had to grin and bear it. Before she hurried back to the ward, where she hoped her absence wouldn't have been missed, Ada turned to Nancy and said, 'Get yourself to bed straight after supper, Nancy, and don't forget to come and see me first thing in the morning.'

When the gong sounded out for supper, Nancy followed Maggie into the dining room. Maggie laid out large plates of meat-paste sandwiches and a pile of crispy hot rock buns on the long refectory table. Usually the girls ate in enforced silence if Matron was supervising; but tonight, in her absence, the room rang with chatter and laughter. Stretching out to help herself to a sandwich, Nancy caught sight of her reflection in the gilded mirror that hung over the dining-room fireplace. How could the pale thin bag of bones reflected in the mirror be her? What had happened to Nancy Wheelan, who less than a year ago had been happily working in Burton's clothing factory in

Bolton? She'd never been a beauty, not like some of the pretty girls she worked with, who curled their hair and expertly applied red lipstick to their pouting lips. Ever the home-bird, Nancy had never been interested in going out dancing or finding a boyfriend; she preferred the company of her mam, who she was especially close to. They shared the same dislike of Nancy's domineering father, Mr Wheelan, who treated them both badly – though never on a Sunday when they went to the Methodist chapel in town, where Mr Wheelan appeared to be a decent, upright member of the community and a good family man. Nancy had always looked forward to Sundays, when she would accompany her parents in their best (but shabby) clothes to the chapel on St George's Road. Nancy proudly played the harmonium and in the afternoon taught Sunday School. It had been a simple enough life, until Walter from Burton's packing department came along and changed everything. He was a spotty young man with buck teeth who took to chatting to Nancy during her tea breaks.

'Watch that bugger, love!' her colleagues warned. 'He'd fancy owt in a skirt.'

Embarrassed by Walter's unwanted attention, Nancy had ignored him but at the same time she was curious: she'd never sought out any man's company and no man had ever shown any interest in her. Over a period of time she had got used to bumping into Walter, and one day he made her laugh when he gossiped about a lad stealing a kiss from a pretty machinist on the shop floor.

'I wonder how many lads fancy stealing a kiss from you, young Nance?' Walter had teased flirtatiously.

Colouring bright red with embarrassment, Nancy had hurried away from his leering gaze, but over time she had started to chat to Walter more; after all, she thought, when she compared him with her bullying, bombastic father, Walter was almost a gent. When he'd asked her to go for a walk with him in Queen's Park to feed the ducks, Nancy had been taken by the innocence of the invitation – what harm was there in feeding some ducks? Though their friendship seemed harmless enough, Nancy instinctively never mentioned her relationship with Walter to her mother, who, she knew, would not approve of her naive daughter talking to strange young fellas. How she wished she had, now. Maybe her mother would have been able to put a stop to it all and she wouldn't be here.

'Dumped and forgotten about for months on end,' Nancy thought bitterly. 'In a home in the middle of nowhere for disgraced unmarried mothers.'

Angry with herself, Nancy pushed aside her plate of dried-up meat-paste sandwiches. If she knew her mother – the person she loved and trusted most in the world – wouldn't have approved of Walter, why in God's name had she dropped her guard and fallen for him?

3. Crow Thorn Grange

In the best and largest first-floor bedroom, Matron prepared herself for Mary Vale's monthly board meeting, which was always held at Sir Archibald Percival's imposing home, Crow Thorn Grange, situated a few miles inland on the lower banks of the fells that rose majestically over the Grange's many turrets and chimney pots. Matron liked the fact that the board meetings were at Archie's, as she fondly referred to him in her private thoughts, though they were marred by the presence of the odious, drink-sodden resident doctor of Mary Vale, Dr Jones. Notwithstanding, Matron enjoyed her time away from the clattering noise of the ever-present girls and the all-permeating smell of dirty nappies soaking in buckets of bleach.

'Still,' Matron reminded herself as she threw off her uniform, 'I am rather well paid, and have my own luxurious rooms with lovely views, which I certainly wouldn't have if I'd chosen to work in a city hospital.'

Matron took pleasure in her preparations. She always dressed carefully for Archie. After slipping into her best claret-red dress, which Sir Percival had previously fulsomely admired, she carefully clipped her silk stockings on to her suspender belt; then, after applying her make-up (racy red lipstick, which Matron was quite thrilled by!), she draped her three strands of pearls around her neck and secured the matching diamond and pearl earrings. Closely examining herself in the large dressing-table mirror that was lit by two tall sidelights with tasselled pink velvet shades, Matron was not displeased with her reflection. She was in her mid-forties and proud of her piercing dark eyes and her thick black hair, admittedly now streaked with grey, and her teeth were still good, albeit a bit yellow. Her eyes, though, were without a doubt her finest attribute; as a nursing sister working at the Front during the Great War, she had terrified doctors of the highest rank with a commanding look from those imperious eyes. Authority and determination were Maud Harding's bywords; with these attributes she believed a professional single woman could move mountains in a male world.

Dabbing Chanel No. 5 behind her ears, Matron held her own gaze for several seconds; though dear Archie was married, to a milksop who fled at the sight of visitors, she knew there was a strong bond between them. She'd had a few romances in her time – none of which had been satisfactory, for she was a hard woman to please. After her appointment as Matron of Mary Vale Hall she had grown to admire Sir Percival: strong, bold, decisive, Archie was a *real* man – *her* kind of man. Picking up her highly polished lizard-skin handbag and a light woollen coat from her canopied bed, she glanced with pleasure at her elegant room, presently bathed in a golden light from the setting sun. Here, in her own private space, Matron could dream her own dreams, which nearly always had dearest Archie at their centre.

Driving over to Crow Thorn Grange in her smart little Austin, Matron took pleasure in the view. The narrow lane running between the rising fells caught the rays of the sun sinking low over the Irish Sea, which blazed crimson in the reflecting light before darkness fell. The night air was rich with the perfume of pungent spring blossom, and, as she drove her car along the winding drive that led up to the Grange's imposing oak-panelled front door slatted with heavy metal bars, owls hooted and a fox barked loudly from the woods that skirted the edge of the fells.

Inside Crow Thorn Grange, Sir Percival was irritated when the butler announced that Dr Jones had already arrived.

'Odious buffoon,' Percival fumed. 'He arrives early every time in order to sink half a decanter of my best sherry before proceedings even get under way.'

Occasionally he wondered how the dubious-looking doctor with his lank, greasy hair, foul breath and puffy, liver-spotted face had washed up at Mary Vale Hall. Possibly because nobody else on earth had wanted him. Instructing the butler to take the doctor into the spacious drawing room, warmed by a crackling log fire and lit by tall standard lamps strategically placed beside low tables on which recent copies of *Horse and Hound* and *Farmers Weekly* were neatly arranged, Percival remained at his desk, glaring at an unpleasant letter he'd received that afternoon from his bank manager.

Percival had married into wealth, but his spending habits, gambling and other life in London, which he worked hard to keep secret from everyone, especially his wife, had quickly eaten up their wealth, and, though there was income from the vast Crow Thorn estate, it didn't begin to cover Percival's lavish needs. Without another source of income he was in imminent danger of losing his Mayfair flat and his mistress, whom he housed there. Stunning, beautiful, slender Marigold, with Titian-gold hair and limpid eyes, had tried her best, poor darling, he thought indulgently, to cut down on champagne and couture gowns, but even her sacrifices hadn't had much impact on Percival's dwindling funds.

Sighing heavily, he stood up and walked over to the windows that looked out over the driveway flanked on either side by rich meadowland, where soon Highland cattle would graze knee-deep in cow parsley. Recognizing Matron's smart little Austin making its way up the drive, Percival gave a loud groan: the thought of having to flatter Maud Harding all night made his already heavy heart even heavier.

As much as he'd like never to host another wretched Mary Vale board meeting again, Percival knew he needed to keep good relations between Crow Thorn Grange and Mary Vale. His role as head of the board brought in a pittance that barely covered his wine bill, but within the county set there was prestige attached to the title, and to be seen working selflessly for a charitable trust for fallen women had its social benefits. Plus, there were occasional unexpected perks bestowed on him by some of the wealthier, sometimes titled parents of the pregnant girls. Grateful for Percival's professional discretion in the matter of their fallen daughters, they'd wined and dined him in some of the best London clubs, where he'd won at the gambling tables and even received expert insider tips on the Stock Exchange. He'd formed a particularly useful relationship with Lord Humberstone, whose daughter, Cynthia, a pretty little thing as he recalled, had been a resident at Mary Vale a year ago. In exchange for Percival's respectful discretion, Lord Humberstone had given him an inside tip on the winner of the Grand National (which happened to be his lordship's horse) and Percival had made a packet. His only regret was that there hadn't been any more passing favours courtesy of grateful parents who'd left their disgraced daughters in his tender care.

Hearing the butler opening the door to Matron, Percival twisted his expression into a welcoming smile; he'd got the old battle-axe wrapped round his finger, but it took patience and effort to keep her happy. As long as his flirting stopped at hand-kissing, it was just about bearable, but there had been sickening moments when Matron's simpers suggested she would be game for a lot more than that. With a swagger he issued forth into the grand entrance hall decked with imperial antlers' heads with multiple points and dead, beaded eyes, where he greeted Matron in the manner to which she'd become accustomed.

'Maud! How do you do it?' he enthused as he took her elbow and led her into the drawing room. Jones was already slumped low in the sofa by the fire. 'Doctor! I was just saying,' Percival boomed, 'how does Matron always manage to look so young and attractive after a gruelling day on the wards?'

Jones made an ungracious snort while Matron responded with a girlish laugh. 'Oh, Archie, you say the nicest things,' she gushed.

Settling Matron on the chaise longue, he mixed her a stiff Gilbey's gin and tonic, then poured himself a double malt whisky. Sitting on the sofa beside Matron, who inched closer to him, Percival chinked his cut-glass tumbler against her cocktail glass.

'Bottoms up,' he joked, as he all but drained his in one.

The meeting proceeded with its usual tedium: monies were discussed and apportioned. End-of-year reports showed that Mary Vale, as usual, just about broke even on the back of the richer girls' fees and the occasional bequest. The convent, an independent body, received rents both from its vast farming land and from the Home itself, out of which Father Benedict was paid and the nursing staff too. On his second stiff malt Percival grumbled about the meagre stipend that was allocated to Father Benedict, who oversaw all of the adoptions at Mary Vale.

'I hardly see why the bumbling old fool should be paid anything,' he barked. 'After all, he is a priest – what's he going to spend his money on, stuck out here in the middle of nowhere?' he added with a sarcastic laugh.

Matron, who agreed with every word that fell from Archie's fleshy lips, nodded effusively. 'My word, the fuss and bother Father Benedict and Sister Ann make, worrying over fitting the right child to the right parents – you'd think they were selecting the royal line of succession!'

Making a disapproving moue with her mouth, Matron continued, 'Some of the babies of the better class of girls end up with the most unsuitable parents – painters and decorators, fishermen, builders, chimney-sweeps and the like,' she sniffed. 'It pains me to see them fall so low in society.'

Percival shot a furtive glance at Dr Jones, who by now was snoring softly against a bank of silk cushions.

'And how would you have it otherwise, Matron?' he asked in a low voice.

'Well, take Cynthia Humberstone,' Matron started. 'You remember her being here only last year, don't you? She gave birth to a fine young son of impeccable breeding – well, at least from one side of the family,' she added, as she drained her glass. 'And where did the illegitimate grandson of a lord end up? With a drab middle-aged couple who ran a corner shop in Atherton!'

Percival stifled a yawn; what with a drunken Jones snoring on one side of him and Matron working up a storm on the other, he was longing for the wretched meeting to be over. 'I suppose if the child is adequately housed, our business is seen to be concluded,' he mumbled blandly.

Matron pressed on undeterred. 'In return for the adoption of the Humberstone boy, the Home received nothing!'

Hard-hearted Matron would never appreciate the joy these new parents had experienced as they wheeled away their son in a brand-new pram they'd spent most of their savings on. After years of a barren marriage the couple hadn't been able to believe that the child sleeping between the softest sheets they could buy was their own precious boy, who would grow up poor but happy and much loved in the back streets of Atherton.

Impatient with the conversation, Percival remarked sharply, 'I thought one of the purposes of Mary Vale was to get the unwanted babies adopted.'

'You're missing the point, Sir,' she replied equally as sharply. 'If the Humberstone child had been offered to a more *suitable* family, we might have received a donation, which has to be better than nothing at all.' Matron sighed before she continued, 'I don't know, it just seems a tragedy that we can't take advantage of the wealth some of our residents have to offer.'

Hearing the word 'wealth', Percival's flagging interest suddenly revived. Giving her a mocking look, he said, 'And how could we do that, Matron? The Home is founded on the convent's charitable trust fund; the Order of the Holy Mother is not a profit-making organization.'

Checking to make sure the stupefied Dr Jones really was asleep, Matron dropped her voice so low that Percival almost had to press his ear to her mouth in order to catch what she said.

'If we were to *very discreetly*, and only in the right circles, let it be known that Mary Vale could offer – for a fee, of course – a child of good breeding, we may be able to reach a group of more discerning parents.'

Percival was flabbergasted by the audacity of her idea. 'You mean cherry-pick the more superior babies?'

Matron bridled. 'They might be bastards, but we could assure our clients that at least one line of their genealogy was respectable.'

Percival shook his head. 'You're suggesting we offer desirable babies with a good blood line to select, affluent customers? For a fee?' he asked incredulously.

Matron, unshaken, held his gaze. 'Exactly so, Sir.'

Slumping back in his chair, Percival slowly lit up a cigarette, and, blowing smoke into the air, he continued to question Matron. 'How do we get round the not so small problem of Father Benedict's role? He is, after all, responsible for all the adoptions in the Home?'

Matron, who was a little tiddly by now, waved a hand in the air. 'I'm not sure on that detail,' she admitted. 'I'd have to give the matter some thought.'

Percival got to his feet. Matron might think she'd come

up with an interesting concept but the old bat was three sheets to the wind! Glaring at Jones now snoring loudly on the sofa, he wished they'd both get the hell out of his drawing room and leave him in peace. He ended the conversation abruptly. 'Let's talk about this matter another time.'

Seeing Matron's expression suddenly harden, he quickly changed his tone: the last thing he wanted to do was get on the wrong side of Maud Harding, no matter how irritating she was. Flashing her his most charming smile, he added, 'Perhaps we could pursue your interesting idea further another time . . . in private?'

'Of course, Archie,' Matron gushed as she wobbled to her feet.

When Sir Percival finally got rid of Matron, who'd rather reluctantly taken Dr Jones home too, he refilled his glass; then, leaning against the ornate marble mantelpiece, he stared long and hard into the flickering flames of the dying fire. Matron's suggestion of selling specially selected Mary Vale babies was something that had never crossed his mind. He'd dismissed the idea as unworkable, but was there a way, he wondered. Stubbing out his cigarette, Percival slowly drained his glass. If they could get around the sticky problem of Father Benedict's role, Matron's idea might be viable. He'd talk to her another time, he decided, when the old bat was stone-cold sober.

4. Edinburgh

In her college digs in Durham, Isla Ross took small sips of water from the glass she clutched in her trembling hand.

'God!' she gasped. 'If only I could stop being sick . . .'

She was trying to pack her belongings into a suitcase in order to vacate her room, which her crabby landlady was keen to repossess.

'I'll be off soon,' Isla had promised.

Secretly, she'd been hanging on for longer than was sensible for one purpose only – to talk to Professor Wiley about her condition.

'God!' She gagged again, as her stomach seemed to rise into her mouth.

For somebody who hadn't eaten for what seemed like days, how could she keep on vomiting like this? After the bout had passed, Isla almost collapsed on her narrow single bed; staring up at the ceiling, she tried to stop the tears welling up in her eyes. What a mess she'd made. What an unbelievable bloody fool she'd been. Up until she'd been twenty-one years old, she'd never even as much as kissed a boy; then, at the beginning of her second year at Durham, she'd fallen head over heels madly in love with her middle-aged English professor, who'd literally seduced her with the poetry of William Shakespeare.

All through her first year at college her friends had tried to involve Isla in their social life, which centred around the local dancehall. To start with, just to show willing, she'd gone along with their giggling plans, allowed herself to be made up and dressed up in borrowed crêpe dresses. At the dancehall she'd drunk only shandy, while her friends downed gin and orange, and she'd actually hidden in the ladies' toilet when the dance band struck up.

All Isla had ever wanted to do was to read books and study English literature: Shakespeare, Byron, Keats, Chaucer, the Brontës, Jane Austen, T. S. Eliot. A star pupil at Benenden, she'd come to Durham to study – not to dance and drink and find a boyfriend. She appreciated her friends' *joie de vivre* (the last thing she wanted was for them to think she was an intellectual snob), but she really did detest those Saturday nights at the dancehall, where she actively avoided men rather than enticed them. When her friends finally realized how shy and retiring Isla was in public, they stopped asking her to join them, for which Isla was truly grateful. And that's how her student life had been: quiet, peaceful, studious and happy – until Professor Keith Wiley had laid eyes on the cleverest student in his tutorial group. Isla Ross, with her silver-blue, dreamy Highland eyes and luscious pink lips set in a sweet, heart-shaped face framed by curling silver-blonde hair. She had a soft young body, with curves in all the right places, and distinctly strong, muscular legs because of all the hockey matches she'd played at boarding school. Though innocent Isla didn't know it, Keith Wiley was famous for his dalliances with clever, pretty girls, whom he charmed with compliments and attention. Nobody could have been more infatuated than Isla when Wiley critiqued her essays or selected her to read passages from Shakespeare and Marlowe in her lilting Scottish voice.

When the professor had asked Isla if she'd like to accompany him to the theatre to see a local production of *The Tempest*, Isla had almost swooned in delight. They'd met on a snowy night and walked into the town centre, the Professor gallantly taking her arm in order to stop her from slipping on the icy roads. The production was mediocre, but Isla thought it was sublime; she knew all the great lines from the play and whispered them under her breath as she watched the actors on stage. 'We are such stuff as dreams are made on,' she murmured.

Taking her hand and softly kissing her fingertips, Keith Wiley had concluded the line for her: 'And our little life is rounded with a sleep.'

Hearing his deep Northern voice in her ear, Isla's pulse raced and her heart beat so fast she was sure he would hear it. During the interval they drank sherry at the bar and discussed the performance; Isla had never been so happy, so alert and so in tune with another human being. He might be double her age and her tutor, but she was quite incapable of resisting his kisses; in fact, she welcomed them with an intensity that surprised her.

'Goodnight, dearest girl,' he'd murmured as they parted, with the snow still falling softly around them. 'Come and see me in my rooms tomorrow; we have so much to discuss.'

Weak at the knees, Isla had agreed and gone to bed in a haze of romantic infatuation.

'And look where that got me!' she thought bitterly now.

Isla wearily dragged her body off the bed, and, throwing the last of her clothes into a suitcase, she tucked her books and files into a smaller case and checked the room to make sure she'd left nothing behind; then she closed the door on her student days and set off for home. On the train journey north Isla tried to make a plan: she'd keep her condition private for as long as she could, but, when her strict Calvinist parents discovered the truth, would they forgive her for what they would surely consider a wicked sin of the flesh? She'd overheard whispered conversations between her mother and her friends, disapproving remarks about local girls from good families who'd got themselves into trouble. Well, now it was their only daughter who was in trouble, she thought ruefully, as the train rattled towards Edinburgh and the parents who had always terrified her.

Once the thrill of the chase had worn off, as it inevitably did, Professor Wiley had started to avoid Isla. When she managed to track him down by following him around campus, he'd bundled her into his office and shouted at her after hearing she was pregnant.

Outraged, he screamed at her, 'It's not mine! I know what you stupid young girls are like, sleeping with every Tom, Dick and Harry. Don't you go laying the blame for your bastard on my doorstep.'

In floods of tears Isla had sobbed. 'But, Keith, I was a virgin! You must know that!'

Even though Wiley had turned his angry gaze away from her tear-stained, imploring face, Isla knew he recalled as clearly as she did the afternoon he'd made love to her on the big sofa in his college rooms, where she now assumed he'd seduced so many other innocent girls long before her. His kisses and caresses had transported her with a passion she'd never experienced before, and it had blazed through her entire body. When she had briefly hesitated, overwhelmed by what she was about to do, her lover had gathered her close to his chest.

'My darling, I promise I will always look after you.'

Catching her breath, Isla gazed adoringly into his tender face. 'Really?'

'*Really*, dearest, darling girl, you're my treasure, I could never bear to part from you.'

And in a daze of romantic love Isla had given herself unconditionally to her amorous professor, who had responded with expert skill and tenderness.

At the end of their love-making, when she lay half naked on the sofa, smiling up at her lover, who traced his hands over her perfect breasts and hips, she had felt sure of his love and devotion. There wasn't a single doubt in her guileless mind that he didn't return her feelings; so when Wiley refused to see her or answer her letters, Isla had been devastated. If she hadn't cornered him in the English faculty building, she doubted whether they would ever have had the grim conversation that would forever draw a line under their romance.

'I suggest you leave Durham immediately,' he'd barked; then, flinging open his door, he'd unceremoniously bundled Isla into the corridor. 'Girls in your condition aren't welcome at this university!'

Too appalled to speak, Isla could only stare at her former lover, who clearly couldn't get rid of her quickly enough. Before he slammed the door in her face, she managed to cry out, 'Keith! Don't you remember? You promised to look after me – you told me you loved me!'

Professor Wiley gave Isla one last humiliating look, then closed the door on her grief-stricken face. A member of staff hurrying down the corridor to his own rooms stopped when he saw the young girl weeping.

'Can I help?' he inquired politely.

Blinded by scalding tears that streamed down her face, Isla numbly shook her head, then, groping her way out of the building, she fled. Staring moodily out of his study window, Wiley watched her, bent double with torment, stumbling across the quad in the sleeting rain.

'The bloody little fool had better keep her mouth shut,' he muttered furiously. 'If this ever gets out, she could ruin me.'

Feeling dreadfully ill and looking pale and dishevelled, Isla was picked up from Waverley Railway Station by her father, who gave her a dry kiss on her cheek before loading her suitcases into the boot of his Rover.

'Isn't that rather a lot of luggage for a brief visit home?' he asked, as he navigated the traffic along Princes Street.

Pretending not to hear his comment, Isla asked about the weather and his friends from church, which successfully took her father's mind off the amount of luggage she'd arrived home with.

Isla repeated her well-rehearsed line, 'The landlady of our digs asked all of us to clear our rooms for the decorators,' she told her father.

In her pristine room, Isla carefully washed her tired face and brushed her untidy hair; smelling the food that the maid, Peggy, was carrying into the dining room, she clutched her heaving stomach. The last thing she wanted to do was eat, but she knew she must join her parents in the dining room. Taking deep breaths, she made her way downstairs, where she bumped into Peggy, whom her arrogant parents always treated in an embarrassing, high-handed manner.

'Nice to see you, Miss,' Peggy said with a warm smile.

Isla smiled back. 'Are you well, Peggy?' she asked.

'Aye,' Peggy quickly retorted. 'In you go, Miss, they're waiting for you,' she added with a knowing nod of her head.

Isla took up her usual place at the gleaming, polished mahogany dining table that sparkled with cutlery and cut glass. Before the smell of smoked haddock and cabbage totally overwhelmed her, she quickly made her apologies: 'I'm so sorry, I seem to have picked up a tummy bug – please excuse me for not eating.'

Her mother threw her a disapproving look, while her father tucked into his food with relish; in between mouthfuls of fish and vegetables, followed by prunes and custard, he barked questions at Isla about her English course and her predicted grades for her forthcoming exams. Taking sips of water, Isla answered as best she could, then, when the meal was, mercifully, over, she fled to her room and remained there all night.

In the days that followed Isla spent as much time as she could outside; the fresh air and long walks seemed to improve her health and clear her brain. In order not to arouse suspicion, she told her parents she was studying in the library, when, in fact, she was drifting around the streets of Edinburgh, wondering what she was going to do with the rest of her life. Even though the Professor had treated her shamefully, Isla was shocked to realize as the days passed that she missed him desperately. She acknowledged she'd been an utter fool, duped by an older man's sweet-talking, but, for all her self-hatred, she longed for the sound of his voice and the touch of his hand. Feeling increasingly lost and lonely, she knew she couldn't go on deceiving her parents; but neither could she summon up the courage to speak to them. She needed advice from somebody she could trust. She waited impatiently for her parents to go out to their twice-weekly church meeting; then, when the house was empty and all she could hear was Peggy washing up in the back scullery, she telephoned her grandmother in Windermere. Using the name she'd always called her by, Isla almost sobbed with relief when she heard her grandmother's clear, strong voice.

'Jeannie!' she gasped.

'Darling girl! How are you?'

At which point Isla burst into tears.

'Jeannie!' she wailed. 'I've got myself into terrible trouble!'

At the end of her distraught granddaughter's outpourings, Jeannie spoke firmly but gently. 'They're not going to take it well, Isla, darling.'

'I know,' Isla gulped. 'It will destroy them,' she added in despair.

'It will hit Eustace hardest,' Jeannie added with a touch of scorn in her voice. 'Him being such an upright member of the Morningside community.'

'Do you think Mummy might support me?' Isla asked nervously.

The silence that followed answered her question.

'She'll do as your father says,' Jeannie finally said. 'My advice is to tell them soon, rather than have them find out for themselves.'

'Yes, you're right,' Isla responded feebly. 'I'm so frightened,' she said, stifling a sob.

'Brace yourself, child,' Jeannie said robustly. 'It's not

going to be easy, but remember you've got me: I'll always be there for you, Isla, I hope you know that.'

Her tender words made Isla start to cry all over again. 'Oh, Jeannie!' she wailed. 'Why can't I come to you and hide away from the world?'

'Darling, you know you can always come to me, but right now, out of respect to your parents, you must tell them the truth.'

Isla dumbly nodded.

'Tell them how you were seduced by an older man, your professor, who wilfully exploited your innocence and abused your trust.'

Isla began to breathe more easily: her grandmother's words made sense. She had been exploited; surely her parents would understand that and help her through this nightmare time?

Jeannie had been perfectly accurate when she'd told Isla that telling her parents she was pregnant was not going to be easy. After she'd poured out the terrible story, there were several long, agonizing minutes of uncomfortable silence in which Isla looked from her stony-faced father to her trembling mother, before her father spoke in a tone of voice Isla had never heard him use before. 'I think you had better leave this house.'

Isla had gazed at him in dumb disbelief. 'Daddy! No, please, no,' she gasped. Turning to her mother who was sitting beside her father on the sofa, she cried, 'Mummy! Help me.'

Mrs Ross looked from her husband, whose face had turned almost grey, to her daughter. Rising, she walked to the door and held it wide open.

'You heard what your father said – leave.'

In a state of profound shock, Isla would never have got out of the house without the assistance of Peggy, who'd overheard the conversation and helped to pack Isla's bags before bracing herself for the conversation to come.

'Come along, Miss: you've got to pull yourself together.'

Isla gulped as she held back her tears. 'It's just the shock,' she cried. 'When I told the man who got me pregnant, he threw me out, and now my parents have thrown me out too.'

'I'm sorry, but you'd better get used to it, Miss,' Peggy said realistically. 'Now what are you going to do?' she persisted.

Isla stared blankly at Peggy, who, with the house to clean, was beginning to panic.

'Are you going to keep it?' Peggy asked point blank. 'Or shall we go somewhere where you can get rid of it?'

It was the first time that Isla had really considered the child that she was carrying. Thinking about the tiny being she had created, a totally unexpected spark of protection flared inside her.

'I don't want an abortion, if that's what you mean.'

'You're clear about that, Miss?' Peggy persisted.

Isla nodded her head. 'I don't want to get rid of it.'

'Right, so where are you going to go, Miss? Clearly, you're not welcome in your own home.'

Isla didn't have to think twice. 'I'll go to Jeannie's!'

Looking hugely relieved, Peggy nodded. 'I'm sure your grannie will help; you've always been close, you two.'

A faint smile of hope played on Isla's soft, pink lips, 'I'll go to Windermere,' she announced. 'Everything will be all right when I'm with Jeannie.'

5. Shirley

Shirley's recovery was slow and her stitches caused her huge discomfort; she was, however, forced from her bed on the post-natal ward by Matron, who was keen to see the girl vacate the Home. The sooner Shirley was gone from Mary Vale, the sooner her place could be offered to another client, hopefully one with money who would pay for her stay, instead of a scrounger who seemed determined not to leave.

Though no longer on the ward and always fearful of Matron catching sight of her, Shirley often slipped into the prep room or the sluice room for a chat with Sister Ann, whom she sought out like a child seeks out its mother. It was in this semi-maternal role that Sister Ann gently explained all the changes that were going on in Shirley's body.

'Your stitches are healing nicely and your milk's drying up too.'

'Is that because of the pills you gave me?' Shirley asked.

Sister Ann nodded. 'Your breasts won't feel quite so tender any more; you'll be back to normal in no time,' she assured the edgy girl.

'I don't want to be back to normal, Sister Ann!' Shirley blurted out. 'Normal means I'll be sent back home, when I'd rather stay here.'

'I understand, child,' Sister Ann told her. 'We'll keep

you for as long as we can string it out, but you have to understand that the Home has rules, and one of them is that you must vacate your place so someone else can fill it.'

Poor Shirley nodded, but her huge, dark eyes filled up with tears as she thought of what she was going back to. Her father had never been an affectionate man, but at least he'd never laid a hand on his daughter. It was when he'd died and her mother had quickly remarried that fourteen-year-old Shirley's life changed very much for the worse; from that moment on she never knew a minute's peace. It started with her drunken stepfather touching her only when her mother was out of the house, but, as his brutish desires increased, he had started to seek Shirley out while her mother was downstairs cooking or cleaning. Shirley's cries of pain and protest were stifled by her stepfather's big, dirty hand, which he clamped over her mouth until he'd sated himself. Shirley couldn't understand why her mother never came looking for her: what did she think she was doing upstairs for so long? But, as the abuse continued with even more hideous frequency, she reached the horrifying conclusion that her mother was somehow complicit; either too frightened of her thuggish husband to protest, or, worse, perhaps she was relieved that her new husband's voracious and distasteful appetite was being fulfilled elsewhere.

When Shirley's shame reached a peak the day she discovered her stepfather had made her pregnant, she hoped her mother would do what a mother should. But that was not to be either: there was no support from her mother. Instead, she had sided completely with her new husband, outraged by her daughter's shameful condition. She had literally thrown her into the street, cursing her daughter for her loose ways, even though they both knew who the father of Shirley's child really was and that she'd had no choice in the matter whatsoever. If it hadn't been for her local priest, whom she'd turned to in desperation, Shirley was convinced she would have died on the streets where she'd been dumped. The priest, who knew Shirley from her regular attendance at Mass and Communion, had pulled a few strings and found her a place at Mary Vale, where Shirley had met the kindest people she'd ever known in her life.

Dragging her mind back to the here and now, Shirley dumbly said, 'Thank you, Sister Ann, I'll always be grateful for my time at Mary Vale.'

Seeing her pain, the nun clasped the tearful girl in her arms. 'We'll pray for you, Shirley, dear, God will guide us.'

Nobody could fail to notice Shirley's complete lack of interest in her new-born daughter, who still didn't have a name. Ada watched Shirley progress through the nursery, glancing into all the little white canvas cots as she did so, but when it came to her own child Shirley scooted past as if she were frightened of seeing her daughter. Catching her in the act one day, Ada drew Shirley aside.

'Your little girl needs a name, Shirley,' she reminded the new mother, who shrugged.

Staring moodily at the floor, she blurted out in an emotional rush, 'I don't care! She reminds me of him and what he done to me.'

Ada completely understood Shirley's reaction – who

would want to be reminded on a daily basis of their rapist? However, she knew from her own professional experience that it was important psychologically for Shirley to talk about her feelings, rather than pretend she hadn't given birth and that her baby didn't exist.

'Shirley, it's not the child's fault,' she said gently. 'She didn't ask to be born –'

Shirley angrily interrupted her: 'And I didn't ask to be raped!'

'I know, I'm sorry,' Ada apologized.

Shirley's bottom lip quivered. 'If I look at her, you might go thinking I want her, and I don't.'

Ada shook her head. 'I would never try to change your mind, Shirley,' she said gently. 'I know you want to have your baby adopted and I agree with you: it is the best option for her. All I'm saying is please don't ignore her. You carried her, gave birth to her, and you've decided to give her away – all these things happened to you and you must acknowledge them. Right?'

She waited for Shirley to reply, which she did with difficulty. 'Right,' she agreed, then quickly turned to go. 'You give her a name, Sister,' she called over her shoulder. 'I ain't got none for 'er.'

Ada and Sister Ann gave Shirley's daughter a grand name: Elizabeth Rose (after the royal princesses), but in no time at all everybody was calling the little mite Lizzie, which suited her far better. Shirley made no comment about her daughter's name, though Ada was relieved to see her casting a cautious glance at her sleeping baby as she hurried through the nursery one afternoon. Ada smiled; at least her message had got through.

6. The Plan

One night, after a long shift, Ada and Sister Ann sat at the scrubbed wooden trestle table in the convent kitchen waiting for the saucepan of milk they'd put on the hob to boil. Sitting opposite one another, they were both worrying about the same issue. Sister Ann spoke up first; sighing heavily, she said, 'Honest to God, nobody in their right mind would let a young girl go back to a home like the one she's got.'

'I agree!' Ada cried in sheer frustration. 'But what can we do, Sister? Shirley's not fee-paying – she has to go when her time's up.'

'Yes, yes, I know,' Sister Ann said with uncharacteristic impatience. 'I've been racking my brains and I think I've found a way around the problem.'

Ada raised her beautifully arched eyebrows. 'Oh?' she said and waited for an explanation.

The nun pulled her chair closer to Ada and whispered conspiratorially, 'I'll pay for Shirley to stay on here myself.'

'YOU!' gasped Ada.

Sister Ann nodded quickly. 'A bit of extra time with us will do the child no harm.'

'But you're a nun, as poor as a church mouse!' Ada exclaimed.

'For the love of God, keep your voice down,' Sister Ann begged, as she looked nervously over her shoulder. 'I've saved a bit of money.'

Ada couldn't help but smile. 'How come you've got money to spare?' she teased. 'You took a vow of poverty,' she reminded her flustered friend.

'Poverty, chastity and obedience,' Sister Ann reminded Ada in turn, when they spotted that the saucepan of milk was just about to boil over. Quickly adding the milk to the cocoa powder in the mugs standing by the range, Ada returned to the table with the hot drinks.

'But we're allowed to keep some money for necessary bits and bobs,' Sister Ann said with a guilty smile. 'And it's enough to pay for a month or so longer.'

Ada smiled softly. 'You're a saint,' she said fondly.

'Rubbish, I'm a sinner and well you know it!' Sister Ann exclaimed. Ada looked thoughtful. 'Anything that gives Shirley extra time I would fully support. In fact,' she added impulsively. 'I'll donate to the Shirley fund too!'

Sister Ann looked concerned. 'You mustn't leave yourself short, Ada, dear.'

'I think it's safe to say a nurse earns a little bit more than a nun,' Ada joked.

The two women took sips from their mugs, then Sister Ann continued, 'I've been asking around schools and convents in the area,' she told Ada. 'Inquiring about whether there might be work available for Shirley. I told them that she's a willing girl, a good girl, prepared to do anything from washing up to chopping wood or cleaning windows.'

'Any luck?' Ada inquired.

Ann wearily shook her head. 'Nothing,' she sighed, as she rubbed her tired eyes. 'The problem is, Shirley's young, innumerate and illiterate; the child's hardly been to school.'

'Well, that's hardly surprising, given her hideous domestic circumstances,' Ada pointed out.

'It's not going to be easy,' Sister Ann admitted. 'But I have to keep on trying. I'm going to write to everybody, far and wide – maybe you will too, Ada?'

Ada nodded her head. 'I'll do everything I can to help Shirley, for sure.'

Sister Ann carefully laid down her mug. 'So, I was wondering,' she started nervously, 'if you could offer my money – our money,' she hastily corrected herself, 'to Father Benedict, tell him it's to cover Shirley's extended stay?'

'ME?' gasped Ada.

'It would be nice to have someone who's laity involved in the arrangement,' Sister Ann explained.

Ada smiled. 'Of course, Sister, I'll see to it.'

'Thanks be to God!' the nun said with a heartfelt smile. 'We have a plan to save Shirley, at least for now.'

The two women parted with a hug, Sister Ann heading into the convent while Ada made her way towards the staff-accommodation quarters. When she passed the statue of Our Lady in the corridor, which separated the secular from laity, out of habit Ada made the sign of the cross and prayed for Shirley and her tiny scrap of a daughter.

Ada wasted no time in telling Father Benedict that she and Sister Ann had sourced some extra funds and could therefore extend Shirley's stay a little. Looking visibly relieved, Father Ben beamed at Ada. 'That's a huge relief, I've been praying the good Lord would keep her safe.'

Taking a deep breath, he continued, 'Now I have good news for you.'

Ada eagerly sat forward in her chair.

'A childless couple from Skipton who have been looking to adopt for some time have expressed interest in Shirley's little girl.'

'That's wonderful, Father!' Ada exclaimed in delight. 'By the way, she has a name now: she's called Elizabeth Rose,' she added with a fond smile. 'But everybody calls her Lizzie.'

Father Ben gave an approving smile. 'Well, now, with God's help, Lizzie might soon be with a kind, childless couple who, I am sure, will give her a happy future and a loving home.' He paused, then continued somewhat anxiously, 'It's just occurred to me, Sister, now that Shirley's going to be in the Home a bit longer, she may well witness her baby leaving Mary Vale with her new parents. Will that be a problem for her?'

'I don't think you need worry on that count, Father,' Ada confidently assured him. 'Sadly, Shirley's never bonded with Lizzie and she's always been adamant about having her adopted – if I'm perfectly frank, I think Shirley will be hugely relieved to see Lizzie go to a good home.'

Father Ben smiled. 'Well, that's good to know. I'll post off the adoption papers right away.'

With a new name and the possibility of new parents, Lizzie, who was much petted and cuddled by the girls in the nursery (especially by Nancy, who felt sorry for the poor little mite), seemed to flourish. By contrast, Shirley, not yet aware that her days at Mary Vale were to be extended, lost the little appetite she had and couldn't sleep.

'We need to put the poor girl out of her misery,' Sister Ann declared once Ada had cleared the new arrangement with Father Ben.

'No time like the present,' said Ada with an excited smile.

They found poor Shirley curled up on her narrow single bed.

'Child!' Sister Ann cried. 'We've been looking everywhere for you.'

Sitting on one side of the bed while Ada sat on the other, Sister Ann raised Shirley into a sitting position.

'We have good news,' she announced.

Accustomed to nothing but bad news, Shirley barely looked up.

'Shirley, dear,' Ada continued softly, 'we've put together sufficient funds to keep you here at Mary Vale for a bit longer.'

Unable to take in the astonishing news, Shirley could only stare at both Ada and Sister Ann in dumb disbelief.

Taking hold of Shirley's cold hand, Sister Ann rubbed it warm. 'Didn't we promise we'd do what we could to help you?' She smiled.

The shock and delight combined with the overwhelming sense of relief that coursed through her body made Shirley crumple with sheer joy.

'Thank you, oh, thank you, thank you!' she cried, as she threw herself into Sister Ann's open arms.

After getting her breath back, she slowly pulled away and stared from the smiling nun to a smiling Ada. 'REALLY?' she asked, in a quivering, tentative voice.

'Really, really,' Ada replied with tears in her eyes.

As the truth dawned, Shirley cried rapturously, 'I can stay, I can truly stay! I don't have to go back?'

Moved beyond words, Ann and Ada repeated their assurances, until Shirley finally relaxed enough to absorb the wonderful news. Her relief was such that it came out in helpless laughter, which she was as unable to control as the tears that had overcome her earlier.

'I can stay,' she murmured over and over again like a soothing mantra.

Sister Ann held her protégée close. 'With God's help we'll keep you safe, dearest child, with God's help we'll protect you.'

Over the coming days, Shirley started to show a new side to herself: she developed an appetite and, as she filled out, she seemed to walk taller, moving about the Home with a permanent smile on her glowing face. For the first time in years she was experiencing hope, and was prepared to do anything at all to repay her patrons' kindness. When Sister Ann and Ada ran out of jobs for her to do on the ward, she would head to Sister Mary Paul's vast Mary Vale kitchen.

'I'll be your skivvy,' Shirley said cheerfully. 'I'll wash and mop, clean and polish, I'll do anything you ask of me,' she promised, and she meant it too.

Sister Mary Paul, who was almost as fond of Shirley as Ann and Ada were, smiled happily. 'To see your sweet face about the place is good enough for me; Mary Vale just wouldn't be the same without our little Shirley.'

The love reflected on the nun's face and her affirming smile flooded Shirley's soul, and, fuelled by affection, she filled up a bucket with warm water and a heavy dollop of pungent disinfectant, then set about mopping the dining-room floor before moving on to washing all the downstairs windows. Returning to the warmth of the kitchen, she sat herself beside Sister Mary Paul and happily helped the older woman to peel a vat of potatoes.

'You're not to go wearing yourself out,' Sister Mary Paul chided her fondly. 'You're a resident here, not a slave.'

Shirley gave the nun a shy smile. 'If I'm a slave,' she joked, 'I'm the happiest one on earth!'

7. A Visitor

Emily, in Manchester, had still not heard back from George. In between hoping and praying she might get a reply from him – something she was rapidly losing confidence in – she forced herself to make inquiries into local mother and baby homes. It wasn't a route she wanted to go down at all, but it was beginning to look as if she didn't have a choice, so she started by visiting hospitals and doctors' surgeries, thinking that they might be able to point her in the right direction. She told the snooty receptionists that she was making inquiries for a 'friend'. When the receptionists looked at her askance, Emily held their cynical gaze until they gave her what she wanted: names, addresses and, in some cases, even phone numbers.

There were quite a few homes in the Manchester area, which Emily visited after work. But she was put off by their dark, brooding façades; a few of the homes actually had bars at the windows so they looked more like prison buildings than places of sanctuary. Unimpressed by her findings, Emily began to feel that a place in Manchester might be a bit too close to home for comfort, so she started to look further afield. One of the homes she saw advertised in a medical journal in her doctor's surgery instantly appealed to her. She couldn't quite put her finger on what it was about the place, but, when she read about Mary Vale, something told her this might be the home for her. She wrote immediately, asking for more information, and when a hefty envelope landed in her pigeonhole at work Emily locked herself in the ladies' toilets so no one could peer over her shoulder and hungrily read through the information, which contained images of the Home and its surroundings. Liking the look of the big old house with its sunny gardens on the edge of the sea, she wrote back to Mary Vale to arrange a visit at their earliest convenience.

As her hope of locating a suitable mother and baby home increased, so her hope of hearing from George rapidly decreased. It was just as Ivy had predicted: LOOSE LIPS SINK SHIPS! BE LIKE DAD — KEEP MUM! the government posters warned. In her case, it was the RAF that refused to talk to her. Even when she stood at the gates and asked the heavily armed guard on duty where Squadron Leader George Holden could be found, she was told in no uncertain terms that it was against orders to issue civilians with any information. Completely at her wits' end, Emily had burst into tears and blurted out that she was pregnant; the guard relented slightly, telling her that all post delivered to the base was always forwarded, so even if the recipient had been moved on, post would reach them, though this process did obviously take longer.

'I'm sure your young man will be in touch when he's had a chance to read the letters you've sent him,' he had said more kindly.

Emily didn't like to point out that she'd already written several letters and she still hadn't heard a word back from 'her young man'. On the bus back to Manchester she cursed herself for not knowing George's parents' address;

they at least might have heard from their son or, better still, know where he had been posted.

'At least he was generous with his money,' Emily thought gratefully. Thank God she hadn't spent his money on clothes and little luxuries; though, occasionally, she'd been tempted to treat herself to a new dress or a smart new handbag, Emily always resisted, instead hoarding every penny for their wedding day. Now she was grateful she had been careful; the money that George had given her would soon be spent on securing a respectable home where she could safely give birth to his baby.

As the long, lonely days passed, Emily became more desperate and disillusioned. How could she not begin to fear the worst – that her beloved had abandoned her altogether? It seemed incomprehensible that George hadn't made contact in what was now months, long enough time for her to begin to show. She was having real trouble squeezing into her nippy's uniform at work; she'd let it out as much as she could, but if her breasts continued to swell she'd have to put in a request for a new uniform, which would immediately arouse suspicion.

Trying to hide her condition at home wasn't easy either. Their small, dingy terraced house had always felt overcrowded, but now, when she was desperate for privacy so that she could rest her aching back or put up her feet, there was nowhere to go. When George was around, Emily had been able to tolerate it – home was just somewhere between work and seeing George – but with him gone and the baby growing so fast home felt unbearable. Even so, she regularly told herself she had to stay for as long as she could bear it; the money she'd saved wouldn't cover more than four months of her stay at Mary Vale and she'd have to pay for the extra weeks of care after the birth of her baby. So for the moment there was no alternative but to grit her teeth and remain at home. To put her mind at rest, Emily decided it was time to pay a visit to Mary Vale, the mother and baby home in which she was putting all her hope and trust.

Telling her family that she was going to Blackpool with a friend for the day, she set off on her journey, but, as the steam train thundered north, Emily was overwhelmed by sadness and despair. How on earth was she going to get through this on her own? Just imagining giving birth brought her out in a sweat of fear. Though she was determined to keep her and George's baby, she wondered in the harsh light of bitter reality how she was going to manage it. Her parents wouldn't want her or her bastard in the house, and in truth it was the very last place on earth she would want to bring up a child – but HOW was she going to support herself and her baby without a job or a husband?

'Whatever happens, I'm keeping our baby; it might be the last link I have with the man I love,' she thought grimly. 'I will find a way.'

Feeling panic rising inside her like a tidal wave that threatened to engulf her, Emily took a long, deep breath and concentrated on the vast sweep of Morecambe Bay against the hazy swell of the green rolling hills that slowly merged with the first fells of the Lake District. The train, puffing its way along a track that was built on a series of piers across the marsh, stopped at Grange-over-Sands, where Emily decided that, instead of staying on to Kents

Bank, the next stop and the one closest to Mary Vale according to the guard she'd spoken to, she would walk to the Home and take in the scenery. Disembarking at Grange Station, she inhaled the fresh sea air and, accompanied by noisy seagulls who swooped around the water's edge, Emily set off with a strong, determined stride. When she reached her destination, she was charmed by the Home's location and the rambling old house that overlooked the sea and the beautiful sun-drenched bay.

'This is a fine place to live,' she thought with relief and, with a nervous smile playing on her lips, she approached Mary Vale's imposing front door.

Knowing that Emily was a fee-paying client (the only kind of client that Maud Harding was genuinely interested in), Matron personally opted to show the visitor around the Home and the maternity wards. When they walked on to the ward where the babies were being fed, Emily was amused to spot a strikingly attractive, tall, slim nurse appear to roll her eyes as Matron processed between the canvas cots, talking in an over-loud voice that made the babies cry.

'Honest to God!' she overheard her say. 'The poor woman's coming here to have a baby, not to be presented at court!'

It was hard for the girls bottle-feeding the babies to keep their faces straight, watching Matron swan around the wards showing off their features as if the Home were a place of luxury and delight rather than a home for unmarried mothers miles away from anywhere.

'This is our dining room,' Matron announced, ignoring the pregnant girls with sweat dripping down their faces as they polished the vast mahogany table and chairs. 'And here's where all the food is prepared,' she said, as she barged into the vast kitchen, where Sister Mary Paul and a fleet of nuns were rolling pastry for seven large meat pies. 'All our produce is local and home grown,' Matron added, as if she personally grew it all herself.

Behind her wimple Sister Mary Paul muttered irreverently under her breath, 'And that includes all the tins of baked beans and corned beef we produce daily!'

Trailing after Matron, feeling distinctly embarrassed by her grandiose manner, Emily was relieved when the tour ended.

'Let's have tea in my office,' Matron said with a cosy smile, which immediately disappeared when she saw Shirley scurrying down the corridor. 'Tea,' she called out imperiously. 'In my office, now!'

Emily cringed at her tone; she felt so sorry for the poor girl, who shot off in terror to do Matron's bidding.

'I'm not sure I trust this woman,' Emily thought uneasily to herself. Following Matron into the office, she firmly told herself that she had to give her the benefit of the doubt. 'Let's see what she has to say next.'

Soon Shirley appeared with a loaded tray of tea and biscuits; trembling, she lowered it cautiously on to Matron's desk. Without even a thank you, Matron rudely dismissed the visibly quaking girl. 'That will be all.'

Emily's anxious gaze followed Shirley, who threw her a shadow of a smile as she bolted for the door.

'Poor kid,' she thought, beginning to wonder how on earth she would fit in with so many girls who, she imagined, weren't that much different to her in age but whose subservient manner was so different to her own confident, independent demeanour. One thing was for sure: Emily certainly wouldn't be cowed by anybody, and that included the woman facing her across the desk, who, oozing charm, was pouring hot tea into delicate china cups.

'We offer an adoption service to all our mothers,' she said, as she graciously handed Emily her tea. 'Mary Vale's resident priest, Father Benedict, is responsible for finding suitable homes for our babies. Unfortunately,' she said with a heartfelt sigh, 'some do end up with poor, working-class couples when, ideally, we would prefer our babies to be housed with a better class of parent, but needs must,' she concluded, and offered Emily one of Sister Mary Paul's delicious shortbread biscuits.

Emily's big blues eyes all but rolled out of her head at Matron's words. By now seriously at the end of her tether with Matron's insufferable snobbishness, she declined the biscuit.

'Actually – I'm working class,' she said with a bit of a swagger.

Matron did a visible double-take.

'Oh! I assumed that, as you were a fee-paying client, you were . . .'

Seeing her struggling to find the right word, Emily helped her out. 'Wealthy?' she suggested; then, without waiting for an answer, she barrelled on. 'No. I'm paying for my confinement out of my savings and, while we're on that subject, you should know that I won't be seeking an adoption for my baby – I shall be keeping it,' she said, a loud ring of pride in her voice. 'Working class I may be, but I certainly know how to love and nurture a baby.'

Though momentarily wrong-footed, Matron still managed to give the bold young woman a level look as if to say, 'HAH! That's what they all say, dear.'

Even though she'd had a serious failure of confidence on her journey north, Emily was not going to let the woman before her know of that; if anything, her hateful attitude had made her more determined than ever. Irritated by the assumptions the older woman had leapt to, Emily continued with a defiant smile. 'As soon as my fiancé in the RAF rejoins me, we shall be married.'

Matron's eyes dropped down to Emily's left hand, where there was no sign of any ring. Nevertheless, her clipped, polite smile didn't slip as she handed Emily the Home's terms and conditions, and a list of fees.

'Good day, Miss Todd – we'll look forward to seeing you when the time is right.'

Emily rose to her feet, thinking to herself, 'That's just another way of saying before you're as big as a house and everybody's asking after the father's whereabouts!'

After her ghastly meeting with Matron, Emily was relieved to meet the rest of the staff, who, unlike her, seemed dedicated and kind; she instinctively took to Sister Ada Dale, the pretty nurse she'd spotted earlier, who thoughtfully gave her a second and more extensive tour of the pre- and post-natal wards and the delivery room, which Matron had whizzed her through. Emily gazed around the delivery room; what would it be like to give birth to the child growing inside her? When Ada took Emily on to the main ward, she was transfixed by the rows of little canvas cots containing tiny babies, waiting to be fed by the girls on the feeding rota.

'It's round the clock here,' Ada joked, as she sat down and expertly balanced a squawking baby on her knee before deftly inserting large safety pins into each corner of its terry-towelling nappy without even pausing for breath.

'They're so small,' Emily murmured, gazing in wonder at the baby's tiny fingernails.

'You'd be amazed how fast they grow,' Ada assured her.

'Do any of the mothers breast-feed?' Emily asked.

Ada shook her head. 'Not a good idea if you're planning on having your baby adopted – best not to bond,' she added in a low voice.

Emily's eyes filled with tears as she watched some of the girls waddling awkwardly about the ward, looking like they were about to give birth on the spot.

'Poor things,' she murmured.

'They're very brave young women,' Ada said, as she settled the baby that she'd just successfully burped into one of the little white cots. 'Generally, they do what's best for their child, even though in most cases it breaks their hearts to be parted from them.'

In a very different tone from the one she'd used when she'd talked to Matron, Emily told the ward sister of her plans. 'I intend to keep my baby.'

Ada gave her a wide smile that revealed her perfect small white teeth. 'Lucky you!' she exclaimed. Quickly checking her fob watch, she added, 'I'm just about finished here – would you like a tour of the grounds?'

Emily nodded eagerly. 'Yes, please,' she replied.

The gardens, mostly wide, well-kept lawns with deep flowerbeds interspersed with sturdy oak trees, were bathed in bright sunshine.

Several residents were wheeling babies in big old prams, or pegging out nappies on the washing line in the kitchen garden; some more active girls were weeding flowerbeds, while others sat on benches chatting to each other as they knitted baby clothes.

'This will soon be me,' Emily thought, as she stood on the lawn that looked over the bay, where high tide was rushing in. Sighing, she turned inland to gaze at the fells, presently drenched in the afternoon sunshine. Here at Mary Vale, built on land between the fells and the sea, she would hide away and await the birth of her baby, all the time praying for the return of the man she loved.

8. Rumbles of War

'More! Please, Mummy, more!'

With her head on the same pillow as her son, Gloria stared into her five-year-old's sparkling green eyes and sighed. With her long, raven-black hair fanned out around her slender shoulders, she had the same stunning Mediterranean colouring as her son, except that his hair was a mass of dark curls. Right now his cherubic little face was lit up with excitement, unlike his mother's, which was drawn with fatigue. She had so much to do before Stan arrived home from work, but how could she resist Robin's beseeching smile?

'Just one more chapter, then I have to go and cook Daddy's supper,' she said with an indulgent smile.

Robin giggled happily and snuggled up closer to his mother. 'What happens next in the Enchanted Wood?' he whispered.

Once again, Gloria opened Enid Blyton's popular book and continued reading until Robin's long, silky eyelashes drooped and he finally fell asleep. Laying the book on the bedside table, she stood up and tiptoed to the door, where she turned to smile adoringly at her darling boy. If she'd got her dates right, Robin might well have a little brother or sister to play with in the new year. Heavens! How would she manage with two? Hurrying downstairs, she checked the meat pie that was baking in the oven in the back scullery, then set about peeling carrots and potatoes.

Excited as she was about the possibility of a new arrival, she wondered how long she would be able to hold down her job teaching infant children at the local school in Battersea. There was no question that she loved her job, especially now that Robin had just started in the reception class right next door to her own classroom. But with a new baby in the house, surely she would have to give up work to take care of her growing family. Stan had advised her not to dwell too much on what she would or would not have to do.

'With war imminent there'll soon be changes beyond our control,' he said whenever Gloria started to worry about the future.

Staring thoughtfully at the bubbles forming in the pan of water she'd put on to boil, Gloria wished that Stan wasn't quite so insistent about war breaking out. Like most people, she wanted peace, after the horrors of the last war, in which so many millions of men were slain (including her own beloved father). Gloria approved of the prime minister's appeasement tactics with Hitler, but recent aggression by the Nazis in Czechoslovakia had caused concern. It seemed increasingly obvious that duplicitous Hitler said one thing and then, as soon as Chamberlain's back was turned, he did exactly the opposite. She knew for sure that her fiercely patriotic husband would be the first to sign up; she'd only to see his expression every time he read an article in the paper or heard a radio announcement about the latest atrocities to know how much he detested the man.

'That fella needs teaching a lesson,' Stan would mutter

darkly. 'A short, sharp shock to put the cocky little upstart in his damned place.'

For all her attempts to turn the conversation away from 'taking on the Hun', Gloria found that Stan remained steadfastly determined that he would not abandon his country when the call came. The thought of her husband marching off to fight the enemy made Gloria almost sick with fear; all she wanted was to keep her happy little family safe and to bring her children up in a country that was at peace. When she heard the familiar sound of the key turning in the front door, her face lit up; quickly wiping her hands on her pinafore, she smiled at her tall, broad-shouldered husband framed in the kitchen doorway. Even now, after seven years of marriage, her heart still skipped a beat at the sight of his wide, generous smile and the mop of jet-black hair that fell carelessly across his dark blue eyes.

'Hello, sweetheart,' he murmured, and stooped to kiss her full on the mouth.

Gloria laid her head briefly against his strong chest, where the familiar smell of soap combined with engine oil assailed her senses.

'Good day?' she asked.

'Long and hard – London's getting too busy,' he joked, as he hung up his coat and washed his hands under the scullery tap. 'Mmm, supper smells good,' he said appreciatively, as Gloria laid the hot meat pie on the table alongside a bowl of vegetables dotted with melting butter. 'How lucky am I?' he joked. 'To have a beautiful, clever wife who can cook like an angel after a hard day teaching little 'uns reading, writing and arithmetic!'

Gloria smiled as she set down two glasses of cold water by their dinner plates; she knew how proud her husband was of her academic achievements. At the same age as Robin was now she and Stan had started school together; she'd always been the brightest student in the class, while he was just an average learner with an overriding interest in football and car engines. Their easy friendship had blossomed into love, and as teenagers they were inseparable. Stan had started working for London Transport as a bus driver as soon as he left secondary school at fourteen, while Gloria had remained on at school until she matriculated, after which she'd attended a nearby teacher-training college.

Everybody had said when they got engaged that beautiful, clever Gloria could do better for herself than marry a bus driver, but Gloria had never strayed from her first and only love, even though other men had regularly tried to court her. And when she qualified as a primary-school teacher she married her childhood sweetheart in the church at the end of the street where she'd grown up. Two years later Robin had been born, but it had taken another five years to conceive again; she and Stan couldn't have been happier or more excited. The only thing that marred Gloria's joy was the constant, worrying talk of a blasted war!

After supper they washed and dried the dishes in the back-scullery slop sink, then – as was their nightly habit – they settled down with a cup of tea in front of the coal fire to listen to the radio. Absorbed in following a complicated knitting pattern for a baby's layette in a neutral cream colour, Gloria wondered dreamily whether the baby she was carrying would be a boy or a girl.

Her reverie was broken by Stan's sombre words: 'There's been talk of women and children being evacuated,' he said, as he lit up a Senior Service cigarette.

Gloria, who had heard the news too but had assiduously avoided mentioning it to her husband, had absolutely no intention of being evacuated. Come what may, she was staying in the city she loved, and in the house she and Stan had saved up and bought just after Robin was born. London was her home, and as far as Gloria was concerned neither Hitler nor Neville Chamberlain would move her out to the country to live in a community where she did not belong.

Stan broke into her rebellious thoughts. 'You might have to consider it, sweetheart,' he murmured.

Laying down her knitting, Gloria glared at him. 'Why? War hasn't even been declared and you've already joined the scaremongers! Packing women and children off to the middle of nowhere before a single bomb has fallen.'

Stan took a deep drag on his cigarette, which he slowly inhaled. 'War's coming, Gloria,' he said. 'For your safety and Robin's, and the baby's too, you cannot stay in London, which is sure to be one of Hitler's prime targets.'

'War might *not* come,' she cried. 'Chamberlain's peace talks might have an effect on other governments; he might succeed,' she frantically insisted.

Seeing the fear and anguish on his wife's lovely face, Stan stubbed out his cigarette and laid a hand over hers. 'Let's hope you're right, my darling . . . let's hope you're right.'

In another part of London, Archie Percival waited impatiently in his stylish Mayfair flat for the return of Marigold, his mistress, who had a long list of afternoon appointments but had faithfully promised she would be back in good time for their trip to the Palace Theatre to watch a production of *Under Your Hat*, a show that was taking the West End by storm. Archie was desperate to get his obliging mistress into bed before they left for the Palace Theatre: after too long in the country with his wife, who locked herself away in the west wing of the house and barely spoke to him, he was desperately in need of Marigold's tender favours. Lovely, lovely Marigold, with her long, white, slender legs, her full breasts and slim hips, would take his mind off his mounting financial problems, albeit briefly.

With the arrival of Marigold bearing bulging bags from Harrods and Fortnum and Mason, Archie forced a smile on to his face; broke he may be, but how could he chide his lover, especially when she arrived bearing bottles of chilled Bollinger? After a satisfactory hour of love-making Sir Percival felt better than he had in weeks. As Marigold took a hot bath, watched by Archie drinking the last of the champagne, she began to speak in her plummy, pouting voice.

'Darling, I hope you don't mind but I've asked the Bennetts to the show – and to supper at the Savoy too.'

'Oh . . .' drawled Archie persuasively, as he smoothed soap on to Marigold's perfectly flat stomach. 'Oh, sweet, I was so hoping to have you all to myself tonight?'

'Darling, this is a mercy call,' Marigold chided, relieving him of his glass and polishing off the contents. 'My dear friends the Bennetts are frightfully sad and demoralized.'

Wondering why he was expected to waste good money

cheering up the Bennetts, Archie looked distinctly unsympathetic. 'And what might have upset them?' he scoffed. 'A little drop on the stock market, perhaps?'

'You are a beast!' she giggled, as she flicked soap bubbles into his face. 'Poor, poor Cicily has just been told by the most famous obstetrician in Harley Street that she and Edgar will never be able to have children.'

'Well, then,' Archie said flippantly. 'They'll just have to adopt.'

Marigold gave him an arch look. 'Oh, of course, you'll know all about that,' she teased in a mock-shocked voice. 'You being the governor of a home for *fallen women*,' she finished melodramatically.

Rising like a perfect Venus, she waved her arms: the sign that she wanted a towel, which Archie tenderly wrapped around her shoulders, but not before kissing each of her soapy nipples.

'Be a sweetie and help me cheer up poor Edgar,' Marigold continued.

Percival waved a hand in the air. 'I wouldn't give a damn about being childless!' he exclaimed.

'Me neither,' she agreed. 'Something we have in common, my darling – we're free spirits,' she whispered seductively, as she snuggled up against Percival, who, hoping they could return to bed, groped clumsily for her breasts.

'No, naughty boy,' she said, tapping him lightly on the arm. 'We mustn't be late,' she added, and finished drying herself before dropping the bath towel on the floor for the maid to pick up.

Sitting on the pink padded velvet stool by Marigold's dressing table, Percival lit up a cigarette as he watched his mistress dress. Picking up where she'd left off, Marigold continued, 'Tell poor heartbroken Edgar that adoption's not as ghastly as it sounds. Heavens!' she said with a roll of her big baby-blue eyes. 'They're as rich as Croesus — they could adopt an Indian prince if they were so inclined.'

No sooner were the words out of Marigold's pretty little mouth than a light flashed on in Archie's head and he recalled Matron's words, which perhaps he'd been too quick to dismiss, desperate as he'd been to get rid of her that night.

What was it she'd said? 'They might be bastards, but we could assure our clients that at least one line of their genealogy was respectable.'

His mind moved fast; Edgar Bennett was the eldest son of the wealthy Earl of Easterbrook and was indeed — as Marigold had put it — 'as rich as Croesus'. The earldom would be passed on to Edgar when his father died, and Edgar would need a son to carry on the noble family line. That his wife was infertile would have been a body blow to Edgar, who was, in effect, an heir without an heir.

'My sweet,' he murmured, his mind going at a million miles an hour as he helped his mistress into an elegant silk dress, 'I will, of course, do everything I can to cheer up Edgar.'

'You're so precious, Archie,' she whispered as she leant forward to kiss his fleshy lips.

Percival smiled; he would unquestionably do everything in his power to help Cicily and Edgar, who might in return be able to help him too.

9. Windermere

It was a mystery to Isla how her independent, open-minded, socialist grandmother could have produced a daughter as feeble as her own mother.

'How did it ever happen?' she asked Jeannie, as they set off over the fells for Orrest Head, where they planned to have a picnic.

'Oh, your mother is just like her father: weak and frightened of everything,' Jeannie answered cheerfully.

'I can't imagine YOU with a weak man!' Isla laughed.

'Well, in truth, I wasn't with him for long,' Jeannie answered honestly. 'We lasted long enough to produce a child, then he died after an attack of flu.'

Incredulous Isla shook her head. 'Why did you marry him in the first place?'

As the land rose higher, Jeannie stopped to catch her breath. 'Darling, he was VERY good-looking, and quite a catch – well, at least to start with – before he became dull and boring.'

Isla giggled. 'You must have made the poor man's life a misery.'

'Oh, I did,' Jeannie said with complete candour. 'He was scared to death of me, but' – she gave a brief sigh of regret – 'it was a shame that your mother never knew him. She would have liked him so much more than she ever liked me.'

Offended on her darling grandmother's behalf, Isla responded staunchly, 'Silly woman!'

'It's the truth, dear: they would have had so much in common. Upright members of the establishment, both terrified of putting a foot wrong, they would have been a great comfort to one another,' Jeannie said with a wry smile.

Isla marvelled that Jeannie could be so objective about her only child.

'I tried SO hard to love Sylvia, and I do, of course – she is my daughter after all – but I don't especially like her,' Jeannie confessed as they strode on. 'As she grew up, she became duller and duller with every passing year. It was almost a relief when she met your father. He was the father figure she never had. He snapped her up and promptly removed her far away from me,' she said with a shrug. 'I know he thought I was a terrible mother – in fairness to him, I probably was!'

As they gained height, Windermere, dotted with pleasure boats and sparkling blue in the spring sunshine, came into view.

'The best thing they ever did was have you, darling child,' Jeannie said fondly, shooting her granddaughter a warm smile. 'Like me, they produced a child who was the very opposite of themselves; you are clever and passionate, not one of the herd, a girl with spirit and determination,' she said proudly.

Tears brimmed in Isla's lovely Highland pale blue eyes. She was so happy here in the Lake District with her beloved Jeannie, who had never judged or condemned her but had opened her door and welcomed her. Even after her grandchild had poured out the whole terrible, disastrous story of her love affair with an older married man, Jeannie had shown no disgust or voiced any disapproval; she had simply wrapped her arms around weeping Isla and held her close.

'Men!' she had scoffed. 'We learn about them when it's too late and then we have to live with the consequences.'

At the top of Orrest Head they found a flat rock to sit on and have their picnic. Now that Isla had got her appetite back and the terrible bouts of sickness had passed, she was unashamedly eating for two and had a much bigger tummy to show for it. After sharing out food from their rucksacks – cheese-and-pickle sandwiches, boiled eggs, tomatoes and fruit cake – plus hot sweet tea that they poured from Thermos flasks, they sat in companionable silence, taking in the view and watching the sunlight sweep across the lake and surrounding fells.

Having not talked about the future or made any plans, Jeannie chose this peaceful moment on top of the fell with puffy white clouds scudding overhead to open discussions about Isla's child.

'Now, what are we going to do about this baby of yours?'

While Isla had been in Windermere, she'd had time to consider her situation; without pressure or prejudice, she'd reached a decision.

'I want to have it adopted,' she said.

Jeannie poured more tea from her flask before looking up. 'Sure?'

Isla nodded. 'Yes, I know it'll be hard, but he or she will stand a better chance of a more balanced life with a loving mother AND father,' Isla added pointedly.

'Well, my dear, I agree, if my opinion helps at all,' Jeannie offered gently. 'And I'm proud of you for making such a brave decision.'

Isla set down her Thermos cup and wrapped her arms around her grandmother. 'YOU help, Jeannie, I love you so much,' she blurted out. 'I couldn't have got through this without your strength and belief in me, even though I have all but ruined my life.'

'Stuff and nonsense,' Jeannie cried, as she brushed crumbs from her tartan skirt. 'You'll get through this, see your child safely adopted and continue with your studies, hopefully at any university other than blasted Durham. We don't want that odious lecherous professor near you again.'

On their way down the fell, they discussed where Isla would give birth.

'I think I should remove myself so I don't embarrass you,' she suggested.

'I'm a bit of a social outcast, so I don't think you should start worrying about my reputation at this stage,' Jeannie told her staunchly. 'Though I do believe you should be in a hospital where you will be safely delivered of your baby by people who know what they're doing and who also have experience in adoption.'

'There!' Isla exclaimed. 'You've come up with an answer: what I need is a reliable mother and baby home, not too far away from you, dearest Jeannie,' she added with a smile. 'I couldn't bear not to see you regularly while I wait for the baby to be born.'

Jeannie linked her arm through Isla's. 'Let's do a bit of research when we get home and look at homes between here and Lancaster – that's not too far away, is it?'

'Lancaster's fine,' Isla replied. 'But no further,' she giggled.

Quickening her pace but still linking arms with Isla, Jeannie said cheerily, 'Good, at last we have a plan.'

Not fifty miles away, in Crow Thorn Grange, Archie Percival was also thinking about adoption. The evening with Cicily and Edgar Bennett had unquestionably been eye-wateringly expensive, but, if things worked out, he comforted himself, he could offset the expense as an 'investment'.

The play cheered them up mildly, but supper at the Savoy was far more uplifting: Archie positively let the wine flow throughout the night. He danced with Cicily, then left her to weep in Marigold's arms, which gave him the perfect opportunity to have a man-to-man conversation with Edgar, who was clearly at his wits' end.

'You see, old man, I have to produce an heir – in fact, an heir and a spare would be the ticket,' he blurted out as he and Archie sat opposite each other, drinking brandy. 'What do I do? Leave the woman I love in favour of a younger, more fecund version? We've always been completely devoted to each other – it's the worst blow possible,' he gulped, downing a good half of the brandy in his glass.

Again, Percival recalled Matron's words. Thinking fast, he realized that if he handled this incredibly delicate situation carefully, there might be something in it for him. Unfortunately, he was lacking in knowledge when it came to the nuts and bolts of adoption, but in order not to waste valuable time Percival reckoned he could research the finer details of the arrangement at a later date; right now he had to win Edgar's confidence. Lighting up a cigarette, he said as casually as he could manage, 'Have you considered adoption?'

Edgar rolled his eyes. 'Never, but with poor Cicily so badly cut up' – he gave a loud groan – 'I suppose adoption is a possibility. The trouble is,' he blurted out, 'it's a bit like playing Russian roulette – you never know what you're going to end up with.'

Making sympathetic noises, Percival laid the seeds of his plan. 'I totally understand, old chap; it can be a pretty random business. I should know,' he said, dropping his voice to add, in a confidential whisper, 'But I may be able to help smooth that path for you. I happen to be chairman of the board of a local mother and baby home near Kendal. We constantly have eager prospective parents knocking at our door looking for the child they can never have themselves. They're usually decent enough folk, salt-of-the-earth sort who don't mind the baby's lineage, but, for the likes of you, where breeding is everything, I can see you wouldn't want to be fobbed off with the bastard child of a scullery maid and a stable boy.'

When Archie saw Edgar's eyes widen in what might have been horror, he speeded up his delivery. 'A man of your rank would need a child of impeccable breeding.'

Looking a little less tense, Edgar nodded his head. 'It would certainly help.'

'Well, speaking from experience, I can tell you that, mingled in with the hoi polloi, there have been some rather fine girls from good families at Mary Vale over the years I've been connected with the place; their presence in the Home is, as I'm sure you can imagine, highly confidential.' Archie topped up their brandy tumblers and pulled his chair closer to Edgar's. 'I've dealt with some of the families on a personal level. Some have been highly connected – of course, I can't mention names – but I can say that one duke, several earls and a couple of knights were the fathers of just a few expectant girls who were placed in my care.'

By this time Edgar was registering considerable interest. 'And the girls themselves, the mothers?' he inquired.

'Fine gels,' Percival announced. 'Good stock but in trouble. Generally speaking, they're frightened, ashamed and in terror of their father's wrath.'

Edgar shook his head in bewilderment. 'How do you match the right child to the right parent? It must be frightfully complicated. And how do I make sure I am, er, allocated the . . . "right" sort of baby for us?'

Sweating with the effort of appearing to know what he was talking about, when, in fact, he was making it up as he went along, Percival glibly continued, 'You can leave that to me – that's if you want me to look into things for you, of course.' He paused, waiting for Edgar's response. When he nodded, Percival carried on with his delivery. 'When we fill in the forms for adoption, we put down as much detail as we can get out of the expectant mothers and their parents too; it helps in the delicate process of finding the right match,' he said, consciously repeating Edgar's turn of phrase. 'And, in your case, I would of course take a *personal* interest.'

By this time Edgar was on the edge of his chair. 'Are you telling me that you could procure a child of good lineage for my wife and me?'

Even though he knew there were obstacles in his path, like Father Benedict for instance, Percival cruised on as if nothing could possibly go wrong. 'Absolutely, old man!' he said with a confident laugh. 'Without a shadow of a doubt.'

Choking back tears, Edgar grasped Archie's hand. 'You could save my marriage,' he gulped. 'You could make Cicily and me happy again.'

'It would be a pleasure to make you both happy, Sir,' Archie fawned.

Making a little awkward noise in the back of his throat, he continued almost apologetically. 'I'm sorry to mention the subject of, er, a donation . . .'

Leaving the sentence hanging, he waited for Edgar to pick it up.

'Not a problem; rest assured, a fine baby, a son and heir to the Easterbrook title, is something one simply cannot put a price on.'

'Quite,' Archie agreed, smiling. 'We'd have to be discreet, and I would have to handle this matter personally to make sure I find the right gel, the right match for you; it all takes time and is extremely delicate, you understand. I can assure you, Sir, it's a service I would only offer to a *special* friend.'

Archie was trying not to salivate at the thought of the funds, which he desperately needed to appease his bank manager, that could be making their way into his pocket soon.

'I am in your hands, Sir Percival!' Edgar exclaimed. 'Let me speak with my wife, then we'll be in touch. Meanwhile, here's my card: phone me any time, day or night.'

Throughout this intense, private conversation with

85

Edgar, Sir Percival had come across as an experienced, dedicated professional, when, in truth, his only interests, so far as Mary Vale was concerned, were the social status it provided him in the county and the little money he could filch from the pregnant girls' admission fees. Up until now he'd never taken the slightest interest in where the bastard babies went: that was worthy Father Benedict's department. But if Mary Vale's adoptions were to become lucrative for him, he would have to find a way to sidestep Father Benedict and legitimately involve himself with the convent's adoption process. He hadn't a clue how he could achieve that end, but one thing was written in stone: he wasn't going to let a nit-picking priest and a bunch of bloody pious nuns get in the way of his making money out of Mary Vale's unwanted bastards!

10. Convent Business

In the cosy convent sitting room, Father Ben, Sister Ann and Ada gathered for their weekly staff meeting. It could not have been more different from the board meetings held at Crow Thorn Grange. There was no alcohol but plenty of tea and cake supplied by Sister Mary Paul. Knowing Father Ben's passion for fruitcake, she made sure a rich cherry Genoa cake was always on the table, alongside china cups and saucers and a big pot of hot strong tea, at every meeting. Relaxing in big old armchairs and warmed by a crackling log fire, the small group appreciated not only the cake and tea but also Sister Ann's precise weekly update. The nun was responsible for logging all the details of the comings and goings at Mary Vale: the number of mothers admitted, the babies born and adopted, the mothers leaving, and how many beds were available at any one time.

Father Ben's first question was, 'Tell me, Sister, how's Shirley getting on these days?'

Sister Ann beamed as she turned to Ada. 'You tell him: you have a better way with words than me.'

'I'd say transformed, Father,' Ada replied. 'Happy and so relieved still to be here.'

'That's just great,' Father Ben enthused.

'The poor girl works her fingers to the bone as a way of

repaying her debt to the convent.' Sister Ann added, 'We tell her not to, but will she listen?'

'As long as she's happy, that's all that matters,' Father Ben said. 'Any progress on the job front?' he inquired.

'Not yet, I'm afraid. We've sent letters far and wide to charitable trust funds that we've heard about. Though I have to tell you, it's an awful, long-winded process,' she confessed. 'I hope and pray something will come up soon.'

'I'll certainly offer up some masses for Shirley's very special intention,' Father Ben promised. Glancing down at his notebook, he said, 'Moving on to other business, are any new residents due to arrive soon?'

Sister Ann ran her index finger down her logbook. 'A Miss Emily Todd from Manchester came to inspect the Home recently,' she replied. 'Her baby's due around Christmas time; she implied she'd like to start her stay here sometime in August,' she added.

Ada grinned cheekily. 'Matron took a shine to Miss Todd when she discovered that she was a fee-paying customer – though I got the distinct impression the feeling wasn't reciprocated by Miss Todd; she was obviously embarrassed by Matron's overbearing and smarmy manner.'

'The way she favours the fee-paying girls is a disgrace!' Sister Ann exclaimed. 'If she prefers to nurse the rich, why in God's name did she ever come here to Mary Vale?'

Knowing how flirty and coquettish Matron was around Sir Percival, Ada giggled. 'Sir Percival might have been the main attraction! Or should I say, "Archie"?'

Sister Ann burst out laughing. 'For the love of God,

stop putting uncharitable thoughts into our heads, Ada!' she begged.

Father Benedict topped up their cups with tea, then helped himself to another slice of cake. 'I'm afraid Matron is the cross we all have to bear,' he said with a resigned smile.

Back at Crow Thorn Grange, Sir Percival wasted no time in arranging to take Matron out to dinner. Matron blushed in delight when she found a letter from him on her office desk.

My dear Maud,

I have something I would like to discuss with you in private. Would you accept my invitation to take you out to dinner at the Commodore Inn in Grange next Wednesday evening? I shall pick you up from Mary Vale if that suits you?

Yours most respectfully,
Archibald

'Archie!' Matron almost collapsed when she read the letter. 'Dinner, alone! Oh, yes, yes!'

In a daze, Matron wondered what Archie could possibly want to talk to her about, and in private too. Maybe he was finally divorcing that milksop of a wife of his and was looking for a woman of calibre to replace her? Maybe he would finally confess his admiration for her? How she'd waited for this moment; she could not have borne the grubbiness of Mary Vale without his noble presence; he alone had made her life worth living, and now she was convinced she was about to receive a sign of his devotion.

The days until their appointed meeting dragged, and when Wednesday finally came round Matron was as excited and gauche as a teenage girl on her first date. She could hardly dress herself for trembling and had to take sips of brandy to steady her nerves before she applied her make-up and jewellery.

'Deep breaths,' she told herself, as she descended the stairs to the Home's spacious entrance hall, where passing girls gaped in amazement at a transformed Matron, with her dark hair swept into an elegant chignon and a fox fur draped over a sparkling black sequinned cocktail dress.

'Gawd Almighty, she looks like bleedin' royalty!' one of the girls gasped incredulously under her breath.

When Archie proffered an arm to escort Matron to his car, her heart fluttered so much she thought she might faint and, sitting beside Archie in his chauffeur-driven old Rover, which smelt of expensive, manly tobacco smoke, she was giddy with pleasure.

The arrival of Sir Percival and his guest caused quite a stir at the Commodore Inn, where the head waiter, aware of Percival's prestigious standing in local society, obsequiously led them to the best table in the house, in a spacious bay window that gave glorious views of the vast bay, where the tide was rushing in over the flat, silvery-green marsh. Once they were comfortably settled, gallant, smiling Archie laid a tender hand over Matron's shaking hand.

'It's wonderful to have you to myself, Maud, dear.'

When Matron smiled tenderly at him, Percival thanked God for the soft candlelight, which hid her rather yellow teeth and the hard set of her mouth. He needed to sweet-talk the old bat if he were to succeed in getting her to do what he wanted, but he bloody well drew the line at physical intimacy, which she seemed to be eagerly working her way towards.

'Archibald,' she sighed softly. 'It's a joy to be alone with you.'

Luckily, the waiter reappeared with the menu and the drinks Percival had instantly ordered when he'd entered the restaurant; pretending to be studying the menu, he wondered how he could play this meeting to his advantage. If he overdid the flirting, he'd be stuck with kissing Matron, the thought of which made his stomach churn. However, if he pursued only the business angle, he could see from her glowing face that she'd be bitterly disappointed and therefore not so willing to play ball with him. He needed to deftly massage Maud Harding's ego if he were to succeed in getting her to work alongside him in a new business venture.

'Christ! If this game's to succeed, I need the blasted woman to help me make it happen. Come on, man, get a grip – you can do it.'

Starting somewhat hesitantly, Percival said, 'Do you recall what we discussed at our previous meeting at Crow Thorn Grange, Maud?'

'Of course, your lovely home,' Matron gushed. 'Always a pleasure to be invited.'

Before she could shoot off at a tangent, Percival quickly added, 'There was something particular you mentioned towards the end of our meeting.'

Looking perplexed, Matron said, 'Oh, yes?'

Steadying his breathing so he didn't rush it, Percival started with an ingratiating compliment. 'I've always been impressed by your intelligence and ingenuity, Maud, gifts rarely found in a woman.' Matron positively glowed as he flattered and praised her. 'Over time and with due deliberation, I've come to the conclusion that your recent proposal for taking Mary Vale into a new era is enormously impressive.'

By this time Matron really was flummoxed; trying to keep a smile on her face, she wondered what on earth she might have said that had had such a profound effect on Archie. Seeing her struggling, Percival leant closer to fill up her glass. 'An elitist sideline to our adoption business,' he murmured in her ear. 'I simply haven't been able to shake off your clever idea, and I'd be grateful if you could elaborate on it.'

The cogs started to turn in Matron's brain. 'Ah, yes, I remember.'

'You suggested – and please correct me if I'm wrong,' he said with a humble smile, 'that Mary Vale could offer – for an enhanced fee – a child of good breeding and status to the more discerning couples seeking adoption.'

'I do recall saying that,' she smirked.

Percival lowered his voice to repeat another thing she'd said that night: 'They might be bastards, you said, but at least one line of their genealogy is respectable.' He gave a soft chuckle.

Looking rather pleased with herself, Matron replied, 'How very bold of me.'

'To use your words again, dear Maud, you said it was such a waste not to exploit what's right on our doorstep.' He stopped to take a thoughtful sip from his glass. 'However, there is one rather large stumbling block.' He paused to look her levelly in the eye. 'As I mentioned before, how do we circumnavigate the little problem of the convent and Father Benedict's role if we want to pursue such a venture?'

Holding his breath, Percival waited; if the old bat didn't come up with a satisfactory answer, he didn't know how he could possibly progress the idea further. 'We can't just smuggle babies out of the Home,' he said, pressing her by stating the obvious. 'We have to find a way for it to appear, at least on paper, a respectable and legitimate operation.'

A look came over Matron's face, which slightly alarmed Percival; he didn't know it, but it was the same forbidding look she'd thrown at any doctor who questioned her authority when she worked on the Front during the Great War.

Dropping the smiles and simpers, she spoke with steely authority. 'In my position I am at liberty to peruse the convent's documents; I also keep details on the Home's adoptions in my office. Their rules are so simple and *Christian*, charitable to the point of homespun,' she mocked. 'I'm sure two clever people such as you and I can find a loophole.'

'Maud,' he murmured as he emptied out the last of the Chablis into her glass. 'I believe you could move mountains if you have a mind to. But . . .' he added with a slightly wistful smile, 'how quickly can you look at these documents? You see, I'm rather anxious to get our new venture under way.'

'I'll have you know, Sir, that when I have a mind to I can indeed move mountains!' Matron answered haughtily. 'Sourcing a few little documents is certainly not a problem for me,' she added with a dismissive toss of her head.

Thrilled at Matron's confident responses, Percival quickly made a suggestion before the food arrived and diverted her attention. 'Perhaps after you've had time to check the files, we could meet again to discuss the matter?'

Matron positively gushed. 'Of course. Another dinner *à deux* would be most enjoyable,' she murmured. 'And, as for getting around the problem of Father Benedict, there are ways and means.'

'Really?' Percival said, a little over-excitedly. 'What do you have in mind?'

Matron wagged an authoritative finger in his startled face. 'Leave that matter with me, Archie, dear.'

Percival made a servile gesture. 'I bow to your wisdom, dear lady.'

As Percival had anticipated, the arrival of their food did indeed divert Matron's attention. Digging into his rare fillet of steak, Percival hoped he wouldn't have to go through another restaurant scenario as Matron had just suggested; he didn't want to be involved in a business relationship with Maud Harding that was blurred around the edges. However, for the time being, Percival, with his ultimate money-making goal in mind, did not have a choice.

'Right now, if the old bag asked me to try to walk on water, I'd no doubt agree to it!'

11. Arrangements are Made

Emily's time to check into Mary Vale had come. She'd been hanging on for as long as she could in order to save money, but she knew with certainty that it would be unwise to wait another week longer. While she'd been just about able to conceal her condition in the early months of her pregnancy, a sudden growing spurt resulted in her developing a noticeably large tummy, which was becoming almost impossible to conceal.

Some of her saucier colleagues had teased her recently. 'Been on the chips, Em?' they'd laughed when they were in the changing room together, as Emily, without thinking, had removed her apron.

A little boy eating a buttered tea cake with his mum had inquired rather too loudly, 'Why has that lady got a big tummy, Mummy?'

If the customers were noticing the size of her, then it was clearly time to go. With her case packed and hidden under tarpaulin sheets in the garden shed (she couldn't trust her sneaky younger sister not to snoop if she left it under her bed), Emily was ready to take flight, but first she had to explain her unexpected departure to her parents, who weren't at all keen on her moving out. Not because they had much affection for their eldest daughter, or for any of their children in particular; they just wanted her wage packet.

'How are we going to survive without your money?' her dad grumbled.

Wearing the baggy old dress that she changed into the minute she got home, Emily sucked in her stomach until it actually hurt.

'It's just a temporary move, Dad, a promotion,' she lied.

'Will you be able to send money home?' her mother whined.

'I'll do my best, Mam.' 'Another lie,' thought Emily. 'But I'll be paying for digs in Leeds, so there won't be much left over.'

'You just said it were a bloody promotion – they can't be paying you less than you earn already?' her dad quizzed her.

Emily gave an inward groan; why had she used the word 'promotion'?

'The extra money, as I've just told Mother, will just about cover my digs and travel costs.' Another lie tripping quickly off her tongue.

Keen to get away from her whingeing parents, Emily bade them a quick goodbye, then left the claustrophobic house she'd grown up in and headed for the railway station. Though she was relieved to get away from her family, tears stung her eyes as the train rumbled out of the station; this essential journey north would take her even further away from George, whom she still hadn't heard a word from. Now firmly convinced he'd abandoned her, or, worse still, was dead, Emily had nevertheless posted a final letter with her forwarding address to Squadron Leader George Holden c/o RAF Padgate, Warrington. Only time would tell if she would ever lay eyes on her beloved again.

Though Emily had made the journey to Grange before, she still gasped at the beauty of Morecambe Bay opening out in front of her; with the tide well in, the sea seemed to meet the sky in a glittering haze of silvery blue. This time, Emily stayed on the train and got off at Kents Bank, just a short walk from the Home, where she was immensely relieved to be met at the door by Ada, rather than Matron. Knowing that all eyes would be on the newcomer, Ada had made it her business to be on hand when Emily arrived.

'Hello, how was your journey?' she said cheerily, as she relieved Emily of her suitcase and led her up two flights of stairs to a large room on the second floor with big bay windows that looked out over the marsh to the Irish Sea.

'This is one of the nicest rooms, with lovely views,' Ada said, depositing the case beside the bed, which had been neatly made up with a bright quilted counterpane by the window. 'It's three-bedded,' she pointed out. 'You'll be sharing with Nancy – she's due before you,' Ada continued chattily. 'In a few weeks you'll be joined by another girl.'

'How old is Nancy?' Emily asked nervously, as she hung her coat on the hook on the back of the bedroom door.

'She's eighteen,' Ada informed her.

'A bit younger than me,' Emily commented, her face showing the growing anxiety she was feeling.

'Not much,' Ada said. 'And you'll love Nancy – she's had a bit of a tough time, with terrible morning sickness and anaemia. But she's much better now and I'm sure you two will get on really well.'

'Thank you,' Emily said, smiling, grateful for the thoughtful reassurance. 'Where's Nancy now? I'd love to say hello.'

Ada checked the fob watch attached to the apron of her nurse's uniform. 'She's probably in the garden on a lovely day like this. The afternoons are free for the girls to do what they please – relax, sit in the garden, knit, go for a walk or attend Sister Ann's fitness and exercise classes.'

Emily raised one beautifully trimmed eyebrow. 'Fitness and exercise classes?' she queried.

'They're an excellent preparation for labour; the girls find them really useful – you should try them yourself,' Ada said. Turning quickly to the newcomer, she added, 'Come on, let's see if we can find Nancy.'

The garden was as Emily remembered it, but now it was a blaze of cream, red and gold roses and richly perfumed summer blooms – lilies, phlox, digitalis, delphiniums and carnations growing in profusion in the flowerbeds.

Used to endless rows of redbrick terraces with only small backyards and front doors that opened on to the street, Emily stopped dead in her tracks. 'Beautiful!' she cried in delight.

Ada smiled too. 'Anything would grow here,' she told the new resident. 'The sun and the position of the secluded gardens are a perfect environment, for babies as well as plants,' she joked.

Emily gazed around the garden – bees droned and songbirds chirruped. A small group of heavily pregnant girls was sitting on benches, knitting and chatting, while one lay on the lawn reading a book with her friend beside her, fast asleep. Some not so heavily pregnant girls were energetically pushing big old-fashioned sprung prams containing tiny babies along the winding garden paths; Emily watched them as they chatted happily to each other, occasionally stopping to readjust a blanket or turn a fretful baby on to its side before they continued with their walk.

'There's Nancy!' Ada cried, as she pointed out Nancy at the back of the pram-pushers. 'Come and say hello.'

Eager to meet her new room-mate, Emily hurried after Ada, who had a long, athletic stride. Nancy stopped when she saw Ada flagging her down. Emily thought she looked younger than her eighteen years, and her burgeoning tummy looked too big for her small frame. Smiling shyly, she shook Emily by the hand.

'It will be nice to have company,' she said pleasantly.

'And how's Lizzie today?' Ada asked, as she peeped into the pram.

Nancy tenderly patted Shirley's little girl's bedding. 'She's fine now we're on the move, but back in the nursery she was screaming blue murder. She gets terrible wind, but Sister Ann's been teaching me how to wind her and it works, thank God,' she said with a laugh. 'She might be small but, once she gets going, she wakes up the other babies.'

Ada was impressed with Nancy's handling of the baby. Nancy's affection for Lizzie had started simply because she felt sorry for the poor mite, but in just a few weeks she seemed to have developed a deep affection for the little girl, who cooed happily at the sound of Nancy's soft, gentle voice. Though Ada was happy for Lizzie to have a devoted carer, she hoped that Nancy wouldn't make the mistake of bonding with the child, who was destined to be adopted quite soon.

'Better get a move on,' Nancy said, and nodded towards the old Silver Cross pram in which Lizzie was making loud protesting noises. 'It's almost time for her feed.'

Before she left, she turned to Emily and said shyly, 'Goodbye, see you later.'

'She's nice,' Emily said to Ada, as Nancy went on her way.

'She's lovely,' Ada affirmed. 'I'm sure you'll both get on. Now, if you'll excuse me, Emily, I need to get back to help Sister Ann with the next round of feeds. See you later,' she said with her beautiful glowing smile. 'Over a cuppa!'

Left alone, Emily settled down on a sunny bench, where a feeling of immense relief flooded through her; she wasn't alone in her situation. All the girls in the Home would experience (if they hadn't already) childbirth with its accompanying pain and joy.

'We're all in the same boat,' she thought.

At last, she was in the right place. She could stop pretending, let her belly grow big and round, relax, eat well, get plenty of rest – even do Sister Ann's fitness and exercise classes. At this point in Emily Todd's confinement, Mary Vale Home for Mothers and Babies was exactly the right place for her.

Just a few miles away, in Crow Thorn Grange, Sir Percival was pacing the floor of his study; he'd just returned from another visit to London, where he and Marigold had been richly wined and dined by Edgar and Cicily Bennett in their stylish townhouse in Chelsea. Tatchbrooke Abbey, Edgar's ancestral home in Derbyshire, was presently occupied by his ageing father, who lived in the hope that before he slipped this mortal coil he would hold a grandson in his arms, secure in the knowledge that the family line would continue well into the twentieth century.

Though dinner (roast duck, new potatoes, home-grown

peas and carrots) was excellent, Percival had eaten little and, uncharacteristically, drunk even less. If he ever needed his wits about him, tonight was the night. Edgar and Cicily weren't the self-conscious, shilly-shallying sort – knowing this, Percival had made sure he had another conversation with Matron before he left for London.

'I'm meeting up with an old chum in town this week,' he had started. 'He tells me his wife is keen to adopt.' He paused briefly before adding, 'They're titled, wealthy landowners; their line probably goes all the way back to William the Conqueror, so they very much want the *right kind* of baby.'

'Naturally! Of course, that makes complete sense,' she'd replied crisply.

'What shall I tell them?' he'd asked uncertainly. 'Have we the makings of a plan, Maud? You said you'd come up with something, re: our biggest stumbling block, the priest,' he reminded her.

'I have,' she replied.

Percival's heart had given a double beat of excitement.

'I can't discuss it over the phone,' she added in her most professional voice.

'Of course,' he agreed.

'Let's just say,' she added slightly cockily, 'I have everything in hand.'

'Excellent, I knew you wouldn't let me down,' he smarmed.

'As I'm sure *you* won't let *me* down,' she echoed.

'My word is my bond,' he boomed pompously.

'Quite.'

Determined to be one hundred per cent sure that he

was in a position to strike a bargain with Edgar, Percival had asked one final question. 'Can I safely say our discreet service is available to the eager couple?'

'Most certainly,' she had assured him and put the phone down.

With Matron's words ringing in his ears, Percival felt in a confident mood as he sat next to Marigold on Edgar and Cicily's sunny Pimlico terrace, drinking the finest champagne money could buy.

'Edgar's told me of your contacts, Archibald,' Cicily said, clearly trying hard to keep the mounting excitement from her well-bred sounding voice. 'We'd like you to procure for us, just as soon as you possibly can, a new-born baby son.'

Marigold slid her lover an adoring smile. Before they'd left his flat (after a wonderful two hours of love-making), Percival had explained to Marigold how the conversation might go later between Edgar and Cicily.

'Darling!' she had cooed as they lay naked in bed. 'How wonderful of you to find them a baby!' she'd declared as if he'd just found it lying around on the streets.

'Dearest, I haven't found it, as you so sweetly say – it's growing,' he chuckled.

'Oooh! Just like a plant!' she shrieked.

'Yes, you could say that,' he replied. 'So, dearest, don't be surprised if talk of babies comes up over supper.'

'Archie,' she pouted. 'You can talk about babies as long as you like, just so long as it's not MY baby,' she said with a steely glint in her eyes.

Percival traced a line of kisses down her pale flat abdomen.

'Never, never,' he purred. 'That would ruin everything.'

After supper, over cigars, brandy and Cointreau for the ladies, Edgar echoed his wife's sentiments,

'We've thought it over, old boy, and we agree that if you can find us a fine boy of good breeding – on at least one side of his family,' he said with a wry smile as he quoted Percival, 'then we would gladly offer you a very large "donation", perhaps even a little more if it would guarantee your personal attention throughout the proceedings,' he added pointedly.

'We'd feel happier knowing that you were steering the ship, so to speak,' dewy-eyed Cicily added.

Percival gave a gallant little bow. 'Madam, you need never doubt that, I can assure you.'

In an emotional rush, Cicily added, 'Ideally, we'd like to have a son, swiftly followed by a daughter'; then, in a more business-like voice, she proceeded to list her questions and requests. They would want details of the child's parents, their occupations and social standing; knowledge of their education was important too. At what age could the child be removed from the Home, and who would nurse him until they came to pick him up? Percival, who, in truth, could barely answer any of her questions, told the anxious pair that all these things would be taken care of by Matron Maud Harding.

'A woman of impeccable character,' he assured them.

'Would you like an initial payment as a sign of our serious intent?' Edgar asked earnestly.

Trying to smother his desperation for money, Percival replied in a voice he did his best to keep calm and devoid of the excitement that was running through his veins,

'That would be most kind; I'll invoice you with my details on my return home.'

In the cab on the way back to Percival's Mayfair flat, Marigold wound her slender, pale arms around his neck.

'My clever little baby-finder,' she whispered in his ear. 'How sweet of you to make Cicily happy, thereby making yourself *very, very* rich.'

Percival felt the swell of her breasts under her white fox fur.

'Find me a few more wealthy, infertile couples,' he said huskily. 'And you can enjoy some of the benefits too.'

'Darling,' Marigold murmured as she stroked his thighs. 'What fun we shall have!'

Now that Edgar had promised to transfer an initial payment, Percival woke early the next morning and, after slipping from Marigold's lingering caresses, he pulled on his silk dressing gown and hurried to the drawing room, where he quickly dialled Matron's office number. Taking deep, steadying breaths as the phone shrilled out, he waited for her to pick up.

'Sir Percival!' she exclaimed when she heard his voice. 'What a pleasant surprise. How are you?'

Impatient to get on to the matter in hand, he answered in his most dulcet tones. 'Dear Matron, I have the best of news!' he charmed. 'I've had a meeting with the couple I mentioned to you the other evening and I urgently need some clarity on how we may proceed.'

'Ah, yes, of course. I thought we might discuss the matter further over a private supper in my suite,' she said seductively.

Already having anticipated that she would be planning some intimate tête-à-tête scenario, Percival deftly side-stepped the potential minefield.

'Sadly, Matron' – he gave a little quivering sigh – 'I'm terribly busy in London at the moment,' he lied. Busy enjoying his delicious mistress and spending money he didn't have – not yet anyway! 'On my return I'm not going to have much free time, especially in the evenings.' Before she could make another suggestion, he ploughed on. 'Maybe we could have a private word in your office as soon as I'm back? Progressing our plan has become a matter of some urgency.'

Clearly disappointed Matron nevertheless conceded. 'Of course, Sir Percival.'

'Perfect!' he exclaimed. 'I'll ring you as soon as I'm home.'

A few days later Percival met Matron in her office after she'd finished her morning rounds. As he took a chair opposite her, he noticed with horror that she was wearing bright red lipstick. It looked terrible on her and she was wearing some frightful pungent perfume that quite turned his stomach. Moving swiftly into business mode, he came straight to the point. 'So . . .' he said, rubbing his palms together, 'how are we going to make this wonderful event happen? Have you had a chance to check those records?'

'I'll come to that in a moment.'

Taking her time, Matron reached for the coffee pot set on a tray on her desk and slowly poured coffee into two teacups.

'Milk? Sugar?'

Desperately impatient, Percival was almost grinding his teeth at the delay. 'Both.'

'Biscuit?' she asked, as she offered him a plate of Sister Mary Paul's shortbread biscuits.

'No,' he answered curtly, quickly correcting himself. 'Thanks.'

Sitting back in her chair, Matron sipped at her coffee before she continued. 'You should bear in mind we have no suitable baby boys at the moment.'

Percival's face fell. 'Damnation!' He'd never thought of that.

Laying down her coffee cup, Matron added, 'A haughty girl and her grandmother paid us a visit recently but I've heard nothing back from them – pity,' she sighed. 'They looked the type who would pay the full residential fee. And a new woman with a rather high opinion of herself has just arrived, but I'm not sure she's quite the right class,' she sniffed. 'And, more to the point, she insists on keeping her child, though how she'll manage that will be interesting to observe.'

Unable to take any more of Matron's controlled diversions, Percival abruptly interrupted her: 'We'll find a boy,' he said with forced optimism. 'Even if we have to be economical with the truth about the parentage. But the more urgent problem is working out how we're going to get around Father Benedict. He's a difficult bugger!' Fawning on her, he murmured, 'I won't have him getting in the way of this marvellous idea of yours, dear Maud.'

'I said I was coming to that,' Matron said, as she nibbled a biscuit. 'It turns out I have had an idea as to how we can get round that particular problem.'

Percival pulled his chair closer. 'Yes . . . ?' he asked with bated breath.

Matron dropped her voice to a confidential whisper. 'We must disgrace him.'

Percival was so shocked he couldn't speak. 'You mean defrock a priest?'

'Yes, that's exactly what I mean. I'm quite sure I could get one, or possibly two, of the more unscrupulous girls in the Home to speak out against the priest, accuse him of accosting them, touching them and making inappropriate suggestions,' she explained.

Percival couldn't believe he was hearing right; was this woman ruthless enough to lie about an utterly innocent priest who, even he knew, had never put a foot wrong?

Clearly without a trace of guilt, Matron breezed on. 'You see, I've checked the official paperwork, which categorically states that, if the person responsible for setting up the adoptions – in this case Father Benedict – should fall ill, an immediate substitution must be nominated. Obviously, we need to make sure that substitution is you, and then you can do what you please,' she smirked.

Following her wicked drift, Percival started to relax. 'Well, after all, I am chairman of the Board of Governors – it would be perfectly right and proper that, after the priest has been, er, disposed of, I would step up to the plate and volunteer to help out with the business of adoptions – on a temporary basis, of course,' he added with a sly smile.

'There could be no better or well-informed person to step into Father Benedict's rather shabby shoes than you, dear Percival,' Matron agreed. 'We'd become responsible for all the adoptions once you were in charge,' she added confidently.

Percival paled. 'ALL?' he spluttered. 'I had hoped we'd be handling only our "special babies".'

With serene confidence Matron sailed on, 'Trust me, we'll be going to no such lengths as Father Ben does.' She rolled her eyes in amusement. 'He makes such a huge palaver about placing children with the right parents – *a match*, he calls it. We won't be wasting our time on that amount of detail, will we?'

'Certainly not!' Percival replied in all honesty.

'We can offload our poorer babies to any Tom, Dick or Harry,' Matron said with a dismissive gesture.

'Absolutely!' he cried. 'We need to be sure we save our time and efforts exclusively for our *special babies*.' He smiled as he tenderly said the words. 'Those we'll take care of ourselves.'

'With the priest out of the way we can do what we want,' Matron announced. 'Oh, and one other thing, Archie: it's vital we set up a joint bank account as soon as possible.'

Swiftly attempting to sidestep her suggestion, Percival pressed on. 'How are you going to get any of the girls to speak out against Father Benedict? They all like him so much.'

Matron gave a shrewd smile. 'We have girls here who could be persuaded to lie for extra food and money. But the bank account, Percy?' she insisted, a small but determined glint in her eye.

Percival couldn't help but be impressed: the conniving, cold-hearted old bag had thought the whole thing through. He would have to give in on the bank account, but he would find a way of keeping the lion's share for himself.

'Leave it with me, dear Maud,' he said with his most suave and reassuring smile. 'I'll sort out the matter immediately.'

'And remember, Sir Percival, the unique advantage of running a mother and baby home is that every single girl inevitably departs; they'll soon go back to where they came from. Ignorant of our actions, so unable to hamper us.'

'Then I'll leave the matter in your capable hands,' Percival said. He finished his coffee and got to his feet.

After pecking her dry cheek he fled Matron's office, feeling just the teeniest bit sorry for poor, unsuspecting Father Benedict, who would soon be experiencing the brunt of Matron's malice.

'Needs must when the devil drives,' he mused, as he drove back home to Crow Thorn Grange.

With the priest gone, Mary Vale's adoptions would be under his control; it was more than he had ever hoped for.

12. Prospective Residents

Firmly convinced that the threat of impending war was very real, Stan was becoming increasingly anxious at the idea of leaving his pregnant wife and young son in London if he was away fighting for his country. He had put more pressure than ever on Gloria to make inquiries about evacuation.

Feeling rather cornered by her husband's insistence, Gloria had no choice but to leave Robin with a neighbour while she set off for the local library. On a lovely August morning, she walked down the sunny road, thinking fondly of the summer holiday she, Stan and Robin had just spent in Brighton. It had only been for a week but without a doubt it had been one of the happiest times of her life. The sun had shone every day; they'd walked on the prom, paddled in the sea, dozed off in deckchairs on the pebbly beach, eaten meat-paste sandwiches gritty with sand and played on the pier, where Stan had won Robin a teddy bear by shooting a line of tins off a shelf.

'My dad's a hero!' Robin had cried proudly as he clutched the teddy in one hand and his dad's hand in the other.

Their B and B in the back streets of Brighton had been relaxed and comfortable, and every night after Robin had fallen asleep in his own little room they'd made love. Being pregnant made Gloria feel sensual and loving; it was sweet to doze off lying in each other's arms with the window wide open to the soft sea breezes. During that week Stan hadn't once mentioned the imminence of war; he'd been upbeat and boyishly light-hearted, and it had been such a relief to get away from the constant worries that beset them at home. But on their return, with the papers predicting doom and gloom across the Channel, Stan's anxieties had resurfaced, and the subject of leaving London raised its head again.

'Better show willing,' Gloria thought to herself. 'Otherwise I'll never hear the end of it.'

The librarian turned out to be most informed on the subject of evacuation.

'Government orders have been issued this month,' she told Gloria. 'If war should break out, the government are keen to get children, the sick and the old somewhere safe; pregnant women too,' she added as an afterthought.

'Well, that's me,' Gloria told her, 'and I have a five-year-old son too. My husband thinks we should organize our evacuation. He's scared of leaving us unprotected if he gets called up.'

'I think your husband's right: you should definitely be thinking about getting out of the city,' the librarian advised, before adding with a heavy sigh: 'It'll be no place to give birth or to bring up a young child if Hitler starts targeting London, which he most certainly will.'

It was now Gloria's turn to sigh. 'So where would somebody like me and my son go?' she asked. 'It's not just about evacuating London; it's also about finding a safe place where I can have my baby.'

'There are mother and baby homes all over the country,'

the librarian replied kindly. 'We've got a few leaflets you can have a look at; you'll find quite a few of the homes are advertised in church magazines,' she added.

'But those wouldn't be right: they're places for young pregnant girls, unmarried mothers, aren't they?' Gloria protested. 'They're usually run by a religious order; they're not the right kind of institution for me and my son,' she said, slightly panicked at the idea of being among a crowd of young women who'd been shut away from polite society.

'There's nothing wrong with making a few inquiries,' the librarian said encouragingly. 'Better to be prepared than to have regrets when it's too late.'

Just thinking of living in a dingy home for disgraced mothers and babies made Gloria feel quite sick. But, knowing that Stan would never let up on the blasted subject, she rather guiltily decided on her way home that she'd twist the truth a little, just to put Stan's anxious mind at rest; she'd say that more information was due out shortly and she'd been advised to wait until it was in the public domain before she made any decisions about evacuating. Little did Gloria know that she would not have the luxury of more time before events overseas would shape the destiny of much of Europe, as well as that of her own beloved family.

In Windermere, Isla was also coming to a decision. Reclining in a deckchair on her grandmother's lawn, which ran down to the edges of the lake, she closed her eyes to the warm sun streaming down on her. This quiet oasis of peace and security was a far cry from the home she'd been asked to leave by her fiercely judgemental father and timid mother. Though she'd been shaken and horridly humiliated at the time, she was, in retrospect, relieved that her parents had kicked her out. They would never have loved and cared for her like her beloved grandmother, who, if it was possible, she loved more with every passing week.

Even so, for all her wrath and indignation, Isla's mother had paid them an unexpected and very unpleasant visit, which would have been unbearable for Isla if Jeannie hadn't been by her side. Over an uncomfortable lunch (made a little more tolerable by the housekeeper's delicious meat pie with rich gravy), Mrs Ross had barely looked at her daughter, despite the fact that Isla was flushed with good health and looking happy and relaxed in a loose day dress.

'She has brought disgrace to our family,' her mother had said, as if her daughter weren't even present.

'Why complain? You're not bearing the disgrace,' Jeannie remarked.

'How could she have done this to us?' Mrs Ross's shrill voice broke. 'We had high hopes for our daughter and now . . .' Her voice faded on a sob of despair.

'Life goes on,' Jeannie answered forcefully. 'Isla will have the child adopted and return to her studies.'

'*Not* at Durham,' Isla quickly interjected. 'I'll go somewhere new, where I feel safe,' she added firmly.

Ignoring any talk of studies or her daughter's future, Mrs Ross spoke sharply, 'You've decided to have *it* adopted?' Her mother stressed the word *it* as if she were referring to something sub-human. 'Well, that's progress.

Maybe we can keep it quiet from our friends and pretend it never happened.'

Fed up with her mother's snippy comments, Isla glared at her. 'You can pretend as much as you like but, as far as I'm concerned, it HAS happened and I'm paying for it.' She paused to turn to her grandmother, who'd given her a lot more help and advice than her own mother was capable of. 'Jeannie and I have discussed the matter and we both think it'll be better for my baby to have a mother *and* a father, and a secure future. I know it'll be hard for me, but I have to think about what's best for my child.'

Mrs Ross moved on to her next concern. 'And where will you go to give birth? You must choose somewhere far away from home, so that no one will hear about it,' she said bluntly.

Irritated beyond belief by this line of brutal questioning, Jeannie rose from the table. 'I think that's enough,' she said firmly. 'You threw Isla out of her home, so I will throw you out of mine. You have no right to care where she goes to have her baby.'

The two women eyed each other across the table, and for the first time Isla could see how much they must have sparred when her mother was growing up. Liberal, generous Jeannie, open to new ideas and interested in the world outside her front door, must have been permanently at odds with her tense, repressed daughter. How miserable they must have been in each other's company. How happy they both must have been to go their very separate ways.

It had been a huge relief when her mother departed and left them to continue living peacefully in the big old rambling house that Isla had loved since her childhood days.

With fat bees droning in the flowerbeds and birds singing in the trees that edged the softly lapping waters of the lake, sleepy Isla laid her hands on top of her tummy, where she felt her baby's fluttery movements.

'Goodness,' she laughed. 'That tickles!'

Jeannie removed her sunglasses in order to peer at her granddaughter's distinctly noticeable bump, which immediately caused her to return to the conversation they'd had several times already. 'Come along, Isla, you've prevaricated long enough,' she chided. 'If you don't make your mind up soon, you'll finish up having that baby of yours right here in Windermere. Which home have you picked?'

Isla giggled. She knew that Jeannie was losing patience with her dithering uncertainty, but her straight talking always made her laugh.

'Try to be serious,' Jeannie urged. 'Out of the four mother and baby homes that we've visited, which do you like best?'

Realizing she wasn't going to be able to fob off her grandmother much longer, Isla said, 'Well, I didn't mind the Salesian home we visited, and Mary Vale near Grange-over-Sands is a possibility too.'

'You can't give birth in two places,' Jeannie pointed out.

'Hmm . . .' Isla considered. 'The only thing about the Salesian home is it looked a bit severe from the outside. And the sisters who run it were a bit daunting too,' she replied thoughtfully.

'True, but surely the ghastly Matron at Mary Vale was a thousand times worse than those well-meaning Salesian nuns?' Jeannie reminded her.

'Matron Maud Harding,' Isla said with a shudder. 'One of the biggest snobs I've ever come across!'

On Isla's visit Matron had excelled herself in the snob stakes. Seeing the new client arriving in a large (and very old) Daimler, accompanied by a well-dressed, upright older woman, Matron had flushed in anticipation. She'd been told in advance by both the Reverend Mother and Father Benedict that Isla Ross was a fee-paying client, but then so was Emily Todd, and look how she'd turned out, she'd thought sourly.

'Well, at least they look the part,' Matron had told herself, as she swanned down the drive to welcome the visitors.

Conducting exactly the same tour as she had with Emily, Matron had whisked Isla and Jeannie through the wards, where Ada was stripping the beds, helped by Shirley and Nancy, who had immediately noticed the new girl with the soft blonde hair and gentle, smiling face.

'She looks nice,' Nancy had observed.

Ada watched Isla pause to look out of the window to see what was going on in the garden; she appeared to be intrigued by the girls outside pushing babies in their prams along the winding footpaths.

'This way!' Matron rudely called to Isla, who jumped, then blushed in embarrassment as she realized she was lagging behind.

'Damn woman!' Ada seethed as she saw Isla scurry to catch up with her grandmother, who had given her a quick sympathetic smile. 'Why doesn't she let the visitors take their time when they inspect the Home?'

Ada shook her head and turned to her work; she knew

perfectly well why Matron was in a rush to complete the tour. What she most enjoyed about showing people around the Home was the final fifteen minutes, when she had them behind closed doors in her private office and could discuss fees and the terms of adoption.

'The way that hateful Matron hurried us through the process of adoption,' Isla reminded Jeannie. 'I know I'm going to have my baby adopted, but I wanted the chance to explain how I'd come to that decision.'

Astute Jeannie succinctly summed up Matron. 'She's an odious, bossy, rude woman, but the other staff were lovely,' she enthused. 'The nun we saw feeding the babies in the nursery was charming.'

'And the ward sister who showed us round the gardens and the bedrooms after Matron had disappeared was sweet,' Isla remarked. 'I really liked her.'

Jeannie remembered her name. 'Sister Ada, I liked her very much.' She paused before she pressed her point home. 'None of the homes are going to be perfect,' she pointed out. 'You just need to decide where you think you might feel most comfortable during your confinement.'

Isla had no trouble coming to a decision. 'Mary Vale,' she replied. 'Apart from that dreadful Matron woman, the staff and the residents were very friendly, and the babies seemed happy too – plus I liked the location, right on Morecambe Bay.'

Jeannie gave a contented smile. 'Good, we're in agreement; Mary Vale it is.'

Isla didn't add what she'd been secretly thinking: that if she hated the Home, she could (*in extremis*) leave and walk back over the fells to Windermere; it would be tough, but it was doable, and she knew the route as she had walked it often in the past, albeit when she wasn't pregnant.

'Though, in truth,' Isla confessed, 'I'd much rather stay here with you,' she said with a wistful smile.

Jeannie patted her hand. 'I know, darling! I'd love that too but this is the best thing, trust me.'

Isla nodded, then quickly turned towards the lake in order to hide the tears that were forming in her pale blue Highland eyes; soon she would be packing her bags and leaving for Mary Vale, the mother and baby home of her choice, just over the fells from her beloved grandmother and Windermere.

13. Room-mate

Emily settled into the Home much more easily than she'd ever expected. To her delight, Ada was right and she really liked her room-mate, Nancy, despite her worries about her being so young. After freely admitting that she'd been dumped in the Home by her dad because he was so ashamed of her, Nancy gave a cold laugh.

'I already feel like the longest-serving resident in Mary Vale,' she joked. 'It'll be nice to have company,' she added with a shy blush.

Sharing the same bedroom and bathroom quickly broke down any initial barriers. Hearing each other snore or dashing back and forth to the toilet all through the night left no room for inhibitions. Emily liked Nancy's quiet, modest manner; she was thankful to have her as a room-mate, as opposed to some of the noisier, more self-opinionated girls she'd seen around the place. Nancy was well ahead of Emily in her pregnancy, so it was useful for Emily to hear from her new friend about the physical changes she could expect to see very soon in her own body.

The girls talked and talked and soon became very close. Emily felt sorry for nervous Nancy, who was racked with guilt about letting down her mother, who apparently would bear the brunt of her father's fury at his daughter's descent into shame. The poor girl picked at her guilt like a dog picks at a scab.

'What's done is done,' Emily said pragmatically. 'And look at me!' she exclaimed. 'Madly in love with a man who doesn't even know I'm pregnant! I've written dozens of letters to him, but I have no way of knowing if he knows – or cares, in fact.' Trying to be light-hearted about their bleak situation, Emily joked, 'What a pair we are!'

'The father of my baby definitely didn't love me,' Nancy murmured in a low, sad voice. 'He just used me and I was stupid enough to believe him when he said that going inside me was just a bit more than kissing.'

Emily rolled her eyes heavenwards. 'Oh, Nancy, you were such an innocent,' she said softly.

'STUPID, more like!' Nancy exclaimed. 'Now that I know the facts of life, I wonder how I could ever have been so naive. Worse still,' she added angrily, 'that pig of a man exploited my ignorance: he chased after me for one thing only – sex. Then he dumped me as soon as he found out I was pregnant.'

'So your mother never told you about the facts of life?' Emily inquired.

'Never!' Nancy cried. 'She's even shyer than I am. When I started my periods, it was the woman next door who told me I wasn't bleeding to death, which I thought I was,' Nancy laughed. 'Thank God she had the foresight to give me some sanitary pads.'

'My mother didn't tell me anything either,' Emily told her friend. 'But the girls I worked with in the Lyons teashop weren't backwards at coming forwards,' she chuckled. 'Talk about graphic! They even told me where I could buy condoms!' Emily rolled her eyes melodramatically. 'Not that it helped,' she sighed. 'The one George used split.'

Nancy's eyes widened in horror. 'Oh, my God! Is that how you got pregnant?'

Emily nodded grimly. 'We thought we were being oh so careful, but look where I am now.'

In Emily's early days at Mary Vale, Nancy introduced her to the other girls, both the ones who were awaiting their confinement and the ones who'd given birth and were preparing to leave. All of the new mothers Emily spoke to were leaving their babies behind, so when they heard that Emily was intent on keeping hers they were intrigued and barraged her with questions.

'How will you manage?'

'Where will you live?'

'What will you do if you've not got a job?'

Passing through the sitting room where poor Emily was being cross-examined by the curious residents, Ada stopped short when she saw Emily's tense expression.

'Ladies, ladies,' she said lightly but quite firmly, 'you'll give Emily a headache with all your questions.' Quickly turning to Emily, she said, 'Could I have a word, lovie? There's something on your file I need to double-check.'

Once she'd got Emily out of the sitting room, the girl's resolve dissipated and she burst into tears. 'Honest to God, I don't know how I'm going to achieve it, but come hell or high water, I'm keeping my baby!'

Ada laid a comforting hand on Emily's heaving shoulders. 'Don't climb mountains until you have to, sweetheart.'

'If I don't hear from George, Sister, I honestly don't know what I'll do!' she tearfully blurted out.

'I've not known you long, Emily,' Ada soothed. 'But it's clear to me that you're a strong woman; I really believe that, once you've made your mind up about something, you'll make it work.'

Emily gripped her hand. 'Thanks,' she gulped. 'I was strong. I am strong. But now I'm so scared.'

'Stand fast,' Ada urged. 'Believe in George – don't give up his baby.'

Emily gazed gratefully at Ada. Only a few weeks ago Emily barely knew her; now she recognized in her both a friend and a professional of the highest calibre.

'I won't give up, Ada,' she cried as she hugged her new friend. 'I'll keep my baby, I promise!'

After getting to know Ada on a deeper level, Emily began to notice how she reacted each time Matron came striding imperiously through the nursery: edgy and tense, the Sister watched her superior like chickens watch a fox.

'She doesn't like her very much,' Emily thought to herself, then laughed out loud. 'But then I don't like her very much either!'

It was a mystery to her that such a cold-hearted woman had finished up in a mother and baby home – what on earth could have been the attraction? Matron Harding was as compassionate as a lump of wood and as generous as a miser. She had her favourites too, particular girls who spoke well and dressed better than the poorer residents; Matron was even nicer to their babies. But, as for the rest of the common rank and file, she barely seemed to notice them.

Emily's dislike of Matron grew when, one afternoon, she witnessed Matron bullying a young, skinny girl who was trembling in fright as the domineering woman harangued her.

'Shirley! When I say I want tea in my office, I mean I want it *now*, not ten minutes later.'

'S . . . s . . . sorry, Matron, I had to go and get the m . . . milk for your tea from the l . . . larder and –'

Impatient Matron turned her back on Shirley and stalked away, insulting her as she went. 'Stupid girl! The sooner you're gone from here, the better.'

Though Matron had little time for Shirley, the sweet-natured girl was very popular among the residents; they appreciated the work the cheerful girl did for them, laying out vast amounts of food three times a day in the dining room and cleaning up after them.

'She works like a dog,' Nancy commented. 'But always with a smile on her face.'

'She's a sweetheart,' Emily agreed.

Determined to get to know Shirley, Emily helped her clear the dining table one day.

'You don't need to do that,' Shirley cried. 'That's my job.'

Emily threw her a rueful grin. 'After the amount of food I've just eaten, I need as much exercise as I can get! That bread is delicious,' she enthused. 'I must have polished off at least half of it, not to mention the farm butter and raspberry jam – you don't get grub as good as that in Manchester!' she joked.

Shirley wiped her hands on her pinafore. 'It's all good stuff,' she agreed with Emily. 'I should know, I help out in't kitchen,' she replied with a happy little swagger. 'Sister Mary Paul's had me pounding dough for weeks, and now that I know what I'm up to she's put me in charge of all the bread-making. I love it!'

'Heck!' Emily laughed as she collected up used crockery. 'I wouldn't have a clue where to start.'

Shirley's dark eyes glowed with love. 'Sister Mary Paul's a right good teacher – she never shouts at me or tells me off, she just encourages me to learn, then praises me when I do well.'

'That's what I call a brilliant teacher,' Emily replied. 'But you don't make the butter too, do you?'

'Nay, that's yon farmer.' Shirley nodded her head in the direction of the fields adjacent to the Home. 'He farms the land that belongs to the convent, so we get the perks – hand-churned butter, local cheese, and milk too, every morning.'

Emily patted her growing tummy. 'I've never eaten so much good fresh food in years,' she giggled. 'I can't seem to stop eating,' she confessed.

Shirley nodded. 'Expecting does that to you,' she agreed.

Emily shot her a curious glance; Shirley looked about fourteen – could she have been pregnant? Shirley's response affirmed that she had been.

'I didn't have much of an appetite when I were expecting,' she admitted. 'I felt sick most of the time.'

Aware she might put her foot in it, Emily asked cautiously, 'Is your baby still here?'

'No,' Shirley told her. 'She's been adopted by some right good folks who Father Ben found, and I'm glad for her,' she said frankly.

A bit baffled as to why Shirley was still a resident, Emily asked, 'And you stayed on here after her adoption?'

'Aye, I were right lucky, mi stay at the Home got extended – thank God,' Shirley told her. 'But I like to earn my keep, do something in return for them letting me stay, so I help out with the cleaning.' She paused to smile. 'I'd do anything for the nuns here, Sister Ann and Sister Mary Paul, and the Reverend Mother too, they're family to me,' she concluded.

Along with Nancy and several other girls, Emily decided to attend Sister Ann's fitness and exercise classes, which, during the summer months, were held in the spacious gardens. Lying on the lawn with her eyes closed and the warm sun on her face, Emily soon relaxed as Sister Ann instructed the pregnant girls on how to improve and strengthen their overall fitness in readiness for the physical ordeal they were soon to endure.

'Now come on, ladies,' she teased the sleepy, reclining girls. 'You're here to prepare for childbirth, so no drifting off!'

A good-natured groan went round the circle.

'Go on, then, Sister, get on with it, then!' one of the girls joked.

'Okay, slowly lift your legs and take some big deep breaths,' Ann started.

As the class slowly breathed in and out, Ann instructed, 'Keep it nice and slow while maintaining that calm, steady breathing. Well done, keep going,' she urged.

As the girls gently exercised, Sister Ann continued, 'Allow all your air to flow out with a sigh as you lower your limbs. Excellent. Now rest.'

'If I carry on like this, Sister I'll be asleep in five minutes,' a friendly girl teased.

'Keep awake and stay relaxed,' Ann advised, as the lesson continued.

Emily smiled at Sister Ann, whose calm voice and warm smile always made her feel secure; nevertheless, she did wonder how she'd feel when it came to her time. Would she panic or feel excitement that at last her baby was about to enter the world and she would soon hold him or her in her arms? One thing she knew for sure: if wonderful Sister Ann was beside her when her time came, she would have all the support she needed and do just fine.

14. A Good Catch

Isla couldn't hold back her tears when she and Jeannie were finally left alone in the big second-floor bedroom that she was to share with Emily and Nancy, who'd tactfully left the two women alone on the pretext that Jeannie would like to help Isla unpack her bags. Despite the brave face she'd been putting on, the minute they were alone together and reality hit her hard, Isla could not stop the torrent.

'Please don't leave me here, Jeannie. Please take me home with you!' she begged.

Jeannie's usually firm resolve cracked when she saw her dearest Isla sobbing like a frightened child.

'Darling girl!' she cried, taking her granddaughter into her arms. 'We have to be strong. I know it's hard, but this is for the best. For both of you,' she soothed.

'I know, but I can't bear for you to leave me,' Isla wailed miserably.

Though on the verge of tears herself, Jeannie held Isla at arm's length and looked her firmly in the eye. 'Listen to me,' she said. 'Your stay here is a necessity; you'll be home before you know it, and then you can start to plan the rest of your life.'

Isla dumbly nodded.

'I'll come often,' Jeannie assured her, her own heart breaking for the poor girl. 'And I'll bring all your favourite food – Mavis's sausage rolls and coconut macaroons.'

Isla managed a weak smile. Jeannie knew how much her granddaughter loved her housekeeper's excellent cooking; she'd piled on weight since her arrival in Windermere and it wasn't all baby weight either.

'Don't forget how near I am, just over the fell,' Jeannie joked. 'And we'll write to each other often, my darling, and I do have a telephone,' she reminded Isla. 'So please try not to worry.'

Their farewell was painful, but Jeannie was wise enough not to drag it out. Leaving tearful Isla with her room-mates, she drove away at speed, praying all the way home that her precious granddaughter would be well taken care of during her confinement.

In her office, with the door firmly closed, Matron was poring over Isla's application form.

'Father, Professor at Durham University; mother, English undergraduate; grandfather, respected Scottish lawyer . . .' Her voice trailed away. 'The girl is perfect!' she muttered joyfully under her breath. 'Or, more to the point – her child will be perfect. If it's a boy, that is.'

Matron was tempted to phone Sir Percival, but then she remembered he'd gone back to London. Blissfully unaware of his double life, Matron had only fond thoughts.

'He's probably doing business with prospective wealthy parents, building up our empire.'

It would be good to give Archie *two* pieces of good news on his return. He hadn't a clue about the arrangements she'd recently made with two of the Mary Vale residents: Olive, a shifty girl with sly eyes who'd recently been caught stealing; and Maureen, who constantly complained that there was never enough food to eat. Knowing they were both greedy, unscrupulous characters, Matron had invited them to tea in her office. After Maureen had gobbled her way through scones heaped with jam and cream, followed by a Victoria sponge and chocolate eclairs, accompanied by endless cups of tea, Matron said her piece.

'How would you like to have more food like this on a regular basis and a nice big single bedroom each on the first floor with a sea view?'

'Yeah!' Maureen enthused with her mouth full.

Olive, who, Matron had deduced, was a cunning little madam, eyed her suspiciously. 'Why?'

'Well, the truth is there's been an on-going issue concerning Father Benedict,' Matron replied. 'It turns out we've had complaints from some girls about his behaving . . . inappropriately, shall we say.'

'What does that mean?' Maureen asked, as she slurped her tea.

'Hands up the skirt – touching 'em up,' Olive crudely explained.

'Ooooh!' Maureen's piggy little eyes rolled in her fat red cheeks. 'A priest wouldn't go and do a dirty thing like that, would he?'

'It has been known,' Matron added. 'Anyway, I wondered if either of you has personally experienced any inappropriate behaviour that you'd be happy to speak up about?'

She calmly laid two five-pound notes on the desktop. 'I'll give you a few minutes to think about it.'

Reaching for the teapot, she rose and left the room.

The wide-eyed girls watched her go; then Olive snatched up the notes on the table.

'What're you bloody doing?' Maureen gasped.

'Don't you see what the old cow's up to?' Olive hissed, as she pocketed the notes in her voluminous grubby smock. 'She'll pay us off if we bad-mouth the priest.'

'But it's not true!' Maureen squawked. 'He's never laid a hand on me.'

'Me neither, but that don't matter,' Olive snapped.

When Matron returned with a fresh pot of tea, she immediately noticed the notes had gone.

'There'll be more when you leave Mary Vale,' she said, as she coolly refilled their teacups. 'If you should remember anything, anything at all, just write it down and pop it into my office.'

'Thing is, Matron, I can't be doing the writing,' Maureen confessed.

'If you have anything to say, you can tell me and I can write it for you,' Matron assured the now eager girl, who was ogling the last eclair. 'All you have to do is sign the document once you agree it is correct.'

'I can write mi own name,' Maureen said with a bit of a swagger.

'And what about you, Olive?' Matron inquired.

'*I* can write,' the girl sneered. 'I don't need any help, ta.'

Not long after Matron's little tea party she received a signed letter from Olive stating that Father Benedict had accosted her several times, in the chapel, and in the garden when nobody was around.

'He trid to kiss me and behaved inaprottly,' Olive wrote, complete with misspellings. 'Disgusting behavor for a man of God.'

Maureen dumbly signed the letter that Matron had written on her behalf.

'Keep this to yourselves,' Matron sternly instructed. 'If I catch either of you gossiping behind my back, neither of you will get the other five pounds due to you on your departure from here. And that will be the least of your worries. Do I make myself clear?'

'Yeah,' Olive scoffed. 'Anyhow, why do you wanna dump the priest? What's in it for you?' she demanded rudely.

'I am merely following the appropriate procedure after complaints and accusations have been made,' Matron stiffly replied.

'Yeah,' Olive cynically scoffed again.

'I don't care,' quipped Maureen. 'I just wanna 'ave this bloody kid and get the hell out of this soddin' place.'

'Quite,' thought Matron. 'And the sooner I see the back of you two little wretches, the happier I'll be.'

Carefully locking the letter and the statement in her desk drawer, Matron waited like a spider in its web for the right moment to pounce. Mercifully, Maureen and Olive were due to have their babies within the next few weeks; if they went over their due dates she would make it her business to see that they were induced, which would be followed by a speedy discharge and their final pay-off; then she would be free to drop her bombshell, secure in the knowledge that her ruthless accomplices were miles away and could not foil her clever plan.

15. Shared Confidences

Emily and Nancy were busy helping Sister Mary Paul and Shirley to lay the dining-room table for tea: cabbage and carrots, mincemeat pie and mashed potatoes.

'The new girl isn't like most of us,' Nancy commented as she carefully manoeuvred her growing tummy around the dining chairs in order to put down glasses, cutlery, cups and saucers. 'She seems a bit posh and stand-offish.'

'I thought she was more nervous than stand-offish,' said kindly Shirley.

Sister Mary Paul nodded her head. 'Entering a home like this can be quite intimidating,' she said sympathetically.

'I agree!' Shirley laughed, 'I was so terrified when I arrived at Mary Vale I could barely speak for a week.'

The nun gave her a cheeky smile. 'But you've made up for it since! She was a little timid mouse of a thing – and now she's virtually running the Home,' she joked. Turning to the other girls, she said confidently, 'I'm sure you'll all get along just fine.'

Emily, who over her working life had come across all types of people and had learnt never to take anybody at face value, added, 'I agree with you, Sister, I think we're going to get along just fine.'

'I hope she doesn't mind sharing with us two,' Nancy said with a nervous giggle. 'I talk in mi sleep and make, you know, rude noises.'

'We ALL do that in this place,' Emily said with a loud laugh.

'Don't you mind sharing?' Shirley asked. 'Three is quite a lot.'

'It's a whopping big room,' Emily pointed out. 'If we all get on, it could be fun, like boarding school,' she joked. 'Not that I've been,' she added with a grin.

'Talking of sharing,' Nancy piped up, 'have you noticed that Maureen and Olive have been moved from a double room to their own private bedrooms on the first floor, with a sea view?'

'How did they fiddle that?' Shirley asked. 'They certainly aren't paying residents – well, not that I know of.'

Nancy, who'd known the two girls longer than the others, said knowingly, 'Couple of little operators if you ask me.'

'I bet Olive wangled it – she's got eyes in the back of her head,' Shirley added. 'And she's been caught stealing too – as for Maureen, she'd do anything for a free meal.'

'Now, now, young Shirley, less of the gossip,' Sister Mary Paul chided.

After the nun had gone into the kitchen to collect more plates, Nancy lowered her voice to whisper to her friends. 'They must have buttered somebody up.'

'I'm surprised Isla didn't get a private room,' Emily remarked. 'She looks like somebody who could pay her own way, and her granny drove her here in a big posh car.'

'She'll be better off sharing with us two,' Nancy laughed. 'If she'd paid for her own private bedroom, she'd be right next to Olive and Maureen!'

Emily grinned. 'We might be poor but at least we're honest, kid!' she joked.

Isla was indeed from a very different background from her two room-mates, but, because of their circumstances and their recent painful experiences, they actually had a lot in common. Nancy and Emily quickly discovered that Isla was a bookworm; they teased her when they found her lying across her bed, or sprawled on one of the old battered sofas in the sitting room.

'If Matron catches you lolling around with your head in a book, she might give you extra chores!' Emily teased.

Over time, the three room-mates opened up about their individual stories. It might be that one of them would pour out her past on a walk across the marsh, dodging grazing sheep and their growing lambs, or when they were in bed in the dark, and confidences would be exchanged and fears for the future too. One afternoon the three of them sat in the sunny garden, Isla avidly reading the daily paper, Nancy knitting bootees and Emily half dozing.

'What do you think you'll do if there is a war?' Isla said, as she laid aside her newspaper.

'There's certainly enough talk about it,' Emily murmured sleepily.

'If war is declared, women will be conscripted, just like they were in the Great War,' Isla told her friends.

No longer sleepy, Emily suddenly sat bolt upright.

'I don't know what I'd do if I was forced to work. Who would look after my baby if I was conscripted?'

'If women replace men in the workplace, the government would have to accommodate them and their children too,' Isla replied.

'How would they do that?' Nancy said puzzled.

'Provide factories with domestic quarters and nurseries for working mothers,' Isla explained.

Nancy, who'd never given conscription a thought, was fascinated. 'What kind of factories?' she asked.

'Factories that build bombs, ammunition, planes and tanks,' Isla told her.

Emily nodded. 'Isla's right: if all the men have joined up, they'll need women to work round the clock.'

Nancy's eyes blazed with excitement. 'I'd love to do something for my country,' she said fervently. 'I hate the thought of Nazis invading our land,' she added with patriotic passion.

'I'm with you, Nancy,' Isla announced. 'I'd like to fly an RAF Spitfire and shoot down every German bomber heading towards these shores.'

Laughing at the idea of Isla gunning down the enemy, Nancy abandoned the bootees she'd been struggling with. 'Could we – we women – *really* do that?' she gasped.

Suddenly galvanized, Isla jumped to her feet. 'Why not? Imagine wearing a WAAF uniform and cap.' She tried to walk as if she were marching off to war, but because of her ungainly body she could hardly keep her balance. 'Well, not right now, fat and pregnant,' she laughed, and settled back down on the warm grass beside her friends. 'If war is declared, we'll face big changes,' she said as she flapped the newspaper she'd been reading in the air. 'Food rationing, training camps, female conscription, the home guard, compulsory take-over of property, including stately homes. Hitler could turn the world we love upside down.'

Talk of war and all the uncertainties that went with it

brought tears to Emily's big blue eyes. Before she could stop herself, she blurted out what was on her mind. 'I still have no idea where my George is! He could be anywhere, The Far East, Germany, Canada.' Ada, hurrying by to hang up washing in the kitchen garden, spotted the three girls in a tight, emotional huddle.

'Everything all right?' she called out.

When Nancy shook her head, Ada put down the heavy washing basket she was carrying and approached the group.

'Now then, Em, darling, what's the matter, dear?'

'I don't know whether my fiancé's alive or dead!' Emily sobbed. 'Life without George would be unbearable in itself, but, on my own, how will I manage to bring up his child, how will I support it in the middle of a war? I can't bear the thought of not keeping George's baby – it's the only link I have with him,' she wailed.

Reaching out, Ada took Emily into her arms. 'There, there,' she soothed. 'Take one step at a time,' she advised.

'That's what I try to do,' Emily told her. 'But sometimes I'm overwhelmed, petrified by what I may have to face in the very near future.'

'You're a strong woman, Em. It will work out, I promise you.'

Even though she spoke so determinedly, Ada honestly did wonder if Emily's boyfriend might have died. The alternative – that he'd abandoned her – was in some ways even worse. She sighed and said nothing further; each of them in their own way would have enough to cope with in the months to come. What fate had in store for them after Mary Vale, only time would tell.

16. War

September 1939

On an idyllic September morning, as churches all over London emptied out their early-morning congregations and barrage balloons already floated ominously high in the bright blue sky, Neville Chamberlain delivered his broadcast from the Cabinet Room of Number 10, Downing Street, at 11.15 precisely. Clearly struggling to keep his voice steady, he spoke solemnly.

This morning the British Ambassador in Berlin handed the German government a final note stating that, unless we heard from them by 11 o'clock that they were prepared at once to withdraw their troops from Poland, a state of war would exist between us.

I have to tell you now that no such undertaking has been received, and that consequently this country is at war with Germany.

During the short length of Chamberlain's speech there were differing reactions all over the country. The older listeners remembered the horrors of the Great War and felt nothing but despair; other listeners, like Stan, were angry with Chamberlain for not having acted sooner.

'The prime minister's given Hitler time to make fools

of us,' he raged, as he sat in front of the wireless smoking one cigarette after another.

Knowing how her husband still grieved for the father he idolized, who had died bravely at the Battle of the Somme, Gloria laid a loving hand on his arm. 'Listen to Robin playing in the back garden with the kids next door,' she said with tears in her eyes. 'He knows nothing of what's to come.'

'Leave him be,' Stan murmured as he caught her hand and kissed it. 'Poor little blighter will know soon enough.'

Grasping her husband's hand, Gloria looked him straight in the eye. 'Promise me you won't volunteer right away,' she said with fear in her voice.

Stan's gaze didn't falter; she caught her breath when she saw the determined look on his face; she knew exactly what it meant: 'I'm not letting the memory of my dad down and I'm not letting my country down either.'

'Sweetheart, you know that I have no intention of dodging my duty,' he replied firmly. 'The Nazis will try to raze this city of ours to the ground; they won't care about the innocent – for God's sake, look what the blighters have just done in Poland.'

Knowing what was coming next, Gloria began to cry. Stan stroked her long, dark hair. 'It would make it so much easier for me to go if I knew that you, Robin and the baby' – he nodded at his wife's growing stomach – 'were safely out of London.'

Gloria sighed as she buried her face against her husband's shoulder. Her world and her lovely, happy life were falling apart; she couldn't send Stan off to war worrying about his family; it was her duty to do as he asked.

'I'll go,' she feebly agreed. 'Robin and I will leave London.'

Turning her tear-stained face to the man she loved with all her heart, she quickly added, 'But only after you've gone, Stan. I'm staying right here in Battersea, and we'll be a family together until the moment you leave.'

Two hundred miles away, in Mary Vale, the girls and the staff alike were gathered around the big wireless in the dining room, listening, as was the rest of the nation, to Chamberlain's speech – at the end of which half the girls started to weep.

'I've got twin brothers. They're only sixteen. How soon before they'll have to go off and fight the bloody Nazis?' Seeing the nuns eyeing her sternly, the tearful girl quickly muttered an apology: 'Sorry, sisters.'

Another girl wailed, 'Mi dad's only forty; he lost his dad and his older brothers in the last war. He's bound to be called up.'

Sensing hysteria was about to break loose, Ada swiftly took control. 'Ladies! Let's not panic,' she urged. Turning to Sister Ann, who was looking distinctly shell-shocked herself, she said, 'Would you please take those who would like to say some prayers to the chapel, Sister?'

Before she hurried away, Sister Ann quickly said, 'I left Emily and Nancy with a couple of girls in the nursery.'

'I'll keep an eye on them,' Ada promised.

After the nun had left with a string of weeping girls, Ada spotted Shirley. 'Can you fetch a pot of tea into the nursery, dear?' she asked politely.

'Course, sister,' Shirley willingly agreed. 'What's going to happen, Miss – will Hitler shut down the Home?' she asked in a voice tight with tension.

Ada couldn't help but smile. 'I should think Mary Vale is way down on Hitler's list of priorities, Shirley. Nothing much will change here, though we'll need blackout curtains right away, and gas masks, and to be prepared for food rationing.'

'You can't ration cows!' Shirley laughed. 'There'll still be milk to be had, and butter and cheese too.'

'It'll be spread a lot more thinly from now on,' Ada warned. 'Time to tighten our belts.'

When Ada arrived in the nursery, she could see immediately that they'd all been discussing the dreadful news too. She heard Nancy saying, 'We'll be all right here in Mary Vale; we're miles away from any action.'

Emily scoffed at her friend's comment. 'You must be joking! We're right on the coast, close to a dozen or so RAF bases dotted around the coastline, and a big shipyard in Barrow too.'

Shirley, who'd just walked in bearing a loaded tea tray, gasped. 'OOOH! Will this area be a target?'

Ada tried as best she could to defuse the girl's fears. 'Calm down, Shirley, and be careful with that teapot,' she warned, as she saw Shirley start to tremble. 'Here, I'll take it,' she said, and relieved the nervous girl of the tray, which she put well out of harm's way. Addressing all the girls, she said calmly, 'Let's not get ahead of ourselves, ladies.'

Later, when Emily was in the sluice room helping Sister Ada hand-rinse the terry-towelling nappies that had been soaking in bleach, she couldn't stop herself from returning to the subject of war. 'I've been reading about the evacuees,' she started. 'If homes like Mary Vale were to take in evacuees, it would become a place for married and unmarried women alike.'

Ada nodded. 'That's a point: it would no longer be a home exclusively for unmarried mothers and their babies. Plus, its secluded location might be very attractive to women and children in need of safety.'

Suddenly seized with fear about the future, Emily's face paled. 'What will happen to our lovely land?' she said in a voice that was choked with emotion. 'Could we British become slaves to the Nazis?'

Ada put a comforting arm around Emily's trembling shoulders. 'Come on, Emily, you mustn't think like that; we're British. Have you forgotten? We *never* give in!'

Leaving some of the girls praying, Sister Ann genuflected, then hurried down the dark corridor, intent on returning to her duties on the ward. Crossing herself as she rushed past the statue of Our Lady, she almost walked headlong into Father Ben, who was as white as a sheet.

'Such terrible news, Father,' she said woefully.

Father Ben leant forwards and said in a low shocked voice, 'I know. And I have some other devastating news too, Sister.'

'What is it, Father?' she asked nervously. 'What's happened to you?'

'I can't speak about it now,' he answered in a flustered voice. 'I must see the Reverend Mother right away.'

Feeling deeply concerned about the priest, Sister Ann hurried back to her ward, where all her demanding duties took her mind off her worries for the rest of the day.

The following morning the Reverend Mother called a

meeting in the convent sitting room for all the nuns in the order, and for the hospital staff too. Father Ben was absent but Matron was present and, oddly enough, Sir Percival too.

Looking quite unlike her normally serene self, the Reverend Mother came straight to the point. 'I'm afraid I have some very upsetting news to report,' she started.

The group gathered around her glanced anxiously at each other: what could possibly be more upsetting than the previous day's terrible news? they wondered.

'I'm sorry to say that Father Benedict has been removed from his post here at the convent with immediate effect,' the Reverend Mother informed the tense group in one long breath.

There was a collective gasp of what was a mixture of shock and indignation. The Reverend Mother held up her hand for silence so that she could continue.

'There have been some very serious allegations directed at Father Benedict; it's been said he's behaved' – the Reverend Mother could hardly bear even to say the word – 'inappropriately. An accusation which of course the convent must investigate.'

Shirley, who'd dropped in with a tray bearing a pitcher of water and some glasses, set it down on the table with a loud clatter.

'That's a LIE!' she cried before she could stop herself. 'Sister Ann says Father Ben's the nearest thing to a saint on earth! He'd never harm a fly.'

Slightly embarrassed by Shirley's passionate outburst, Sister Ann quickly put a warning hand on her arm. 'Shhh, child,' she hissed.

Wild with anger, Shirley muttered mutinously, 'You know it's a lie, Sister.'

The nun pressed a warning finger to her lips. 'Shhh!'

Stony-faced Ada, also livid at the accusations directed at good Father Ben, demanded, 'What kind of allegations?'

'I'm afraid I'm not at liberty to speak,' the Reverend Mother responded.

Though outraged that the priest could be dismissed without any adequate explanation, Ada carefully modified her tone. 'Please excuse me, Reverend Mother, I'm sure you know how loved and respected Father Ben is by residents and staff alike; it would help if we knew a little more.'

Looking flustered and embarrassed, the Reverend Mother answered stiffly, 'I'm sorry, Sister Dale, I can give no further explanation.' Addressing the group in general, she concluded, 'For the moment, while the inquiry is on-going, Father Benedict has been advised to return to his seminary.'

A stunned silence followed; nobody could believe that, whatever the accusations were (and they must have been weighty if the priest had been removed from his office), dear, loyal, modest, self-effacing Father Ben, who'd been so much a part of Mary Vale life, would not be with them for the time being. Sir Percival broke the silence, stepping forward and saying in a soft, reassuring voice, 'I appreciate this has been an awful shock to you all. God knows no one here could fail to appreciate the work that Father Benedict has done for the Home over the years.'

A collective murmur of agreement ran round the room.

'We have no choice but to leave the matter with the

religious authorities, who will thoroughly investigate the case. Meanwhile,' Percival quickly added, 'as chairman of the Board of Governors, it is my responsibility to take over the administration of Mary Vale's adoptions.' Bowing in her direction, Percival added with a grateful smile, 'With the assistance of Matron, of course.'

Ada exchanged a long look with Sister Ann: how had all of this vital reorganization been achieved so swiftly?

As if reading Ada's mind, Matron stepped forward. 'The information that Father Benedict meticulously filed away will help us to soldier on until his safe return,' she announced.

As the meeting broke up and they returned to the ward, Ada turned to Sister Ann and Shirley. 'What are we going to tell the girls?'

'They're bound to ask questions,' Shirley said knowingly.

'We can't fob them off with lies,' Sister Ann replied. 'We have to tell them the truth.'

'What? That Father Ben's been sent back to his seminary pending inquiries?' Ada asked.

Sister Ann nodded miserably. 'Yes, though I don't believe a single word of it!'

Shirley looked troubled. 'Why is Sir Percival taking over? He doesn't know anything about adoption. He won't care what happens to those babies. There's no way he'll do the job as well as Father Ben,' she said loyally.

'Well, he is chairman of the Board of Governors,' Sister Ann reminded her. 'And hopefully it is only a temporary position until Father Ben's name is cleared and he can return to us with his name unblemished.'

Crossing themselves as they passed the statue of Our

Lady in the corridor that connected the convent to the Home, they all paused briefly to gaze up at the statue of the smiling Madonna holding the child Jesus to her breast.

'Please God,' Ada silently implored. 'Please bring dear Father Ben safely back to Mary Vale, where he's loved and much needed.'

17. Fear

Over the next week, as word spread about Father Ben's sudden dramatic departure, Shirley was unusually vocal in her loyalty to the priest, who, she believed, had been publicly maligned.

'He's the nearest thing to a saint on earth,' she repeatedly told anyone and everyone at the drop of a hat.

Nancy, whose baby was due soon, was particularly agitated about Sir Percival taking over the adoptions.

'HIM!' she scoffed. 'He knows nothing about any of us girls.'

Determined to keep irate Nancy calm, Ada quickly added, 'I'm sure it's only a temporary arrangement until Father Ben returns.'

The announcement of Percival's new role threw Isla too, especially so soon after having parted from Jeannie. When she and Jeannie had briefly met Father Ben on Isla's preliminary visit to the Home, both women had been impressed by his sensitive and thoughtful inquiries and had instinctively trusted him.

'He's obviously had years of experience when it comes to placing babies,' Jeannie had said.

Isla had agreed with her grandmother. 'Listening to him talking about finding the "right match" for my baby was very comforting,' she admitted.

'And he's fastidious about records and dates,' Jeannie

added. 'His filing system is astonishing,' she laughed. 'Much better than mine!'

'He's obviously an extremely organized administrator,' Isla remarked. 'I liked him a lot.'

Little did Isla know that in Matron's office, just off the main ward, Sir Percival was at that very moment poring over Isla's records, which had been lifted from Father Ben's famously neat and organized files.

'Do you see what I mean?' Matron asked with the smuggest of expressions. 'Miss Ross – or should I say Child Ross – is perfect for our purposes.'

'Indeed,' Percival agreed with a smile. 'Good breeding on both sides, highly presentable and highly desirable. I'd say a perfect match for the Bennetts, as long as it's a boy – though a clever girl from good stock might change their mind,' he added as an afterthought. 'When's the baby due?' he asked.

'Around Christmas,' Matron told him.

Percival, who'd been hoping to bank another hefty cheque, swore under his breath. It was clear he'd have to wait a bit longer for further funds to drop into his bank account. His disappointment was mingled with irritation; he hadn't planned on sharing the down payment with Matron, but she had been so persistent in the matter, pestering him daily about the bally joint account, that it had become impossible for him to wriggle out of the arrangement. Trying to smother his irritation, he returned to his questions.

'And the young woman has definitely made her mind up about adopting? She's not likely to bolt at the final hurdle?'

'I haven't spoken to her personally about the adoption of her child,' Matron told him. 'But, as you can see from her file, she appears to be quite certain about not keeping it.'

'Excellent,' Percival murmured as he accepted the cup of coffee Matron held out to him.

'And there is another piece of good news,' Matron added. 'We've had an inquiry from a family in Northampton; the father phoned me last night, asking if we could immediately place his daughter, who ran away from the mother and baby home they had chosen for her.'

Percival smothered a yawn – what had all this nonsense got to do with him? He might be in charge of Mary Vale adoptions, but did he really need to know every single detail of every single resident?

But Matron's next comment made him suddenly sit bolt upright.

'They're a titled, landowning family.'

Inertia gone, Percival was literally on the end of his chair, agog for more information. 'Really?' he spluttered. 'How titled?'

'I'll find out more when they register here tomorrow.'

'Tomorrow!' Percival asked in surprise. 'So soon?'

'The girl, Daphne, is expecting her baby very soon – this month, in fact.'

With pound signs swimming before his eyes, Percival loudly announced, 'Then she must come here straight away!'

'The sooner the better,' he thought to himself.

Feeling vastly relieved that he now had another arrow to his bow, Percival waxed lyrical in his thanks to Matron. 'I must congratulate you on your marvellous work, Maud,' he smarmed. 'Getting rid of the priest and clearing the way for me was a stroke of sheer genius; and now we have, thanks to your good management, two desirable babies on our books.'

Matron smiled at his flattering comments. 'We make a good team, Archie,' she said primly.

'Let's hope the bloody war doesn't get in the way of our plans.'

Looking distinctively put out that a world war might get in the way of her arrangements, Matron bristled. 'And why should it?'

Percival shrugged. 'The government is already shipping thousands of evacuees out of London to safe houses such as Mary Vale; you could soon be overrun by hordes of filthy, hungry city children,' he pointed out. 'More mouths to feed could leave us less time to focus on our little venture.'

Matron's expression remained cold and haughty. 'I'm sure they won't send evacuees here,' she announced, as if she herself were in charge of war operations in Europe. 'We're too far north to be of interest to anybody. Anyway,' she insisted, 'the Home is permanently full of pregnant women and squawking babies. Given the choice between overcrowded Mary Vale and a large sheep farm in Wales, most evacuees, I'm sure, would opt for the latter.'

'Don't count your chickens, Maud. Mary Vale could be requisitioned by the government and turned into a training centre. You could lose your job and all our plans could go up in smoke.'

Matron's face set hard as concrete. 'We'll see about that!' she declared.

In London, Stan was walking home deep in thought. As Gloria had predicted, he'd wasted no time in signing up. Quickening his pace, he hurried along the familiar

Battersea streets; he needed to tell his wife what he'd done before an official letter from the War Office dropped through his letterbox. But the first thing Stan saw when he got home was an official-looking letter propped up on the mantelpiece. Catching a glimpse of Robin playing happily in the back garden with a friend from across the way, Stan was relieved to have the opportunity to talk in private to Gloria.

'I always suspected that you might be the first man in London to sign up,' Gloria said in a hurt voice. 'But I didn't ever think you'd go behind my back,' she added tearfully.

Full of guilt, yet determined to do the right thing, Stan started to explain himself to his wife. 'The Royal Army Service Corps urgently need experienced drivers to transport vital equipment to the Front Line – food and men, ammunition, tanks, medical equipment and what have you. I'm sorry, sweetheart,' he gulped. 'I've joined up along with half the men from the bus depot.'

'I know you, Stan,' Gloria said, as she slumped on to a kitchen chair. 'You'd die for your country and I love you for your loyalty, but I'm frightened,' she burst out. 'What with the baby' – she laid a protective hand on her tummy, which was quite a considerable size these days – 'and Robin, how will we cope without you?'

Across the table Stan clasped his wife's hand. 'I know, love, we're all frightened, and quite rightly so too.'

Seeing his wife so terrified and sad broke Stan's heart. Hurrying to her side, he kissed away her tears. 'I'm sorry, darlin',' he murmured into her glorious, long, dark hair. 'I have to do my duty.'

Clinging on to her husband, Gloria wondered how many

women and young girls were in the same emotional turmoil as she was. *Of course* he had to fight for his country – it was the right thing to do – but *why* so soon, why now?

Drawing away from her, Stan gave his wife a long, level look. 'Promise me you won't back out of leaving London when the time comes?' he whispered.

Gloria held her handsome husband's hand. 'When have I ever broken a promise to you, Stan?'

He shook his head. 'Never.'

'I told you I'd go, and I will,' she concluded, then burst into tears all over again.

With the start of the war, petrol was rationed and suddenly there were sandbags everywhere, and everybody had a gas mask with strict instructions not to leave home without it. Morale, which had been robust, began to falter with the devastating news of the slaughter of 66,000 people in Poland when it collapsed to Hitler's armies. This was rapidly followed by news closer to home: the sinking of HMS *Royal Oak* hit the nation hard. The battleship, part of the British Home Fleet in Orkney's Scapa Flow, was sunk on a night raid. The enemy's U-boat had cunningly threaded its way through anti-submarine defences and, after firing off torpedoes, the battleship went down in just two minutes, taking all 833 officers and men on board with her.

There was a feeling that the Germans were everywhere, creeping closer and closer, making their way along the coast, waiting to pounce and invade. The new, spooky sound of air-raid sirens practising in anticipation of enemy attack made Gloria's skin crawl, and the heart-breaking pictures of evacuees in the daily papers brought tears to her eyes.

Gloria's friends were constantly urging her to choose a safe home out of London for her and her son. 'If you don't make a decision soon, you might be forced to separate,' one friend warned. 'It would be awful if you and Robin were evacuated to different parts of England.'

Starting to panic, Gloria decided that she was going to jump before she was pushed. Returning to the local library, she scoured through some up-to-date catalogues and registers and spotted a home called Mary Vale, which she immediately liked the look of. Quickly jotting down the details in her little notebook, Gloria made contact with the Home right away. On paper it looked better than most; she just hoped they had room for one more pregnant woman and her young son too.

It wasn't long before Gloria got a reply from the Reverend Mother.

'You and your young son will be our first evacuees at Mary Vale,' she said in her letter. 'You are most welcome, and we pray you'll be happy with us.'

Now that they'd come to terms with one another's decision, Gloria and Stan felt there was less tension in the air, but both dreaded the moment of parting. They tried to stay focused on practical details, in Gloria's case washing, mending, ironing and packing Stan's civvy clothes, which would soon be replaced by a soldier's uniform once he arrived at his training centre outside London. As Gloria packed her husband's case, she struggled to fight back tears.

'I can't tell you the relief I feel now that I know you and Robin have got a safe place miles away from London to go to,' Stan said gratefully.

When the moment of parting finally came, Gloria and

Robin accompanied Stan to the bus stop, where Robin broke down and wailed, 'Can I come with you, Dad?'

Luckily for Stan, the bus loomed up before he broke down and wept too.

'Look after Mum,' he said in a choked voice; then, after hugging his son, he grabbed hold of Gloria, whom he clung on to.

'I love you both so much,' he said in a voice that was choked with emotion.

Knowing she had to stay strong, Gloria said gently, 'Get on the bus, love – you don't want to miss it.'

Reluctantly releasing her, Stan slung his bag over his shoulder and hopped on to the platform. 'Take care of our baby!' he cried, as the bus pulled away.

'Bye, Dad!' Robin called. 'Come back soon!'

'I love you, Stan,' Gloria whispered, as the bus turned the corner and her husband disappeared from sight.

With Stan gone, the house felt sad and empty; memories rattled in every corner and Gloria knew she was ready to leave London. As she tidied up before their departure, she prayed that when she returned to Battersea her home would still be standing and not bombed to a pile of rubble. After locking up for the last time, she took hold of Robin's hand and, with her free hand, she picked up her heavy suitcase. Blinded by tears, she gave her precious home one last, lingering look before she turned her back on the life she'd lived as a wife and a mother in London and set off for the North of England, where she hoped she and her son would find sanctuary.

18. Lady Daphne

Nobody could quite believe their eyes when Daphne Wallace swanned into Mary Vale like a ship in full sail. Her father, ensconced with Sir Percival in Matron's office for well over an hour, had left his wife and daughter in Matron's tender care and nobody could doubt from the smile that wreathed Matron's normally formidable face that she was in her element. As the Wallace party toured the Home, the girls looked in amazement at the new arrival: here was no shy, shamed, wilting violet. Tall and rangy, with cropped brown hair, gappy front teeth and sharp brown eyes, she strode like a man, shifting the weight of her belly as she moved briskly about the Home with her mother, Lady Wallace, who had a voice that could easily have shattered crystal.

'I do apologize for the undignified haste of our arrival, Matron,' she said, as her eyes swept in a peremptory way around the delivery room. 'We really had no choice, given the circumstances,' she added, throwing her daughter a disapproving look.

'I told Papa I wouldn't stay in the ghastly place you sent me to,' Daphne snapped. 'You wouldn't listen, so what else was I to do but leave?'

'In the dead of night, sneaking away like a felon,' her mother retorted.

'It was the only time I could get out of the blasted building,' Daphne remonstrated.

Lady Wallace threw a shuddering glance at her daughter's vast tummy. 'And arriving home in *that* dreadful condition.'

'You should have thought of the consequences before you locked me up in that prison of a home!' Daphne grumbled.

Seeing the pair of them (who were so like each other in temperament) on the point of exploding, or, worse still, scratching each other's eyes out, Matron stepped in. 'May I offer you a cup of tea, in the garden?' she suggested, thinking it might be a good idea to get mother and daughter out of the Home and away from the goggling girls they would come across.

'That would be most kind,' Lady Wallace replied. After giving the delivery room a final glance, she said with another shudder, 'I think I've seen quite enough.'

As the three of them marched through the large entrance hall, Daphne barked, 'Where exactly is my room?'

In the privacy of the garden Matron explained that Daphne's room was presently being prepared for her. 'It's a single room with a sea view,' she told her.

It was, in fact, the single room that scheming Olive had just vacated; she and Maureen, keen to pocket the final payment from Matron, had left Mary Vale just as soon as they could after giving birth. Instructed by Matron, Dr Jones had signed them off as hale and hearty and they'd left the Home within a week of each other, neither with any regret that their scandalous lies had brought about Father Benedict's tragic downfall.

'I don't mind where you stable me,' Daphne told Matron. 'With a bit of luck I'll be here only a month, then I'll be back in the saddle,' she said with a cheerful snort.

Her mother cringed at her daughter's crass expression. 'I don't think so!' she vehemently protested.

Ignoring her mother, Daphne cheerfully crashed on. 'Bad luck giving birth bang in the middle of the hunting season!' she exclaimed. 'Still, I should get a sniff of the hounds before the season ends,' she said with an optimistic beam.

'If it weren't for the wretched hunting season, you wouldn't be in the mess you're in now,' Lady Wallace sniped.

Sensing an almighty row was about to explode, Matron hurriedly ferried the visitors out of the garden and into her office, but not before popping into the kitchen to demand tea for three in her office *now!*

In the cool, capacious kitchen pantry Shirley was very carefully wiping down the deep shelves stacked with neatly labelled jams, pickles and chutneys, not to mention bottled blackberries, plums, cherries, and red and black currants, whose richly coloured juices glowed like little stained-glass windows. When she heard Matron's imperious bark outside, her heart skipped a beat. 'What does the old witch want now?' she wondered.

Like a sniper coming up for air, Shirley cautiously waited a few minutes before popping her head around the pantry door. 'Has she gone?' she whispered to Sister Mary Paul.

The nun, who never spoke an unkind word about anybody, simply rolled her eyes. 'She wants tea for three *now!*' she said, repeating Matron's exact words.

'Oh, Sister, don't go asking me to take it into her. I nearly dropped the lot last time,' Shirley implored.

Sister Mary Paul raised her hands, sticky with pastry dough, in the air. 'Look at me, child! she exclaimed. 'I'm up to mi elbows in pastry.'

Shirley gave a little sheepish nod. 'All right, I'll do it,' she murmured.

Waiting for the kettle to boil on the big old range, Shirley neatly set a large wooden tray with a snowy lace cloth, the best delicate china cups and saucers, and a little cream jug and sugar basin decorated with the tiniest pink rosebuds, which Shirley adored.

'Don't forget the shortbread biscuits,' Sister Mary Paul reminded her, and Shirley reached up for the biscuit tin on the high shelf over the kitchen worktop. She brewed the tea; then, taking a deep breath, she lifted up the heavy tray, which started to rattle in her trembling hands.

'Put it down before you drop it, child!' Sister Mary Paul cried. As poor Shirley set down the tray, she added reassuringly, 'You can do this; it's just a question of mind over matter.'

'It's easy saying that, Sister, but I'm terrified of the old bat,' the girl blurted out. 'She stares at me with eyes as cold as a dead fish and complains about everything I do, even when I know I've done it right! She enjoys picking on me, frightening me – and that's the truth!'

Knowing only too well what a bully and sadist Maud Harding could be, the nun concentrated on building up Shirley's confidence in herself. If Shirley were to remain a fixture at Mary Vale, she had to learn to survive, and that meant facing her demons.

'Do you know how to say the Hail Mary?' the nun suddenly asked.

Shirley nodded. 'Yes, Sister Ann taught me the prayer. It's lovely. Hail Mary . . .' she started with a sweet smile.

'Good,' said Sister Mary Paul. 'Now, here's what to do: say the prayer in your head all the time you're in Matron's office.'

Shirley's eyes opened wide in surprise, but the nun rolled on.

'Praying the Hail Mary all the while?' Shirley quizzed.

'Not out loud!' Sister Mary Paul laughed. 'Concentrate on Our Lady and she'll get you through it. Now, off you go,' she added, as she gave her favourite helper a gentle pat on the back.

Shirley obediently picked up the tray and, with a timid but determined expression, she left the kitchen. It was only as she approached Matron's office at the end of a long corridor that she started to pray, 'Hail Mary, full of grace, the Lord is with thee . . .'

Sister Mary Paul was right: the prayer worked and kept her steady and focused, so that when it came to setting down the laden tea tray her hands barely shook. Without even looking at Matron or the two other women in the room, Shirley gave a quick bob, then all but flew back to the kitchen, where Sister Mary Paul was waiting for her.

'It worked!' Shirley laughed, as she spun around in a circle like an excited child. 'I did as you said, Sister, and it worked.'

Looking not the least bit surprised, Sister Mary Paul smiled at Shirley, who looked as triumphant as a warrior king.

'I did it!' she exclaimed.

Returning to trimming the crusts on the plates she'd just covered with pastry, Sister Mary Paul nodded. 'I've never known Our Lady to let a good soul down yet.'

*

Smiling Sir Percival was also drinking tea, though, after the arrangements he'd just made with Lord Wallace, he thought he truly deserved a triple gin! He'd agreed to take Wallace's pregnant daughter into the Home. 'Even though we're full to capacity, we're more than happy to make special arrangements for your daughter,' he'd lied through his teeth.

'And can you keep the little madam for a few weeks after the damn thing's born?' Wallace had asked.

Percival, who hadn't shown the slightest interest in post-natal care up until now, smirked. 'Post-natal care is one of our major priorities; I can promise you your daughter won't be allowed home until she's been declared fit by Matron and our in-house doctor, Dr Jones.'

'Who'd sign anything for a bottle of brandy,' Percival thought to himself.

'And you'll see to the adoption,' Wallace continued. 'She doesn't want the bastard, and we certainly don't, not after knowing who's fathered it.'

Percival gave an understanding smile; Wallace had already informed him that the master of the local hounds had had his way with his daughter.

'A bounder and a cad!' Wallace had raged. 'Old enough to be her blasted father, married – with a family too.'

Percival had quite different thoughts: the bounder and the cad in question would probably have some good breeding on his side, while the Wallaces were at the top of the tree in that department. The child (hopefully a boy) would be prime material for adoption. With luck, the Bennetts would have a son and heir in time for Christmas, and Percival would be in credit in the bank.

Wallace wrote out a cheque for his daughter's stay in Mary Vale, and then another, much more generous cheque payable to Percival. 'For your discreet service, Sir. This delicate matter must be kept strictly secret. If word should get out, my daughter's chances of a good match in the future will be in tatters. You understand, I'm relying on your honour, Sir,' he said sternly.

'Rest assured, here at Mary Vale discretion is our byword,' Percival replied with an obsequious smile.

'Make sure she doesn't bolt,' Wallace added as he rose to go. 'She's a damned handful, always has been. You'll have your work cut out managing her,' he warned.

When the booming parents finally departed, Matron led Daphne into the noisy dining room, where the girls were finishing their midday meal. Leaving hearty Daphne unashamedly heaping her plate with fish pie and cabbage, Matron hurried off to grill Sir Percival.

With not a shred of nervousness about her, Daphne plonked herself down next to Nancy, who almost fainted in terror when the new girl turned her big horsy face towards her.

'When's your brat due?' she asked.

Poor Nancy was so shocked by Daphne's abruptness she stammered her reply, 'Th . . . this month.'

'Mine too,' Daphne said, as she glared at her tummy. 'Bloody hell!' she guffawed. 'I can't wait for the whole ghastly business to be over!'

In her office Matron found Sir Percival leaning back in his chair smoking a Pall Mall cigarette with a wide smile on his face.

'Wallace couldn't wait to offload his troublesome daughter,' he announced with a triumphant smirk.

Matron gave him a cunning look. 'Was money exchanged?'

'Of course!' Percival exclaimed. 'A very generous initial *donation* to the convent, via our account.'

Referring to the Bennetts, Matron demanded, 'And the rest? When do we get the full amount?'

'The full *donation* will be made when we exchange the goods, so to speak,' he told her.

'*If* we exchange,' Matron added cryptically. 'The new girl could give birth to a girl – or a horse,' she muttered under her breath.

'Horses for courses,' Percival clumsily joked.

'Thank God she won't be here long,' Matron continued. 'She's got a voice like a fog horn, eats like a gannet and defers to nobody.'

'A chip off the old block, I'd say,' chuckled Percival, who, in the best of spirits, bade Matron farewell and left Mary Vale with a skip in his step and the *donation* safely in his pocket.

All the girls nervously circumnavigated the new girl, but Isla liked her; having been to a girls' boarding school on the Borders, she wasn't unfamiliar with hearty girls with loud voices. Isla made it her business to introduce Daphne to all the girls, who, to start with, made fun of her behind her broad back, but they soon grew to like her breezy approach to life. Her lack of shame was refreshing and her cheeky ways and irreverent attitude to those in charge made the other girls laugh.

When Isla showed Daphne the list of chores that

Matron compiled every week, she didn't question it as Isla had done on her arrival.

'I'm convinced Matron believes that mopping and cleaning the Home, demeaning ourselves like servants, is a way of paying penance for our sins.'

Daphne burst out laughing. 'Penance! What a load of old tosh!' she snorted. 'The moment I'm minus this great lump,' she said, as she shifted the weight of her baby from one side to another, 'I'll be keen to have another roll in the hay.' She winked saucily. 'But next time I'll make sure a romp doesn't result in a blasted pregnancy.'

'There are ways and means,' Isla replied with a grin.

'I'm not just talking about a packet of johnnies!' Daphne replied robustly. 'I'll get the old tubes snipped, solve the baby problem for life.'

Isla's eyes grew big and round. 'You mean you'd get yourself sterilized?'

'Absolutely!' Daphne retorted with a grin. 'Never again,' she vowed.

Having made this heartfelt announcement, she peered myopically at the list of chores pinned to the dining-room wall.

'I'm down to do the fires,' she remarked. 'What does it mean?'

'Cleaning out the grates, removing ashes and cinders, sweeping *all* the fireplaces, then resetting the grates with paper and kindling *and* hauling in buckets of coal from the coal shed too.'

Daphne threw back her shoulders. 'I don't mind!' she announced. 'Better than the damn embroidery and lace-making classes that were compulsory at the last home.

Dreadful dump.' Rubbing her hands together, she said, 'Right-i-o, let's get started.'

Isla – on laundry duty hand-washing sheets in an ancient, old-fashioned boiler and putting them through a mangle that creaked with age and use – explained where the main fireplaces were, then left Daphne to get on with it. It was in the dining room that Daphne, her face smudged with soot and cinder dust, met Shirley, who'd come in to lay the table for dinner. Shirley jumped in surprise when she saw the figure of a woman with a big swaying bottom in front of the fireplace, and heard an indignant voice booming, 'Bally filthy dirty job, this is!'

Seeing the stranger struggling to find a place to dump the cinders, Shirley picked up a discarded newspaper and hurried forward to help her.

'Put them in here,' she said, as she spread the newspaper on the floor for Daphne to use.

Daphne turned her sooty face to Shirley and grinned gratefully. 'Awfully kind of you, old bean,' she said. 'Never done this job before – usually leave it to the servants.'

'I am a servant,' Shirley said with cheerful pride. 'I'll show you how it's done.'

With neat precision she cleared the grate of all the cinders, which she wrapped in the newspaper, then, picking up the little brass brush that was propped up against the side of the fireplace, she dusted down the grate and the fire surround before rising to her feet and polishing the mantel shelf.

'There, all done,' she announced.

Daphne was impressed by the small girl's deftness of touch. 'Good work!' Struggling to her feet, she continued,

'I could tack up my mare in as few minutes as it took you to do that – afraid domesticity is not my forte.'

Taking hold of Shirley's little hand, she pumped it like she was filling a bucket from a standpipe. 'Daphne Wallace, by the way, pleased to meet you.'

Awe-struck, Shirley gave a nervous bob. 'Shirley . . .' she replied. Then, to her complete astonishment, Daphne asked her another question. 'Had a baby?'

Shirley's jaw dropped. 'What?'

'Well, that's what we're all here for, to drop a filly, so to speak.' Daphne's keen eyes swept the length of Shirley's skinny frame. 'You're certainly not carrying one, not like me,' she said, patting her huge bump. 'Think I might have three in here!'

Though transfixed by the new woman, who was a tour de force of energy and conversation, Shirley managed to reply. 'I had a baby, but she was adopted.'

'That's my plan too: get the little blighter adopted and me back into the saddle.' Before Shirley could catch her breath, Daphne blasted another question her way. 'Like horses?'

Shirley, who was scared stiff of all animals except Teresa the kitchen cat (named after Saint Teresa of Ávila by Sister Mary Paul), shook her head.

'Better than babies, believe me,' Daphne assured her. 'Now where do I dispose of all this rubbish?'

'I'll take it,' Shirley volunteered.

'Awfully grateful,' said Daphne, as she bundled the newspaper into Shirley's hands. 'Might just nip to the lav for a gasper,' she added with a saucy wink.

Left on her own, Shirley smiled. 'What a character!' she

said out loud, then giggled as she had a wicked thought. 'Oh, my God! She will drive Matron round the bend!'

Daphne could make friends as easily as breathing; she had no qualms about breezing into different girls' rooms for a chat and a smoke, and, as her friendship with Emily, Nancy and Isla, who were a floor up from her, grew, she spent more and more time with them in their roomy bedroom. Shirley, who was fascinated by Daphne and what she might say next, made a point of doing her cleaning very near any room Daphne might be in. It was while she was doing just that one day that Shirley heard Daphne loudly discussing the inconvenience of an unwanted pregnancy.

'A bally blip to be got through, then move on as swiftly as possible.'

Riveted, Shirley laid aside her mop and crept into the bedroom to join in the discussion. When Nancy saw her, she threw Shirley a welcoming smile before continuing with the ongoing conversation.

'Don't you ever feel guilty about, you know, doing it when you weren't married?' she whispered, red-faced, as they were sharing a box of chocolates that Daphne's mother had sent in the post. 'A guilt gift!' Daphne had called it.

'Not at all!' Daphne retorted, as she took the last coffee cream and popped it into her mouth. 'Couldn't get enough of it.'

Shirley's dark brown eyes almost rolled out of her head. 'You mean you actually enjoyed it?' she gasped.

'Golly, yes!' Daphne cried.

Seeing Nancy and Shirley's startled faces, Daphne asked, 'Not so in your case, huh?'

Shirley kept her mouth firmly shut, while Nancy recalled horrible, gap-toothed Walter on the packing floor in Burton's clothing factory in Bolton.

'It was horrible,' she said with a shudder. 'I didn't even know you could get a baby that way.'

Daphne gave her a rather forceful clap on the back, which made poor Nancy almost choke on her nut truffle. 'You should have been brought up with dogs and horses; there's no doubting where babies come from after you've seen a stallion cover a mare!'

Seeing Nancy going slightly green, Emily swiftly added, 'Sex can be wonderful when you're in love with somebody.'

'Can't say I've noticed the difference, one way or the other,' Daphne joked.

Not wanting to frighten timid Shirley and Nancy, Isla tried hard to recall the only good part of her relationship with her unfaithful professor.

'Emily's right: making love can be special when you really care about the other person.'

'You shouldn't be put off, Nancy,' Emily urged.

'One of the best things in life, if you ask me!' boomed Daphne.

Seeing Nancy and Shirley squirming with embarrassment, Isla completely changed the subject. 'Why did you run away from your previous mother and baby home?' she asked Daphne.

'It was my idiot Papa's decision; nobody consulted me,' Daphne cried indignantly. 'He thought the stricter the Home, the better the place, a punishment for my sins of the flesh,' she scoffed. 'The bloody nuns frog-marched us into church every morning at six, where we yawned our way through half a dozen prayers, then it was out into the garden for gymnastics before a breakfast of bread, marg and water. Absolute bally nightmare!'

'How did you get out?' Nancy giggled.

'Knotted a couple of sheets together and climbed out of the window,' Daphne replied. 'Then ran as fast as this wretched bump would allow.'

'Will you run away from here too?' Nancy asked nervously.

'Nah, this place isn't so bad. I'll stay the course, get it over with,' Daphne replied pragmatically. 'Not long now, eh, Nancy?' she said with a conspiratorial grin.

'Don't talk about it,' Nancy wailed. 'I'm so frightened.' She gazed down at her tummy, which was nothing like as big as Daphne's. 'How will something this size ever come out of me?'

'The same way that it got in!' Daphne joked. 'Nature's way.'

Nancy paled. 'I just wish it was all over,' she sighed.

'Stiff upper lip, girl,' Daphne urged. 'Just a few more weeks, then we'll be free as a bird!'

19. The New Boy

Robin adored the train ride across the wide and spectacular expanse of Morecambe Bay.

'Look, Mummy, the train's on the sea!' he gasped, and stared in wonder through the window at the big engine that was sending up great plumes of smoke as it made its way towards Grange-over-Sands.

'It's not really on the sea, darling,' Gloria tried to explain. 'The train's on railway tracks that are on top of strong wooden piers built into the sea.'

Robin, who obviously preferred his version of things, insisted that the train was somehow making its way magically through the sparkling blue water that was so bright he had to squint to see the station they were approaching.

'Not this stop, laddie,' the cheerful passenger, whom Robin had made friends with on the journey, told the little boy. 'Yours is the next stop, Kents Bank, but I'm getting off here at Grange.

'Have a nice time,' the genial man called as the train pulled away from the platform and chugged slowly past the marsh, which, at high tide, was covered in seawater.

'Have a nice time,' Gloria mused. That wasn't quite how she imagined her immediate future. Comfortable and safe would do for the moment, and until her baby was born early in January. 'Born in wartime,' she thought with a heavy sigh. 'How old will he or she be when the war ends?'

Robin roused Gloria from her stream of sombre thoughts. 'Mummy! The train's stopping!' he cried.

With a grinding of breaks the train groaned to a halt and the porter on the platform called out, 'Kents Bank! Kents Bank! Disembark here for Allithwaite and Cartmel.'

Seeing Gloria struggling with a small boy and two suitcases, the porter hurried forward to relieve her of the cases, while she held tightly on to Robin. As the train moved off on its way to Barrow-in-Furness, where the Royal Train regularly delivered the King and Queen to the famous shipyard to launch the latest battleship, she thanked the helpful porter.

'Do you know where we can find Mary Vale Hall?'

'Aye, lass, reet there,' he replied in a thick Northern accent. 'Straight through yon gate, it's that big owd house yonder.'

Gloria gazed at the big, redbrick, multi-gabled house that was just about visible through tall beeches and holly bushes.

'Follow me, Mummy,' Robin called out, as he skipped along the narrow path that the porter had pointed out.

Staggering under the weight of the cases, Gloria arrived out of breath at the front door. Robin was already knocking on it, but, before she could tell her son to wait, it was flung open by a vastly pregnant girl, who smiled when she saw a small boy standing on the doorstep.

'I'm Robin,' he announced. 'And my mummy's here to have a baby!'

Blushing crimson with embarrassment, Gloria quickly held out her hand. 'Hello, I'm Gloria Baxter and this is my son, Robin. I think we're expected.'

'Come in,' boomed the cheerful girl. 'I'm Daphne. I'll get Sister Ada for you.'

Ada was, in fact, busy in the sluice room, so Sister Ann welcomed the newcomers, whom she took into the sitting room, where Shirley and Sister Mary Paul brought them tea. When the old nun laid eyes on cherubic Robin with his rosy-red cheeks, green eyes and a front tooth missing, she all but dropped the tray in delight.

'I wasn't expecting a fine young man,' she said, as she set the tray down and ran her hands through Robin's silky dark curls.

'I'm staying here to look after my mummy,' he told Sister Mary Paul.

'Well, I'm delighted to hear it,' the old nun said. 'A big boy like you will be very welcome,' she told him. 'Now, I've forgotten to bring the biscuits – will you come and help me find them?'

Skipping after the old nun, Robin chirped, 'Why are all you ladies wearing nighties?'

When they'd left the room, Shirley and Sister Ann burst out laughing.

'Little monkey!' Shirley giggled.

Sister Ann smiled in delight. 'He's a sweetheart,' she murmured.

'I'm sorry, he never stops talking,' embarrassed Gloria apologized. 'It's been a long journey too, which he'll be full of,' she added.

'I'm sure you're exhausted,' Sister Ann sympathized. 'After you've had your cup of tea, I'll show you to your room, where you can rest, and then later on, at tea-time you can meet the other ladies.'

'Is Robin the only child on the premises?' Gloria inquired.

'For now, yes,' Sister Ann told her. 'But, with the number of evacuees increasing, we might get more mothers arriving with their offspring. It will certainly change the nature of the Home,' she added thoughtfully.

'I hope Robin won't be too disruptive,' Gloria fretted. 'Once we're settled, I intend to teach him every morning. I'm an infant teacher,' she added. 'If other children should turn up here, I'd happily teach them too – the more the better,' she smiled. 'I had forty-two children in my class in Battersea, so I'd welcome more; it would be company for Robin too.'

Robin came bursting back into the room clutching a plate of Sister Mary Paul's biscuits. 'The smiley lady in the nightie is making apple pie for tea!' he announced as he bit into a crumbly biscuit.

Thinking she'd better get things clear from the start, Gloria hunkered down and explained the status quo to her son. 'Sweetheart, the smiley lady is Sister Mary Paul, and this is Sister Ann. They're not wearing nighties, they're wearing habits, that's what nuns wear.'

'What's a nun?'

'A lady who belongs to God,' Sister Ann chipped in.

'I'm baptized,' the boy proudly informed her. 'I belong to God too, but I wear pyjamas!'

Sister Mary Paul patted Robin on the head. 'I can see we're going to have hours of fun with this little chap, aren't we, Shirley?'

Shirley nodded and smiled at Robin, who was now frantically hopping from one foot to the other.

'Mummy!' he cried. 'I need a wee-wee!'

The newcomers were given a large corner room on the first floor that gave them views of the sea and the sandy bay one way and the garden of Mary Vale the other way. There were two narrow single beds; a wardrobe, dressing table and sink were in the room too. Across the hallway were shared toilets and a bathroom. Before they went down for tea, Gloria insisted that Robin wash his face and comb his hair, which always sprang back into tight curls. She too washed her face and brushed her long, dark hair before taking a deep breath and descending the stairs to meet the women she would be spending quite some time with.

Matron had kept to her office, even though she'd been informed by one of the kitchen staff that the new woman – an evacuee along with her son, newcomers Matron certainly had no time for – had arrived.

Right now, with so many other things on her mind, two evacuees were not at the top of Matron's priority list. True, she was concerned about how many other pregnant evacuees, plus their screaming, snotty-nosed brats, might turn up at the Home, but her overriding concern at the moment was establishing a secret suite at Crow Thorn Grange where the 'special babies' would be – albeit briefly – privately nursed until the adoptive parents discreetly arrived to pick them up.

Sir Percival had been surprised when she'd made her request. 'Why Crow Thorn?' he'd demanded. 'You already have a post-natal ward at Mary Vale. Why complicate matters, Maud?'

Matron sometimes had her doubts about her business

partner, who seemed to see no further than the end of his rather large nose.

Taking a deep breath, she patiently pointed out the obvious. 'We need to keep our babies separate from the rest in order to allow prospective parents to visit them in private. We don't want every resident in the Home over-hearing our arrangements, do we? It would cause a riot if the girls were to see some babies being given preferential treatment, don't you see?'

Percival nodded. He could see Matron's reasoning, but it was nevertheless rather awkward keeping this secret with his wife on the premises. Matron had shrugged dis-missively when he'd mention Lady Percival – surely a man like Archibald could handle a pathetic milksop such as her?

'I could allocate a couple of rooms at the back of the Grange,' he suggested. 'And I'd ensure that we have exclu-sive use of the back door.'

'I'll provide a cot and some bedding, and equipment to make up feeds,' she added.

'Who will nurse the children?' he asked.

'I'll supervise the nursing initially,' she replied. 'But I can't be there all of the time; we'll have to employ somebody.'

'That would cost money,' Percival complained, before adding, 'What if the minder's a big mouth and gossips about what goes on at the Grange?'

'I have my eye on somebody who'll keep her mouth shut for a price,' she assured him.

'When might we expect our first "visitor"?' he asked coyly.

'The way the Wallace girl is thundering about the place, her waters could break any minute,' Matron declared.

Cringing at Matron's graphic detail, Percival moved swiftly on. 'Leave the equipment you need near the toolshed at the back of the Home. I'll send my gardener down with a truck; he can load it up and bring it all back here.'

'Can you make sure the rooms are thoroughly cleaned and aired?' Matron bossed. 'Hygiene with a new-born is vital.'

Percival nodded; suddenly, after what seemed like weeks of discussion, reality was beginning to kick in.

'The Bennetts are foaming at the bit to pay a visit,' he told Matron.

'They'll have to curb their impatience,' Matron retorted sharply. 'Daphne needs to give birth first – hopefully to a strong, healthy boy. And, if not, let's hope Isla will produce the goods, and soon.'

Robin did indeed take the dining room by storm. At first he was shy – hiding behind his mother's skirts, he peeped out when they entered the room, then darted back behind Gloria (who was feeling quite nervous herself) when he saw so many people staring at him. But at the sight of Sister Mary Paul bustling in with a plate of bread and butter, Robin, who only came up to her waist, dashed forward and hugged her. The delighted nun went pink with pleasure and took the boy by the hand.

'You're just the man I'm looking for!' she announced. 'Will you help me bring out the pasties and the apple pies?'

With a bit of a swagger, Robin trotted after the nun, leaving Gloria wondering where she should sit at the big communal table.

'Sit anywhere – don't stand on custom,' Daphne said, as she waved Gloria towards a chair beside Nancy and Emily, who moved up so that there would be enough room for Robin to sit down too.

Over cups of strong tea and good wholesome food, Gloria chatted to the women around her, who were intrigued by the fact that she'd just been evacuated from London. Shirley, who was wiping down the tabletops with a damp cloth, was fascinated too, moving closer to the group to listen intently to what Gloria had to say.

'The government thinks that the city's not a fit place for women and children; there are over a million people on the move right now,' Gloria told them.

Surprised at what she'd just overheard, Shirley gasped, 'I never imagined evacuees would be sent this far north.'

'They're being sent everywhere,' Gloria told Shirley. 'Scotland, Wales, Cornwall, Devon, the Midlands – even *this* far north,' she joked.

'You were sensible to leave London as soon as you did,' Daphne commented.

'I didn't have much choice!' Gloria laughed. 'My husband insisted that we go after he was called up.'

Greatly amused, Daphne hooted loudly, 'Husbands! They're as rare as hens' teeth round here!'

After the laughter had subsided, irrepressible Daphne continued, 'God knows what snooty Matron would do if evacuees were to arrive en masse. Especially if they looked . . . *poor!*'

Shirley couldn't stop herself from bursting into laughter. 'She'd run for the hills!'

Laughing too, Emily agreed. 'You're dead right there, Shirley.'

Emboldened by the women's camaraderie. Shirley dared to add a cheeky comment. 'Or maybe she'd run to Crow Thorn Grange; she's got a soft spot for the big fella who lives up there.'

Daphne all but fell off her chair. 'You are joking!' she cried. 'Who in the world of God would fancy Percival? He's an absolute cad!'

Her remark caused even more raucous laughter, which assailed Sister Ada, who had just walked into the dining room in search of a cuppa. Seeing the bright, happy faces of her patients, she smiled.

'What's making you all so lively?'

'Shhh!' Emily hissed melodramatically. 'We're talking about you-know-who.'

By this time Shirley, who loved to hear naughty gossip about Matron, was bent over double with laughter.

'Matron!' Daphne hissed. 'And her love of the poor and downtrodden.'

'Starting with me!' Shirley tittered.

'And me!' Nancy cried, as she clutched her tummy. 'Please stop, it hurts to laugh.'

Ada filled up a mug with hot tea, then sat down with her patients, who had fast become her friends.

'You'd better be careful, ladies,' she warned with a wink. 'If you-know-who catches you taking the mickey, you could get put on nappy duties and be locked in the sluice room for a week!'

Listening to the happy, relaxed women chatting easily around her, Gloria began to relax too; it was going to be all right; she was among good people and she had her son safely with her. She was lucky. Nevertheless, her thoughts flew to Stan. Was he driving his truck (loaded with food, ammunition, uniforms and medicine) aiding the British Expeditionary Force, which had been moved across the Channel and was concentrated as part of the Allied line in the area around Lille and Arras? She and thousands of others had been moved out of London to avoid German bombing-raids, but, in the months after war had been declared and men were called up, there'd been no military action; people were even referring to the state of affairs as a 'Phoney War'. Why had things gone so eerily quiet after Neville Chamberlain had made his sombre announcement?

A great wave of tiredness suddenly descended on Gloria; it had been a long, long day and her back ached after their journey. Ada noticed the new arrival trying to smother a yawn.

'You need to get some rest,' she advised. 'When you're feeling less tired, let's have a chat, Gloria, and maybe I could examine you and see how Baby's progressing?' Ada suggested.

'Yes. I'd like that, thank you.' Rising to her feet, Gloria added, 'Meanwhile, I must find that boy of mine. It's way past his bed-time.'

Saying goodbye to her new friends, Gloria followed Shirley into the kitchen, where she found Robin digging into his second helping of apple pie.

'Say night night to Shirley and Sister Mary Paul,' Gloria told her son, as she wiped crumbs off his face.

'Night night, Merry Paul!' he said simply, which made the nun smile indulgently.

'Night night, Robin, see you in the morning,' she replied, as she gave Robin a gentle pat on the back.

Watching mother and son leave the warm kitchen hand in hand, Shirley called after them, 'Sleep well, God bless.'

After a quick bath in rather tepid water, Gloria settled her yawning son on his narrow bed, then curled up beside him. In no time at all she could hear his gentle snores as he drifted off to sleep. Lying still and peaceful, Gloria listened to the new sounds around her: the clatter of footsteps on the stairs; the clink of crockery as the dining room was cleared; girls calling to each other in the garden; and, through the open window, the steady, relentless lapping of water as the tide went out and the moon came up over Morecambe Bay.

20. Births

Daphne and Nancy went into labour within twenty-four hours of each other. Daphne's waters broke just as she was filling up two buckets of coal in the shed with Gloria giving a helping hand.

'Take it easy, Daphne,' Gloria cried, as Daphne heaved a load of coal into one of the buckets. 'You're not mucking out stables – that's heavy stuff.'

'Good exercise!' Daphne replied robustly, as she continued shovelling. 'Exercise, that's what we're all short of in this place.' She stopped suddenly and her face contorted with pain. 'Dammit,' she groaned. 'Think I've got a touch of wind, must be that wretched porridge that the nuns slop up every morning.'

Seeing the colour drain from Daphne's normally rosy-red face, Gloria quickly removed the shovel from her hand. 'Describe the pain to me,' she said calmly.

'Sharp, stabbing, in the small of the back,' Daphne said. 'Ouch!' she yelped. 'There's another one.'

Gloria guided Daphne out of the coal shed and into the garden.

'That's not wind, sweetheart,' she smiled. 'You're going into labour.'

'Labour!' Daphne cried in genuine astonishment. 'Now?'

'Well, it is nearly your time,' Gloria said with a wry smile. 'Let's get you into the house.'

'No, wait – here comes another.' Daphne protested as she bent over double and held the small of her back. 'OWW! It bloody well hurts.'

Gloria waited for the contraction to pass, then tried to move Daphne on before another one kicked in, but half-way up the path Daphne's waters broke; Daphne, a woman very rarely lost for words, stared in horror at the amniotic fluid dripping down her legs.

'Is that what I think it is or have I just peed myself?' she gasped.

'You're not imagining anything,' Gloria assured her. 'That's your waters breaking,' she said, steering Daphne through the back door.

'I feel like I'm wearing wellies,' Daphne cried, with the fluid squelching in her shoes.

'Be serious,' Gloria implored.

'It's hard to be serious when you've got wet knickers!' irrepressible Daphne replied.

On the ward, Gloria was immensely relieved when she found Ada bagging up laundry.

'Sister Ada!' Gloria, still supporting Daphne, called out. 'You have a patient in need of your attention.'

Ada turned and smiled when she saw Daphne hobbling towards her, grimacing.

'OUCH! And buggeration! Hope you have a spare bed handy, Sister, looks like the little blighter's on its way.'

Sister Ada abandoned the laundry bag and took hold of Daphne by the arm.

'She started with back pains about quarter of an hour ago, lugging buckets of coal,' Gloria explained with a smile.

Ada grinned. 'Typical of our invincible Daphne.'

'I don't feel invincible at the moment,' Daphne admitted. 'In fact, I'd quite like to lie down.'

'This way,' Ada said, and she led her patient to a freshly made-up bed, then drew the curtains around her.

'I'll leave you to it,' Gloria whispered through the curtains.

Ada popped her head around the curtains to whisper back, 'It's Sister Ann's day off, so I'm in charge of the ship. You have experience of childbirth – you know what it's all about. It would be really useful if you could stay with Daphne, hold her hand and chat to her while I get a few things sorted out, then I'll take over.'

Gloria's big, dark eyes widened. 'You won't leave me for long?' she asked. 'The hand-holding and chatting I can manage, but not the rest.'

Ada gave her a reassuring pat on the shoulder. 'Don't you worry, I won't. I just need to get rid of this dirty laundry and check up on the girls in the nursery, then I'll be back. Okay?'

Feeling calmer, Gloria nodded. 'Okay, I'll stay.'

'If you can get her into a clean nightie and back into bed, that would help,' Ada said, as she turned to go. 'I'll have somebody fetch you both a cup of tea soon. See you shortly.'

'So this is what it's like,' Daphne joked. 'I would have brought *War and Peace* to while away the hours if I knew I was going to be flat on my back all day.'

'Don't kid yourself,' Gloria replied with a knowing smile. 'Believe me, you won't have time for reading.'

She was right too; going by the clock on the wall, Gloria guessed Daphne's contractions were coming every four minutes already. 'Eleven o'clock now,' she thought to herself. 'If she's lucky, Daphne might well have had her baby by supper-time.'

She was astonished, and so was Daphne, when Matron suddenly dropped by to check on the patient's progress. Seeing Gloria at the bedside, Matron snapped, 'What are you doing here? Where's the ward sister?'

Bristling with indignation at the woman's appalling rudeness, Gloria coldly answered her question. 'She's just clearing away the dirty laundry; she'll be back soon.'

Knowing that Daphne was more than likely to give Matron (whom she loathed) a mouthful, Gloria quickly added, 'Daphne's doing a great job.'

Though Matron smiled at Daphne, she didn't get a smile back from the glowering girl.

'Right-i-o,' she said breezily, as she went on her way. 'Well done.'

Daphne scowled at her departing figure. 'Stupid bitch!' she seethed; then, forgetting Matron, she grabbed Gloria's arm. 'I need to lean against something,' she gasped, struggling to her feet. 'I need to be upright.'

'You don't have to stay lying down; you can walk, squat, bend, do what makes you comfortable.' Supporting Daphne's bulky body, Gloria did her best to help her friend. 'Lean across the bed, see if that helps.'

It did help. Daphne grunted her way through the quickening contractions, taking sips of water in between while steadying her breathing in readiness for the next onslaught. Genuinely impressed, Gloria praised her friend. 'You're doing really well – sure you haven't done this before?' she teased.

'No, but I've seen plenty of mares give birth: they're usually calm, taking things as they come,' Daphne responded. 'Nature's way.'

When Ada returned, Gloria left her to examine Daphne while she brewed more tea in the kitchen just off the ward. Gloria's thoughts drifted back to the wonderful day when her son was born in Battersea General Hospital, or the 'Old Anti', as it was commonly known in the parish, nearly six years ago. Robin had become such a powerful force in her life she couldn't imagine life without him. Smoothing her hand over her tummy, Gloria wondered what it would be like to have a second child, another boy or a little girl. Before he'd left, Stan had expressed a yearning for a daughter, but she didn't really mind at all. What she most wanted in all the world was her family to be reunited and a happy little unit again, but that wasn't going to happen any time soon, she thought, as she poured hot water on to the tea leaves in the pot. When Robin had been born, Stan had rushed on to the ward as soon as visiting time allowed, but when would he see his second child? How old would he or she be before they were held in their father's arms?

'Oh, Stan,' she murmured, tears threatening to engulf her. Picking up the tray, she told herself firmly: 'Concentrate on Daphne for the moment; she'll need your help.'

When she returned to her friend's bedside, Gloria was amazed to find Daphne nearing the last stages of labour. Quickly abandoning the tea, she helped Ada to move Daphne into the delivery room. Impressed by her strength and determination, Ada praised her warmly. 'You're doing so well – not long now before we see that baby of yours.'

Even Daphne, as tough as old boots, was feeling the strain. 'God! This is so much tougher than I ever imagined.'

'It'll soon be over, darling,' Ada assured her when they reached the delivery room and Daphne was settled on the bed.

Daphne suddenly reared up. 'Oh-o!' she cried. 'I want to push – I need to push!'

Ada gave her a reassuring pat on the back. 'Then go ahead and push,' she advised. 'Push as hard as you can.'

Gloria, who'd stayed by her friend's side, gripped her hand tightly. 'Push until you feel like your eyes will pop!'

With Sister Ada on one side of her and Gloria on the other, Daphne pushed hard.

'Excellent!' Ada exclaimed. 'You're a model patient. Nearly there – one more push should do it.'

Gloria was quite right in her calculation; by supper-time Daphne had produced a big, bouncing baby boy with a bellowing voice that easily equalled his mother's.

'Fine set of lungs,' Ada said, as she held the screaming baby up for Daphne to see. 'Heavy too, nearly ten pounds,' she added.

'Jesus!' Daphne laughed. 'That's two large bags of spuds!'

'You're lucky you didn't tear,' Ada said, gently cleaning down her patient with warm, soapy water.

Gloria, who'd stayed throughout the entire delivery, smiled at Daphne. Completely exhausted by her ordeal, the girl was now lying back against her bed pillows.

'Clever girl, you were brilliant,' she said.

'Thank you,' Daphne said feebly.

Ada looked up from her work. 'Would you be an angel, Gloria, and fetch us all a strong cup of tea?' she asked.

'Of course,' Gloria replied as she got to her feet.

'Slip a double brandy in mine,' Daphne said in all seriousness. 'I feel like the world has just dropped out of my bottom!'

After settling Daphne, Ada turned her attention to Daphne's son, whose vitals she expertly checked. 'You're a strong little fella,' she murmured examining his squirming body. 'A big strong lad.'

'Just like his bally father, built like a gable end,' Daphne, already back on form, joked from her bed.

Their intimate conversation stopped abruptly as Matron breezed into the delivery room.

'What have we got here?' she asked.

Irritated by her untimely intrusion, Ada's reply was clipped. 'A boy,' she replied. 'Now, if you'll excuse me, Matron, I need to attend to my patient.'

Matron peered over Ada's shoulder. 'Hah! He looks like a fine, healthy boy too!' she exclaimed; then, after a few more checks, which Ada was more than capable of doing herself, she turned and left the room, leaving Daphne scowling.

'I wish she'd bugger off!'

Unknown either to Daphne or to Ada, Matron virtually ran back to her office where, after shutting the door, she immediately phoned Sir Percival at Crow Thorn Grange.

'He's a strong fellow,' she announced with as much pride and emotion as if she herself had just given birth.

'A boy!' Sir Percival exclaimed in delight. 'How long till we get him?' he asked eagerly.

'Post-natal patients can stay up until six weeks,' Matron started to explain but was interrupted by Percival's reaction.

'Christ! That long?'

'I've told you all this before,' Matron said snippily.

'Is there any way you can hasten her departure?' Percival rudely inquired.

'I won't have to do that,' Matron said with a smile. 'Daphne will leave here just as soon as she can walk. To quote the dreadful woman – she's dying to get back in the saddle!'

On the other end of the phone Percival gave a long, slow smile. 'Excellent,' he murmured. 'Excellent.'

'By the way,' Matron added before she put down the phone, 'she's called him Bertie!'

With Sister Ann absent, Ada's feet hardly seemed to touch the ground. While keeping an eye on sleeping Daphne and her baby, now in the nursery, she also had to check up on the other new mothers and oversee the feeding rotas and sterilize the instruments she'd used in the delivery room. When Gloria turned up on the ward, Ada assumed she'd popped by to say goodnight to Daphne, so she was stunned by her announcement.

'Nancy's started –'

'What? Nancy too?' Ada stopped in her tracks and, looking at Gloria, she gasped, 'Can you believe it? Two births on Sister Ann's day off!'

Gloria nodded sympathetically. 'Is she not back?'

'No, she's visiting family; she might not be back till the morning,' Ada sighed. 'Never mind, needs must, babies choose their own time to be born and there's nothing you can do about it. Is she coping so far?'

Gloria shook her head grimly. 'Panicking something awful.'

'I see. Let's get her down here,' Ada said quickly. 'Gloria,

I hate to ask, but you were so good with Daphne – I don't suppose you'd help me out again, would you?'

'I'd love to,' Gloria said truthfully, 'but I need to check on Robin. I haven't seen him all day and I suspect he's driving Sister Mary Paul round the bend by now. Maybe I can come back when I've got him to bed?'

Shirley, who'd been quietly mopping the ward floor, startled them both when she chirped up: 'Don't worry, Gloria, you see to Robin; I'll stay on and help Sister.'

Ada did a double-take. Shirley helped out everywhere in the Home, but she'd always sensed that Shirley actively avoided the delivery room. Though Shirley's offer of help was most welcome, Ada was nevertheless a little anxious about anything that might set Shirley back when she'd been doing so well.

'Are you quite sure, Shirley?' she asked carefully.

'Quite sure,' the girl replied confidently. 'I used to be squeamish about going anywhere near babies being born, but I'm long past that. Life goes on,' she added sweetly. 'Just let me get rid of the mop and bucket and I'll be with you, Sister.'

Ada gave her a quick, grateful smile. 'You'll have to swab up and wash your hands thoroughly,' she instructed.

'I know: I've seen you and Sister Ann do it a hundred times,' Shirley replied with a knowing smile.

Shirley turned out to be a good nurse; it was as if everything she'd witnessed on the wards over the last few months had been absorbed into her memory bank and she automatically knew what to do. If Ada hadn't been so busy attending to Nancy, she would have been astonished by the young girl's skilful insight. After a long, hard labour,

Nancy finally gave birth and her son was delivered by Ada and Shirley as dawn broke over the Irish Sea.

No two boys born within twenty-four hours of each other could have looked more different: Daphne's big, bouncing Bertie, with his flailing arms and kicking legs, and Nancy's wailing boy, Tom, who, at six pounds and twelve ounces, was much slighter.

'Oh, God,' Nancy groaned when she first laid eyes on her son. 'He looks like his dad.'

'Babies quickly change,' Ada assured Nancy, who displayed little interest in the new-born. 'Do you want to hold him for a minute?'

Ada was saddened by Nancy's highly emotional reaction. 'NO! I don't want to hold him,' she cried. 'I just want my mam!'

Ada quickly handed the baby over to Shirley, who swaddled him in a warm shawl before taking him off to the nursery.

'I've missed Mam so much all the time I've been here, but now I miss her more than ever,' Nancy wailed. 'She's the only person who understands me.'

Feeling sorry for the poor girl, Ada kindly asked, 'Does she have a telephone? I could phone her with the news?'

Nancy shook her head.

'Not to worry; I'll drop her a line as soon as I'm off-duty,' Ada promised. 'I'm sure she'll be longing to see you. Will that make you feel better?'

Nancy nodded. 'Thank you, Sister, mi mam will want to know what's going on.'

'Now, sweetheart,' Ada continued, 'I really do have to tidy up a bit.'

'Stay right where you are, lovie,' Shirley added. 'While Sister's seeing to you, I'll go and make us all a fresh brew.'

Nancy smiled weakly. 'Believe me, Shirley, the way I'm feeling, I'm not going anywhere!'

Sister Ann couldn't believe her eyes when she saw the two new babies in the nursery on her return.

'Glory be to God!' she exclaimed, looking from one to the other. 'How did that happen?'

'God arranged for me to do all the work while you swanned off to see your family!' Ada teased. 'I was worried about how I'd cope without you, but Gloria was such a help with Daphne, and then, believe it or not, Shirley assisted with Nancy. She was marvellous!'

'Shirley!' the nun cried. 'Well, well,' she mused. 'God really does move in mysterious ways.'

After checking the babies, she came back to join Ada. 'How are the new mothers coping?'

'Daphne's fighting fit and ready to walk out of the Home if we'd let her, while Nancy's wailing for her mam,' Ada replied with a yawn.

'Go on – off with you,' Sister Ann said firmly. 'I can manage on my own while you get some rest.'

'Really?' Ada asked yearningly.

'Go!' Sister Ann cried with mock severity.

Ada nodded obediently and left the ward, but before she went to her room she managed to scribble a note to Nancy's mum in Bolton and even popped out to post it in the hope that it might arrive at its destination within the next day or two.

*

Over the next few days nobody could fail to notice how very different the new mothers were with their babies: Daphne handled Bertie like a chubby puppy, feeding him and winding him and changing his nappy with some amusement as she joked about his genitalia – 'He's certainly a big boy, just like his father!' she chuckled – while Nancy was all thumbs when it came to anything to do with her son, who seemed to sense he wasn't wanted and wailed piteously most of the time.

'He might be small but he's pretty vocal,' Isla commented, when she popped in with Gloria and Emily to see their friends on the post-natal ward.

Nancy blushed in embarrassment. 'He keeps waking up the other babies.'

'He'll be fine once he gets into a good feeding regime,' Gloria assured her nervous friend, who still couldn't walk without wincing, whereas Daphne was up and about, striding around with her characteristic vigour, as if nothing had happened.

Nancy didn't look convinced. 'I don't feel anything for him,' she whispered miserably. 'I just wish the adoption was over and done with and he'd been taken away from Mary Vale.'

Ada tried not to worry about the girl she'd come to care for over the course of her long stay at Mary Vale. She told herself it was a good thing for her not to bond with her son if he were adopted, but she couldn't help wishing Nancy looked happier.

So she was relieved a few days later when she spotted a slight woman walk on to the ward who turned out to be the spitting image of Nancy. Thrilled that her efforts had been rewarded, she approached the woman.

'Hello,' she said warmly. 'I think I can guess whose mother you are.'

'I've come to visit my Nancy,' the woman announced shyly.

'Of course, she'll be thrilled to see you,' Ada assured Mrs Wheelan. 'Nancy's just over there,' she said, pointing towards a bed by the window.

When Nancy caught sight of her mother walking nervously towards her, she all but fell out of bed. 'MAM!' she cried, as she clung on to her tightly.

'Nance, darlin', how are you, lovie?'

'Oh, so much better for seeing you, Mam,' Nancy sobbed, and tears poured down her cheeks. 'I can't believe you're here,' she whispered, and gripped her mother's hand.

'The ward sister kindly sent me a letter telling me you'd had the baby,' Mrs Wheelan explained. 'When your dad left for work this morning, I hopped on a train and here I am,' she said, looking very pleased with herself.

Nancy's face fell. 'Was Dad angry?'

'Aye, but when is he not?' her mother replied. 'Anyway, let's not spoil our time together talking about him; I've come to hear about you, my sweetheart.'

Sitting as close to her mother as she could get, and still holding her by the hand, Nancy told her about the birth. 'It bloody hurt, Mam!'

'You do surprise me,' her mother said knowingly. 'Where is the little lad?'

'Over there,' Nancy replied, and nodded in the direction

of the little cots lined up at the end of the ward. 'He looks like his dad,' she said in disgust.

'Well, you can't blame the kid for that,' her mother protested.

After she'd inspected her grandson with only a little more enthusiasm than her daughter, Mrs Wheelan returned to Nancy's bedside. 'Well, the good news is, the lad that got you in the family way has signed up and buggered off to France, they say,' her mother said with genuine relish. 'So you won't have to see him for a while.'

Nancy's face grew pink with relief. 'Oh, well, that's something.'

'Eh, and I've got summat for you, lass,' Mrs Wheelan said, as she rummaged in her old shopping bag and produced a package, which Nancy eagerly opened.

'Oven bottoms!' she exclaimed in delight.

'Spread thick with best butter and a bit of Lancashire cheese, the creamy sort that you like,' her mother added with a grin.

In between mouthfuls of the fresh oven bottoms, Nancy told her mother in whispers what her thoughts for the future were.

'I'll never go with another man,' she declared passionately. 'I hated it and I hated the outcome,' she confessed. 'I'll get a job as soon as I get back home and I'll save every penny I earn, I promise, Mam.'

'There's plenty of work going for lasses now that all the men are off to war,' her mother informed her cheerfully. 'They say that owd mill, the Phoenix out on't moors, is being set up as a munitions factory.' Mrs Wheelen leant in closer to add, 'Folks says it's as big as a village, with living accommodation for hundreds of workers; indoor lavvies and posh bath tubs with running hot and cold water. They say there's nurseries for the kiddies and a bar, even a picture house!'

Nancy's eyes grew wide with amazement. 'One of my friends here, Isla, she's right clever, reads all't time, she went to university,' she said with a swagger, as if Isla's knowledge had rubbed off on her. 'She's been saying that they'll be calling up lasses to do fellas' work, Mam,' she said with an excited gleam in her eyes. 'I'd love to work for my country,' she announced.

'Oooh, lovie, in't it dangerous working alongside bombs?' Mrs Wheelan fretted.

'It can't be as dangerous as firing the bombs on the Front Line,' Nancy declared with genuine passion. 'If Chamberlain wants me, he can have me! I'll sign up just as soon as I'm discharged.'

'Ooh, Nance, don't tell your dad your plans; he won't like it,' Mrs Wheelan warned.

'I'll hide as much of mi earnings as I can from Dad.' She lowered her voice to a whisper. 'But he won't stop me working. I plan to save up so that one day I can buy a nice little terrace up Tonge Moor Road, just me and you, Mam!' she said breathlessly.

'Oh, lovie, I'd like that very much,' her mum said with tears in her eyes.

Nancy cried like a baby when her mum took the train back to Bolton, but the visit had done her good; it focused her attention on returning home and on her ambitions to become a Bomb Girl on Pendle Moor!

*

Leaving their babies in the nursery, Daphne and Nancy were discharged from the ward and in less than a week they were back to doing light chores around the Home. When they were strong enough, Ada liked to see her patients on their feet, though she insisted they got plenty of rest, which aided their recovery. After the clattering noisiness of the ward, Nancy was delighted to be back in the big, comfortable bedroom she shared with her best friends.

Still rather sore, she carefully settled herself on her narrow single bed, sighing with relief. 'Eeeh, it's good to be back,' she said to Emily and Isla. 'Away from all them bloody screaming babies.'

Though it was nice to be among her friends again, Nancy realized that the time left to her with Gloria, Daphne, Emily and Isla was fast running out. Sister Ada had promised her that when she was fully recovered and her stitches had healed she would be allowed to leave Mary Vale. Like Nancy, Daphne was also in a lather to go home.

'Not that I don't like this place,' she declared as she lay across Nancy's bed, smoking a cigarette. 'But my heart is aching for Hermione,' she told her friends.

'Who's Hermione when she's at home?' Emily laughed.

'My mare, of course!' Daphne exclaimed.

'I don't understand why you are both in such a rush to leave. You could stay longer and enjoy being taken care of,' Emily reminded the two girls.

Nancy vigorously shook her head. 'Thanks – but no thanks,' she answered briskly. 'I've been here quite long enough – I'm ready to go home. Anyway, there's a war on and I want to build bombs to blast Hitler to kingdom come!' she announced with patriotic zeal.

'Good for you, girl!' Daphne boomed. 'Make a bomb big enough to take out Hitler and we'll all be dancing in the streets!'

Nancy laughed along with her friends, who, she knew, she would sorely miss – but it was the real world that called her now, and, in truth, she just couldn't wait to begin her life over again.

21. Farewells

To Percival's disgust, Daphne stayed on at Mary Vale a little longer than she had planned. Her father was adamant that she wouldn't be allowed home until he'd discussed 'the state of play', as he called it, with Sir Percival, who was more than keen to sign the girl off for reasons not known to Lord Wallace.

'She's as fit as a fiddle; she can leave any time,' Matron informed Percival. 'In fact, if the wretched girl isn't discharged soon, she's more than likely to jump out of the window and run away.'

'Oh, dear, we can't have that,' Percival said with mock sincerity. 'I'll notify Lord Wallace right away.'

Jubilant as she was to return to her horse-and-hound life, there was an unexpected sadness in Daphne when she visited the nursery to say goodbye to her son.

'He's a fine chap,' Ada said, when she spotted Daphne at the changing table, where Bertie, kicking his chubby bare legs and chortling happily, was blissfully unaware that his world was about to change forever. Biting her lip, Daphne turned to Ada. 'Will you keep an eye on him for me, until he goes?' she asked.

'Of course I will,' Ada promised, touched by the request. 'We all will. That's our job here: to look after all of Mary Vale's babies until they leave us.'

Daphne picked up her son, gave him one last cuddle,

kissing him tenderly, before returning him to his cot, that more familiar look of resolve back on her face.

'Mummy's waiting for me in the car,' she said with a grimace. 'It'll be a hell of a journey home, with her rabbiting on about the ghastly deb balls she's lined up for me.'

Her friends could hardly conceal their smiles.

'Oh, heck, Daphne, for the life of me I can't see you in a tiara and a long white frock,' giggled Nancy.

'Mother's under the illusion that, just because I've had a baby, I've had a brain transplant too! It drives her mad that I've always resisted society balls and parties; a good ride to the hounds and a bit of slap and tickle in the tack room is more my thing,' she guffawed.

'We'll miss you so much,' Gloria said, hugging her friend goodbye.

'Who will make us laugh when you're gone?' Isla asked sadly.

'I would say I'll come and visit you, but one thing's for sure: I'm never coming back to this place as long as I live and breathe,' Daphne boomed as she strode towards the door. 'You've all got my address. I expect you to write after you've had your own babies, and give me an update, and you, Nancy,' she added bossily, 'keep in touch too, once you're back home.' And, with a final goodbye to Bertie, she swept out of the room.

In the hallway Daphne completely ignored Matron, who'd come to see her off, but she thanked Ada and Sister Ann profusely. Not one for sentiment, she bade her last farewells, then picked up her suitcase and set off down the garden path to join her mother, who was waiting for her in a gleaming chauffeur-driven Daimler. To her surprise, Shirley came hurrying down the path after her.

'Daphne, I just wanted to say goodbye too,' the girl called out. 'I've never met anybody who made me laugh so much,' she added with a shy smile.

Touched by Shirley's sincerity, Daphne gave her a thundering smack on the back. 'Keep up the good work,' she barked, as she clambered into the Daimler, which drove off at top speed, Daphne waving her hankie out of the open window.

'What a character,' said Sister Ann to Ada.

'I've never known anybody who could turn the air as blue as Daphne with her foul language,' Ada giggled. 'Mary Vale will be a quieter place without her, that's for sure.'

Sister Ann smiled fondly. 'We've still got Bertie to remind us of his mum.'

Neither of them noticed that Matron was standing right behind them.

'You're quite right,' she said. 'We still have little Bertie . . . and life goes on.'

Nancy's leaving was a much quieter affair.

'I just want to go now,' she confided in Shirley, whom she'd grown to trust. 'I've been here longer than anybody but you!' she joked. 'You can't get enough of it, and I've had more than enough of it!'

Though Sister Ann pointed out to Nancy that her accommodation was still covered for a few more weeks, Nancy remained firm and politely declined the offer.

'It's not that I'm not grateful to you, Sister, and Ada too,' she said humbly. 'I'll never forget how good and kind you've been to me, but I really want to go home to mi mam now.'

'Pick up where you left off,' Sister Ann said optimistically.

'No, definitely not that,' Nancy corrected her. 'A new life is what I want, a completely new life: building bombs to beat Hitler!'

After helping Nancy pack her few things and making sure she had a packet of sandwiches to eat on the train home, Emily and Isla accompanied her to Kents Bank Station.

'Promise you'll write,' Isla begged.

'Tell us if you get called up to the munitions factory,' Emily added.

'I will,' Nancy promised. 'I hope your births go well, and you both have bonny, healthy babies,' she said, a lump in her throat as she boarded the train. 'I'll never forget you,' she gulped through her tears as the train moved off. 'Take care!'

Emily and Isla waved and managed to keep up the smiles until the train disappeared round the bend in the track. But, as silence fell, a sense of anticlimax mixed with some sadness descended on the two women. They hoped Nancy would be okay – and that they would see her again. Standing forlornly on the empty platform, they looked out over the darkening marsh, which was loud with the sound of the incoming tide and the call of oyster catchers and dunlins dipping and diving over the waves.

'We're next, kiddo,' Emily said, as she looped her arm through Isla's.

'That's just what I was thinking,' Isla agreed. 'Me, you, Gloria and all the other girls in the Home too, an endless cycle of mothers and babies and inevitable farewells.'

Squinting her pale blue eyes, Isla gazed at the vast marsh as it rapidly filled up with seawater. 'Living here in this remote part of England, quietly waiting for our babies to be born – it's hard to imagine there's a war on out there.'

At the mention of war Emily's eyes welled with tears. 'I think about it all the time . . . And wonder where my George is.'

Seeing she'd put her foot in it, Isla was quick to apologize. 'I'm so sorry, Em, that was thoughtless of me.'

'The truth is, Isla, I'm permanently upset,' Emily confessed. 'I just try not to show it.' She gave a weary sigh. 'We all have our troubles at Mary Vale.'

Isla leant over to give Emily a kiss on the cheek. 'You're not wrong. Come on,' she said more cheerily. 'I've still got some cake left that Jeannie sent over last week. Let's get back and polish it off with a nice pot of tea.'

Everybody missed Daphne's booming voice and Nancy's earnest ways, but life went on at Mary Vale, just as it always did. Gloria finally got around to setting up her little school in the dining room, which at the moment was exclusively for Robin, who, if left to his own devices, would have stayed all day long with Sister Mary Paul and the other nuns in the big kitchen that always smelt of something baking.

'This isn't a real, proper school,' Robin said mutinously, when he and his mother sat at the dining table on the first day with his schoolbooks spread out before him.

'It's Mary Vale's School,' Gloria coaxed. 'And this is where we'll carry on with your reading, writing and arithmetic while we stay here.'

'Want to play in the garden,' he added sulkily.

Knowing she had to lay the law down right from the start, Gloria drew Robin on to her knee. 'You know Daddy's gone off to war, don't you?'

Robin's bottom lip trembled but he didn't say anything.

'He would want you to carry on being his big, clever boy,' Gloria continued gently.

Robin stopped looking cross and smiled his heart-melting, cherubic smile. 'All right, Mama, I'll be a big, clever boy for Dada – and for Merry Paul too!'

Gloria burst out laughing; she knew exactly where she came in the pecking order of her son's affections, and it delighted her to hear Robin's improvised name for his favourite nun. Merry Paul was the perfect name for Sister Mary Paul, who brought happiness out of her kitchen as well as food.

School was only half a day, with playtime at 10.30. After a glass of milk and a biscuit provided by Sister Mary Paul, who clearly thought Robin would fade away if he didn't eat something (provided specifically by her) every two hours, Robin went tearing out into the garden, where he pretended to be a bomber plane for a full fifteen minutes.

'I thought he might be hungry – all that learning taxes the brain something awful,' Sister Mary Paul said, handing Gloria a cup of tea.

'He'll never be hungry with you around,' Gloria laughed.

'I brought this for you; it's just arrived,' the nun added.

Instantly recognizing the handwriting, Gloria eagerly clutched the airmail letter. 'Thank you! It's from my husband,' she cried gratefully.

'I'll leave you to enjoy it in peace,' Sister Mary Paul said, as she discreetly left Gloria in private.

Shaking with excitement, Gloria tore open the letter she'd been waiting for and a lump rose in her throat as she started to read it.

My dearest darling Gloria,

God! How I miss you. I know it's not long since we parted but it seems like a lifetime ago. Everybody's talking about the 'Phoney War', and I expect you're grumbling to yourself about leaving London when you did, very much at my insistence. But, believe me, my sweetheart, this is no phoney war; it might be quiet in London but there's so much action this side of the Channel. Almost as soon as we got here, we were moved closer to the Belgian border in anticipation of an invasion of the West. I can't say more than that – otherwise the censors will destroy my letter – so I'll talk about something else. I'm longing to hear how you and Robin are settling into the Home; are there any other evacuees there? I just hope you've got good company and that you and the baby are being taken care of. Is Robin being a good boy? As long as he's with his mum I'm sure he'll be happy. Write to me, my darling, I ache to hear how you are. I'll write as often as I can but I'm not sure how reliable or how regular the post is from this end.

I love you ALL so very, very much.

Your loving husband,
Stan xxxxx

Gloria kissed the letter, then held it to her heart; it was such a relief to know her beloved was alive and well. When Robin came back in from his 'bombing raid', she'd suggest they write a letter, and maybe Robin could draw a picture of his new home for his daddy? Gloria smiled to herself as her baby gave a hearty kick; he or she was alive and well too, thank God. Stan's little family was all safe and sound in Mary Vale, where life held many surprises and some unexpected pleasures too.

A few days later, after Sister Ann's fitness and exercise class, which was now held in the sitting room, as it was too cold to use the garden any more, Ada approached Gloria, who was looking beautifully calm after the class.

'Sorry to interrupt,' she said with an apologetic smile.

Gloria struggled to her feet. 'Sister Ann's classes are the best part of the day,' she said gratefully. 'Apart from preparing me for the birth of my baby, I feel so completely relaxed afterwards.'

'I'm pleased to hear it,' Ada said, as she drew the young woman aside so she could speak to her in private. 'I have a request to ask of you,' she added, lowering her voice so the girls leaving the room couldn't hear what she was saying. 'I hear you've started up a little school in the dining room.'

'It's just to keep Robin on his toes,' Gloria told her. 'I'd love it if there were more than one person to teach; I'm used to big classes after teaching in Battersea.'

'With your permission, I would like to add another pupil to your class.' Ada paused, then said, 'It's Shirley.'

Gloria's big, dark eyes widened in surprise. 'Shirley?'

She'd never imagined she'd be teaching the quiet, unassuming girl, who seemed to be part of Mary Vale's furniture; always there with a mop or a duster, cleaning and tidying with a smile on her face, as if she actually enjoyed doing hard work.

'She's more than welcome, but, to be honest, she always seems to be so busy – she's here, there and everywhere!' Gloria laughed. 'Cleaning, helping out on the ward, working in the kitchen – I've even seen her gardening. Will she have time to come to school?'

'I'm sure she'll make the time,' Ada answered confidently.

Gloria gave Ada a direct look. 'I'm aware that Shirley's arrangements here at Mary Vale are rather unusual,' she said frankly.

Ada nodded. 'That's right: she was a resident here but stayed on after she'd had her baby adopted. She seems to like the place,' Ada smiled fondly. 'However, when the time comes for her to leave Mary Vale, we'd like to keep an eye on her: she's so young and inexperienced, we'd prefer it if she could stay close by. But having barely been to school could seriously hold her back,' she added. 'Being able to read and write would stand her in good stead in the workplace, don't you think?'

'Of course,' Gloria assured her.

'And, God willing,' Ada thought to herself, 'she might never have to return home again if we can find her work locally.'

'She's a sweet girl; I'd love to help,' Gloria said generously. 'If she can put up with Robin, she's most welcome to join us.'

'I think your little boy will make Shirley feel easier, less self-conscious, if you know what I mean?' Ada said with a knowing smile.

'He'll probably finish up teaching her,' Gloria joked. 'Once he gets going, I can barely get a word in edgeways. We start at nine and finish just before dinner-time;

depending on her chores, Shirley can stay for as long she wants.'

'Thank you, Gloria. We've been wondering how to help Shirley find work, and this might be just the thing,' Ada said gratefully. 'I'll go and ask her if she'd like to start tomorrow.'

Shirley appeared in the dining room the next morning, without her usual pinafore. She carried a notebook and a pencil and had a shy smile on her face that disappeared the minute Robin started chatting. Thrilled to have company, he took Shirley's hand and sat her down in the chair next to his. 'My mum's the teacher,' he said. 'So we can do what we want!'

'Robin!' Gloria chided her adorable, irrepressible son. 'Shirley's here to learn to read and write, so be serious.'

'I'll learn her!' Robin declared, and he started to reel off the alphabet. 'A for apple, b for ball, c for cat . . .'

Shirley giggled, then chanted in the same manner as the little boy.

'Let's do it together,' said Gloria, as she took out the reading flash cards. 'And Robin, not so fast, please.'

School took on a whole new meaning with Shirley's arrival. Robin loved her company and Gloria enjoyed teaching the shy girl, who was an eager learner and, once she'd become accustomed to the alphabet, quickly linked the letters to make words, and in no time at all she was reading.

At the end of the week Gloria congratulated her new student on her rapid progress. 'You're doing really well.'

Shirley positively glowed with pleasure. 'I'm loving it,

Gloria,' she confessed. Smiling, she turned to bright-eyed Robin. 'And I'm loving being with Robin,' she said with genuine affection.

The little boy beamed proudly. 'I'm a good learner, Mummy. Shirley can spell CAT!'

22. Bertie

A few days after Daphne's departure a letter arrived for her friends.

Dear Gels,

Just wondered if any of you poor things has given birth since I left? Life back home is worse than I feared. I was hoping to gallop off and escape the dreaded parents, but, after struggling to mount Hermione, my favourite mare, I realized that the old whatsit down below needed a bit more recovery time.

All the girls burst out laughing.
'She's irrepressible,' giggled Isla.
'Never changes,' Gloria said fondly.

I can muck out and groom the horses – Lord knows, I need the exercise – but that's my lot for the moment; at least it gets me out of the draughty old wreck of the so-called stately home we were cursed to inherit. Hope you're keeping an eye on the boy – that's if he's still with you? He might well have left Mary Vale for pastures new. Good luck to him I say!'

After reading the letter, Gloria, who'd been so involved in Bertie's birth and had grown fond of him, popped into the nursery to see how he was so she could write back to

Gloria with the latest news. However, when she arrived there she was puzzled to find Bertie's cot empty.

Seeing Shirley wiping down the windowsills with what smelt like strong disinfectant, Gloria frowned.

'Morning, Shirley. Where's Bertie?'

'I'm not sure, Gloria,' Shirley replied. 'Maybe Ada's got him.'

Not having the time to search further, Gloria turned to go.

'Will you be joining us later for lessons?' she asked Shirley.

'Of course, Miss Teacher,' Shirley joked. 'Highlight of my day.'

Promising herself that she'd pop back and see Daphne's baby later on, Gloria set off for the dining room to find Robin.

In point of fact, Gloria was not the only one looking for Bertie. Ada was also puzzled when she turned up for duty on the ward and found him absent.

'Where is he?' she asked Sister Ann, who had been helping the girls on the feeding rota in the nursery.

'He wasn't in his cot when I arrived on duty either,' she remembered. 'Maybe Matron's taken it upon herself to move him,' she suggested drily.

'I'll see if I can track her down,' Ada volunteered.

She found Matron making herself a pot of tea in the little staff kitchen just off the ward.

'Excuse me,' Ada said with a polite smile. 'Do you happen to know where Bertie might be?'

Turning towards her ward nurse with a tight smile on her face, Matron answered casually, 'Oh, he's gone.'

Dumbfounded, Ada stared at her. 'Gone *where?*' she demanded.

'To his parents, his adoptive parents,' Matron replied. 'It was rather hurried,' she admitted, as she popped a tea cosy over the pot of tea she'd just brewed. 'They arrived late last night and were quite insistent about returning home right away. I telephoned Sir Percival, who was kind enough to drive over with the adoption papers that he'd organized and had signed by Daphne Wallace's father before the girl left.'

Ada couldn't believe she was hearing right. 'We are normally informed and given time to get the baby ready.'

'Yes, but in this case, as I've already said, the parents arrived sooner than expected and simply wouldn't take no for an answer. I could hardly inform you in the middle of the night,' Matron reasoned. 'I don't quite see what all the fuss is about, Sister.'

Before red-faced Ada could open her mouth to protest further, Matron picked up her tray and brushed past. 'Now, if you'll excuse me, I have things to attend to.'

For a few seconds after she'd gone, Ada could only stare incredulously after her.

'The damn cheek of the woman!' she fumed, as she stood in the corridor, where Sister Ann found her looking hot and bothered. 'You'll never believe what Matron's gone and done with Bertie,' she all but exploded.

After she'd told her friend of Bertie's hasty departure, the nun looked saddened. 'When Father Ben was in charge, we nearly always had an opportunity to meet the new family, or at least to say goodbye to the child.'

'Sadly, Sir Percival's not made of the same stuff as Father Ben,' Ada reminded her friend.

Sister Ann gave a heavy sigh. 'Now we'll never know who Bertie's going to grow up with.'

Completely baffled by the events, Ada shook her head. 'I simply don't understand the rush.'

At Crow Thorn Grange, Matron was grilling Olive, who'd been tracked down and drafted in to care for the 'special babies'. It didn't take much of a financial offering to make sure Olive kept her mouth shut.

'You do understand this arrangement here at the Grange is strictly confidential,' Matron reminded the girl sternly, but she showed no sign of being intimidated by her employer.

'Yeah, we've already been through this, Miss,' Olive snipped impertinently.

'Matron, to you!'

Olive rolled her eyes. 'It's not like I'm at the 'ome any more, thank Christ!'

Resisting the temptation to slap the cheeky little madam, Matron continued, 'If you want the second half of your payment, you will behave yourself and do *exactly* as I say, understood?' She paused before adding in a milder tone, 'The boy is being secretly kept here at the parents' request; they're a rather high-profile society couple who want their adoption to be kept out of the public eye.'

'Posh, eh?' Olive inquired.

'Yes, and powerful too,' Matron replied. 'So, are we clear about your routine?'

'Yeah, just like at the 'ome. Feeding, bathing, changing, burping,' Olive chanted off in a bored voice.

'Watch him like a hawk, and sleep in the bed alongside his cot so that you can keep an eye on him through the night,' Matron instructed. 'And on no account must you use any door other than the back door.'

In his cradle, Bertie began to cry.

'Right, I'll leave you to it, Olive – don't let me down.'

After leaving Olive to give Bertie his bottle, Matron slipped down the back stairs and left the hall by the back door. Some minutes later she re-entered the Grange via the front door, where she asked the butler if she could have a word with Sir Percival. Eager for news, Percival bustled Matron into his private study and quickly closed the door.

'The Bennetts are hoping to arrive tomorrow,' he said in a voice that was bristling with excitement. 'Once I told them the child was in my charge, they simply couldn't wait.'

Matron was visibly relieved. 'Good. I'll be easier in my mind when Bertie is miles away and we've banked the second cheque we are due.' At this, she very pointedly made eye contact with her partner in crime.

'That joint account is set up, all ready and waiting for the next instalment,' he assured her. 'With luck, the future Earl of Easterbrook will very soon be on his way to London to start a wonderful new life and we'll both be enjoying the fruits of our labour.'

Matron gave him a hard look. 'I would certainly hope so after all the effort I've put in, Archibald.'

Back at Mary Vale, all the girls shared Ada's sadness that Bertie had been whisked away without any of them having had a chance to say goodbye.

'I suppose that's what happens here,' Isla said thoughtfully. 'A quick handover and a new life begins elsewhere.

No doubt that will happen to my child after I've left him or her here.'

Gloria and Emily exchanged an uncomfortable look; it was awkward to talk about adoption with Isla, when they both knew they were keeping their babies. Sensing their discomfort, Isla was quick to reassure them. 'Don't worry, I can't grumble,' she said realistically. 'It's what I chose to do and I know it's the right thing for my baby, and for me.'

'Well, I hope at least it won't happen quite so abruptly as it did with Bertie,' Emily said indignantly.

Isla was pragmatic. 'I guess once the adoption papers are signed, wheels quickly start to roll and there must always be pressure on the Home to free up beds for new arrivals.'

'Should we write back to Daphne to let her know Bertie's been adopted?' queried Gloria.

'Yes,' Emily said firmly. 'She'd want to know.'

'We can't pretend we've met the parents, but we'll just say we're praying that Bertie's in a good place, with loving parents who'll look after him for the rest of his life,' Gloria suggested.

Emily and Isla nodded in agreement with her. 'And it's true,' Isla murmured. 'Our prayers are with Bertie, wherever he is.'

Sadly, all their prayers and hopeful wishes for Bertie's future were not enough for the little boy. Only just over twenty-four hours after Bertie left the warmth and safety of the Mary Vale post-natal ward, Olive started awake in the dawn light. Wondering why Bertie hadn't woken her up for his 2 a.m. feed, she swung her bare feet out of bed and leant over to see him apparently sleeping peacefully in his cradle. As her short-sighted eyes adjusted to the grey light in the room, she came to the slow but alarming realization that this baby was not only too perfectly still, but also alabaster white. Hoping against all hope that her instincts were wrong, she dashed to the light switch by the door, then gingerly leant over to stroke the baby's cheek – at which point her worst fears were confirmed. Bertie was stone cold. Though hard-hearted and calculating, Olive simply couldn't bear to look at the baby's sweet innocent face; trembling, and her mind racing, she hastily pulled on her clothes and a coat, left the Grange and ran down the fell road to Mary Vale to tell Matron about the tragic event. Knowing full well that leaving the house and the baby were specifically going against Matron's instructions, Olive had no choice. Anyway, what did it matter now?

23. Dark Plots

In the bleak early-morning light, Olive, gasping for breath after her long run from the Grange, burst into the Home through the back door and found Shirley already busy baking bread in the kitchen. Startled by the sight of Olive, who had left Mary Vale some months ago and who had been disliked by many of the girls, including Shirley, she could only gasp, 'What are you doing here?'

'I have to see Matron immediately,' Olive answered, her eyes wild. 'It's urgent.'

Shirley gave the unpleasant-looking girl with sly eyes and a vicious tongue a long, suspicious look. She had to admit, though, that Olive did look genuinely distressed.

'Get on with it,' Olive snapped rudely. 'Tell her I'll wait for her in the garden.'

Matron, who'd been in her office most of the night and had barely slept due to her nervous agitation, joined Olive, who wasted no time in breaking the awful news. Visibly shaken, Matron smothered a cry of anguish with her hand. 'NO!' she rasped. 'That's impossible!'

'It's the truth,' Olive assured her.

'What did you do to the poor child?' Matron demanded.

'Nothing! I done like what you told me to do.'

'You couldn't have,' Matron protested. 'You obviously did *something*, you stupid girl!'

Furious with Matron, Olive hit back with a snarl. 'He was fine when I settled him down for the night! He'd fed well and I'd winded him, I was there right by his bloody side throughout the whole soddin' night, but when I woke up he was gone.'

Almost out of her mind, Matron paced the garden, running her hands through her hair.

'I employed you to watch the child's every move. God! Oh, God!' Turning venomously on Olive, she lashed out further. 'I'll drag you through every court in England if you're responsible for Bertie's death.'

Olive stuck out her chin. 'Try it, and I'll tell any court who asks how you sneaked the kid out of Mary Vale like a thief in the night.'

By this time, Matron was literally ranting in fury. 'He was a strong, robust child – he showed no indication of any abnormality or infection, his vitals were good,' she gabbled to herself. 'His breathing . . . his colour . . . they were both good . . . how could he possibly die?'

Leaving a scowling Olive in the garden, Matron ran back to her room, where she immediately phoned Percival, whom she woke from his sleep, with Olive's grim news.

'Jesus Christ!' he cried explosively. 'What're we going to do? The Bennetts are planning to arrive here later today to pick him up!'

Tense and white-faced, Matron was thinking fast. 'Then put them off immediately,' she commanded.

Percival was so panicked he had trouble understanding her. 'Put them off?'

'YES!' she cried. 'We've nothing to show them. Tell

them the baby's not well enough to travel – tell them anything to stall them,' she added wildly.

Eventually seeing the logic in her suggestion, Percival said, 'Yes, of course, I'll phone them right away . . . but we'll have to come up with another plan.'

Matron quickly corrected him. 'Don't you mean another *baby*?'

Percival didn't mince his words. 'Precisely. Another *baby* – if we're to get the Bennetts' money.'

Matron, who'd already thought of Tom as a possible replacement, added cautiously, 'Actually, there is another baby boy in the Home.'

Percival gasped in relief. 'Can we pass him off as Bertie without arousing suspicion?'

'We can but try,' she said smoothly.

'Then get the bastard up here as soon as you can!' desperate Percival begged.

'I'll do my best, Sir Percival, but we must act carefully,' she told him. 'For the time being, I'm sending Olive back to the Grange, where she'll await further instructions. I can't keep her here, where residents might start asking her questions.' She paused before adding, 'Could you make sure the room Bertie occupied is back to normal before her arrival, please?'

Before Percival could start to bluster and protest, Matron bade him a brisk good morning and quickly put down the phone. Having dispatched Olive, Matron locked her office door so she could be certain of no tiresome interruptions. Thinking fast, she grabbed Nancy's and Daphne's files, which would soon join Bertie's file, safely locked away in her own private suite. But having the files safely in her hands wouldn't get Tom up to the Grange, which was Matron's burning priority.

'Stay calm,' she told herself. 'Think!'

The phone shrilling out on her desk made her jump sky-high. Grabbing it, she barked, 'Yes. Who is it?'

'Dr Jones here,' came back the reply.

Matron's heart dropped; at this moment in time she needed to talk to the drunken doctor like she needed a hole in the head. Just the sound of his slurred voice put her teeth on edge.

'I wondered what time would be convenient for me to conduct my rounds?' he asked.

Normally, Matron would have referred him to Sister Ada and have done with it, but it suddenly occurred to her that having a doctor as an ally (albeit a drunken one) could work to her advantage.

'Dr Jones,' she began in a tone of voice he'd never heard her use with him before, 'would it be possible for you to come tomorrow morning?' Making it up on the air, she babbled, 'I'd like your advice on, er . . .'

WHAT? she thought frantically. Playing for time, she added vaguely, 'There's a child I'm a little concerned about . . .'

Jones innocently volunteered the very information she needed. 'Oh, dear, I hope it's not got an attack of the measles,' he remarked. 'There's a lot of it about at the moment. Have you checked for Koplik spots yet, Matron?' he inquired.

Matron's heart raced. 'I haven't, but I will right away, Dr Jones.'

'If you spot them at the back of the throat, then I need to see the child urgently.'

'We certainly wouldn't want that spreading through Mary Vale's nursery,' she added earnestly.

'Let's catch up in the morning, Matron,' he suggested.

'First thing,' she replied, as she put the phone down.

Who would have believed that idle, drunken Jones could have come up with a solution to her problem? Babies could go blind as a result of the infection; some even died. In homes like Mary Vale, where babies were at risk, it was essential that any contagious infant was immediately isolated in order to prevent the infection from spreading throughout the entire nursery. Getting to her feet, Matron paced the room as she made plans that would enable her to take exclusive charge of Tom. She would nurse him round the clock in a private room off the main ward, and, with him in her sole charge, she would be able to secrete him up to the Grange when the coast was clear. It would take planning and careful synchronization but it was do-able – if she kept her nerve.

Shirley wasted no time in telling Ada about the visit that morning from horrible Olive (who everybody had been glad to see the back of).

'She seemed all of a flutter,' Shirley remarked.

'How odd she should ask to see Matron,' Ada mused. 'As I recall, they couldn't stand the sight of each other.'

'I wouldn't say they were on friendly terms now: from what I saw of the two of them in the garden, there was a lot of shouting,' Shirley told her. 'Matron soon sent her packing.'

Ada couldn't help but laugh. 'Well, that's a relief: the

last time Olive was in the Home she pinched anything she could get her hands on!'

Joking apart, Ada thought to herself, 'Why has Olive visited the Home?' Throughout her entire stay at Mary Vale, Olive had never made a secret about how much she loathed the place and just about everybody in it, and that included Matron too. So why on earth had the two former adversaries met in the garden, and what exactly had they been arguing about?

Matron spent the rest of the day executing her plan, which she had to do with great subtlety in order not to arouse suspicion among the staff. While Ada was busy on the ward, Matron found the key to the room she planned to use. After unlocking it, she slipped inside to find a single bed and a baby's cot, which was all she needed.

Before tea-time she went to see Tom in the nursery, which surprised Ada, who was busy assisting the girls on the bottle-feeding rota.

'Matron?' Ada politely inquired when she entered the busy room.

Walking in between the line of little cots, Matron peered very closely at each baby in turn.

'I've heard some rather alarming news from Dr Jones: it appears an epidemic of measles is rife in the area.'

Ada's prettily arched eyebrows shot up. 'Really? I've not heard anything.'

'Dr Jones mentioned it only this morning,' Matron answered airily, as she stuck her head into Tom's cot in order to get a good view of the child, who was fretful and mewling. 'Is Tom all right?' she asked sharply.

'Yes, he's fine,' Ada replied scooping Tom into her

arms, then carried him to a comfortable chair, where she settled herself before commencing bottle-feeding the baby. 'Just hungry.'

'He looks flushed,' Matron commented.

Concentrating on the baby, who was having trouble connecting with the rubber teat, Ada answered quickly, 'He's a little overheated, nothing more than that.'

Having finished her inspection, Matron strode to the nursery door. 'I'll pop back later to see how Tom is; he doesn't look quite right to me,' she informed her ward sister.

Ada eyed Matron as she went, then turned her attention to Tom, who was finally sucking successfully from his bottle.

'There's a good boy, you're fine, aren't you?' she crooned. 'A very good little boy.'

Back in her office, Matron sat down and drummed her fingers on her desk. She was satisfied that she'd sown the seeds among the staff of a possible measles epidemic, and she'd certainly pop back and see Tom in the nursery before she went off-duty tonight. She would have to make sure that the baby boy was indeed hot when the doctor examined him in the morning: a hot-water bottle applied a few minutes before his examination should do the trick, she thought. As far as she could see, everything was in place to facilitate her plan, and she only hoped that Percival had kept his part of the bargain and managed to postpone the Bennetts' arrival.

The next morning Matron was on the ward bright and early. She said a polite good morning to Sister Ann, who'd completed her night shift and was hurrying off to the convent to get some rest. Sister Ada had just taken over from her, and was busy with a team of girls bathing babies in the sluice room. Checking that nobody was in the nursery, she opened the briefcase that she had tucked under her arm and quickly removed a small hot-water bottle. Slipping it under Tom's bedding, she watched him wriggle in discomfort as the heat reached him.

'Excellent,' she thought. 'He's going red in the face.'

Standing guard over Tom's crib, she waited until the baby started to cry, then she snatched the bottle from under his body and slipped it back into her briefcase, which she quickly hid in a cupboard.

'Poor little boy,' she said somewhat over-dramatically, as she reached down and picked up the child.

Seeing Shirley entering the ward with a mop and bucket, she strode past her with Tom in her arms. 'He's dreadfully overheated: tell Sister Ada I've taken his temperature and will be seeing to him,' she declared. Astonished Shirley could only stand and stare at the departing figure.

In the sluice room Ada was concentrating on drying a little girl who was laid across her lap with a towel underneath her squirming body. She caught sight of Matron hurrying past the sluice room with a baby in her arms.

'Where's she off to?' Ada wondered.

The fretful baby claimed her attention and Ada returned to the task of drying and dressing her.

When Dr Jones arrived, he found Matron in the room off the ward that she'd carefully prepared for Tom, who was now in a little canvas cot, red-faced and screaming.

'I brought him in here just to be on the safe side,' she said in a voice that brooked no argument.

As Jones searched for his stethoscope in his medical bag, he asked, 'Have you checked for Koplik spots?'

She nodded. 'They're very much in evidence at the back of his throat and he has a roaring temperature.'

Matron was confident that lazy Jones wouldn't trouble himself to double-check the accuracy of her statement, which is exactly what happened. In fact, anxious to avoid picking up the unpleasant infection himself, Jones quickly signed all the forms she proffered.

'Best to keep him away from the other babies if he's incubating measles,' he swiftly concluded.

Matron almost smirked. 'My thoughts entirely. I shall personally nurse him round the clock,' she added rather self-importantly. 'After all, it is ultimately my responsibility to ensure that this disease remains contained.'

Bundling his stethoscope back into his bag, Jones nodded his approval. 'Quite right, Matron. I bid you good day,' he said, as he all but bolted from the room.

'Please alert Sister Dale right away,' Matron called after panicked Jones as he hurried away.

Ada was astonished when the doctor made his sudden announcement.

'Tom seemed perfectly fine when I gave him his morning feed, and there was certainly no sign of his having a high temperature then,' she stressed.

'I have no choice but to isolate the child,' Dr Jones insisted. 'I've just examined him,' he lied. 'And there is no doubt at all about his condition. We don't want a full-on outbreak. Tom is under Matron's sole care in a private room just off the ward.'

'I'm happy to nurse Tom,' Ada volunteered.

Knowing better than to disobey Matron's strict instructions, Dr Jones stuck to the plan. 'Heavens, no need for that, Sister! You have more than enough to do as it is,' he gushed. 'Matron wants to take care of this matter personally. Now, if you'll excuse me, I need to make my report.'

A bewildered Ada could only stand on the ward and watch him go. Gathering her wits, she turned on her heel and dashed to the room Dr Jones had mentioned, only to discover that the door was firmly locked. Sighing, she retraced her steps; Matron really was serious about isolating Tom, even to the point of locking the door. It would have been nice to check up on the little boy, whom she'd grown very fond of, and, besides, something was niggling her: something just did not feel quite right. Still, given the seriousness of the illness and the potential danger Tom could be to the other new-borns, she supposed she had to go along with the plan to keep him in isolation, for the time being anyway.

Now that her plan was swinging into action, Matron made herself highly visible as she hurried busily back and forth looking after Tom, who, mercifully, slept soundly once he'd cooled off.

'This time,' she vowed to herself, 'there'll be no slip-ups.'

A knock at the door made her jump. 'Who is it?'

'Sister Dale,' came the reply.

Matron opened the door and cautiously poked her head around it.

'I just wondered if I could get anything for Tom?' Ada asked.

Not wanting Ada to see the baby peacefully sleeping, Matron slipped out of the room and quickly shut the door behind her.

'He's not at all well,' she lied. 'If his temperature goes any higher, I may have to call the doctor back.'

'Poor lamb,' Ada murmured.

'I just hope he makes it through the night . . .' Matron sighed. 'He's never been a particularly strong child, I fear. But we must keep him here, for the benefit of all the other babies in the nursery.'

'We're all saying prayers for the little chap,' Ada said earnestly. 'I'll be going off-duty soon, but I'll bring Sister Ann up to date before I leave.'

'Would you be so kind as to ask her not to disturb us during the night?' Matron added, as Ada turned to go.

'Certainly, Matron. Goodnight,' Ada replied.

The hours that followed seemed endless – though Matron was kept busy attending to the little boy, whom she fed and changed in order to make him comfortable for his move to the Grange. Obviously, the quietest and safest time to remove Tom was in the dead of night, between the midnight and the 4 a.m. feeds. With her heart pounding, she checked her wristwatch over and over again as she waited for silence to descend on the ward. Around 1 a.m., when all was deadly quiet, Matron wrapped her capacious nurse's cape around herself; then, after peeping through the curtains to make sure the lights on the ward were out, she lifted a slumbering Tom from his cot.

'Shhh,' she murmured, as she tucked the sleeping baby underneath her cape; then she opened the door and, assuming an air of authority, hurried along the dark corridor that led to the back door. Carrying Tom under one arm, she slid the bolt with her free hand and emerged through the tradesmen's entrance, where she'd had the foresight to leave her car unlocked and as close to the door as possible. Sighing with relief, she slid into the driver's seat; then, after carefully settling Tom in the passenger seat, with her cape wrapped around him, she started the ignition.

Little did Matron know that, for all her carefully laid plans, somebody was watching her every movement. In the dimly lit kitchen, Shirley, sleepily waiting for her batch of bread to rise, had been startled by a shadowy figure passing the kitchen door. Spotting it was Matron, with every hair on the back of her neck rising, Shirley followed. Once outside in the cold night air, she hunkered down behind a bush, from where she watched Matron quickly settle a small bundle on the passenger seat. Before Matron closed the car door, Shirley was quite sure she saw the bundle stir; wondering if she was imagining things, she watched intently as Matron got into the driver's seat and started up the engine. It was only then that she heard the shrill cry of a baby.

'That's Tom!' she gasped, laying a hand over her mouth to smother her cry.

Having only recently been in the nursery cleaning around the baby's cribs, Shirley instantly recognized

Tom's mewling cry, which was distinctly weaker than that of the other, more robust babies.

Watching the car drive slowly out of the grounds with no headlights to guide the way, alarm bells sounded in Shirley's head.

'Jesus! She's taken Tom!' she muttered and, without stopping to think, she grabbed the gardener's old rickety bike and set off, at a safe distance so as not to be seen, along the road after Matron.

Matron made her way to the back of the Grange, where Shirley, now hidden behind a belt of rhododendron bushes, saw her knock on the door, which was opened by Olive. Hardly able to believe her eyes, Shirley stood rooted to the spot. If scheming Olive was involved, she knew deep in her gut that something bad was going on at the Grange and Matron was at the heart of it. Staying hidden behind the rhododendron bushes that were dripping with a fine rain, she waited until Matron reappeared. Hurrying past her, Matron made her way to the front of the Grange. Dodging in and out of trees and bushes, Shirley followed Matron, who was admitted through the front door of the Grange by a footman. With the rain now teeming down, plastering her hair into lank, wet strands, Shirley, frozen to the bone, saw Matron reappear about half an hour later. Still in hiding, she watched her get into her car and drive away, again with the headlights off.

When the sound of the car engine had faded away, Shirley jumped on to the bike and cycled back to Mary Vale, where, shivering with cold, she dashed into the kitchen to warm herself by the old range where she'd left her bread to rise. Checking the clock on the kitchen wall, she put the bread into the oven to bake, then sat by the range to wait for it to be ready. It was there that Matron found Shirley, fast asleep, with her hair still streaky wet from her night out in the rain.

'What are you doing?' she barked, as she shook Shirley awake.

Fuddled and frightened, Shirley babbled, 'Waiting for the bread to cook.'

'Are you usually up in the middle of the night?'

'Only if I'm minding the bread,' Shirley replied.

Matron's eyes swept along Shirley's skinny little body. 'Why are you wet?' she asked suspiciously. 'Have you been out?'

Shirley's tongue felt like it was stuck to her palate, but eventually she managed to stutter, 'N . . . no.'

Matron made a grab for some dry dead leaves that clung to strands of Shirley's hair. Waving them in front of the girl's pale face, she asked the question again: 'Have you been outside?'

Shirley knew she had to explain herself somehow or worse would follow. 'Only to fetch in the milk,' she spluttered.

Contemptuously flicking the leaves at trembling Shirley, Matron brought her own face as close as she could to the girl's. 'If I find out you're lying, or, worse still, spying, you will live to rue the day, madam.'

After Matron had stalked off, Shirley, weak with relief, virtually sank to the ground, where, filled with deep foreboding, she fearfully hugged herself.

'I need to talk to Ada – I need to tell her where I've been right away.'

But, as she rose to leave the kitchen, her eyes caught sight of the clock on the wall. 'It's too early to wake her now; she needs her sleep.'

Slumping back down, she said to herself, 'I'll tell her first thing, as soon as she comes on duty.'

Matron hurried back to the room that Tom had previously occupied.

'Snivelling, lying, interfering little bitch,' she seethed under her breath. 'It's so damned obvious she's been out of doors – and, knowing her, she's been snooping too.'

There was now absolutely no doubt in her mind at all: she would get rid of the damned girl once and for all. And, Matron thought as she entered the room where she had 'nursed' Tom and quickly locked the door behind her, she had to do it fast, just in case Shirley had seen something she shouldn't have and started blabbing to her friends.

Knowing it would soon be dawn, Matron needed to prepare the room for others to see; right now, it looked too spick and span, as if she hadn't slept in it – which she hadn't – but she didn't want anybody else to know that. After rumpling the sheets and blankets on her bed, and on Tom's cot too, she set a stone-cold, half-empty feeding bottle on the bedside table alongside a thermometer and a stethoscope. When she was satisfied the room gave off the appearance of frantic nocturnal activity, she sat on the edge of the bed, where, after taking a notepad and pen from her handbag, she composed a letter to the Reverend Mother, insisting that Shirley be removed from Mary Vale immediately. Matron wrote that the girl's stay, extended for far too long, would set an unwanted precedent. The matter had been referred to Sir Percival, who'd expressed a wish that Shirley's stay at the Home should be curtailed with immediate effect.

Though Shirley had hardly slept, she was still on the ward first thing, cleaning, as usual, and hoping to see Ada just as soon as she started her shift. After her terrifying encounter in the kitchen with Matron, her jangled nerves were soothed by the steady, rhythmic swish-swish of the mop, which she regularly dipped into a bucket of heavily disinfected hot water. It was there that Matron (having just delivered her letter to the Reverend Mother at the convent) tracked her down.

'Miss Miles,' she boomed without any preamble.

At the sound of her icy voice Shirley's blood ran cold in her veins; beginning to shake in every limb, she gripped the mop handle to support her quaking body.

Matron came straight to the point. 'I've just informed the Reverend Mother that we've received an official complaint concerning your extended residency here. I'm afraid funds have run out and you will have to vacate the Home at once.'

With her head reeling in shock, Shirley tried to speak, but her tongue seemed to be stuck to the roof of her mouth.

'It's the precedent, you see,' Matron rolled on. 'What if every girl in Mary Vale took a shine to free board and lodgings, like you have?' she asked maliciously.

Eventually, outraged Shirley found her voice. 'That's just not true!' she cried. 'I would *never* cheat and lie. I love Mary Vale, and all my friends here.'

Matron gave an unconcerned shrug. 'Yes, well, that's as may be. I've informed Sir Percival and the Board, who, of course, are in complete agreement with me. I'm here to personally remove you from the premises before breakfast.'

Pole-axed with shock and fear, Shirley laid aside her mop before she dropped it. Her worst fears were now confirmed; the very thing she'd been dreading was about to become a reality. Unchecked tears streamed down her face.

'Please, Matron, please don't make me go, I beg you,' she implored.

Anxious that nobody should witness the scene, Matron quickly herded Shirley out of the ward.

'Come along – let's pack your things, and I'll see you on to the train,' she said in a steely voice, as she virtually frog-marched the staggering girl up the stairs to her bedroom.

As Matron flung Shirley's few belongings into a battered old suitcase, which she'd found tucked away under the neatly made bed, Shirley, now out of her mind with terror, immediately tried to snatch them back.

'NO! NO!' she screamed. 'Please, *please* don't send me back home.'

At which point Matron, sensing that she had a hysteric on her hands, slapped Shirley hard around the face.

'Listen to me, young lady,' she snarled, gripping Shirley's hands hard. 'I've had more than enough of your dramatics.' Pushing her hard face close to Shirley's, she dropped her voice. 'I am NOT Sister Ann or Sister Ada, or any of your gullible friends. You will do as you're told or I will call the police and have you forcibly removed,' she threatened.

Shirley crumpled on to her bed. 'Can I at least say good-bye to Sister Ann?'

'What kind of a fool do you take me for?' Matron scoffed. 'Why would I allow another show of your wild emotions? Isn't that your game? Deceiving good, honest people to get your own selfish way?'

Dumping the remainder of Shirley's clothes into the suitcase, she slammed it shut and then literally threw Shirley's coat, hanging on the back of the door, at the girl.

'Get up,' she commanded. 'And get out of Mary Vale.'

Before the residents of the Home had even come down for their breakfast, Matron had all but dragged Shirley down the garden path to Kents Bank Station, where she boarded the first train south. Not taking her eyes off Shirley for a minute, vengeful Matron stood on the deserted plat-form until the slow-cranking train disappeared into the mist swirling in from the marsh, where mournful seabirds swooped over the tidal waters slowly rolling in. Only then did Matron turn away and, with a triumphant smile on her face, retrace her steps back to Mary Vale, where she could prepare herself for all the questions that would inevitably be asked about Tom.

Shirley sat in her freezing-cold, empty compartment like a condemned prisoner going to the gallows. All the happiness and joy she'd experienced over the last few spe-cial months – the love, laughter and friendship – they were gone forever.

'I always knew it was too good to be true,' she thought to herself. 'It was like a dream, one I prayed I would never wake up from, but now I have.'

Wiping the steam from the window, Shirley caught a last glimpse of Mary Vale disappearing from sight, and from her life too.

24. Shirley

Sister Ann was busy supervising the eight o'clock feeds when Ada arrived to take over. Ann smiled at her friend, who, as usual, was stuffing her glorious, thick, auburn hair under her white, starched cap. Even in the stark early-morning light, Ada's blue eyes sparkled and the smile that was never far from her lips lit up when she saw her friend.

'Good sleep?' Ann inquired.

'Yes, after all the comings and goings of yesterday, I virtually passed out and slept right round the clock,' Ada admitted. 'Any sign of Matron, or news of Tom?'

Sister Ann shook her head. 'No, nothing. I left them alone as she requested.'

'I'll go and tap on the door,' Ada said, once she'd finally fixed her cap with several kirby grips.

Sister Ann nodded. 'She might be grateful for a cup of tea.'

After giving a few discreet knocks on the door, Ada called softly, 'Is there anything I can get you, Matron?'

The door opened slowly and Matron appeared, looking unusually bleary-eyed and tousle-haired.

'Excuse my appearance,' she said wearily. 'I've been up most of the night with little Tom.'

'How is he?' Ada asked, peering eagerly over Matron's shoulder.

'I'm sorry, Ada, the poor child died just before dawn,' Matron said mournfully.

Ada clamped a hand to her mouth. 'God! NO,' she cried.

'He just hadn't the strength to fight any more; the infection finally got the better of him,' Matron added with a heavy sigh.

'Where is he?' Ada exclaimed, as she bustled past Matron to peer into the empty cot.

'He's not here, Sister. Dr Jones arranged for him to be taken away,' Matron told her. 'He said I couldn't have done any more for the child,' she added in a martyred tone.

Ada wiped a tear from her eye. 'Poor little chap,' she murmured. 'Did he suffer much?'

'By the time the fever took hold of him, he wasn't aware of much.' Matron laid a stiff hand on Ada's shoulder. 'Be assured, Sister, he is at peace now.' Rubbing her tired eyes, Matron added wearily, 'If you'll excuse me, I have a few things to do before I retire to my quarters and catch up on my sleep.'

Ada stepped out of her way. 'Certainly, Matron. You must be exhausted.'

After she'd gone, Ada stood a few moments in the room where she'd been told that Tom had spent his last night on earth. 'Goodbye, Tom,' she breathed. 'Rest in peace, darling.'

Having successfully dispatched Shirley back to where she came from and dealt with questions from her nursing staff over Tom's whereabouts, Matron now had to turn her attention to preparing Tom – masquerading as Bertie – for his first meeting with his future parents. She desperately needed some sleep, but she couldn't rest until she had covered all her tracks. And there was another reason Matron didn't want to be in the Home that morning: she knew full well that, when Shirley's absence was discovered, an emotional storm would break loose, not to mention a shower of awkward questions that she was determined to avoid. It was a mystery to Matron, who congratulated herself on being able to spot a manipulative operator from a mile away, how a poor, stupid girl like Shirley had wound her way into the residents' and the staffs' hearts. Matron dismissed them as simple, sentimental fools who could weep and rail till kingdom come – the girl was gone and any secrets she had were gone with her.

When the Bennetts arrived later that day, Matron left Sir Percival to welcome them with a proper Northern tea, sandwiches, rich fruit cake and scones, while she concentrated on preparing their son and heir for his introduction to a new and wonderful life. On her arrival at the Grange, she immediately ordered Olive to bathe Tom, then she personally dressed him in one of Bertie's laundered white nighties, which was way too big for him. Looking at him with a dispassionate eye, and worried that the Bennetts might think the child a bit of a runt, Matron wrapped Bertie's soft white shawl around Tom to give him some extra bulk before delivering him to Sir Percival.

Standing in the large marble-floored entrance hall, she whispered, 'How does he look?'

Lowering his voice too, Percival replied, 'Nothing like as impressive as the other one.'

'Given the circumstances, we're lucky we've got him,' she sharply reminded him. 'Make sure the Bennetts' final fee is paid before they leave the premises,' she bossed as Percival took the child into his arms.

'Don't worry – they're keen to settle up,' he confidently

assured her. 'They want no untidy loose ends,' quoting Edgar's own words.

Nervously holding Tom, Percival processed into the drawing room, where he grandly introduced the child to his new parents. Mercifully, in their desperate eagerness to claim a son, the Bennetts were thrilled with the baby, who slept sweetly and charmed them with, using Edgar's words, 'his noble visage'.

Watching the proceedings from the hallway, Matron could just about see the beaming Bennetts receiving their son in the drawing room. Smothering a smile, she thought to herself, 'If they but knew that Tom – who, the Bennetts had announced, would be baptized Rupert Edgar Easterbrook – was the bastard son of two dirt-poor workers from Bolton, they might well have fainted right there and then on the spot! Nancy's baby, Tom, would soon be growing up with a new name in a grand new home in London with the proverbial silver spoon stuck firmly in his mewling mouth.

Back at Mary Vale, there was deep, deep sadness at Tom's passing, which it was Ada's sorry task to announce to the residents after breakfast.

'I'm told the poor little chap just couldn't fight off the fever that gripped him,' she said despairingly.

Gloria, who'd helped bring Tom into the world, was especially distraught. 'It would have been nice to have had a final cuddle with Tom.'

Ada shook her head. 'Once he was in that private room being nursed by Matron, nobody got a chance to see him.'

'Well, somebody should write to Nancy and tell her what happened to her son,' Isla said anxiously.

'I'll do that,' Ada assured her.

Relieved, Emily exclaimed, 'Thank God! At least you'll find the right words to comfort her.'

'If I found out that my baby had died before being adopted, I'd be utterly devastated,' Isla blurted out.

'Of course you would,' Ada soothed. 'Any mother would; it's a natural reaction to want the best for your child, whether you've given them up for adoption or not.'

Little knowing of Tom's real new circumstances, Gloria spoke up. 'I suppose you'll have to inform the family who were planning to adopt Tom what's happened to him?'

'That's Sir Percival's job now that he's taken over from Father Ben,' Ada told her.

'Poor things,' Emily murmured. 'They're bound to be bitterly disappointed. Let's hope another baby can be found for them soon.'

Seeing Isla's startled expression, Emily suddenly realized what she might be thinking. 'God! Isla's baby might go to them,' she thought, and could have kicked herself. 'Me – and my stupid big mouth!'

With Tom's loss on everybody's mind, it took until lunch-time before anybody noticed that Shirley was missing. When Gloria saw Sister Mary Paul breathlessly laying out crockery and cutlery on the vast dining-room table, she said cheerfully, 'You're hard at work, Sister. Where's Shirley?'

'I've no idea,' the flustered nun replied. 'She never showed up for work, which is quite unlike her.'

'She didn't come to the dining room for her lessons either,' Gloria remarked. 'She might be ill,' she added, suddenly worried. 'I'll go and check her room.'

When she found the girl's room bare and her chest of drawers and wardrobe empty, Gloria began to panic; quickening her pace, she ran as fast as her big tummy would allow downstairs to the ward, where she found Sister Ada and Sister Ann in the office making their notes.

'Have either of you seen Shirley?' she asked. 'Her room's empty and her clothes are gone.'

After an extensive search, it was clear that Shirley had left. Everybody was troubled, but Sister Ann was particularly devastated. In the privacy of their shared office, with the door firmly closed, she collapsed in floods of tears.

'The child would never leave here of her own accord,' she blurted out to Ada. 'I absolutely know she wouldn't. Somebody must have forced her or frightened her – I know it!'

Ada nodded in total agreement with her friend; both knew better than most exactly why Shirley had chosen to stay on at Mary Vale.

'And to leave without a note or an explanation,' Sister Ann cried. 'It's not as if Shirley can't write now. I just don't understand it,' she sobbed. 'It makes no sense.'

Seeing the poor, heartbroken nun weeping into her hands moved Ada to tears. 'Dearest,' she murmured, as she drew Ann into her arms. 'Let's be hopeful – she may come back as quickly as she went,' she said, though in truth she didn't believe a word she spoke.

Sister Ann slowly nodded. 'I'll pray for her safety and for God's guidance,' she said feebly.

So it was once more Ada's woeful task to break further bad news to the residents of Mary Vale.

'Why on earth didn't she tell anybody?' Sister Mary Paul exclaimed in a voice choked with emotion.

With a home full of pregnant women all on the point of giving birth, Ada's first job was to calm them down.

'Ladies, if any of you would care to join Sister Ann, she'll be leading prayers in the chapel for the repose of baby Tom's soul, and now' – she caught her breath as words momentarily failed her – 'for Shirley's safe homecoming.'

Unable to understand what was going on, poor Robin stamped his foot in frustration. 'I want Shirley to come back!' he cried.

Forcing herself to stay balanced in the midst of a highly emotional storm, Gloria gathered her son into her arms and comforted him.

'Shirley's just gone home for a little holiday,' she murmured. 'When she's back, we'll read *The Enchanted Wood* together, just like we always have.'

'And I'll carry on learning her,' Robin staunchly insisted.

'Yes, darling,' Gloria agreed as she gazed up at Sister Mary Paul, who, seeing her favourite little boy so upset, managed to swallow her own tears and hold out her hand to him. 'Come on now, Robin, I've got a few eggs to spare – let's go and make some pancakes.'

Later that evening, as they prepared for bed after a long and sorrowful day, Gloria, Emily, Isla and Ada – who'd taken a quick ten-minute break with her friends before she went back on duty – confided in each other over comforting mugs of cocoa.

'I wish I could have said goodbye to Shirley,' Emily confessed. 'She was such a cheerful little soul.'

'I still wonder why she left so abruptly?' Isla said, puzzled.

'Maybe she just couldn't face telling us?' Gloria speculated.

'Perhaps she'll write once she's settled back home?' Emily said hopefully.

Ada, who knew the real truth about Shirley's background, very much doubted that Shirley would be in any state to write letters now she was back home, if indeed that was where she had gone.

Isla suddenly got to her feet and started to pace restlessly around the room.

'What is it, Isla?' Ada, concerned, inquired. 'Have you got cramp? Can I get you anything?'

'No, thanks,' Isla answered almost impatiently. 'We're going around in circles asking lots of questions about Shirley, and I just had a thought – could she have been discharged?'

'I don't think so!' Ada answered robustly. 'That's very much my domain. If Shirley had been discharged, I would have had to enter the date on her admin file; as it is, I'll now have to record the day she left Mary Vale. I keep all the admin files in my office,' she went on to explain.

As Ada returned to her duties on the ward, she could only conclude that somebody had forced Shirley or frightened her away from Mary Vale.

'And only Shirley knows who that was,' she thought with a mournful sigh.

At the Grange, after smoking his way through half a packet of Pall Mall cigarettes, Percival had barely given a thought to the couple who'd originally been selected to be Tom's adoptive parents and who would now have to be told of his 'demise'. Basking in the knowledge that, after months of anxiety, he finally had a sound amount of money in his bank account, he decided he'd attend to the matter later; right now, he had better things on his mind. He'd calculated that if he could get the same amount every three months, he could live comfortably for the rest of his life. He was hoping that, on the back of his success with the Bennetts, he'd be able to dip into their vast social network of wealthy contacts, but he'd have to be discreet and Matron would have to do her bit too. There'd be no point in sourcing an eager couple if there wasn't a suitable baby on offer. They'd passed Tom off as Bertie, but it would be dangerous to make a habit of deceiving their clients, who'd take a very dim view of being duped. The consequences of being discovered smuggling and selling babies for his own profit would bring ruin and imprisonment; he had to tread warily – and keep Matron in check too.

Percival was well satisfied with the way things had worked out: Tom was safely miles away; Olive had been sent packing with the promise of more money if she kept her mouth shut; and the convent had kindly taken it upon themselves to organize a funeral service in the convent chapel for the child that they believed to be Baby Tom.

He was pleased to note that Matron was already confidently plotting her next business venture. She had gone down the register of women presently resident at Mary Vale with him and had pointed out that, apart from young Isla Ross, most of them were dirt poor. Gloria Baxter and Emily Todd were ruled out anyway, as they'd both declared their intentions of keeping their babies. Returning her focus to Isla, who had already signed adoption papers, Matron had flicked through her file. She was certainly of good stock, university educated, and the father of the child was an acclaimed academic. Matron decided to lock Isla's file away in her desk with the other two, in her personal suite, when she went off-duty. Percival was more than happy for her to do this. He knew that if their elite baby business was to succeed, it was vital always to have a suitable child on their books, and Isla Ross's baby might just be the next one to offer for consideration.

The chapel service and funeral, attended by the Reverend Mother and her order, plus all the staff and residents from Mary Vale, was deeply moving and reduced many to tears. Ada made sure she sat with the women who had known Tom well: Emily, Isla and Gloria. She knew they would feel his loss the most, and she kept a watchful eye on them throughout the sad little service. The women stayed strong throughout, singing hymns and joining in all the prayers, but in the small chapel cemetery, when the nuns stood singing 'Ave Maria' around the little grave covered in flowers, all three women, and many more too, completely broke down. Sad though she was, Ada was relieved when the ceremony was over and she could get her charges back into Mary Vale, where, as she knew better than most, life went on.

25. Life Goes On

The atmosphere in Mary Vale turned oppressive. Nobody wanted to make things worse by talking about Shirley's departure, but there wasn't a person in the Home who didn't feel her absence everywhere they looked. They missed her smiling face in the entrance hall that she used to mop and polish every morning; they missed her in the kitchen where she washed up and cleared away pots, pans and crockery after every meal; they missed her in the dining room pouring out tea and handing around plates at breakfast, dinner and supper; and they missed her in the garden where, even in the winter months, she could be found weeding out the flowerbeds. Though young, small and completely unassuming, Shirley had filled the Home with her presence, which had been so gentle and benign that nobody had really appreciated it until she was gone.

It was sweet relief to have visitors to lift the heavy atmosphere in the Home, so Jeannie's visit with a hefty hamper was most welcome. After struggling to get the hamper out of the boot of her car, Jeannie staggered indoors, where she was met by her smiling granddaughter.

'Heavens above, darling,' she exclaimed, as she lay aside the hamper to embrace Isla. 'You're the size of a house!'

Isla grinned. 'I know: I swear I'm eating for an army!'

Jeannie looked with pleasure at her grandchild, who, in her final months of pregnancy, looked like a flower in full bloom; Isla glowed with health and energy, and her soft blonde hair had grown long and had a pretty shine to it.

'In that case you'll love my housekeeper's hamper, full of all your favourite treats,' Jeannie told her. 'She made extra for your friends too. There'll be a mutiny in my house if the government start rationing sugar and butter,' she joked.

In the sitting room, warmed by a crackling fire, Isla shared out cakes, sandwiches and cheese scones with her friends, which they enjoyed with several pots of tea provided by kindly Merry Paul, as everyone (thanks to Robin) now called the genial nun.

Referring to the recent letters she'd received from Isla, Jeannie spoke gently. 'It sounds like you've had a sorry time here recently?'

Emily, Gloria and Isla exchanged sad looks.

'Everything happened very quickly,' Isla murmured tearfully. 'We never got a chance even to say goodbye to the little boys, and now Shirley's gone too.'

'The staff have been wonderful,' Emily added staunchly. 'Sister Ada keeps a beady eye on all of us, making sure we don't get over-emotional and upset our babies.'

'She's a wonderful nurse,' Jeannie said admiringly. 'You can see it the minute you set eyes on her: so strong and competent but with warmth and compassion – they're very rare qualities.'

'We all love her to bits,' Gloria said fondly. 'I'm having trouble keeping Robin out of the maternity ward now that he's found out where Sister Ada lives.' She burst out laughing. 'I swear he thinks Merry Paul sleeps under the kitchen table and Sister Ada sleeps in a cot with the babies!'

Taking a sip of tea, Emily mused, 'You get really close to people in this place and then – before you know it – they're gone from your life.'

'I suppose that's the nature of the establishment,' Jeannie said.

Sensing their gloom, she tried to talk of other events outside of the Home. Not wanting to dwell on the recent depressing report of the Luftwaffe and German U-boats mining the Thames Estuary, she instead told them about the new film *Goodbye, Mr Chips*, which everybody was raving about.

'I'd love to go to the cinema in Grange to see it too,' Isla said, as she rolled her hands over her huge stomach. 'But I know I couldn't sit in a small, cramped seat with this big bump for more than five minutes.'

'And I'd be nipping to the ladies' toilets all the time,' Emily laughed.

'Never mind,' Jeannie chuckled. 'There is life after pregnancy.'

All three women briefly imagined their lives post-childbirth. Fearing the worst, Emily wondered how she and her baby would survive if George didn't come home to them: where would they live, what would she do? Isla thought of starting her academic life over again, maybe in Oxford or Cambridge this time round; while Gloria thought longingly of returning home to Stan with Robin at her side and a new baby in her arms.

When it came to saying goodbye, Jeannie had a private word with her granddaughter. After giving Isla a firm hug, she said, 'Not long now, my precious.'

'I know,' Isla answered excitedly. 'I can't wait for it all

to be over, to have my body and my life back, but after all the ghastly events that have happened here I do wonder about the future of my child. Don't get me wrong,' she quickly added, 'I haven't changed my mind – I still want it adopted – but I hope she, or he, will be safe as well as loved.'

'You made that perfectly clear when you talked to Father Benedict,' Jeannie reminded her.

Isla nodded. 'I trusted him completely,' she said. 'I'm quite certain Father Ben would always put the happiness and wellbeing of Mary Vale babies first and foremost. I wouldn't be at all worried if he were still in charge.'

'The sooner that good man returns to the Home, the better,' Jeannie said, as she clambered into the driving seat of her car.

'Come and visit me again soon,' Isla begged.

'I will, sweet child,' Jeannie promised. 'Even if the roads are blocked with snow, I'll struggle over the fells with a hamper that will keep you all going till Christmas!'

26. Midwinter

As December set in, national morale was raised when news came through of the first Canadian troops arriving in Europe.

'It makes you feel safer when you know another nation is joining in the fight against Hitler,' Emily said to her friends.

'The Canadians are a good, loyal lot,' Gloria said, as she raised her cup of tea in a salutation. 'Bless 'em all!'

Emily and Gloria exchanged a look as their thoughts flew to their beloved men. Stan's letters were now few and far between, but at least she got letters, whereas poor Em had still not heard news of her George. The Winter War was now under way, and in Britain conscription was expanded to cover men from nineteen to forty one years of age. Seeing Em's strained expression, Gloria reached across to squeeze her friend's hand.

'Now the Canadian Air Force is on our side, we're bound to hear more of our own RAF boys,' she whispered reassuringly.

'Oh, I pray so, Gloria,' Emily said fervently.

Fearful that she was raising false hopes, Gloria added with a warm smile, 'It makes sense: they can't report on the Canadian Air Force's progress without passing on a bit about our own RAF, can they?'

Wanting to believe anything that gave her hope, Emily

gave a bleak smile. 'Fingers crossed,' she responded. 'Anything would be better than nothing.'

As one cold and frosty day followed another, the girls began to plan for Christmas. Ada informed them that the convent farm always supplied a tall, sturdy Christmas tree from nearby Cartmel Fell, and that it took pride of place in the large entrance hall. The thought of Christmas sent a burst of welcome cheer around the Home.

'Maybe we'll be lucky enough to get a few chickens from the farm along with the Christmas tree?' Emily said.

'There's plenty of allotments round here; we might be able to trade a pair of baby bootees for a big fat hen,' Isla joked.

In a buzz of activity, motivated particularly by Robin, who even wanted to decorate Merry Paul's kitchen with streamers and balloons, everybody threw themselves into making decorations and Christmas cards with great gusto. Along with letters, Christmas cards were arriving at Mary Vale too; when Emily received a letter her heart almost stopped beating.

'Oh, dear God!' she gasped, clutching the letter in her trembling hands.

After all these long, lonely, agonizing months, was this the letter she'd been hoping and praying for? Had her George finally managed to make contact? Struck by the thought that hardly anybody else knew where she actually was, Emily looked more closely at the letter, which was marked URGENT. Praying and trembling, she ripped open the envelope with fumbling, clumsy fingers and her heart hammering in her chest. Hardly daring to breathe, she unfolded the headed sheets of paper.

Mr and Mrs Reginald Holden,
The Briers,
Didsbury Road,
Chester

Stunned, she stared at the heading for several seconds. 'George's parents!' she thought to herself, and her excitement turned to blind terror. It was months since her brief meeting with them in Manchester on that carefree, happy day when they'd all met up in a pub in the city centre and George had proudly introduced them to his girlfriend. WHY were they writing to her now? Oh, God! Had George perished in the war? Or did he want nothing to do with her? Feeling her baby reacting to her wild emotions, she gently rolled her hands over her stomach to calm the child inside her. When she felt steadier, she finally plucked up the courage to read the letter.

Dear Miss Todd,

We are delighted to inform you that George is fighting for his country somewhere in the Far East; the location and other details have been censored, so that is all the information we can give you at this time.

Feeling weak with relief, Emily could only murmur, 'Thank God, he's alive! My George is alive.' Quickly turning her attention back to the letter, she read on.

Because George was only allowed to write one letter home to his family, he was most keen that we passed on information to you

249

and suggested we got in touch with you at your place of
employment, so we have taken the liberty of sending our letter
to the Lyons café in Manchester, where he told us you worked.

'Oh, my God!' Emily gasped. 'If he's telling them to contact me at the café, George must still think I'm working in Manchester!'

As the penny dropped, Emily realized that if George didn't know she had moved on from Manchester, he very likely hadn't got the news about her pregnancy either, and clearly neither had his parents. They were all under the impression that she was skipping round the Lyons café serving tea and toast to all and sundry, when, in fact, she was in a mother and baby home in the far North-West of England.

'All those letters,' she murmured. 'What happened to them? Where have they all gone?'

Thanking God she'd left her Mary Vale address with Ivy, who'd kindly forwarded the letter, she read on.

We're so sorry we've not been in touch previously; we would have
liked to but we didn't know your home address and we weren't
sure which of the cafés in Manchester you worked in. When we
heard from George that it was the Lyons café in Piccadilly, we
immediately posted our goods news off to you. We've never
forgotten the happy time we spent with you and George, and
remember with affection him calling you 'The most Beautiful
Girl in the World!'

Emily glowed with pride; it felt like years, centuries even, since she'd been described as a beauty, since she'd felt like a woman whom a man might desire. During the months of her pregnancy she had lost sight of the slim, shapely girl with long legs and a trim waist, but George describing her as beautiful to his parents brought back a rush of heady memories and sensations that made her feel quite dizzy not only with pleasure but also relief. He hadn't abandoned her – he just hadn't got the letters! Eager to hear more, Emily quickly returned to reading the letter in her trembling hand.

George was anxious to explain why he suddenly disappeared from Padgate. As we said, his letter was heavily censored, but reading between the lines it appears his squadron was removed to a secret destination in the UK before being flown out to the Far East. We knew nothing about this; we even travelled to Padgate in Warrington to try to find out more about our son, but we were met with a stone wall.

'Me too,' sighed Emily, recalling how months ago she'd begged the guard on duty at the base to help her find her fiancé.

From the date on the postmark, we can see that it has taken months for George's letter to filter through. We pray our son continues to be safe in the time that has passed since he posted the letter to us. As you know, George is our only child and we miss him dreadfully. We would love to meet you again, Emily: the three of us could support each other during this awful time of waiting. Hoping to hear from you soon.

With our very best wishes,
Reggie and Margaret Holden

In a daze, Emily folded the precious letter, which she held without knowing it to her heart. 'George still thinks of me; he hasn't abandoned me. And, even better than that, I'm not alone any more,' she thought. 'George's parents want to see me again, we could be friends – except . . .'

Emily's bubble of joy began to fade. How could she possibly follow up on such a warm invitation to meet George's parents if they didn't know the truth about her condition?

When Gloria and Isla found Emily in the sitting room clutching a letter, they couldn't help but fear the worst. Exchanging a nervous look with Gloria, Isla was the first to speak.

'Em, is everything all right?'

'Yes, yes,' Emily assured them. 'Everything's *wonderful*!' she laughed, Dampening down the anxiety she felt about how George's parents might react to her pregnancy, she focused on the positive, at least for now. After so many months of worrying that George no longer cared for her, or that he might not even be alive, she had evidence to the contrary, even if it was somewhat out of date. Weak with relief and occasionally fighting back the tears that threatened to overcome her, Emily quickly read the letter to her delighted friends.

'Oh, Em! I'm so happy for you!' exclaimed Gloria, when she'd finished.

'How marvellous that George's parents want to see you soon,' Isla added.

'Mmm,' Emily said cautiously. 'Though they don't know about the baby; neither does George, from the sound of things.' She continued, 'I don't think I'd want to see them after so long looking like this.' She nodded at her vast tummy. 'It would be too shocking for them.'

'But you must write back to them,' Isla urged.

'I will, of course,' Emily assured her friends. 'And perhaps I can visit them once I've had the baby.'

'But what will you give as your address?' Gloria inquired. 'They might see that the postmark isn't Manchester,' she pointed out.

'You're right,' Emily replied, thoughtful. 'I'll tell them I'm spending Christmas with a friend in the Lake District,' she grinned. 'It's almost the truth!'

Feeling in desperate need of fresh air to clear her conflicting emotions, Emily leapt to her feet. 'Let's go for a walk before dinner-time,' she suggested. 'Come on, girls,' she urged. 'You can help me plan my letter.'

'Sorry, Emily, I'd love to but I can't,' Gloria apologized. 'I've got to check up on Robin. I left him doing some homework but I bet you half a crown he's scoffing his favourite potato cakes in the kitchen with Merry Paul,' she joked.

'Please come with me, Isla,' Emily said, as Gloria hurried off to find her son.

Isla groaned. 'It's too cold,' she grumbled.

'A walk will do you good!' Emily exclaimed. Grabbing Isla's hand, she gave it a playful tug. 'Be a pal, keep me company,' she begged.

Groaning and moaning, Isla staggered to her feet, 'All right, but I want to be back in time for dinner – and Sister Ann's fitness classes.'

Emily nodded. 'Me too,' she quickly agreed.

Wrapping up in big, warm winter coats and scarves, the

girls trudged across the road towards Kents Bank Railway Station, where they heard the loud rumble of an approaching steam train and blasts of smoke told them it was very close. Isla stood on her tiptoes and peered up the track that skirted the large stretch of silver marsh now visible with the tide out.

'I love watching the trains pull in,' she said, as excited as a little girl.

Further conversation was drowned out by the train, which slowly ground to a halt before heading on its way again to Grange, and onwards to Arnside, Silverdale and Lancaster. Once it was safe to cross the line, the heavily pregnant girls set out along the marsh, where the wind almost blew them off their feet. Laughing and swaying, Emily clutched Isla's arm as they made their way across the tracks that threaded around the tidal creeks. When the howling wind snatched their breath away, they fell silent and listened to the call of the wild fowl, while oyster catchers and dunlins swooped and dived over the sparkling water that was so bright and luminous it almost blinded them.

'Don't tell me this doesn't make you feel better?' Emily exclaimed, as she threw back her head and breathed clean fresh air into her lungs. 'It's cold and windy, but it's great to be outdoors. Especially when I know that my George is alive – and that he loves me still!'

She stopped short as she realized that Isla was no longer listening to her, but was stock still, staring across a stretch of sand littered with birds pecking for food in tidal creeks filled with seawater that the outgoing tide had left behind.

'There's something over there!' she heard Isla exclaim.

Emily, who had poorer eyesight than her friend, squinted but shrugged. 'I can't see anything. What can you see?' she replied.

'I don't know, but something doesn't look right. We should take a look,' Isla urged.

Seeing her friend striding boldly off, Emily panicked. 'Isla, stop!' she yelled. 'Stay on the tracks – there's quicksand out there.'

Though frightened, she hurried after Isla as much as her bulk would allow. Breathless and sweating, Emily struggled through the biting wind that whipped around her, but before she could reach Isla she was horrified to see her dear friend stumble and fall to the ground. Thinking she was stuck in quicksand, Emily screamed out, 'ISLA!'

Running and stumbling herself, she finally caught up with Isla, who gripped her hand.

Almost hysterical with fear, Emily cried, 'What is it?'

White and trembling, Isla could only point to a nearby creek.

Following Isla's finger, Emily gasped, then clutched her belly as if the shock of what she'd seen would cause her to go into labour. She could just about make out the horrifying sight that Isla had spotted. There was a body lying prone on the sand near the rising tide.

27. The Marsh

White-faced, trembling and in shock, the two girls stumbled forwards, and, as they neared the body, their distress grew one hundred times worse when they saw who it was lying there.

'God Almighty!' Isla shrieked. 'It's Shirley!'

Gasping and spluttering for breath, Isla and Emily took hold of Shirley and tried to help her into an upright position. Horrified by their dear friend's alabaster-white face, Emily, almost too terrified to ask the question, whispered, 'Is she alive?'

Isla didn't reply; instead she stripped off her coat and wrapped it round Shirley's skinny body. 'We've got to keep her warm,' she said urgently. 'Put your coat around her too and lay her down.'

Shivering in the wind, Emily watched her friend tilt Shirley's face backwards; then, after pressing Shirley's nose shut with her fingertips, she breathed deeply into the girl's open mouth several times. Hardly daring even to breathe herself, Emily, silent and tense, prayed with all her heart.

'Please God, don't let little Shirley die. Please let her live.'

Isla took another deep breath and repeated the first-aid procedure she'd been taught at school, and at the end of the second breath Shirley suddenly groaned.

'She's alive!' Isla cried. 'Shirley! Shirley!' she cried.

Hearing the girl making gagging noises, Isla quickly rolled her on to her side, 'She's choking!'

As Isla worked to clear Shirley's airway, Emily knelt beside the girl, whose hands she firmly grasped. 'SHIRLEY!' she implored. 'Stay with us, darling, please don't die.'

In what seemed like hours but was, in fact, a few agonizing seconds, they waited for some sign of life. And then, suddenly, Shirley took a noisy breath.

'ARGHHHH!' she moaned.

'Get her upright again,' Isla instructed.

Emily, still on the ground, helped Isla to get Shirley to sit up.

'She's freezing,' Emily said in a panic. She rubbed the girl's cold hands with her own warm ones.

Looking frantically about, Isla said urgently, 'Can you manage to stay here with Shirley while I run back to the hall?'

Emily quickly nodded. 'Yes, of course I'll stay.'

'Here – take my scarf,' Isla said, and wrapped her woolly scarf around Shirley's neck.

Worried that Isla might catch a chill, Emily cried, 'Won't you need it?'

'I'll be warmer once I get moving,' Isla replied. 'Wrap your arms around Shirley, hold her tight and keep talking, and try to make her talk too – I'll be as quick as I can.'

As Isla set off back across the sands, Emily called after her, 'Be careful of the quicksand! Stick to the tracks.'

Left alone, Emily gazed into Shirley's pale face, lifting her closer into her embrace and wrapping the coats even more tightly around her shivering body. 'I'll keep you warm. There now,' she crooned gently rocking Shirley, 'Shhh, lovie, you're safe now.'

After almost running all the way back to Mary Vale, Isla just about collapsed in the entrance hall. Clutching her belly, which felt like it was on fire, she groped her way on to the ward.

'Heavens above!' exclaimed Sister Ann, when she saw Isla bent over double and gasping for breath. 'What on earth has happened to you?'

Helping Isla into a chair, the nun went white with shock when she heard they'd found Shirley on the marsh.

'She's alive, but only just,' Isla quickly told her. 'Emily's with her; we need someone to get her safely back here. It's freezing out there and she's so weak.'

Instantly galvanized, Sister Ann picked up her heavy skirts and tore down the ward, calling at the top of her voice for Ada.

Minutes later, after getting directions from Isla (who wanted to accompany them but was firmly told otherwise), Ada set off running like a thing possessed across the marsh, where the wind was blowing even more strongly and sheets of icy grey rain had started to fall. Following the tracks that skirted the quicksand, Ada ran and her nurse's cape billowed in the wind like a dark cloud; her long auburn hair whipped free of her starched cap and blew wildly about her tense face. When Emily saw Ada approaching, she frantically waved her scarf.

'OVER HERE!' she shouted.

Seeing Shirley cradled in Emily's arms lent wings to Ada's feet: she flew across the ground that separated them.

'My dearest child,' she murmured, as she relieved exhausted Emily of her burden.

At the sound of the voice she loved and would always remember, Shirley briefly opened her eyes, and her hand reached out to grasp the nurse's hand. 'Ada . . .' she sighed.

Taking her pulse, Ada cried urgently, 'She's freezing! Come on, can you help me get her up? Here, take my cape and wrap it over the top of the coats – we've got to get her moving.'

Clutching Shirley, who weighed very little, Ada and Emily supported her back across the blustery marsh.

As they made their way home, with the icy wind almost blowing them off their feet, poor Emily panted with exhaustion. Seeing her tired, strained face, Ada spoke softly and very calmly. 'You did well, Em: both of you girls have been very brave. Now I need to get you back to Mary Vale, where you will need to be checked, as well as poor Shirley. You've had quite an ordeal.'

Rushing past the gaping girls who had gathered in the entrance hall to see what was going on, Ada and Emily hurried on to the main ward, where they gently lowered Shirley on to a vacant bed and quickly drew the curtains around her.

'Shall we call an ambulance?' Emily gasped as she stared at poor Shirley lying limply on the bed. 'Or Dr Jones?' she added desperately.

'I don't think we need an ambulance now that we've got her on to the ward,' Ada assured her. 'And as for Dr Jones,' she added cryptically, 'I'm not quite sure how helpful he might be.'

Knowing of the doctor's drinking habits, Emily gave a quick nod.

'I can take care of her,' Ada said with cool professional confidence. 'But you, madam,' she said with mock severity, 'need to get out of those wet clothes and into a hot bath immediately.'

Stripping off Shirley's soaking-wet clothes, Ada laid hot-water bottles in the bed, then gently wiped her face and body dry with several warm towels. Feeling the warmth slowly returning to her patient's skin, she slipped a snug winceyette nightdress over Shirley's shoulders and settled her back on the bed, which was piled high with blankets.

'Better?' she asked softly, as she tucked Shirley up.

Shirley's eyelids fluttered open. 'I wanted to die,' she confessed in a tiny whisper. 'I'm sorry . . .' she said, as her voice trailed away.

Rearranging the hot-water bottles around Shirley, Ada soothed her fretful patient. 'Shhh, now, snuggle down and keep warm while I get you something to eat and a nice cup of tea.'

No sooner had she stepped out from behind the curtains than she saw Sister Ann hurrying towards her, an anguished look on her face.

'She's alive,' Ada quickly told her.

'Thank God for that,' Sister Ann replied, as she proceeded to roll back her sleeves and wash her hands in the large sink. 'I'll take over from here, Ada – you're needed elsewhere.'

Ada threw the nun a puzzled look. 'What?'

'Isla's gone into labour,' Sister Ann explained.

'She's three weeks early!' Ada exclaimed.

'Her waters broke just after you left,' Sister Ann added.

'She's in the delivery room.' The nun gave a knowing smile. 'She's asked for you,' she said.

Ada set off at a run. 'Get Shirley some food, Ann, and some hot sweet tea,' she called over her shoulder. 'And keep the hot-water bottles going.'

Sister Ann found Shirley fast asleep, and, as she tenderly brushed mud from her streaky wet hair, she couldn't help but notice the girl's neck and pinched little face were covered with black-and-blue bruises. Hot tears stung the back of her eyes as she imagined the horrors Shirley must have endured once she arrived back home.

'My poor girl,' she whispered. 'We'll look after you now, I promise.'

Briefly leaving Shirley peacefully sleeping, Sister Ann hurried to the kitchen to put on the kettle for tea. She stopped dead in her tracks when she entered the kitchen and saw Matron there, looking extremely irritated.

'Where have you put the wretched girl?' she snapped.

'On the ward, of course,' the nun retorted. 'Isla and Gloria found her half dead on the marsh.'

'If she was half dead why was she brought *here*?' Matron fumed. 'Why not the local hospital?'

Sister Ann gave her a pitiful look. 'Because we take care of the ones we love,' she answered with sweet simplicity. 'And,' she added pointedly, 'she trusts us. And thanks to young Emily and Isla, she survived her awful ordeal.'

After the nun had left bearing a loaded tray, Matron swore out loud. 'Damnation!' she cried, thumping the tabletop. 'Just when I thought I'd got rid of her!'

*

In the delivery room, Ada was monitoring Isla's contractions, which were already starting to come regularly and with increasing ferocity.

'How's Shirley?' she gasped in between two of her contractions, when she could just about think straight.

'She's sleeping off her terrible experience; you did a wonderful job,' Ada assured her sweating patient. 'You and Emily saved Shirley's life.'

'And I went into early labour as a consequence,' Isla said, with an anxious expression on her face. 'We were both running around like things possessed on the marsh,' she admitted guiltily.

Ada patted her hand. 'Nothing to worry about: a week or two either side of the due date is neither here nor there,' she said with a confident professional ease that immediately put her patient's mind at rest.

Isla gave a sad sigh. 'What could have happened to the poor kid once she left here?'

Ada shook her head. 'That's for Shirley to tell us in her own good time.' As another contraction gripped Isla's body, she said gently, 'Come on now. For the time being, let's just concentrate on you and your baby.'

Recalling the steady breathing Sister Ann had taught in her classes, Isla took some long, deep breaths; she hoped her baby wouldn't take too long to come into the world, which was all the better a place for having Shirley back at Mary Vale where she rightly belonged.

28. Heather

Though born nearly three weeks early, Isla's daughter was a good, healthy weight; she had her mother's silvery-blonde hair and her eyes promised to be as blue as Isla's. Ada smiled softly as she cradled the sweet little girl she'd brought into the world.

'She's beautiful,' she congratulated Isla, who lay back exhausted after a long and difficult breech birth. 'I was worried you might need a C-section, or that at least I'd need to use forceps, but your clever daughter suddenly turned herself around and saved me the trouble.'

Isla smiled feebly. 'Every time I saw those wretched forceps I thought I was going to die,' she admitted.

'Don't worry about all that now,' Ada urged cheerfully. 'You have a strong, healthy baby you can be proud of.'

'For now,' Isla said with a catch in her throat.

Familiar with the sadness and regret that often swamped the young mothers who would be parting with their babies shortly after the trials of childbirth, Ada quickly popped Isla's baby into a bassinet. 'I'll take her into the nursery while you get some sleep.'

Isla nodded gratefully. 'Please, will you let my grand-mother know?' she asked as her eyelids drooped.

'Of course, dear, rest now,' Ada said softly.

Wheeling the tiny new baby into the nursery, Ada felt a

sudden stab of sadness; usually, she had no problem in acknowledging that adoption was the best alternative for most of the babies born at Mary Vale, but, looking at Isla's sleeping daughter, she felt differently. Isla's grandmother, Jeannie, was a free-thinking, independent woman of means and Isla was a clever young woman with a fine future ahead of her: between them, they'd make a splendid job of rearing a child. Ada gave an audible sigh of regret; it was not meant to be. The die had been cast and Baby Ross was destined for another life far away from her mother and her remarkable grandmother too.

Though weak as a kitten herself, Shirley insisted that she paid a visit to one of the women who had saved her life. Seeing how desperate she was to see Isla, Sister Ann pushed Shirley on to the ward in a wheelchair and left the two women to have their own private conversation.

'I'm sorry I put you to so much trouble,' Shirley said nervously. 'No wonder you had your little girl early,' she added guiltily. 'Running across the marsh in the driving rain, trying to save my life – it couldn't have done you any good.'

'It was worth it, just to see you here, alive and well,' Isla replied with tears in her eyes. Embarrassed but nevertheless determined to know the truth, Isla asked in a whisper, 'What happened, Shirley?'

Looking tense, Shirley reached under her pillows. 'I had this letter that I wrote in my coat pocket; it was addressed to Sister Ann,' she said, as she handed it to Isla. 'She dried it out and gave it back to me, but only after she and Sister Ada had read it. I want you to read it later – you and Emily and Gloria too: you're my friends and should all know the truth,' she urged. 'In private. It explains everything.'

Taking the letter, Isla gave a bright, determined smile. 'Well, all I can say is I'm glad we found you and saved you – the world would be a smaller place without you, Shirley.'

Shirley looked at her for several long seconds. Genuinely puzzled, she asked, 'Did people really miss me?'

'You were missed so much,' Isla answered passionately and truthfully.

Looking flabbergasted, Shirley again said, 'Really?'

'YES!' Isla laughed. 'You're part of Mary Vale's furniture! Without your cute, smiling face peeping over the teapot every morning, we all felt glum,' she joked.

Shirley gave an incredulous smile. 'I'm so lucky!' she exclaimed.

'I'd personally fund you to stay on here at Mary Vale for the rest of your life,' Isla said, and she meant it too. 'But if they can't have you, I'm sure I could persuade my grandmother to give you a roof over your head until we found work for you locally.'

Shirley's wide eyes glistened with tears. 'Would you REALLY do that for me, Isla?'

Isla hugged her tight. 'Of course – we're friends, aren't we?'

Isla, Gloria and Emily read Shirley's letter in private the next morning, when Emily and Gloria dropped by to visit the baby, who had been named Heather, on the maternity ward. With the curtains drawn tightly, they sat close together on the edge of the bed, where, in silence, broken only by their gasps and cries of dismay, they read Shirley's suicide note.

Dear Sister Ann,

*I'm grateful to Gloria and Robin for helping me to learn to read
and write, I know I am a bad speller but I can write enough to
tell you my story in my own true words. Sister Ann, I have made
up my mind, I don't want to live on this earth any more. I want to
go to God, who I know loves me as I love him. I wish I could have
died before I left Mary Vale, because I knew what was in store for
me. But after Matron kicked me out I had no choice but to go
back to the home I hate. Dearest Sister Ann, there's something
else I need to tell you all, something really important. I witnessed
something quite wrong the night before I left; I was going to tell
you at the time but Matron made sure I was well gone before I
could speak to anybody about what I witnessed.*

'Oh, God!' Emily murmured. 'My skin's starting to creep.'

*That night, I was half dozing in the kitchen, waiting for the bread
to rise, when I saw Matron sneak out the back way in the middle
of the night. Even though I'm scared to death of the woman,
something made me follow her outside, where I crouched down
behind a bush and watched her. I saw her lay a small bundle on the
passenger seat of her car, and I thought it stirred, then I distinctly
heard a baby crying and, as God's my judge, I would swear on the
Bible that the baby was Tom; believe me, I've heard him wailing
often enough when I've been cleaning in the nursery. When Matron
drove away in the dead of night with no headlights on, I had no
choice but to follow.*

After they'd read open-mouthed about the events of
that fateful night, the girls were visibly shocked.

'She was brave!' Emily exclaimed. 'I don't think I would have had the courage to follow Matron in the dark.'

'Me neither,' Gloria said. 'I'd be terrified.'

I prayed I'd get safely back home without Matron seeing me but she caught me in the kitchen, soaked to the skin and muddy, and she started asking me questions. I made some excuse, but I knew in my gut she didn't believe me for a minute, and it turns out I was right to be scared. Matron sent me packing the next morning before I could see any of you to pass on what I saw at the Grange. I didn't even have a chance to say goodbye to the people I love. She told me to get out or she'd have the police on me! There was nothing I could do but go back home.

With a face like thunder, Isla looked up from the letter she was clutching in her shaking hands. 'That damn cold-hearted bitch of a matron,' she swore.

'She kicked out poor little Shirley because she'd seen her up to no good,' Emily seethed.

'She did it to protect herself!' Gloria cried.

Isla, with the bit now firmly between her teeth, declared, 'Well, girls! Wouldn't it be interesting to get to the bottom of whatever it was Matron was up to that night?'

Emily agreed. 'It's obviously a secret she's keen to keep, because Shirley paid such a high price for it,' she said grimly.

Galvanized, Isla was in war mood. 'Then we have an obligation to find out what it is, for Shirley's sake. The poor girl's back here; we don't want her picked on again!'

'Please, let's finish the letter,' Gloria begged.

I hope you don't mind, Sister Ann, that I've chosen to drown myself. That way the pain will stop and I can go to sleep in heaven with the angels that you told me about. I loved your stories, Sister Ann. I hope God will forgive me for drowning myself, I will explain to him why I was forced to do such a bad thing, he might understand. I want to end my life close to you, the mother I never had, in the only place I've ever felt safe, Mary Vale, my one true home.

Forgive me, Sister Ann.
Your loving servant,
Shirley

'God! The poor kid!' Isla murmured, folding the letter and returning it to its dirty, crumpled envelope.

'Christ! Who can blame her for wanting to end it all?' Gloria said with a sob.

'Why would anybody do that to an innocent young girl?' Emily said, puzzled. 'It's damn inhuman.'

Deep in sad thought, the girls jumped as the curtains around Isla's bed were swished open.

'Hellfire! I hope it's not Matron come visiting again,' Isla hissed, then sighed with relief as Ada appeared carrying a metal kidney bowl containing warm water.

When she saw their guilty faces, Ada joked, 'Who are you three whispering about?'

The women looked at each other.

'Shirley gave us this to read,' Isla said, as she held up Shirley's letter, which she knew from Shirley that Ada had read.

Ada slumped down on the bed beside her friends.

'It truly beggars belief!' she exclaimed.

'So we need to work together to get to the bottom of Matron's dark secret,' Emily told Ada.

'I agree!' she cried. 'You don't know what she's going to do next; she needs watching like a hawk – one thing's for sure, we can't trust her.'

Her friends nodded in agreement with Ada's sentiments.

'And whatever we find out, we should pass on to each other,' Isla urged. 'Keep a mental file of where Matron's been and who she's talked to, but without arousing suspicion,' she warned.

'Talking of files,' Emily said, 'isn't it time we checked Tom and Bertie's adoption records? You must know where they're kept, Ada?'

Ada nodded. 'Copies are kept in the convent and in Matron's office.'

'Is there any chance you could have a peek at Matron's files?' Isla asked.

'I think I would risk losing my job if I did that,' Ada answered honestly. 'But,' she added with a cunning smile, 'if I could lay my hands on Sister Ann's skeleton key, you could do the job yourself.'

'Yes!' daring Isla exclaimed. 'One of us can do it. We might get dragged through the coals if she finds us at it, but at least she can't sack us.'

'Matron's off-duty tomorrow afternoon; if Sister Ann agrees, I could slip you the key once Matron's left the ward.'

Emily and Gloria looked at each other, then nodded conspiratorially.

'You're on!' said Em.

'And when Shirley's back on her feet,' Gloria added,

'we'll involve her too. She'd make a perfect spy, wandering around the Home with her mop and bucket!'

'Oh, how I wish the darling girl could stay here for-ever!' Gloria said with passionate fervour.

'Well, clearly she can't if wretched Matron's got any-thing to do with it,' Isla pointed out.

'One thing is for sure,' Ada assured her friends, 'Shirley's going nowhere that Sister Ann and I don't approve of.'

'I told her she could stay with me at Jeannie's until a safe place is found for her,' Isla announced.

'Now that is a wonderful idea!' Ada cried. 'But you must check with Jeannie, Isla,' she added anxiously.

'Of course,' Isla replied. 'Jeannie's due to visit soon, to see Heather,' she said. 'I'll ask her then,' she promised.

'Now if you'll excuse me, ladies,' Ada said, getting to her feet, 'I need to examine Isla.'

Isla groaned as she lay back on the bed. 'I had a feeling this wasn't just a social call.'

Ada grinned. 'Open wide!'

'Think that's my cue to go!' Emily groaned, as she hauled herself to her feet. 'I envy you having a baby out-side of your body rather than inside, Isla.'

Ada smiled at the two heavily pregnant women. 'Your turn will come soon enough,' she teased.

While Ada deftly examined her patient, Isla mentioned to her that Matron had popped in to see Heather.

'I can't stand the sight of the woman!' she declared. 'I've never liked her, but, after reading poor Shirley's tragic letter, I could cheerfully strangle her! She was here three times yesterday,' she grumbled. 'She said she wanted to examine Heather, even though I told her you'd already been in and checked her. I wish she'd leave me and my baby alone,' she muttered crossly. 'The wretched woman just gives me the creeps!'

Seeing that Isla was getting irate, Ada said calmly, 'Don't worry, darling, given the discussion we've just had, we'll all be keeping a beady eye on Matron – and Heather – from now on.'

The following afternoon, after receiving Sister Ann's skeleton key from Ada, who winked, then went about her business, Gloria and Emily made their way to Matron's office, where Emily would stand on guard while Gloria slipped inside to check the files.

'Be as quick as you can,' Emily urged. 'I'll hang about in the corridor pretending I'm waiting for somebody,' she promised.

With a nod, Gloria slipped the key into the lock and opened the office door. Once inside, she made her way to the filing cabinet, which, to her enormous relief, slid smoothly open: before her were a great number of paper files all arranged in neat alphabetical order.

'W . . . W . . . W . . .' she murmured as she went through the surnames beginning with the letter *w*. 'Wallace and Wheelan,' she whispered as she double-checked. 'Wood . . . Wilmer . . . Walker . . . Waters . . . ?' Starting to feel hot and shaky, Gloria checked the files beginning with *u* and *v*. 'Maybe they've been put back in the wrong place?' But the files didn't appear to be anywhere in the cabinet. 'They're both missing!' she said out loud, before moving quickly to cover her tracks and hurry out of the room to join Emily who was loitering at the end of the corridor.

'You're never going to believe this,' she gasped, as she and Emily made their way into the main corridor that led away from Matron's office. 'Bertie's and Tom's files aren't there – I couldn't find them.'

Emily stopped dead in her tracks. 'And it doesn't take a genius to guess who removed them, does it?'

Catching Ada on the ward, Gloria repeated her news. Ada's brow creased in dismay. 'Oh, God,' she breathed. 'She would only have gone to the trouble of removing those files for one reason – she took the babies!'

'Thanks to brave little Shirley, we know that Matron took Tom to the Grange on the night he was supposed to have died,' Gloria said darkly.

'If Shirley heard him crying, he couldn't have been dead,' Emily pointed out. 'Who knows if he ever died at all!' she exclaimed.

An angry flush spread across Emily's high cheekbones. 'It's not safe to turn our backs on that evil woman – we don't know what she'll do next!'

Ada's face set hard. 'There's another new baby in Mary Vale.'

With the same terrifying thought in their heads, the three women looked at each other.

'Heather,' Gloria whispered fearfully. 'I checked under Isla's surname, Ross. Her file wasn't there either.'

'Without alarming poor Isla, we've got to watch her baby like a hawk, day and night – we can't risk taking our eyes off the child, not for a minute,' Ada finished grimly.

29. God

When Jeannie arrived one bitterly cold afternoon shortly afterwards, with blustery snow blowing at the windows, she had to fight back tears when she saw her great-grandchild lying fast asleep in her bassinet. Overcome with emotion at seeing her grandmother so moved, Isla threw herself into her arms.

'Oh, Jeannie, it's wonderful to see you,' she sobbed, as all the pain and anxiety of the last few days poured out of her in a torrent of relief.

Jeannie held her close for several minutes before she spoke. 'I all but had a heart attack when I heard you'd gone into labour three weeks early,' she admitted. 'Only you, silly girl, would go striding over the marsh in the middle of a raging storm!'

'Good job we did, though,' Isla reminded Jeannie, who'd heard the full story over the phone from Sister Ada.

'And how is Shirley – and poor Emily?' Jeannie inquired. 'Imagine if you'd both gone into labour out there in the cold!'

'Emily's fine,' Isla laughed. 'You'll see her before you go; she pops down to see Heather at least twice a day.'

'Heather!' Jeannie exclaimed in delight. 'What a lovely name.'

'I named her after you,' Isla said proudly. 'Her full name is Jennifer, like yours, then Heather . . .' Her happy smile faded as she added, 'Though what her adoptive parents will name her, I have no idea.'

Looking at the baby, who had fallen fast asleep, Jeannie had the urge to snatch her up and keep her close, but she knew that was not what Isla wanted; Heather was destined to be adopted in a few weeks' time, and Isla would come home to Windermere for a brief spell before she resumed her university education. Completely changing the subject away from such a painful thought, Jeannie opened the hamper of food she'd brought along with her.

'If you've an appetite, I have three kinds of sandwiches, a ginger cake and some scones.'

'IF I've an appetite!' hungry Isla joked. 'I'm ravenous!'

'You're not eating for two any more,' Jeannie joked, as Isla tucked into the delicious egg-and-cress sandwiches.

Munching appreciatively, Isla took the opportunity to discuss Shirley's potential short-term future with Jeannie.

'She's had a shocking time,' Isla confided. 'And she might need a bolt hole until things settle down.'

Jeannie cocked her head to one side. 'So, I could end up with TWO Mary Vale girls instead of one?' she teased.

Isla gave an apologetic nod. 'If you wouldn't mind?'

'Of course I'll help the poor girl out,' Jeannie answered with her characteristic generosity. 'Now, come on, give me a sandwich before you scoff the lot!'

Surrounded by loving, caring friends, Shirley recovered quickly from her awful ordeal. Though she was absolutely terrified of bumping into Matron, she insisted that she wanted to get back to work in the kitchen, where Matron rarely went, and do some cleaning around the Home too, as long as Matron wasn't around.

'If you're sure?' Ada asked.

'I can't loll around in bed all day when there's work to be done,' Shirley cried. 'Anyway, I've got some serious thinking to do,' she added with a mysterious smile. 'And I always think best when I've got a mop in my hand!'

The fact was, Shirley had something very important to discuss with Sister Ann, something so profound she was almost too scared to talk about it. One evening she slipped out of the kitchen (where she'd been preparing trays of cheese-and-onion pies for the following lunch-time with Sister Mary Paul) and waited in the corridor that connected the convent to the Home for Sister Ann to appear. When she did, Shirley stepped out from the shadows and startled the nun.

'Jesus, Mary and Joseph!' Sister Ann exclaimed clutching her heart. 'You put the fear of God in me, child.'

'Sorry, Sister, I was waiting for you,' Shirley said shyly. If it hadn't been so dark, the nun would have seen that poor Shirley was blushing bright red. 'I have to speak to you about —'

Thinking she knew what was coming next — a plea not to be sent back home — Sister Ann gently laid a hand on Shirley's shoulder. 'We're in the process of sorting things out: try not to worry, dear.'

Terrified that she'd lose her strength and determination, Shirley stopped the nun mid-flow and blurted out in a loud voice that echoed around the cold, dark corridor, 'Sister!' she exclaimed. 'I've decided. I want to be a nun!'

Speechless, Sister Ann gazed in wonder at Shirley, who, now that she'd started talking, was finding it hard to stop. 'I know what you're thinking, I only want to be a nun so

I can stay here and get free bed and board at Mary Vale – well it's not true! I want to join your order – I want to dedicate my life to Christ. I know I'm not suitable, I'm stupid and I'm stained with sin –'

Now it was time for Sister Ann to interrupt Shirley. 'Stop, Shirley,' she said firmly. Taking hold of the girl's hand, she squeezed it hard. 'This might be one of the most important decisions of your life; we need to talk about it clearly and calmly.'

Seeing Shirley's expression fade from happiness to fear, she quickly reassured her. 'Not that I'm doubting you. I'd just prefer to have this conversation in the cold light of day, if that's all right with you, child?'

Shirley nodded, then asked, 'Please, may I come to chapel with you while you say your office?'

'How would you know that's where I'm going now?'

'Because I've been following you every night and I know that's where you go to say your evening prayers,' Shirley shyly admitted. 'Please let me come with you?' she begged. 'It would make a nice change from hiding from you behind the back pew!' she added with a mischievous giggle.

'Of course,' Sister Ann replied.

Arm in arm, they walked past the statue of Our Lady, before which they both stopped to make the sign of the cross, before entering the candle-lit chapel, where they knelt down on a wooden bench and said their night prayers together.

Over the next few days Sister Ann had several long, intense conversations with Shirley, asking her what had prompted her to reach the enormous decision to become a nun. 'You never mentioned it when you lived among us,' she pointed out.

'I never even thought of it!' Shirley said with a laugh. 'I was happy just to be here and clean for you all. I vividly remember thinking how much I loved being among you and the sisters – it felt like family.'

Though it was a joy to see Shirley speak so openly, Sister Ann had to take a hard line; if she was to be the child's spiritual mentor, she had to prepare her for what lay ahead; Shirley could start her postulancy only if she really had a true vocation. No matter how much she loved the girl and rejoiced in her decision, Sister Ann couldn't afford to be soft or sentimental; for Shirley's sake, she had to remain objective and honest, and that meant asking tough and uncomfortable questions.

'I suppose I only really seriously thought about becoming a nun when I was sent back home,' Shirley admitted. 'I was grateful that you'd taught me to pray, Sister,' she said. I prayed a lot in those terrible times. I prayed he'd leave me alone, which he didn't, and I prayed during him, you know, doing it.' She blushed to the roots of her hair to say such crude things to a nun. 'I began to realize that prayer helped me. You'll never believe this, Sister, but it was prayer that led me to thinking about taking my own life.'

'Well, that's a contradiction in terms!' Sister Ann exclaimed.

'I know suicide is a sin in the eyes of the Church, but I thought, like I wrote to you in my letter, that if I was dead, I'd be safe with God in heaven,' Shirley said with such simple, naive conviction that Sister Ann had to turn away to hide her tears. 'Then, when I was lying on the marsh, I stared up at the sky and I swear I saw God in the clouds. I thought He was waiting for me and I was so, *so* happy to go to Him. The last thing I remember before everything went black was holding out my hand and saying, "Take me, please take me home."'

'But God saved you,' Sister Ann reminded Shirley. 'He clearly wanted you to live.'

Shirley's plain face glowed with joy. 'Yes, he saved me because He has a job He wants me to do for Him,' she announced. 'God's given me a lot of gifts – I can read and write, clean and polish, but most important of all, I can *pray*,' she said happily. 'I'm good at praying, Sister,' she said with a modest smile. 'Prayers go round my head like a joyful song night and day.'

Sister Ann, who'd been struggling for the kind of prayer Shirley had so blithely described, couldn't believe she was hearing right; this simple, uneducated girl, who had suffered abuse and ill treatment all her life, was speaking with such clarity and conviction, with a love so palpable – who could doubt her sense of vocation? Concealing a pleasure that edged on awe, Sister Ann told Shirley that her next step was to talk to the Reverend Mother. 'She might take some convincing,' she warned.

'I'll put all my trust in God,' Shirley answered with a confident smile.

30. Latin Lessons

Anxious that her interest in the new arrival might have drawn too much attention, Matron avoided any further visits to Heather and her rude, unsociable mother. However, it was pleasing to see that Isla was a picture of health and would no doubt soon be discharged, leaving charming little Heather in Matron's tender care. Percival was also enthusiastic about the new arrival. Courtesy of the grateful Bennetts, who fawned on their new son (no longer plain Tom but Rupert with a title), they'd provided Percival with two new clients. One of them definitely wanted a son, so Heather was out of the question, but the second couple had stated that the sex of the child was unimportant but good breeding was essential.

'Well,' Percival thought smugly. 'Nobody could fault Baby Ross's breeding; she might have been born on the wrong side of the blanket, but she has good blood running through her veins and she's probably got a fine brain too.'

Telling the eager (and wealthy) childless couple that they might have a little bundle of joy by Christmas, Percival sat back and, like Matron, eagerly awaited Isla's departure.

While Shirley made preparations to start her postulancy, she was under the convent's wing and, though she lived in constant fear of Matron, who gave her looks of sheer malice every time she passed by, Shirley was, to some extent, freer than she'd ever been before. Though nobody asked her to, she still continued devotedly to wash, mop, polish and scrub Mary Vale's floors daily, but she always made sure she had time for her schoolwork, which now, with her heart set on joining the religious order, was more important to her than ever. Robin was ecstatic to have his friend Shirley back in the schoolroom.

'Come and sit here,' he begged tapping the bench next to him.

'We've missed you so much,' Gloria said with genuine warmth.

'It was boring, just me and Mum!' cheeky Robin added.

Gloria gave her irrepressible son a mock-glare before she addressed Shirley. 'So, is there anything special you want to study now that you're back?'

'Bomber planes and submarines,' Robin suggested with a hopeful smile.

'That would be fun,' laughing Shirley agreed. 'But, now that I'm hoping to be a nun, I need to really improve my reading and writing, and maybe you can teach me Latin too?' she asked in all innocence.

Gloria burst out laughing. 'Heavens! You really have got the bit between your teeth!' she exclaimed. 'I can do as much reading and writing as you want but, sadly, Latin's way beyond me, sweetheart,' she admitted.

Robin's green eyes all but fell out of his head when he heard that Shirley wanted to be a nun. 'Are you going to wear a big nightie like Merry Paul?' he asked in amazement.

'Oh, I do hope so, sweetheart, if the convent will have me,' Shirley answered in all sincerity. 'Though I have to prove to the Reverend Mother who's in charge of the convent that I'm good enough and clever enough to be a nun, and it takes years and years; you'll be a teenager by the time I've taken my final vows,' she joked.

Robin's green eyes lit up. 'I'm going to join my dad when I grow up. I'll drive tanks and bomb all the Germans who get in my way,' he announced with a heroic swagger.

Gloria's face clouded at the very thought of her little boy going to war. 'It will all be over with by then,' she said firmly. 'Daddy will be home and England will be at peace.'

'Will you have had the baby by then?' Robin asked.

Gloria and Shirley looked at each other, then fell about laughing.

'Heavens above, I hope so,' Gloria cried. 'Otherwise it will be the longest pregnancy in history!'

Bringing order back to the classroom, Gloria said, 'Are you really serious about becoming a run, Shirley?'

The girl nodded. 'I've never been more serious about anything in mi life.'

'But won't your parents try and put a stop to it?' she persisted. 'After all, you're very young.'

'Sister Ann said that if they try to stop me, the convent can write to the police and tell them what my stepfather did to me. The police won't believe me, of course – they'd never believe a girl like me – but my stepfather still won't like the idea of the police being involved.' Her eyes shot to Robin, who was hanging on her every word. 'That's enough of that for now,' she said briskly. 'Come on, young man!' she added, as she recalled Robin's words from the past. 'Time to start *learning* me!'

*

With Heather's formal adoption form, as well as her file, safely removed from her office to her own private suite, where it was secreted away alongside Bertie's and Tom's files, Matron turned her thoughts to other pressing matters. When Isla and her sharp-tongued grandmother were gone, the path would be clear for her and Percival to proceed, though the return of Shirley niggled Matron, who had thought she'd successfully got rid of the sly little minx. The girl was now apparently intent on becoming a nun, and Matron could only hope that the stupid thing might have forgotten anything she saw the night she stole Tom away. Anyway, Matron comforted herself, if Shirley did decide to talk, who would believe her? Matron had thoroughly covered all her tracks; there was nothing to arouse suspicion; and if the little madam did snivel, she would roundly accuse her of lying and deception.

Emily and Gloria spent as much time as they could spare with Isla, who was kept busy looking after her daughter and who, they knew, they would soon have to say goodbye to. In the privacy of her own room, Emily confessed to Gloria how sad she would be when Isla left Mary Vale.

'She's a marvellous woman,' she told Gloria. 'Clever but not big-headed, educated but not a show-off, funny and honest. I'll miss her so much.'

'I couldn't agree more,' Gloria replied. 'We'll just have to make sure we keep in touch – maybe we could visit her once she's settled back home in Windermere?'

'We'll have to take our cue from her,' Emily said sensitively. 'If she's just getting over parting from Heather, us two bouncing up might bring back painful memories.'

Gloria gave a sigh. 'I suppose so,' she said. 'But I can't bear the thought that we might not see each other again.'

A tap at the door interrupted their conversation. 'May I come in?' Ada called.

'Of course,' Emily said, opening the door to a grinning Ada, who, over the months they'd all been together in the Home, had become more of a friend to them than their ward sister.

'Oh, it's nice to get away from work, even if it is just for five minutes,' Ada cried, as she flopped on the nearest vacant bed, where she kicked off her brogues and removed her starched cap, so that her long hair could hang loose and free. 'So, ladies, come on, tell me your news.'

Emily gave her a big, excited smile. 'I've heard back from George's parents, a Christmas card this time – they want to meet me soon.'

'Wonderful!' Ada cried. 'Any more news of George?'

Emily looked disappointed. 'Nothing new. What with all the talk about the Winter War and the Soviets attacking Finland, I've been worried sick. The trouble is not knowing where George is or where he might be. I worry about every bit of news that comes up: is he fighting the Hun or the Soviets?' she said with a desperateness in her voice. 'I feel so stupid and helpless not knowing.'

Ada quickly moved to restore her friend's spirits. 'At least you've got his parents, Em, that's something. It means you're part of George's family,' she said enthusiastically, as she gratefully accepted the mug of hot tea that Gloria had brewed on the little electric hotplate they kept in their room.

'And I've had news of Stan,' Gloria told Ada. 'Like Em,

'I don't know exactly where he is. He mentioned in his letter that they were desperate for more back-up troops, so I'm guessing that means he's in the thick of it somewhere.'

'Well, now that conscription's covering men from nineteen to forty-one, there are bound to be thousands more troops deployed,' Ada said. 'Though nineteen seems young – thank God my little brother's only eighteen – I couldn't bear to see him go marching off to war.'

'So you do have a young man in your life?' Gloria teased.

'Well, I suppose my brother is a young man,' Ada conceded. 'Though I always think of him as a kid,' she said with an indulgent smile.

'Ada's married to her job,' Emily joked.

Ada looked thoughtful as she sipped her tea. 'I'll have you know I've had boyfriends,' she admitted. 'They've just never come up to scratch.'

'You're a woman with high standards,' Emily laughed.

'I think we've all got high standards when it comes to men,' Gloria murmured. 'I couldn't bear to live with a man who didn't love his country, even though I never stopped nagging poor Stan about being too patriotic. What a cow I was,' she said sorrowfully, recalling their bitter disagreements about Stan joining up.

'Stop scourging yourself, woman!' Emily cried. 'I would have willingly laid down in the road and been reversed over by a tank if it would have stopped George from flying over enemy territory.'

'We're a couple of hypocrites,' Gloria continued. 'We want peace in our time but we'd prefer it if somebody else's fella did the fighting.'

Ada laid aside her empty cup. 'Moving on to an entirely different subject – can you believe Shirley is hoping to become a nun?'

'I don't know why it never crossed her mind before,' Gloria said. 'She's as innocent as the day the world was created.'

Cheeky Em couldn't stop herself from smiling. 'I wonder what name she'll take if she does make it through?'

A mischievous smile played around Ada's full, rosy-red lips. 'Possibly Sister Mopalot!'

'Or Sister Brillo Pad!' Emily laughed. 'Nobody cleans better than our Shirley; she could go straight to heaven on that basis alone.'

31. Jingle Bells

Prior to Shirley's forthcoming interview regarding her entering the religious life, the Reverend Mother had a very blunt conversation about the girl with Sister Ann.

'One of the rules of the convent is that nobody entering the order can have dependent children,' she started.

'As you know Shirley did have a child, a little girl, earlier on this year; she was legally adopted,' Sister Ann explained.

The Reverend Mother came straight to the point. 'And how do we know the poor child's not pregnant again after her recent visit home?'

'Sister Ada examined Shirley on her return to the Home; mercifully, after all that happened to her, she isn't pregnant.'

The Reverend Mother crossed herself, muttering, 'God help the poor child.'

'Indeed,' Sister Ann fervently agreed.

Sticking to the facts, the Reverend Mother moved swiftly on. 'How are Shirley's studies progressing?'

Sister Ann smiled proudly. 'She's grasped her subjects quickly and shows a great eagerness to learn more, even Latin, which she may well struggle with.'

The Reverend Mother smothered a smile. 'I've struggled with Latin all my life, Sister!'

In the schoolroom, blissfully unaware of the conversation that was taking place in the convent, Shirley and Robin were singing Christmas songs in readiness for the service that always took place in the convent chapel on Christmas Eve. Shirley had a remarkably melodic voice: she could sing harmonies and hold high notes, which lent the traditional carols like 'Silent Night' and 'Angels from the Realms of Glory' great beauty; but when it came to the fun songs it was Robin who took the credit. His forte was 'Jingle Bells', reading the words that Gloria had chalked up on the portable blackboard she'd set up in the dining room. He and Shirley belted out the song until the rafters rang.

Delighted by their singing, Sister Mary Paul popped out of the kitchen and stood by the piano so she could applaud them when they finished and hand out the warm jam tarts she'd just taken from the oven.

'To give them a bit o' strength after all their fine efforts,' she said, sending an adoring smile in Robin's direction.

After Robin had gulped down his glass of milk, he dragged Shirley out into the garden to play snowballs.

'Come on,' he yelled. 'We'll build a snowman too!'

Pretending to resist but loving the fun, Shirley – like the child she was at heart – tore after him, yelling, 'Hey, wait for me!'

Watching her go, Sister Mary Paul murmured, 'God love the girl.'

Turning to Gloria, who was sipping the cup of tea the nun had made for her, she added, 'You know, I've been thinking,' she said, going off at a tangent, 'it would be nice to have a Nativity Play on Christmas Eve.'

Robin, who'd just bounded in from the garden with glowing red cheeks and sparkling green eyes, caught Sister Mary Paul mid-sentence.

'What's a Nativity Play?' he asked eagerly.

'It's a play about the birth of the baby Jesus in the stable at Bethlehem,' the nun explained.

Gloria jogged her son's memory. 'We had a Nativity Play at your old school in Battersea – you played the part of the donkey last year.'

Robin's eyes lit up. 'I remember!' he exclaimed.

'Sister Mary Paul would like us to have a Nativity Play here at Mary Vale,' Gloria explained.

'YES!' Robin squeaked. Talking to Shirley, who'd followed him indoors, he continued, 'Shirley can be an angel 'cos she sings like one and Mummy can be Mary 'cos she's got a baby in her tummy!'

'Mine isn't Jesus!' Gloria laughingly protested.

'Glory be to God!' Mary Paul giggled. 'What will the child say next?'

Unperturbed Robin babbled on. 'Sister Ann can be God and Merry Paul can be a camel!'

'I thought the kings and the camel came later,' Mary Paul reminded Robin, who ignored her and rolled on. 'And I'll be Father Christmas' he announced.

'Was Father Christmas in Bethlehem when Jesus was born?' Shirley cheekily asked.

'No,' Gloria giggled. 'But, believe me, that won't stop Robin.'

Taken with the idea of treading the boards for the first time in her life, Sister Mary Paul chuckled. 'Well, I don't mind being the camel, but I think you might have your work cut out persuading Sister Ann to be God!'

*

Isla, who had bounced back to health after her daughter's birth, expressed a wish to Ada that she wanted to leave Mary Vale soon.

'I'd like to spend Christmas in Windermere,' she said. 'Is that very selfish of me?' she asked with a guilty flush.

Ada's bright blue eyes opened wide and she smiled. 'Of course not, dear! As long as you're fit and well enough to leave, I'll discharge you whenever you please.'

'What I mean is . . .' Isla struggled to find the right words to express herself. 'Is it wrong of me to leave Heather at Christmas time?' Tears flooded her eyes and she blurted out, 'I feel if I have her over Christmas, I'll never be able to let her go!'.

Ada laid an arm around Isla's shaking shoulders. 'You have to do what's best for you AND for Heather too,' she said firmly. 'Christmas is a highly emotional time. If you can't deal with that on top of leaving Heather, then it's sensible of you to separate off the two issues.'

'That's exactly what I was thinking,' Isla said with obvious relief. 'I don't want to mix sentiment with love. It's going to be hard enough as it is,' she confessed with a sad, heavy sigh.

'I understand, I really do,' Ada assured her friend and patient.

'I knew you would,' Isla said. 'You are an amazing nurse, Sister Ada – I shall miss you so very much.'

'Well, I hope you'll come and see us,' Ada said cheerfully.

Isla shook her head. 'I don't think so: it would be an agony coming back to Mary Vale and finding Heather gone – best avoided,' she concluded.

'Make sure you tell the girls what your plans are,' Ada

urged. 'They'll miss you something rotten, especially Em. I suspect she'll be lost without you.'

'Em and I bonded almost right away when we first met,' Isla said with great affection. 'But our experience out there on the marsh with Shirley made us closer than ever – she's a great girl!'

When her friends heard that Isla was planning on leaving the Home before Christmas, they were shocked.

'Oh, no!' Emily gasped before she could stop herself. 'I thought you'd be with us at least until after Christmas.'

Isla squeezed her friend's hand. 'I'm sorry, Em. I've just explained to Ada that I simply can't do that, not without bonding even more with Heather.

Pulling herself together for her friend's sake, Emily immediately said, 'Of, course, I understand, Isla. But, God knows, how I'll miss you, sweetheart!'

Later, when Isla was busy elsewhere, Ada called Emily, Shirley, Gloria and Sister Ann into her office.

'Now we know that Isla's leaving,' she started, 'I want us to put our heads together and work out a plan of action that will protect Heather.' Lowering her voice, Ada continued, 'We must not frighten Isla; she mustn't hear us talking like this. She's got a lot on her plate and we don't want to add to it.'

'Nevertheless, she *must* be worried,' Gloria insisted.

'I'm sure she is, but it's our job to convince her that we'll look after her baby in her absence – Isla must leave Mary Vale feeling as confident as she can be, given the circumstances,' Ada insisted.

The women grouped around her nodded in agreement with her sentiments.

'We'll do our best,' Emily promised.

'Once Isla's gone, we've got to focus on Matron – but she mustn't guess what we're up to!' Ada warned.

'Look what happened to me once she got suspicious!' Shirley angrily reminded her friends.

'Gloria and I can tail Matron about the Home, possibly with Shirley's help when she's able?' Emily suggested. 'While you and Sister Ann watch her on the wards and in the hospital area.'

'And somebody needs to monitor her movements around the back of the house and the tradesman's entrance,' Sister Ann chipped in.

'We could ask Sister Mary Paul?' Shirley suggested, 'She's a regular Rottweiler when it comes to protecting her brood,' she giggled.

'So, we have a basic plan?' Ada asked.

Her friends solemnly nodded.

'From the moment Isla leaves the Home, our priority is Heather,' Shirley said.

'And under NO circumstances must Heather ever be left alone with Matron, Dr Jones or Sir Percival,' Ada concluded.

Hearing of Isla's imminent departure, Matron was determined that she should not be the one to remove Heather from the nursery. It had been a nightmare with Tom, and she'd got away with it, but she couldn't pull that trick a second time. She couldn't afford to spirit away another child on the flimsy excuse that the adoptive parents had arrived in the middle of the night; and she couldn't use the death-by-measles excuse again; it would have to be an altogether different scenario, and one that didn't include her. Matron wished they didn't have to do the handover at the Grange, but where else could money, papers and a baby be exchanged? It was too much of a risk to bring the parents to the Home; the business was better conducted in the privacy of the Grange, even if it was nerve-racking.

Matron's nagging problem was solved when, on her daily ward inspection, she spotted Isla fumbling to change Heather's nappy; as she awkwardly tried to balance the baby on her knee, Heather rolled forwards, and if Isla hadn't snatched hold of her, she would most certainly have landed on the floor.

'Take care, Isla,' Matron said, approaching the new mother, who was flushed and shaking. 'That could have resulted in a very nasty accident.'

An eager-to-impress, know-all girl beside Isla who was also changing her baby's nappy said, 'A girl not long ago dropped her baby and the poor little mite broke its arm. Poor kid never stopped bawling.'

Blushing with guilt, Isla mumbled, 'It was an accident.'

'Make sure it doesn't happen again,' Matron said, not unkindly. 'If you feel inadequate about changing Heather, ask Sister Ada to assist you.'

Continuing with her inspection, Matron suddenly realized the solution to her problem was right before her. Heather could be diagnosed with a fracture! It would mean colluding with the doctor again, but it might work. She could lie to Jones (he'd believe anything for a bottle of whisky), tell him that Heather had had a fall and she suspected a possible fracture. He could drive the child to the cottage hospital, apparently for an X-ray, when, in fact, Percival would be waiting for him and Heather in a prearranged place. Heather could be secretly transferred into his car and taken to the Grange. Heather's extended absence from Mary Vale would be explained away by another lie: that her injury needed specialist treatment and she had therefore been transferred to Lancaster Infirmary for an indefinite period – something Matron would instruct Jones to relate to the staff at the appropriate time.

'And the best thing of all about the whole plan is I won't have to set foot out of Mary Vale!' Matron rejoiced.

On the day of her formal interview with the Reverend Mother, poor Shirley was a nervous wreck. It hadn't been a problem to open her heart to Sister Ann, but would she be able to speak so articulately to the Reverend Mother, who might well think she was stupid, tainted, uneducated or, even worse, believe – as Matron did – that she was using the order to secure free board and lodgings.

'Will you be there with me?' she asked Sister Ann, as they sat in the dark, timbered corridor waiting for the wall clock to tick round to 11 a.m., which was the time scheduled for her interview.

Sister Ann nodded. 'The Reverend Mother agreed I could be with you, but this is about you, child, not me. I can't speak of your vocation; it is for you to express that wish and explain your motives as best you can.' Seeing Shirley's small white hands trembling on her lap, the nun gripped them in her own. 'Just be yourself and speak the truth, as you did to me.'

Though the Reverend Mother was kind, she nevertheless grilled Shirley on why she wanted to enter their religious order and why she thought she had a vocation. When Shirley answered her questions with the same clarity and love as she had previously with Sister Ann, it was clear that the Reverend Mother was affected by the girl's innocence and utter sincerity.

Later, over a cup of tea in the sitting room (recently vacated by the highly overexcited Nativity cast rehearsing their play), Sister Ann explained to Shirley what might happen next.

'That went well,' she started. 'Congratulations. I think the Reverend Mother was touched by what you had to say.'

'She did ask a lot of questions!' Shirley exclaimed.

'Quite right too!'

'So what next, Sister?' Shirley asked impatiently. 'When can I become a nun like you?'

Sister Ann smiled at her eagerness. 'Don't get ahead of yourself,' she warned. 'You've a long way to go. If you're accepted, you'll undergo a form of training. This is when you will learn about the life of a nun and our order from the inside. It's a testing time for a new postulant, a period of prayer and introspection, when you decide whether or not you really want to be a nun.'

'I do!' Shirley blurted out.

'I know that, you know that, perhaps God knows it too, but this early part of your postulancy is vital for your spiritual development,' Sister Ann said patiently. 'It's good that you can now read, as there is a lot of wonderful material in the Scriptures that will guide and inform you.'

Sister Ann reached into her capacious pockets and handed Shirley a weathered leather copy of the Bible. 'This was mine,' she said. 'I read it continually throughout my postulancy – the New and the Old Testaments. I'd like you to have it now, child.'

Overcome, Shirley reached out to take the book. 'Will I really be able to read this?' she said, squinting at the tiny print written on delicately fine paper.

'Of course, you're a quick learner – and you have plenty of time,' Sister Ann assured her student. 'I'll help you with any difficult passages and I'm sure Gloria will too.'

'Thank you, Sister,' Shirley murmured emotionally, as she clasped the book. 'I'll treasure it forever,' she promised.

Sister Ann continued, 'Once you're sure you want to become a nun, you'll take temporary vows of chastity, celibacy and obedience. After fulfilling your temporary vows, you'll take your final vows and be ready to lead a totally religious life,' she concluded. 'As I just said, you'll have plenty of time in which to think about this momentous decision.'

Slightly deflated at the thought of a long wait, Shirley groaned. 'Years and years.'

'It's a long and wonderful journey,' Sister Ann said. 'And you might ponder as you pray what work you'd like to do as a novice and as a nun.'

Seeing Shirley looking startled, Sister Ann added, 'For example, I became a midwife.'

Shirley quickly shook her head. 'I could never do that!' she exclaimed, then burst out laughing. 'I'll clean – that's what I'm best at.'

'Shirley, with an education you could teach if you wanted to,' Sister Ann suggested.

Again Shirley shook her head. 'No,' she repeated. 'I'll clean for God!'

*

Though Isla tried hard to prepare herself for leaving her daughter, she struggled; it was clear to all her friends that the poor girl was upset, and, even though she thought she was doing the right thing, it still hurt her to do so. Isla had tried to put a distance between herself and her daughter, but she had inevitably fallen in love with the little girl, who gurgled and burbled in her cot and wriggled with pleasure at the sight of her smiling mother.

As Emily and Gloria helped Isla pack her suitcase, which had been hidden under her bed since her arrival at the Home months ago, Emily cautiously asked, 'Will you come and see us?'

Isla answered her as honestly as she had Ada when the ward sister asked the same question. 'I know it sounds rude, Em, but I think, once I leave here, I will never come back. The thought of returning to Mary Vale and not seeing Heather in the nursery would break my heart.'

Emily nodded; she could completely understand Isla's motives.

'But we must keep in touch,' Gloria insisted. 'We can't pretend none of this ever happened.'

'Maybe you – and your children too – could come and stay with me in Windermere? Jeannie's house is big enough for an army,' Isla suggested. 'Promise you'll come?'

'Promise!' her friends replied.

As Daphne had with Bertie, Isla begged her friends to keep an eye on Heather. 'I know she'll be collected by her adoptive parents soon after I leave, but while she's here in the Home, please will you cuddle her if she cries after I've left?'

Knowing the potential danger Heather might be in

once her mother departed the Home, Isla's friends exchanged a quick conspiratorial look; remembering Ada's words about not alarming poor Isla, they all kept tight-lipped. Fortunately, Isla was too upset to notice their awkward expressions. Unable to hold back her sorrow a minute longer, she fell on to the bed and sobbed her heart out.

'I thought I was going to be all right,' she wept. 'I thought it was all organized. I was sure I was doing the right thing, but the thought of never seeing her again, never smelling her again, never holding her again, just crucifies me.'

Gloria, who couldn't even imagine parting with a beloved child, sat on the bed beside her friend and stroked her silky blonde hair.

'It will get better once you leave her,' she assured Isla. 'These last days have been a torture, but when you're back in Windermere you can start looking to the future.'

A rap at the bedroom door distracted them. 'Come in,' Emily called.

They were all surprised to see Sister Mary Paul standing, looking flustered, in the doorway.

'Sorry to bother you, ladies, but the farmer from Cartmel Farm just down the road has come calling,' she announced. 'He said he found Robin wandering around his stables.'

Jumping guiltily to her feet, Gloria cried, 'ROBIN!'

The last time she'd seen her son he was playing in the garden; checking her watch, she realized with a shock that that had been hours ago. Heavy and lumbering as she was, Gloria tore down the stairs, coming to a breathless halt at the door.

'He's out in the garden with the farmer,' Sister Mary Paul said with a secretive smile.

Gloria hurried into the garden, where, to her amazement, she found Robin, grinning from ear to ear, sitting on a little donkey. The cheery farmer grinned as he affectionately patted the donkey's big bottom.

'Yon lad 'ere ses yer after wanting a donkey for Christmas, is that reet, missis?'

32. The Cottage Hospital

As Emily and Gloria waited rather tensely for Jeannie to arrive to take Isla home, Gloria said, 'Thank God Isla's not leaving Mary Vale on Christmas Eve – what with the play – and now the blinkin' donkey – I don't think I could take one more thing!'

'That boy of yours should be sent to Berlin to deal with Hitler – he'd sort him out in no time!' Emily chuckled.

'I blame Sister Mary Paul for indulging Robin's every whim,' Gloria said fondly. 'It turns out she was the one who introduced him to the farmer – and she's the one that's cleared a shed in the back garden for Big Ears – that's the donkey's name, by the way.'

By this time both women were in convulsions of laughter.

'Are we really going to have a donkey trot into the chapel on Christmas Eve?' Emily said, mopping tears of laughter from her eyes.

'Have you seen Sister Mary Paul's camel outfit?' Gloria giggled. 'Talk about getting the hump!'

Emily clutched her stomach. 'For heaven's sake – stop it!' she begged. 'I shall go into labour if I laugh any more.'

They quickly sobered up when they saw a car pulling into the drive of Mary Vale.

'Oh, God! Jeannie's here already,' Emily gasped.

'We must be brave for Isla's sake,' Gloria whispered urgently.

'Brave is the last thing I feel,' Emily confessed. 'God only knows how Isla's feeling right now, poor kid.'

When Ada saw Jeannie arriving, she hurried to the nursery, where she knew she'd find Isla. Looking down on her sweetly sleeping daughter, who had the faintest shadow of a smile playing at the edges of her lips, Isla was blinking back tears.

'I don't want to leave her,' she blurted out when she saw Ada. 'I never thought I would love her the way I do.'

Ada, who'd seen many a young woman in the same heartbroken state, quickly moved Isla away from the sleeping baby.

'I promise you we'll take the greatest care of her,' she said fervently to the weeping mother, who, after taking one last lingering glance at her baby, fled the nursery in floods of tears.

In the bedroom that she was just about to vacate, Isla hugged Emily and Gloria in turn.

'Goodbye, goodbye,' she cried. 'I could never have got through these last months without you both.'

Also in tears, Emily burst out, 'And how would we have survived without YOU, Isla?'

'We'll keep in touch,' Gloria assured Isla, who was being firmly shepherded out of the bedroom and down the stairs to the front door by Jeannie. 'Goodbye!'

Downstairs, Jeannie whispered to Ada, 'I need to get her away as quickly as possible; otherwise she'll be hysterical all the way home.'

As Isla walked out of Mary Vale, she recalled the moment

of walking in, with Heather safely inside her; now that her baby was born, she no longer had any claim over the daughter she'd grown to love. Taking one last look at the Home, she climbed into the car before she could run back inside to grab her baby – as she so longed to do.

'Drive carefully,' Ada said, quickly slamming the door; then, with a quick wave, Jeannie roared away in a swirl of falling snowflakes.

When Isla had gone, Emily returned to the bedroom she had shared with Isla and also Nancy when she had first arrived at Mary Vale months ago. As she stood in the cold, echoing room, she smiled softly as she recalled Daphne's hooting laughter combined with Nancy's nervous giggles. How she missed them both; but how much more would she miss Isla. They'd been through so much together – not just their pregnancies but the perilous adventure they'd had on the stormy marsh the day they'd saved Shirley's life. She hoped they would remain friends for the rest of their lives, but she realized that keeping her baby would inevitably put a strain on their friendship. If Isla were to see Emily's baby grow up, how could she not make painful comparisons. How could she not think that her Heather would be the same age? Determined to shake morbid thoughts from her mind, Emily walked over to the window, which gave spectacular views of the fells etched out in dark silhouette against the sharp winter light.

'Isla might have left but Heather's still here, and I owe her a duty: I will watch and protect her every minute she's in Mary Vale – this time, I will NOT let an innocent child down,' she vowed.

Thoughtful Ada was concerned that, until the new

arrivals appeared, Emily might start to feel lonely left on her own in the big bedroom, so she suggested that she move closer to Gloria and Robin.

'There's a large single room on the same corridor as Gloria and Robin,' she told Emily, who instantly liked her idea.

By dinner-time she'd moved into the comfortable room and looked a lot more cheerful for it.

'I was beginning to get gloomy,' she confessed.

'You won't be gloomy for long with Robin around,' Gloria chuckled. 'He'll have you on donkey duty before you know it!'

'Actually' – Emily dropped her voice to a conspiratorial whisper, 'Now that Isla's gone, I'm on another kind of duty – I'm keeping an eye on Heather,' she confessed.

Gloria gave her a sideways glance. 'That makes two of us,' she said with a sly smile.

Christmas Eve dawned bright and beautiful. Half the residents of Mary Vale were awakened at dawn by Big Ears braying loudly and continually, until Sister Mary Paul and Robin arrived with his breakfast, after which he was taken into a section of the garden cordoned off exclusively for his use.

'Father Christmas is coming tonight, Merry Paul!' Robin chanted as he literally danced up and down, wild with excitement.

'And Baby Jesus too,' the smiling nun reminded him.

Wide-eyed and suddenly still, Robin asked, 'Will Mummy's baby come tonight with Jesus?'

'Mummy's got a few more weeks to go before her

baby's born,' Sister Mary Paul gently explained. 'Hopefully, no babies will be born at Mary Vale tonight and we can all enjoy ourselves singing carols in the chapel once it goes dark.'

In various parts of the Home, watchful eyes continued to follow Matron's every movement. When she bustled into the nursery with Dr Jones, Ada hovered over Heather like a protective mother hen, while Shirley, as usual mopping the hospital floor, moved in closer to hear what was going on, and Sister Ann pretended to be busy reading notes at the nearby nursing station. The three women, alert for any misdemeanours, were taken aback when Dr Jones (sufficiently prepped by Matron) announced that he'd like to give Heather a full examination.

'Why?' Ada asked.

'I shan't be visiting the Home over the Christmas holidays, unless there's an emergency,' he replied. 'So, if it's not too inconvenient, Sister, I'd be grateful if I can examine the child now. If all is well, I can close her medical file in readiness for her to be collected by her adoptive parents.'

Ada trusted the drunken doctor as far as she could throw him.

'I'd like to attend while you perform the examination,' she said curtly.

After a cursory examination, with Ada breathing down his neck, Dr Jones nervously cleared his throat. 'The child appears to have something wrong with her right arm.'

Completely astonished, Ada protested. 'She was perfectly all right this morning when I fed and changed her.'

'Well, she's not all right now,' Jones said, nodding in

the direction of Heather, who, after his clumsy examination, was howling furiously. Turning to Matron, he said sharply, 'I suspect she's got a fracture.'

Matron rolled her eyes in deep disapproval. 'It doesn't surprise me, Doctor. Some of the girls are quite careless with the new-borns, throwing them around as if they were nothing more than bags of sugar.'

Though Ada bridled at her waspish comment, her thoughts were entirely on the upset baby, who was now sobbing her little heart out. Catching sight of Sister Ann's tense face and Shirley watching wide-eyed with fear, Ada made a move to pick up the baby.

'I think she might need changing,' she said briskly.

'Not so hasty, Sister,' interjected the doctor. 'With your permission, Matron, I'd like to take the child immediately to the cottage hospital for an X-ray.'

Matron put a hand to her face before she gushed, 'Of course, Doctor. We can't leave her in pain all over Christmas.'

Ada's blood boiled; this was exactly what she had vowed would not happen and yet, before her very eyes, Heather was on the point of being removed from Mary Vale, just like the other two babies who'd been in her care. Striding forwards, she said in an over-loud voice, 'NO!'

Astonished, Matron and Dr Jones glared at her.

'Excuse me, Sister!' Matron snapped.

'Are you saying, Sister, that you don't agree with my diagnosis?' Jones queried.

Ada swallowed hard. 'Yes, I am,' she declared. 'I am quite sure Heather doesn't have a fracture and I would prefer it if the child stayed here to be nursed. Sister Ann and I could arrange round-the-clock care, just as Matron did when Tom had measles,' she added pointedly.

Holding her breath, Ada could almost see Matron's hackles rise.

'Well, well, well,' she mocked. 'Rarely in my working life have I seen such a gross display of poor practice.' Turning to Jones, she threw up her arms in a dramatic show of displeasure. 'It would seem, Doctor, that our senior nurse would prefer to see the poor child crying in pain here rather than having specialist treatment for her injury elsewhere.'

Picking up on Matron's tone, Jones shook his head in seeming despair. 'For the child's sake, Matron, you might have to override Sister Dale's determination to keep her under Mary Vale's roof; as you yourself just said, she needs specialist care – and she needs it urgently.'

Wide-eyed with terror, and with every instinct railing against what was unfolding, Ada took a deep breath and tried a softer, humbler approach. 'May I accompany the little girl, please, Dr Jones?'

'Oh, my word, we can't have that,' Matron said, with a phoney, indulgent smile. 'Your services are required here at Mary Vale, Sister Dale.'

'But . . . but . . .' Ada babbled, at which point Heather started to scream her head off.

'Matron,' Jones urged, 'I really must insist that we deal with this child right away.' Closing his doctor's bag with a decisive snap, he added, 'Would you be so kind as to settle her in a travelling cot – make sure she's well wrapped up, it's cold out there,' he warned. 'I'll go and fetch my car – please meet me out front.'

Matron quickly nodded. 'Of course, Doctor,' she replied.

Exchanging a look of panic with Sister Ann, Shirley abandoned her mop and bucket and hurried after Ada and Dr Jones.

'I shan't be long, Sister,' he said to Ada, as he set off down the drive.

Left alone, the two women turned to each other. Shirley was almost hysterical. 'We can't let that man take Heather! We might never see her again!'

Frantic with fear, Ada cast wildly about for an idea. 'How can we stop him?'

Thinking fast before Matron appeared with Heather, Shirley frantically whispered, 'You can drive! Take the gardener's old van – it's out the back. Follow Dr Jones: make sure he goes to the cottage hospital.'

'And what about my shift? Matron will notice if I'm gone – we can't risk it, Shirley.'

'Gloria can drive,' Shirley gabbled. 'She can follow Jones! I'll go and fetch her, and Em too,' she muttered, as she took the stairs two at a time. 'Stall them till I've got back!'

Breathless Shirley burst into Emily's bedroom, where she gasped in relief at the sight of both women with their feet up on their beds. 'Come quickly: Ada needs you, now – Jones is taking Heather!'

When the two wide-eyed girls appeared, Ada furtively pushed the keys to the van into Gloria's hands. 'For God's sake, don't lose sight of him: every nerve in my body is telling me there's something bad going on.'

'I swear we'll not lose her,' Emily said through gritted teeth.

Almost in tears, Ada cried, 'I'm sorry to do this to you both – please stay safe.'

While Ada was issuing instructions to Gloria, Shirley had dashed outside to the car, where she was doing a great job of buying even more time, clucking and fussing. She must have rearranged the bedding in the carry-cot that Matron had placed on the back seat of the car at least three times. Growing irritated, Jones budged her impatiently aside.

'Excuse me!' he barked. 'This is an urgent business. I really do need to get on.'

Hardly able to take in what was happening, Gloria and Emily located the van; then, following Ada's instructions, Gloria drove out of the back gate and on to the path, which, as Ada had said, joined up with the main road, where she could see Jones's car just up ahead.

'Pull your scarf well over your face, Em,' she said nervously.

'Don't get too close,' Emily warned. 'We don't want the old bastard spotting us.'

'I'll try and keep a safe distance between us,' Gloria said, as she changed gears, and they sped on their way following innocent little Heather, who, exhausted by all the commotion, lay fast asleep in her carry-cot on the back seat of Jones's car.

33. Christmas Eve

Emily was surprised at how empty the roads were.

'Where's everybody gone to?'

Tensely watching Jones just up ahead, Gloria muttered distractedly, 'Probably indoors decorating their Christmas trees.'

The sporadic falling snow gave them some cover from Jones's car, which the girls were puzzled to see turning off the main road – long before the turning for the cottage hospital.

'What's he doing?' Gloria cried. 'You can't get to the hospital that way?'

Indicating right too, Gloria followed Jones, who swung on to the verge, where he pulled up. Thinking she'd been spotted, Gloria quickly reversed the van behind a garden wall.

'Bugger!' she swore. 'Has he seen us?'

'Pull back a bit further,' Emily urged. 'I'll sneak out and take a peep.'

Once Gloria was safely parked, Emily struggled out of the car and walked to the end of the wall, from where she peered out. What she saw all but made her blood freeze. Jones was handing the carry-cot to Sir Percival, of all people, who was parked a short distance from the doctor's car in a clearly pre-arranged lonely spot. Terrified, Emily tried to slow her breathing so that she could catch what they were saying.

'Matron said you'd know what to do with her,' she heard Jones mutter as he all but shoved the carry-cot on to the back seat of Percival's Daimler.

'Did anybody follow you?' Percival barked.

'No,' the doctor replied as he hurriedly backed away. 'Nobody.'

Obviously desperate to leave, Jones virtually ran back to his car, which screeched loudly as he drove off at top speed. Percival waited until the doctor had disappeared, then he too drove off, at which point Emily belted back to Gloria, who was already revving the engine of the old van.

Gloria drove on, filled in en route by Emily.

'Are you all right, sweetheart?' Gloria inquired when she heard Emily give a sharp gasp.

'Yes, yes, I'm fine, just a stitch in my side,' Emily replied. 'Shouldn't be running around at this stage in my pregnancy,' she said with a feeble smile.

The country road was narrow and circuitous but at least it went only in one direction; the signposts all read GRANGE and CARTMEL, which baffled Gloria. 'We're heading back to where we came from,' she muttered.

About a mile later, as the countryside became more familiar and they recognized some of the landmarks, the penny dropped. 'Percival's heading back home,' Gloria cried. 'He's taking Heather to Crow Thorn Grange!'

Knowing that it would be too dangerous to follow Percival up the drive, Gloria parked Ada's car behind some thick rhododendron bushes near the imposing metal gates of the Grange.

'Stay here – I'll creep up to the house and see what's going on.'

'No!' Emily protested. 'You can't go on your own. I'm coming with you.'

'Em, you're exhausted; it's my turn now,' Gloria pointed out. 'Watch out for anybody leaving – you'll be safe – the van's tucked well out of sight.'

Before Emily could argue, Gloria set off through the undergrowth, leaving her friend peering out of the car window.

'For God's sake, be careful,' Emily called softly after her.

Back at Mary Vale, Matron could not have been more pleased with herself. She had remained there the entire day; she'd even been there when the Christmas tree, still covered in a pretty frosting of sparkling snow, had been delivered by the beaming farmer who owned Big Ears. Nobody could accuse her of ill practice this time, she thought smugly. Heather's departure was seemingly nothing to do with her or her judgement. When Jones phoned to say, in a muffled, somewhat drunken whisper, that the handover was complete, Matron immediately put the phone down on the old fool; he'd done what was required of him and he was of no further use to her.

Throughout the day Matron's thoughts constantly drifted to Crow Thorn Grange. Would Olive, who'd been recalled for the task, handle Heather with kid gloves as instructed? Were the adoptive parents still due to arrive on Christmas Eve, as planned? If they did manage the journey on the snowy roads, she hoped that Percival would be sure to take the full payment from them. He was turning out to be such a blundering fool – so disappointing in a man of his status. Noisy laughter and a sense of heightening festive excitement provided a timely diversion from Heather's sudden departure; though nobody could fail to notice how upset Sister Dale was. She'd put her foot down good and proper, Matron recalled – for a moment she'd actually thought that she would seize the baby and bolt – but Matron's timely professional chastisement had soon put an end to any silly ideas she might have had, Matron thought smugly.

On the ward, Sister Ann and Ada were taking it in turns to comfort and reassure one another.

'The tension of waiting is bringing on a headache,' Sister Ann confessed.

'I'm worried sick there might not be enough petrol in the van,' Ada admitted. 'Imagine if it broke down in the middle of nowhere and Jones got clean away with Heather.'

Agitated Shirley came scooting by with Robin. 'Any news?' she asked in a nervous whisper.

'Nothing so far,' Ada quickly told her.

Looking anxious, Shirley was dragged away by Robin to clip streamers on to the tree that stood in pride of place in the hallway.

'We need an angel to go on top,' the child called out.

Sister Ann smiled indulgently at the little boy, who had successfully wound his way around everybody's heart. 'I hope his mother's back soon,' she fretted. 'The last thing we want is Robin making a fuss and drawing attention to Gloria's absence.'

Robin's mother, at that precise moment, was creeping up the snowy driveway that led to the Grange. Her bulky tummy made it virtually impossible for her to bend over from the waist, but, if she skirted the edge of the drive, there were enough sturdy trees and rhododendron bushes to hide her presence. When she reached the front of the house, she was surprised to find the Daimler wasn't parked up there; studying the tracks in the snow, she realized Percival must have driven his car round to the back of the house. Still avoiding the open drive, she made her way around the bushes to the back of the Grange, where she stopped dead when she heard voices close by. Dropping on to her haunches, she strained her ears to listen in on a conversation that was taking place not twenty feet away from her.

'Here's the child; you'd better take good care of her,' he snarled. 'No slip-ups, like before.'

'That were now't to do with me,' Olive snarled back.

Recognizing the familiar whining voice talking with Percival, Gloria peered out through the snowy leaves, from where she got a brief glimpse of Olive. Gasping in shock, she ducked back down again. Her blood froze when she heard what Olive said next.

'It weren't my bloody fault that Bertie went and died!' she snapped. 'That were Matron's fault for taking the poor kid out of the 'ome in't first place.'

As the pair bickered on the doorstep, Gloria's head spun as pieces of the puzzle fell into place. Bertie had been stolen from Mary Vale and removed to the Grange, where – Gloria had just heard with her own ears – the poor little boy had died. So what had happened to Baby Tom after he'd been removed from the Home? Had he ended up at the Grange, and had he died too?

'Oh God,' Gloria groaned in terror. 'What're they planning to do with Heather?'

Trying to suppress the hysteria that was rising up in her like a hot wave of fear, Gloria headed carefully back down the drive in the fading light; if it hadn't been for the brilliant white snow guiding her, she might have stumbled and fallen but, luckily, she made it back to the car with only a few scratches to her face caused by overhanging brambles. Relieved to see Emily safely in the passenger seat, Gloria hurried to open the door. When she saw Emily's strained white face, she froze. 'Em! What's wrong? What's happened?'

Emily clutched Gloria's hand. 'My waters have broken,' she gasped in fear.

Without a second thought, Gloria jumped into the driver's seat and switched on the ignition.

'NO! NO!' Emily cried. 'We can't leave – we've got to rescue Heather!'

Ignoring her protests, Gloria reversed the car, then set off as fast as she could for Mary Vale.

'Gloria!' Emily implored. 'We can't leave Heather – please go back,' she begged as she started to cry.

Pressing hard on the accelerator, Gloria drove as fast as she dared in the falling snow.

'Don't you worry, I'll go back for Heather – but only after I've dropped you off at Mary Vale. I need to think about what to do.'

Events were in full swing at Mary Vale. Though Robin had shed a few tears when his mummy failed to turn up to dress the tree, he was quickly distracted by clever Shirley, who said that Big Ears needed a good grooming in readiness for the evening play. Shirley, Sister Ann and

Ada had only one thought in their minds throughout the afternoon, constantly checking the driveway and praying for Heather's safe return. Shirley, fearful that Gloria might not arrive back in time for the play and thereby cause Robin to have a tantrum, suggested to the edgy little boy that she could play the part of Mary, which outraged Robin.

'You can't be Mary!' he loudly protested. 'You haven't got a baby in your tummy!'

Grabbing at straws, Shirley said, 'I know, but your mummy's a bit too big and heavy to ride a donkey in the dark; she might fall off Big Ears and hurt herself!'

Robin gave her a long, sad look. 'I wish Mummy was here.'

Frantic Shirley completely agreed with his sentiments. 'Me too, sweetheart,' she said, hugging the disappointed child. 'Me too.'

Driving back to Mary Vale, Gloria didn't care who saw her arrive. Em needed help: that's all she could think of. Screeching to a halt by the front door, she cried out to Ada, who'd come running to open it.

'Em's in labour.'

Ada's heart went out to poor Emily, sweating and exhausted in the passenger seat. Reaching out to take her hand, she said softly, 'Come on, lovie, let's get you indoors.'

Yet Emily hung back, incensed beyond words. 'Tell them what you saw,' she cried to Gloria.

'It was all a con,' Gloria explained, as she hurried after Ada, who was supporting Emily. 'Jones had no intention of going to the cottage hospital; we saw him meet up with

Sir Percival just after he left here. Percival left Heather with Olive at the Grange. Jones is just the go-between.'

As if winded, Ada gasped in terror. 'What in God's name are Matron and Percival up to?'

Frantic with fear, and terrified of wasting precious time, Gloria blurted out, 'I heard Olive telling Sir Percival that it wasn't her fault that Bertie died.'

Ada paled and swayed on her feet. 'Bertie *died*!' she cried incredulously.

Desperate Gloria hurried on. 'We've got to get Heather out of there before she disappears, just like Tom and Bertie did. I'm going back to the Grange, no matter what you say.'

Though utterly exhausted, Emily grabbed Ada's hand. 'Don't let her go alone,' she beseeched. 'It's too dangerous.'

Seeing the pain in her patient's face, Ada moved swiftly. 'Let's get you settled on the ward and concentrate on that baby of yours, eh?'

Emily gratefully leant on Ada, who led her slowly down the corridor to the ward, where Sister Ann swiftly took the situation in hand.

'You look worn out, lovie,' she said gently. 'I need to get you out of those clothes and into bed.'

Before she disappeared behind the curtains that she was drawing around the bed, Ada quickly whispered, 'Can I leave you to manage for a few hours, Sister?'

'We're fine, Ada, off you go – God go with you,' she said with tears in her eyes.

Ada gave her a brief smile before she dashed back to Gloria, who was pacing the hallway.

'Em's right, Gloria, you've done more than enough, I'll take over from here.'

'NO!' Gloria loudly protested. 'I'd wear myself out if I stayed here worrying about you up there on your own – please let me come with you. I promise I won't do any more dashing about. Please . . . ?'

Seeing the steely determination in her friend's dark eyes, Ada sighed. 'You could finish up in the bed next to Emily if you carry on at this rate,' she said wearily.

'We can't stand here arguing when Heather's life is in danger,' Gloria cut in impatiently.

Grabbing her cape, Ada said resignedly, 'On your own head be it.'

34. Sanctuary

Fortunately, Gloria had had the foresight to grab a towel before she left the Home, and she laid it over the passenger seat, still damp from when Emily's waters had broken earlier on. Utterly weary yet wound up as tight as a clock spring, Gloria thought wryly to herself, 'Christmas Eve, the day Robin's been counting down to for weeks.'

'How many more days, Mummy?' he'd been asking as soon as he woke up every morning and she would laughingly reply, 'Ten, nine, eight, seven, six, five, four, three, two, one.'

Now here she was, the day before Christmas, on a rescue mission to save Isla's baby from what? Who knew? Only Matron and Percival knew the truth. Thinking about Isla made Gloria's insides flip; Isla, in Windermere, was oblivious to what was going on just over the fells from her. She hadn't a clue that her baby had been kidnapped and was being cared for by Olive, of all people, in an old rambling house on the edge of the dark moors. Ada dropped down a gear in order to ascend the bumpy and uneven fell-side road, which caused Gloria to support her swaying tummy with her hands.

Incandescent with anger, Ada seethed as she drove. 'How could they do that to Heather? Putting an innocent baby's life at risk; driving her around the countryside in the freezing cold, poor lamb. I NEVER did trust Matron!'

Ada raged. 'When Bertie and Tom disappeared, her excuses were too glib, too damn well rehearsed. Oh, Tom's got measles!' She copied Matron's imperious tone of voice perfectly. 'RUBBISH!' she cried. 'And only this morning some nonsense about Heather having a suspected fracture! And those wicked lies about Tom dying, when all the time he was up at the Grange!'

Though Gloria agreed with furious Ada's sentiments, her thoughts were elsewhere; worried sick about the friend she'd just left behind in labour, she blurted out, 'I feel so sorry for poor Em! Do you think she'll be all right?'

Ada shook her head in disbelief. 'It's no wonder her waters broke after all this drama. There's something about you mad Mary Vale girls,' she mused. 'Isla goes into labour three weeks early on the marsh rescuing Shirley, Emily's waters break while she's dashing about in the snow trying to rescue Heather – I just hope you're not going to go haring off and give birth in a bush! Far too impetuous, the lot of you,' Ada chided with a fond smile.

'Listen to you!' Gloria exclaimed. 'Driving through a dark, snowy night on a dangerous mission to rescue an innocent child.'

As the gloomy outline of Crow Thorn Grange loomed up, Gloria grew nervous. 'So what's the plan?'

'You stay in the car and I'll do the talking,' Ada said firmly. 'I'm hoping that when Olive lays eyes on me, I'll come over as official in my cape and uniform.'

Gloria couldn't argue with Ada's logic; even in the dark, she looked commanding in her ward sister's starched white cap and uniform with a dark navy-blue cape thrown over her shoulders to keep out the chill.

'You look like you could move tanks across Northern Europe,' she answered confidently.

'I just hope Olive thinks so too,' Ada replied, as she negotiated the drive to the Grange.

'How are you going to persuade her to hand over Heather? What will you say?' Gloria asked anxiously.

'I've been thinking just that too,' Ada admitted. 'I could say Percival sent me to pick up the baby.'

Gloria gave a brief nod. 'Good idea: that might work . . . either Matron or Percival.'

Keeping the car lights dimmed, Ada followed Gloria's instructions and drove slowly round to the back of the building, where she pulled up under a line of trees and quickly switched off the ignition. Straightening her shoulders, she stepped out of the vehicle.

'Wish me luck,' she whispered, as she strode boldly up to the back door, which was starkly illuminated by an electric light that shone down on to her as she rapped loudly against the door. When she got no reply, she rapped again but still got no response. Not in the mood for being ignored, Ada banged the door hard with the flat of her palm.

'I'll stay all night if I have to,' she muttered furiously.

Eventually, the door slowly swung open and Olive appeared, her scowling face falling in surprise when she saw who it was.

'You! Bloody Sister Dale, eh?'

Ada gave a haughty nod. 'How are you, Olive?'

'All the better for not being up the bleedin' duff,' Olive cackled. 'What the 'ell do you want here?' she quickly added.

All that Ada wanted was to get her hands on baby

Heather. Speaking with a supreme confidence she didn't feel, she squared her shoulders. 'Heather, of course. Percival sent me to collect her from you, as Matron is tied up.'

Olive's pinched little face contorted into an expression of contempt. 'That owd cow!' she sneered.

Ada quickly played her second card, just as Gloria had suggested. 'Sir Percival wants the baby right away.'

Olive threw her a nasty suspicious look. 'He never said anyfink to me about a bleedin' nurse,' she growled. 'All he told me was some posh folks from down South are coming up here to take the kid away with them.'

Though her mind was reeling at what she'd just heard, Ada appeared to smile patiently. 'Exactly,' she said smoothly. 'Which is why I'm here to take Heather to them.'

Olive shuffled uneasily. 'I'm not sure . . .'

Ada gave a dramatic shudder. 'I'll catch my death if I stand here much longer. Don't worry,' she added in an unconcerned voice, 'I'll go and fetch Sir Percival himself; I'm sure he won't mind coming out in this foul weather.'

Olive looked scared. 'I 'ate that bastard!' she exclaimed. 'Treats me like dirt.' Olive's next words surprised Ada. 'At least you treat me with respect,' she said. 'Wait there, I'll fetch the kid for you.'

Hardly daring to believe she'd heard right, Ada glanced nervously around; what if Percival were to appear now? He'd catch her red-handed.

'Hurry up, please, God, make her hurry up,' she prayed under her breath.

When Olive reappeared bearing the carry-cot containing a sleeping Heather, Ada had to control an overwhelming urge to grab the baby and run.

'I've just fed and changed her,' Olive informed Ada. 'She should sleep for a good few hours now.'

'Thank you very much, Olive,' Ada said in all sincerity, and, trying to control her heightening nerves, she quickly mumbled her goodbyes.

Seeing Ada approaching the car gripping the carry-cot, Gloria ducked down as far as she could in order to avoid being seen by Olive, who stood uncertainly on the door-step for a few seconds before going back inside.

'You got her!' Gloria whispered triumphantly, as Ada laid the carry-cot on the back seat of her car, then quickly climbed into the driver's seat.

'Christ! That was the most terrifying thing I've ever done,' she muttered faintly, as she started up the ignition.

Gloria turned to look at Heather sweetly sleeping in the carry-cot on the back seat. 'Thank God – she's safe!'

Desperate to get away, Ada struggled with the gear stick. 'I'm afraid to go back the way we came,' she admitted.

'There must be a back road out of here,' Gloria suggested.

When she switched on the headlights, Ada was able to make out an open farm gate that led on to a farm track; driving slowly to avoid the hedges that overhung the lane, Ada gathered speed as the track widened into a road, where she put her foot down and drove as if the devil himself were on her tail. Concentrating hard on her driving, she was also trying to formulate a plan. 'It's not safe to take Heather to Mary Vale,' she told Gloria, who'd been thinking exactly the same thing.

'Matron's there, and Percival might well turn up with some cock-and-bull story and reclaim Heather,' Gloria fretted.

'Over my dead bloody body!' Ada exclaimed through gritted teeth. 'They'll have to kill me first!'

Seeing car lights looming up behind them, both women started to sweat in terror – could it be Percival trailing them through the night, intent on snatching Heather back from them?

Gloria reached over and laid a protective hand on Heather's carry-cot. 'You're safe with us, sweetheart,' she whispered into the inky darkness.

They both gasped in relief when the car behind hooted, then, revving loudly, overtook them and roared on its way. Once she'd stopped trembling with fear, Gloria breathlessly picked up where they'd left off.

'So, *where* can we take Heather?'

Ada was quiet for a minute, thinking, and then pushed her foot down on the accelerator. 'I don't know why I never thought of it before – it's so obvious. There's no safer place than the convent – that's where we'll take Heather!' she said triumphantly. 'Everybody's there for the Nativity anyway; you never know, if our luck continues, we might catch the end of it!'

Draped in Gloria's blue cloak, Shirley was carried into the chapel on Big Ear's broad back; Robin, dressed as Joseph in a number of colourful tea towels (all donated by Sister Mary Paul), firmly held on to the reins as he led the donkey down the aisle to the sweet singing of 'O Little Town of Bethlehem'. Shirley might have enjoyed the experience a lot more if Robin hadn't had a mighty tantrum just before the Nativity Play started. Completely at the end of his tether, the little boy, who'd waited so long for his mother's return, stamped his feet and mutinied just as they were about to enter the chapel, where the nuns, local residents and girls from the Home were all eagerly assembled.

'I can't be Joseph if Mummy's not here,' Robin bawled.

Having heard from Sister Ann that Emily was home and in labour, Shirley had a brainwave.

'Mummy can't be here right now because she's helping Aunty Emily have her baby,' she whispered to Robin, who instantly stopped crying.

In an awe-filled tone, Robin whispered back, 'Is Aunty Emily giving birth to Jesus?'

Shirley shook her head and smiled. 'No, but she's giving birth to a nice baby who needs your mummy's help.'

Happy with this explanation, Robin took up Big Ear's reins and finally did as they'd rehearsed a dozen times during the week: he walked down the aisle to the altar and helped Shirley (with a tummy as flat as an ironing board) to dismount so she could apparently give birth off-stage, in the stable at Bethlehem. Everybody, especially ecstatic Robin, cried out in wonder and delight when, moments later, 'Mary' reappeared on stage with a baby in her arms. But 'Mary' looked rather different – for the part was now being played by Gloria, with baby Heather playing the starring role of Jesus. Ada had, in fact, without even knowing it, timed their arrival to perfection; entering the convent via the chapel, Gloria and Heather were just in time to be the stars of the show.

'MUMMY!' Robin cried.

'HEATHER!' Shirley gasped.

While still cradling Heather, Gloria pressed a finger to

her lips and, in what looked like a well-rehearsed, stage-managed direction, Shirley draped the blue cloak around Gloria's shoulders, after which Gloria settled on the nearest hay bale with Joseph proudly standing guard at her side. As the choir sang 'Away in a Manger', Sister Mary Paul waddled in as the camel. Nearing the altar, she said in an over-loud theatrical whisper, 'Sister Ann sends her apologies – she can't play God tonight as she's otherwise engaged in the delivery suite!'

Smiling down at Heather, who had woken up and gurgled when the singing began, Gloria held the baby close to her breast; Isla's wonderful little girl was safe – the Church had given her sanctuary.

Having safely deposited Gloria and Heather in the chapel and returned the van to the yard, Ada ran into Mary Vale, which was virtually empty: apart from the girls on duty rota, all the other residents were at chapel enjoying the Nativity Play. Hurrying through the quiet wards, she made for the delivery room, where she found Sister Ann busy with Emily, who was groaning loudly. Quickly removing her cape, Ada washed her hands before joining the nun at the bedside.

Seeing Emily's tense expression, Ada was quick to re-assure the patient. 'Heather's safe – she's in the chapel with Gloria.'

'Oh, thank God!' Emily exclaimed.

'Get yourself over there, Sister,' Ada added with a smile.

'As I'm supposed to be playing God, I'd better not let the team down,' Sister Ann joked, hurrying away. 'I'll leave you in Ada's competent hands, Emily, dear,' she called over her shoulder.

When the next contraction came, Emily gripped Ada's hand and held it tightly. 'I never thought it would be this hard,' she groaned.

Ada, who'd had a chance to glance at Emily's notes, reassured her brave patient. 'You're doing beautifully, Em,' she said softly, stroking her hand. 'George would be so proud of you.'

Emily gave her a grateful smile, which quickly gave way to a gasp of pain. Emily's fingers cut into Ada's flesh. Grunting like an animal, and in the space of just an hour or two, she was ready to push.

'AAAARRRGGGHHHH!!' she cried, pushing so hard she thought she'd explode with the effort.

'The head's crowned,' Ada cried, and, within moments and just a few more contractions, the baby slithered into her waiting hands. 'Emily, you have a son,' she said. 'A perfect little boy.'

After cutting the cord and gently cleaning the baby, Ada laid him in his mother's arms.

'My baby,' Emily said, as tears coursed down her tired but radiantly happy face. 'George's son!' she whispered, kissing the top of his warm head, then all of his fingers and toes. 'My beautiful son.'

35. Christmas Day

Barely an hour after Ada had fled with Heather, Percival came knocking on the back door of the Grange, which was opened almost immediately by a yawning Olive, who could smell the whisky on his breath immediately.

'The people we were expecting have been delayed by the bad weather, so you'll have to take care of the child for a while longer,' he told her curtly.

Confused by all the recent activities, Olive said sharply, 'What yer talkin' about? The bloody kid's already gone. And anyway, I'll have you know I'm not working 'ere on Christmas Day.'

Percival was stunned for a second before literally appearing to sway before her eyes. 'Gone? Gone where?'

'The sister from Mary Vale took her not long ago.'

As the horrifying reality of her words sank in, the blood drained from Percival's face.

'You mean Matron?' he asked, hoping all his instincts were wrong.

'Not 'er. T'other one, Sister Ada,' Olive said with a grumpy shrug. 'She said you'd sent her round to fetch the baby for't posh folks who'd arrived.'

Any colour that was left in Percival's face fled. 'Where did she go? How long ago was this?' he asked urgently. Thinking if he stayed one minute longer he would throttle the stupid woman with his bare hands, he snarled, 'I swear you'll pay for this, you senseless bloody bitch!'

Getting nothing more out of Olive, he ran back like a madman through the snow to his study, where he grabbed the phone and, with trembling hands, dialled Matron's number. In her office, where she'd spent most of the evening pretending to be catching up on her paperwork but in reality desperately waiting to hear from Percival, Matron jumped when her telephone shrilled out.

Not bothering with any preamble, Percival broke the news.

Clutching the phone like a life-line, Matron simply couldn't believe she was hearing correctly.

'Taken where? By whom?'

'One of your damned nurses! A sister,' he snarled. 'The idiot girl you left in charge told me. She just handed the child over to her.' His voice wavered as he began to sob. 'Christ, oh, Christ! Where is she? Who's the wretched nurse who took her?'

Matron didn't need to think twice: there was only one woman in Mary Vale who had the determination to pull off such an audacious trick – and that was Ward Sister Ada Dale!

'Leave it with me – I'll find her.'

On the maternity ward, Emily lay in bed with her son sleeping peacefully in her arms. Overwhelmed with love and the sheer wonder of childbirth, she gazed adoringly at her baby's teeny, pearly fingernails, at the swoop of his delicate, dark eyebrows which already reminded her of George, and his silky thatch of dark hair which she gently stroked as she nuzzled his soft, warm cheek.

'It's like a miracle,' she told Gloria when she came to visit after the play had finished and Robin had finally gone to bed. 'I know you've experienced childbirth,' she added. 'But I never imagined I would ever feel such emotion and such a fierce, protective love.'

Gloria smiled and nodded. 'Childbirth brings out the lioness in all of us,' she agreed. 'Have you got a name for him yet?'

'He was born an hour into Christmas Day,' Emily replied. 'So I thought I might call him Noel – Noel George Holden,' she said proudly.

'That's a fine name!' Gloria exclaimed. 'Wait until his daddy sees him.'

Emily's wide blue eyes filled up with tears. 'Oh, Gloria, I'm aching to see George,' she sighed. 'Holding his son makes me miss him more than ever.'

Gloria was determined not to let Emily dwell on sad thoughts. 'Hopefully, you'll be able to show George's parents their beautiful grandson very soon,' she soothed.

'I'd like that,' Emily answered shyly. 'But I'm scared they'll disapprove of him – you know, being born out of wedlock.'

'Nobody could ever disapprove of a baby as beautiful as little Noel,' Gloria answered staunchly.

'You and Ada did so well, Gloria,' Emily congratulated her brave friend. 'If I hadn't been in labour, I'd surely have come with you.'

'You were definitely better off here, sweetheart,' Gloria teased. 'Ada was incredible: just strode up bold as brass and told Olive she needed to take Heather urgently. I thought I'd faint with fear,' she admitted with a grin.

'Can you imagine Olive handing Heather over just like that?' Emily exclaimed. 'I would've sworn she'd pick a fight.'

'When Ada's in professional mode, she's a tour de force,' Gloria said proudly.

Emily looked anxious. 'Now what, I wonder?'

'Heather's definitely not coming back into the Home.' Gloria dropped her voice to a whisper. 'Ada's staying with her at the convent until we can think of a better plan.'

'Thank God!' Emily whispered back. 'The further away Heather is from Matron, the better!'

Exhausted but happy, Gloria crept back to her bedroom, where Robin, worn out by an exciting day, lay fast asleep in his bed. After changing into her warm winceyette nightie, Gloria filled his stocking, which was hanging on the end of his bed with little treats: some walnuts, an apple, a small bar of chocolate, a tin soldier and some glass marbles. Yawning, she lay down beside her son and reflected on the day with all its fears and triumphs. Heather was safe; Emily had a son; and today was Christmas Day.

'Peace on earth and good will to all men,' she whispered, thinking sadly of those at the Front, fighting for their families; she prayed for their safety in the country they were battling to defend. 'Goodnight, my darling Stan,' she murmured into her pillow. 'Merry Christmas, my love.'

Ada knew that once Olive spoke to Percival or to Matron, they would be on her tail and would do everything in their power to track her and the baby down. Even though it was late and she was emotionally exhausted, Ada had to speak urgently to the Reverend Mother, who needed to be made aware of the grim events that had taken place under her own roof. After she'd related everything she knew about Percival's and Matron's actions, both at the Home and the Grange, culminating in the abduction of Heather, the Reverend Mother's dark eyes blazed with righteous anger.

'We'll make sure Matron gains no entry here,' she announced. 'After what that woman has put the Home and this convent through, I'm delighted to be in a position to protect you and the baby!' she informed Ada, who, after a long and stressful day, almost burst into tears.

Grateful as she was for the Reverend Mother's assurance, Ada knew in her bones that nothing would deter Matron from her plans, not even an order of nuns! For Heather's safety, she had to get her as far away from Mary Vale as possible.

In a bedroom allocated to her, Ada settled Heather in her carry-cot on the bed and, with Shirley standing guard, she and Sister Ann made a plan while they boiled up cocoa in the tiny kitchen just along the corridor. Too tired to be bothered with explanations, Ada came straight to the point.

'I'm taking Heather to Isla in Windermere,' she announced.

Sister Ann almost dropped the mug she was holding. 'But you've just got her here – why move her again?'

'With Matron on the prowl, Heather might be at risk even in the sanctuary of the convent!' Ada exclaimed. 'Ann, I know from what Olive let slip that Heather was on the point of being adopted by parents none of us knew about.'

The nun's trembling hands flew to her mouth as Ada continued.

'Percival and Matron are running some shady under-hand business up at the Grange – why else would they be stealing babies out of the Home?' Shaking her head, Ada added, 'They're not going to give Heather up without a fight, I know that in my bones.'

Sister Ann crossed herself. 'God forgive them for their evil ways,' she murmured, then added urgently, 'You should set off for Windermere in the car as soon as it's light.'

'There's a chance the roads might be blocked,' Ada pointed out.

'I should have thought of that!' Sister Ann exclaimed.

Ada stared out of the window at the dark, stormy sky. 'I'll walk over the fells to Windermere if necessary,' she said determinedly.

'WALK!' Sister Ann spluttered in horror. 'Are you out of your mind, Ada?'

'I've done that walk over to Windermere so many times I could do it in my sleep,' she assured her anxious friend.

'That's as maybe! But NOT in the snow with a baby!'

'Really, Sister, it's not that far – once you're over the tops you can even see Windermere,' Ada said confidently.

'But it will be freezing!'

'I'll wrap Heather up in blankets, tuck her into a sling and keep her warm under my coat.' Ada grinned as she added, 'One thing I'm sure of: Matron certainly won't come chasing up the fells after me.'

Sister Ann wasn't amused. 'Ada, this is not a laughing matter.'

'Let's see what tomorrow brings,' Ada said, draining her mug.

'Will you be able to manage without me? I can't promise when I'll be back.'

'We'll manage; we have no choice. Heather comes first, and if somebody goes into labour, I'll drag Shirley into the delivery room to help me!' the nun replied.

'Merry Christmas, sweetest friend,' Ada said, leaning over to kiss Sister Ann on the cheek.

'God bless,' the nun replied as she gave Ada a hug in return.

Though Matron searched Mary Vale, she found no sign of her ward sister and, mysteriously, nobody seemed to know where she was.

Furious and frustrated, she had to wait for morning to dawn, then she hurried to the maternity ward, where she found Sister Ann and Shirley organizing the feeding rota with her team of helpers. Shirley scurried into the sluice room the minute she saw Matron approaching, but Sister Ann went calmly about her business.

'Morning, Matron, Merry Christmas to you,' she said with a sweet smile that hid the contempt she felt for the conniving woman standing before her.

Ignoring the festive greetings, Matron looked around. 'I need to speak to Sister Dale – where is she?'

Sister Ann took a deep breath. 'God forgive me for telling fibs on Christmas morning,' she thought before replying. 'On leave, Matron.' Glancing at her fob watch, she cringed as she told another bare-faced lie. 'I think I'm correct in thinking she'll be well on her way to Sheffield by now.'

Matron spun around so that the nun wouldn't see the

fury in her face; the wretched girl could be well on her way to Timbuctoo for all she knew, but one thing Matron knew: wherever Ada Dale was, Heather would be close beside her. Walking purposefully back to her office, Matron wondered how far away Ada could be. With the snow falling the way it had been, she could still be in the vicinity, in which case there was still a chance of reclaiming Heather. Beginning to lose her nerve, she paced back and forth nervously across her office floor.

'What happens if we're reported? Olive would yap to anybody for the price of a drink,' she thought to herself. 'Maybe I should slip away too and leave Sir Percival to face the music on his own? After all, it's due to his repeated incompetence that we're in this mess.'

But it was exactly his incompetence that made her stay. She knew she could never trust him to deal with the problem on his own; whether she liked it or not, she had to stay.

As Ada had predicted, the roads were blocked and the telephone wires were down.

'Be a love,' Ada asked Shirley, who'd stayed by Heather's side all night long and was due to join Sister Ann on the ward. 'Pop down to my office and look out my admin file on Isla; I needed Jeannie's address in Windermere. Here's the key to the filing cabinet,' she said, handing it over. 'And, while you're down there, Shirley, can you pick up a warm layette from the nursery, and a couple of blankets too?' she quickly added.

Shirley gave her a worried look. 'What're you up to, Ada?'

'I'm taking Heather home to Windermere – I'm walking there.'

Shirley's jaw dropped. 'You're mad!'

'Please don't you start,' Ada pleaded. 'I've had enough nagging. I can't sit around here – it's not safe for the little girl.'

Agreeing entirely with Ada, Shirley didn't argue for a moment. 'Best to get her well out of here and to safety as soon as possible.'

'Jeannie's house is the safest place I can think of, and it's not that far once you're on the tops . . . But I'm worried about what this will do to Isla. I don't think I have a choice, though,' she admitted.

The girl nodded. 'Turning up out of the blue with Heather when Isla thinks she's been adopted,' she guessed. 'I'd have a fit if somebody turned up with Lizzie,' she replied in all honesty. 'But, really, Ada, if Isla breaks down and rejects Heather, I'm certain they'd at least let you stay with them until it's safe to move her to another home. One thing's for sure – she can't stay here!'

Ada gave her a hug. 'And that's exactly what I think too. Now be a love and get that address; otherwise I could be explaining my motives to Sister Ann till Boxing Day!'

While Shirley hurried to do her bidding, Ada got out her warmest trousers, a roll-neck woolly jumper, a waterproof jacket, gloves, scarf and her beloved leather walking boots. After feeding and changing Heather, she waited feverishly for Shirley to return, which she did, bringing baby clothes and Jeannie's address scribbled on a scrap of paper.

'Good job I learnt to write,' Shirley said with a bit of an un-nun-like swagger. 'While you're getting Heather dressed, I'll go and fetch you some food for your journey.'

'Thanks, Shirley,' grateful Ada replied. 'I'd completely forgotten about eating – though I've made up several bottles of milk for Heather, hopefully, they'll stay warm for a while wrapped in a couple of old jumpers that I'll stuff into my knapsack. I've got some milk formula too.'

Heather didn't like the improvised sling which Ada had concocted from two soft woollen shawls but, once she was against Ada's body, the baby calmed down, and, after Shirley had helped Ada into her coat, which she buttoned up tightly, Heather seemed quite content. Heaving the rucksack on to her back, Ada put on her gloves, then wrapped the scarf around her neck.

'If anybody apart from Emily, Gloria or Sister Ann asks where I am, be sparse with the details and stick to the plan that I'm heading home for Sheffield,' she told Shirley. 'If the phone lines are in operation on the other side of the valley, I'll phone you when I get there. Do your best to keep Sister Ann from having kittens – she's bound to worry,' she said fondly.

Anxious to be on her way without being spotted by Matron, who would surely be on the lookout for her, Ada slipped out of the convent grounds shortly after dawn on Christmas morning. On the verge of tears, Shirley smiled at the baby, whose little face emerged over the edge of Ada's coat. Her dazzling Highland blue eyes, so like her mother's, shone against the ice-blue sky.

'I'll pray to God to keep you in his love, to keep you safe, and to Saint Christopher to guide you on your way!' she said, brightened by the thought of having another spiritual force to address. 'He's the patron saint of travellers, you know.'

335

Before sweet, earnest Shirley started reeling off a list of her favourite saints, Ada gave her a kiss.

'Bye, Shirley – keep those prayers rolling,' she chuckled, and, with a wave of her hand, she strode confidently across the fields to Allithwaite.

36. Hamps Fell

As church bells rang out in the little villages she passed, Ada hummed Christmas carols to herself. She'd told the truth when she'd said she'd done this walk many times, but on previous occasions it had been springtime with birds singing and daffodils in bloom, or in high summer, when sheep with their scampering lambs grazed the fells. Now it was cold and icy, but Ada felt invigorated. Energized by the necessity of her mission to get Heather to safety, she made good progress over Hamps Fell; then, after crossing the road, she covered the low hills to Newton Fell, from where she could make out Newby Bridge to the west. The ice-cold wind got stronger as she gained height and reached the ridged pathway above Newton in Cartmel. Normally, it would be comfortable walking, but, with the snow and ice underfoot, Ada almost slipped several times, until she came across a stout stick that she used to keep her balance as she climbed higher and higher. She couldn't let anything happen to little Heather, nor to herself.

Looking down from the ridge, she gasped at the first sight of Lake Windermere stretching out long and wide until it disappeared into the hazy distance that was Grasmere, fringed by the majestic Northern Fells. Heather wriggled, as if waking up, and caused Ada to put on a spurt of speed; she had to make the most of her time while the baby slept. Once Heather was awake and restless, she'd probably have to stop to give her a bottle-feed.

The higher she climbed, the better the view was; she could even see little boats moored on the shimmering blue water, and far down below she spotted a few cars, like children's toy cars, weaving their way along the narrow country lanes.

'Good,' thought Ada. 'That means the roads are open on this side of the valley.'

It was the perfect scenario, she mused with satisfaction: the roads around Cartmel and Allithwaite, which undoubtedly Percival and Matron would take to pursue her (if they'd second-guessed her plan), were blocked with deep snow, while on this side they were open.

'The wicked pair are stuck with no way out!' she said out loud. 'I hope it stays that way,' she added, because the next thing she planned to do (after delivering Heather to Isla) was to notify the police of all that she knew about what was going on at Crow Thorn Grange.

'The sooner it's in the police's hands, the better,' Ada thought vengefully.

In Matron's office, where Percival eventually turned up after she had threatened him, the two faced each other across her desk. Looking like he'd been drinking all night, he barked, 'So, have you found the brat yet?'

'NO!' she snapped back. 'And I can't go turning the place upside down without arousing suspicion.'

'Have you questioned the nurse who took her?' he demanded.

'She's gone off on holiday leave,' Matron coldly told him.

'And what if she blabs to somebody? Or, worse still' – he paled at the thought – 'takes the baby to the police?'

Desperate to calm his escalating anxieties, Matron spoke in her ringing, professional voice. 'Leave the finding of the child to me, Sir!'

Percival gave her a mocking look. 'And how do I get around the small problem of telling the eager adoptive couple that, for the moment at least, we don't have a baby to give them?'

'Buy time,' she snapped. 'They already know the weather's bad – tell them it's getting worse – tell them bloody anything to stop them from turning up here!'

After a few hours of brisk walking, Heather grew restless, so Ada made a brief stop to feed her. The baby devoured her bottle of milk, then, knowing she had to make the most of daylight, Ada set off once more, hungrily eating the egg sandwiches and the apple that Shirley had so thoughtfully prepared for her. How Shirley had changed, Ada mused: the little nervous wreck of a girl had gone, replaced by a stronger, braver and more focused young woman. Life's hardships had made Shirley grow up fast, and after her near-death experience she'd discovered a love of God and a desire to become a nun. Ada smiled to herself: Shirley's journey had been a torturous one, but at last there was happiness in sight.

'A bit like Heather's journey,' she thought. 'She could have been lost forever, but we found her and, one day soon,' she promised herself, 'I'll find out where Bertie and baby Tom went too.'

At Tower Wood, Ada started her descent to Ghyll

Head, then onwards to Windermere itself. When she reached the country lanes, Ada sighed with relief – it was good not to be slipping and sliding on ice and snow – but she was beginning to feel tired and Heather, fed up with being restricted for so long, was wailing loudly.

'All right, all right,' Ada soothed, as she jiggled the restless baby.

The sound of an approaching car made Ada draw back into the hedgerow to let it pass, but to her surprise the vehicle, an old, rusty farm truck covered in mud and smelling acridly of sheep's droppings, pulled up.

'We'er art thou heading, lassie?' the cheery farmer driving the truck asked.

Ada scrambled in her pocket for the scrap of paper on which Shirley had written the address.

'Thou's a few miles to go,' he muttered, recognizing the address. 'Hop in: I'll drive thee yon afore it turns dark.'

'Oh, thank you,' sighed weary Ada. 'That's so very kind of you,' she added, as she opened the passenger door, then stopped short as a wet collie dog slurped her hand with its warm tongue.

'Shift, yer owd bugger!' the farmer said with rough affection. 'Make room for't lass, wil't?'

After the collie had mooched over on to the back seat, Ada sank gratefully into the passenger seat he'd just vacated.

'It's very kind of you, Sir,' she said again, releasing Heather from her makeshift sling, then blushing as she realized how very smelly the baby was. 'I'm sorry,' she said apologetically. 'She's needs a nappy change.'

'Doesn't fret this'elf, cock,' the farmer chuckled, as he

clanged gears and they rattled slowly along the road that skirted the now-darkening lake. 'Owt's better than the stink of sheep shit!'

After a few stops for the farmer (accompanied by his faithful collie) to chuck hay into the snowy fields for his sheep to graze on, Ada arrived at her destination.

'Is that babby somebody's Christmas present?' the farmer teased, as Ada staggered out of the car clutching Heather, whom she'd managed to change during one of the stops.

Gurgling and contented now, Heather wiggled her feet in the woolly leggings that had kept her warm all day.

'You could say more of a Christmas surprise,' Ada laughed, as she abandoned the sling and settled Heather on her hip before looking around to get her bearings.

'It's yon big 'ouse over yonder,' the farmer said, and pointed to Jeannie's house, which, Ada could see, ran all the way down to Lake Windermere.

After thanking him again, she waved off the farmer and his dog, then took deep breaths to steady her nerves. What would Isla say? How would she react when she saw her baby again? What if she were in the throes of getting over leaving Heather and Ada's appearing so unexpectedly like this would rip the wound open all over again?

'It's too late for that now,' she declared, and, with her stomach churning, she walked to the front door and rang the bell.

'Okay, kiddo,' she muttered to Heather. 'Time to see Mama again.'

It was Jeannie's housekeeper who opened the door, but, on seeing Ada standing on the step holding a little baby, she quickly beckoned them in out of the cold.

'Could you tell your mistress that it's Sister Ada from Mary Vale?'

'Yes, Miss,' the housekeeper replied, and hurried away to make her announcement. Hardly a minute passed before Ada heard running footsteps approaching and Isla's soft, lilting voice calling excitedly down the long echoing hallway. 'ADA!'

Just as she was about to throw herself on to Ada, Isla spotted the little bundle now resting in the curve of her friend's arm; going as white as a sheet, Isla visibly rocked on her feet with shock. 'Heather . . .' she gasped.

'Isla, dear, what is it?' Jeannie's voice rang out, as she too came hurrying into the corridor. 'Is it really Ada, come visiting on Christmas Day?' she inquired in a delighted voice.

'It is Ada,' Isla replied, her face now transformed by a radiant smile that brought the colour rushing to her cheeks. 'Jeannie, darling, Ada's brought . . .' She paused as Jeannie caught sight of Heather. 'She's brought my daughter home to me.'

That night Isla fed her baby with the formula that Ada had had the foresight to bring with her along with the bottles of prepared milk she'd fed little Heather on their journey over to Windermere. As starry-eyed Isla gazed adoringly at her daughter, flushed and asleep after she was sated, Ada began her long and frightening story.

Isla shook her head incredulously. 'And there we were, thinking that Heather would soon be established with her new family, when all the time Matron was planning her own particular scenario.'

'In retrospect, I think there was something fishy going

on right from the moment Father Ben was hoisted out of his role. With the priest out of the way, Percival and Matron more or less had a free hand to pull the wool over everyone's eyes – that is until brave little Shirley started to unravel the mystery. We know from her that Matron sneaked Tom out of the Home and took him to the Grange, where a horrid girl called Olive looked after him; Gloria heard the same girl talking about Bertie's death while he was in her care, and it was the same unscrupulous girl who told me that Heather was going to be adopted.'

Jeannie shook her head as she gazed into the crackling fire, which the housekeeper kept well stoked up. 'Good God!' she cried out in anger. 'Why would anyone in a position of power as they are steal a child away from Mary Vale?'

'To make money, of course,' Ada answered bluntly. 'What other possible motive could they have?'

Holding her baby tightly, as if frightened she might lose her a second time, Isla recalled, 'At the time, I really believed Matron about the measles scare. Though I remember you didn't, Ada.'

'I was very uneasy but I felt I had no choice but to go along with it – measles is serious!' Ada exclaimed. 'But now I feel so guilty I didn't act. It's my ward – wouldn't I, as sister in charge, have spotted Tom's symptoms? Just as I would have spotted that Heather had a fracture, which is what Matron told Jones to say. I knew something wasn't right when Matron said Tom needed to be isolated, but I would have come across as grossly unprofessional if I'd complained, especially as she kept insisting, in a martyred

343

voice' – Ada rolled her eyes as she recalled Matron's words – 'that she was doing it for the "benefit of all the other babies in the nursery".'

She gave a heavy sigh as she took a sip from the glass of sherry Jeannie had filled for her.

'And then poor old Shirley paid such a price for seeing what she did,' Isla murmured.

The memory of Shirley lying on the marsh caused Isla's face to drain of colour, and, seeing her change of expression, Jeannie quickly suggested she make some cocoa, asking Ada if she'd come to help.

Once they were in private, Jeannie spoke in a whisper to Ada. 'I know we have to get to the bottom of all this ghastly business, and we will, you mark my words. But my Isla is so vulnerable right now; it's taken a while to recover from the experience of seeing Shirley in such a terrible way,' she advised. 'And then having to give up Heather, which she had no idea would be so hard, and now having her back – the poor child doesn't know if she's coming or going.'

'She'll need time to come to terms with it all,' Ada replied softly.

While they waited for the pan of milk to boil on the big old Aga that warmed the kitchen, Jeannie earnestly thanked Ada for bringing Heather home. Ada blushed as she confessed how arduous the journey had been.

'I knew I was taking a risk coming here, especially with little Heather, but an overwhelming instinct told me it was the right thing to do, I couldn't think of anything other than getting Heather as far away from Matron and Sir Percival as possible in order to keep her totally safe.'

Jeannie gave her a comforting pat on the hand. 'You absolutely did the right thing, and you were very brave. Who knows what would have happened to our precious Heather if you hadn't had the courage to do that?' Her voice turning more sober now, she continued, 'You have no idea what a difficult time it has been here. Isla was simply inconsolable about leaving Heather; we were going to head over to see you all just as soon as this blasted weather calmed down. I initially thought that once her hormones had settled down and her milk had dried up, she might start to feel better, but every day seemed, if anything, worse than the day before. The longer she was away from her baby, the more depressed Isla became. So perhaps it's partly fate that's brought you here. I can't see her being able to let the little mite go a second time, especially after all this.'

Ada slowly nodded her head. 'I've seen things like this happen before,' she confessed. 'Not baby snatching!' she quickly corrected herself. 'But mothers changing their mind at the last minute and asking to have their babies back. In the end, only Isla can decide what is right for her and for her baby,' she concluded.

Quickly lifting the pan from the heat before it boiled over, Jeannie made three mugs of cocoa. 'I'll take this to Isla and be right back,' she said, leaving the room. When she reappeared, Jeannie had a big smile on her face. 'Both fast asleep,' she said tenderly.

'They need this time together,' Ada commented. 'Isla struggled with her conflicting emotions in the Home: she never allowed herself to bond fully with Heather, yet at the same time she felt huge love for her.'

'Poor darling,' Jeannie sighed.

Ada gave a resigned shrug. 'That's what mothers who are planning to hand their babies over for adoption have to train themselves to do: keep a check on their emotions for their own sake and for their babies' too.'

'I've been wondering, now that we know something fishy was going on at Mary Vale, if Isla somehow intuitively sensed the danger her daughter was in – you know, like a sixth-sense type of thing?'

'That wouldn't surprise me at all,' Ada replied. 'One thing I've learnt from experience is that childbirth brings out an animal instinct in new mothers. I've heard some say that their wombs contract when they hear their baby crying; even though their baby is outside of them, their body reacts as though the child were still inside the womb. I have no doubt about Isla sensing her baby was in danger,' she concluded. Laying down the mug she'd been cradling in her hands, Ada outlined her next plan of action to Jeannie.

'Now that Heather's safe, I intend to go to the police tomorrow. To be honest, if the phone lines hadn't been down, I would have got in touch right away; as it is, I'll now have to wait until tomorrow morning. I know it's Christmas, but there's got to be somebody on duty,' she insisted.

'I'll come with you,' Jeannie said without a moment's hesitation. 'First thing in the morning, we'll go to the police station together.' Seeing Ada's weary face, she added, 'You look like you haven't slept in days, dear.'

Ada nodded. 'I feel like it,' she laughed.

'I'll make you up a bed.'

'Thank you, that sounds lovely,' Ada said, as a slow smile of satisfaction spread across her face.

'I'd say, with all the evidence we have from Shirley, Gloria and Emily, and maybe even Olive, we have quite a lot to say to the police, wouldn't you, Jeannie?'

37. The Local Constabulary

At Crow Thorn Grange, Sir Percival had sent Olive packing, dismissing her with heinous threats ringing in her ears if she should ever speak to anybody of what had taken place during the time of her employment there. Percival had dismantled the cot that Bertie had used and instructed the gardener to burn it immediately. With all evidence removed, he began to breathe easier.

One thing that comforted him was his standing with the local constabulary, with whom he'd always had a good working relationship. As County Sheriff, he was a well-respected member of the community; he was quite confident that the police would favour his side of the story, rather than listen to a bunch of hormonal pregnant women with an axe to grind. He would discreetly slip the officers (with whom he was on first-name terms) a fiver plus a fine bottle of malt whisky apiece. With luck and careful handling, they might just get away with it – IF Matron worked with him rather than against him.

In Ada's absence, Sister Ann had a very disturbing conversation with her superior in the Reverend Mother's panelled oak study.

'I've already heard Sister Ada's side of this tragic, sorry story, but I'd like to hear yours too,' she began. 'When do you think all this ghastly business started?' the Reverend Mother asked.

348

'Really,' Sister Ann answered slowly, 'I think it started when Father Ben was removed from office; things started to slip and Matron started behaving erratically. Whenever Ada questioned her judgement, Matron always fobbed her off with some excuse. None of it felt right,' she said, as she recalled the recent sequence of events. 'Ada and I had our suspicions, but we only knew for sure on Christmas Eve, when we heard from Emily and Gloria that Heather had been taken to Crow Thorn Grange instead of to the cottage hospital. Once Dr Jones was caught handing Heather over to Sir Percival, and Gloria overheard the woman who was supposedly looking after Bertie talking about his death, it didn't take long to realize that something was very wrong indeed.'

'Holy Mother!' the Reverend Mother exclaimed as she crossed herself. 'So you think the little mites were all taken to the Grange?'

'I think that must have been what happened – well, it certainly happened to little Heather.'

'But *why* did they need to be taken to the Grange?' the Reverend Mother said, puzzled. 'Adoptive families usually pick up from Mary Vale.'

She paused to stare out of the convent window that gave a view on to the chapel and the small graveyard. 'Hmm,' she murmured. 'And all of this took place after the very surprising allegations against Father Ben, when Sir Percival was appointed to take over the business of Mary Vale's adoptions?'

'Yes – and, as for Father Ben, I never did believe a word about his behaving badly. The man's a saint. And he kept good records of all the babies born at the Home, and the names and addresses of their adoptive families,' Sister Ann reminded her. 'Father Ben was scrupulous with the details; everything was open and above board.'

'Knowing what Ada told me about Sir Percival, I'd say there's money behind this dreadful business,' the Reverend Mother announced. 'However, Sister, this matter falls squarely on our shoulders: we run a mother and baby home, not a baby-snatching service,' she continued guiltily. 'I agree with you. None of this would have happened under Father Ben's good and loyal care. We've been duped, Sister, roundly duped, and we must make it our business to put things right; and, when we've done that, to clear our convent's good name.'

Almost in tears, Sister Ann muttered her reply, 'Absolutely, Reverend Mother. What happened at Mary Vale is a sin against God!'

In Windermere Police Station, with Jeannie at her side, Ada gave a full report on all the proceedings she and the others had witnessed at Mary Vale and at Crow Thorn Grange too.

'There are at least four other witnesses I can call on,' she told the officer in charge, and gave him their names. 'And, hopefully, once I'm back at Mary Vale I'll be able to furnish you with more information.'

After assuring Ada that he would immediately link up with his colleagues in Grange, the officer congratulated Ada, shaking her firmly by the hand.

'I promise we'll do everything we can, Miss.' With a wink, he added, 'It's quite an ordeal walking over the fells with a new-born baby in the snow.'

'My sentiments entirely!' Jeannie exclaimed.

'You're an impressive woman to do what you did, Miss,' the officer said with genuine admiration, which made Ada blush to the roots of her auburn hair.

'It seemed the only thing to do,' she responded modestly. 'All I could think of was that Heather needed to be safe – that's what drove me on.'

Jeannie gave Ada a huge hug. 'Thanks to you, darling girl, Heather's *very* safe now.'

After saying an emotional farewell to Isla, who had plans for all the girls to meet up once Emily was back on her feet, Ada turned to Heather, whom she'd grown to love very much.

'Shall we go fell-walking again?' she asked, softly kissing the baby's pink fingertips. 'I'll take you over Hamps Fell when you're a bit bigger,' she promised. 'And I'll buy you your first pair of fell-walking boots too.'

After giving mother and baby a final kiss, Ada walked with Jeannie to the station, where she managed to get on a crowded train bound for Lancaster; there, she would be able to pick up another train for Grange.

'The line's only just been cleared, so it's chocka on board,' the porter warned.

'I'd be happy to stand all the way,' Ada said to Jeannie with a laugh. 'If I don't get back to Mary Vale soon, I know Sister Ann will have every rescue party in the North-West combing the fells for me.'

'How can we ever thank you enough?' Jeannie said, as she clung on to Ada. 'My blood runs cold when I think of what might have happened to my little granddaughter.'

'Seeing Heather safe is all I wanted,' Ada replied. 'Though there is one thing I would ask, Jeannie. Be patient with Isla: she'll need time to come to the right decision about her baby.'

'Of course,' Jeannie answered staunchly. 'But I have to admit that, if she does decide to put Heather up for adoption again, I just might adopt the darling child myself!'

Percival's confident hopes that his cordial relations with the local police would save him were quashed when Grange Police Station sent over a couple of officers who showed not the slightest interest in Percy's smarmy name-dropping.

'Excuse me!' he roared as they frog-marched him out of his comfortable home in order to interview him at the station. 'I have friends in high places. You'll live to regret this,' he threatened, as they ducked his head down in order to push him into the back seat of the police car.

'I don't hold out much hope on that, Sir,' said the police officer who was handcuffed to Percival. 'Not from what we've heard.'

Percival and Matron were questioned separately several times and then together. Initially, they stuck to the same story: that they were doing friends a favour, fast-tracking their cases in order to secure an adopted child for them sooner rather than later. As the weight of damning circumstantial evidence provided by the residents of Mary Vale overwhelmed them, they both panicked (the holes in their story got bigger and bigger) and finally resorted to blaming each other. Matron's resolve eventually broke down entirely and she confessed that the children's files were locked away in her desk in her private suite at Mary Vale. She was removed from her post and asked to leave the Home immediately, while Percival went into hiding after the newspaper headlines condemned him as 'A Baby-Snatcher' and 'A Wicked and Unscrupulous Man!' With no money to pay for his Mayfair flat and champagne-style London life, Marigold quickly moved on to pastures new, while poor, long-suffering Lady Percival sued for a divorce.

'If Percival gets banged up behind bars, Lady Percival might well hold on to Crow Thorn Grange, which is by rights her ancestral home,' the Reverend Mother told Sister Ann; the older nun had trouble wiping a smirk of deep satisfaction from her face. 'Now wouldn't that be God working in deep and mysterious ways?' she remarked with a wicked smile.

The Reverend Mother was further gratified when Shirley, accompanied by Sister Ann, appeared in her office, eager to explain the role she'd played in the recent dramatic events in her own words. After hearing of Shirley's involvement and the hideous price she'd paid for it, the Reverend Mother reached across her desk to grip Shirley's hand.

'You suffered greatly, child,' she said with tears in her eyes.

But Shirley astounded her by answering with a smile that bordered on beatific. 'But God took care of me, God led me back to you – and Mary Vale.'

'Indeed, praise be,' the Reverend Mother replied. 'Now answer me honestly, dear girl: are you brave enough to say what you've just told me in a court of law?'

Little as she was, Shirley stood up tall and straight, and, sticking out her chin, she answered boldly, 'I'm not afraid, Reverend Mother. As God's my judge, I will speak out in a court of law against Matron and Sir Percival – neither of them can hurt me any more.'

38. New Year

There was a happy holiday atmosphere in Mary Vale during the week after Christmas. Ada, now temporarily acting as Matron, went about her work with a grin on her face and a skip in her step, despite her increased workload. Sister Ann wore a similarly large permanent smile and Shirley virtually danced around the place. When she wasn't with her mentor inquiring about the teachings of the Church or discussing a Bible reading, she was either deep in private prayer or accompanying the nuns singing their daily office in the chapel. In her spare moments she would dash into the schoolroom to join Robin, who brightened up at the sight of his friend; in truth, so did Gloria. In her last month of pregnancy, she was enormous: her small frame seemed all baby, and when she sat down her legs stuck out sideways in a rather comical way.

'Honestly, I swear I look like Donald Duck!' she joked with Shirley.

Though Shirley's reading was getting more sophisticated by the day (with all her missal studies), she still enjoyed her lessons with Robin, particularly history, geography and handwriting, a subject, she insisted, in which she needed improvement.

'Your handwriting's perfectly all right,' Gloria said in all honesty.

'Not if you've seen the Reverend Mother's,' Shirley laughed. 'I'd love my writing to be as artistic as hers.'

'I'm a good writer,' Robin announced, as he scrawled a row of letters. 'Copy me, Shirley,' he said like a bossy little teacher. 'And you might get a gold star!'

Gloria rolled her eyes. 'Is there nothing he thinks he can't do?' she muttered under her breath.

Even though her life was crammed with one activity or another, Shirley absolutely refused point blank to give up cleaning the Home.

'It's my way of relaxing and I get to chat to all the residents,' she insisted to Sister Ann. 'And I have my best conversations with God when I'm on my hands and knees scrubbing the floors.'

Though the nun shook her head in despair, it was difficult not to smile at Shirley's sincere comments.

'You'll wear yourself out,' she warned.

So Shirley was a regular sight on the wards, clanking along with her mop and a bucket containing hot water laced with pungent disinfectant.

'Wouldn't it be marvellous if you were made Matron permanent like?' she remarked one day when she bumped into Ada in the sluice room.

'I don't think it's quite as simple as that, Shirley,' Ada chuckled. 'The Board of Governors and the convent would have to advertise the post and interview the candidates; they can't just give the job to somebody they like,' she giggled. 'Anyway, to be honest, I'm not sure I'd like a job that involved so much desk work. I love working on the wards, I love my patients, and I love midwifery – I'd miss all of those things if I were behind a desk a good part of the day.'

Shirley gave a shy smile. 'I like it when you're in charge – we have more fun!'

'I'm not sure FUN should be top of the list in a maternity home,' Ada joked.

Shirley laid aside her mop in order to give Ada a hug. 'Well, it is in Mary Vale these days – and I for one have never been so happy nor had so much fun in my life!'

Emily was full of happiness and energy too. When she wasn't feeding, bathing and changing Noel, she generally helped out where she could.

'You've only just given birth; you're supposed to be resting,' Ada chided the new mother when she found her sterilizing feeding bottles in the prep room.

'I like to keep busy,' Emily admitted. 'And I like being near Noel too – I love watching him sleeping – he's got the sweetest little mouth, which I find it hard not to kiss.'

'How's the feeding going?' Ada inquired.

'Only days old and he has the appetite of a horse!' Emily replied.

'Don't go overdoing it,' Ada warned. 'Sister Ann told me you'd got cracked nipples the other day.'

'It was so painful, I nearly cried!' Emily exclaimed. 'But Sister Ann gave me some marvellous cream that really helped. Though I sometimes worry that I might not be producing enough milk,' she fretted.

'The more Noel sucks, the more milk you'll produce,' Ada assured her. 'Now stop worrying, Em: you're a wonderful mother.'

'It's not difficult when you love your baby as much as I do,' Emily murmured dreamily.

After they'd finished sterilizing the feeding equipment,

Ada suggested that they make a quick cup of tea in the kitchen. Emily set out the tea things on the table, deep in thought.

'Do you recall how nervous I was about telling George's parents I was pregnant?'

Ada nodded. 'Yes, I remember.'

'Well, I've realized I'm not nervous any more,' Emily continued. 'I'm so proud of my son – George's son – that I could shout it from the rooftops! Anyway, I've decided to tell Mr and Mrs Holden. I want them to know they have a fine grandson.'

A smile spread across Ada's lovely face. 'Don't waste time writing, Em, she said. 'Phone them!'

'Phone?' Emily gasped.

'Yes, from my office. Think how happy it might make them.'

'Or not,' Emily pointed out.

'Emily, it's your decision,' Ada solemnly replied. 'But consider this: we're at war, and George's parents are worried sick about their only son, whom they haven't seen in months, and they don't even know they have a grandchild sleeping sweetly in his cradle here.'

Emily gazed into Ada's sparkling blue eyes for several seconds, then she leapt to her feet. 'You're right!' she exclaimed.

After Mr and Mrs Holden had got over the shock of hearing Emily's voice on the other end of the phone, they were even more shocked when she broke the news of Noel's birth to them.

'Grandparents!' they gasped.

'Yes!' Emily exclaimed, adding the details of Noel's birth and his birthplace too.

'I had to book into Mary Vale home for mothers and babies,' she explained. 'I didn't give you details in my letter, as I thought you would be ashamed of us, but after giving birth to Noel I know there's no shame in his being alive. He's a joy – the living image of George – and I love him so much,' Emily told them proudly.

After she'd concluded her highly emotional conversation with Mr and Mrs Holden, Emily left Ada's office with a big smile on her face.

'It went well?' Ada cried when she saw Emily's happy expression.

'They want to see him!' Emily exclaimed. 'They asked if they could come and visit us here in Mary Vale and I said yes!'

'I'll take a photo of the pair of you with my little Box Brownie camera,' generous Ada suggested. 'A picture of their new grandson will make their Christmas.'

Radiant Emily said, 'He's certainly made mine!'

Though Gloria and Emily were busy throughout the day in their different ways, they always made sure they had a cup of cocoa together before they went to bed.

'Put your feet up, lovie,' Emily insisted when she saw Gloria's pale, drawn face. 'I'll make it tonight.'

With a stiff back and swollen feet, Gloria was more than grateful to be able to climb into her bed next to Robin; the little boy, worn out by the day's constant activities, lay fast asleep.

As Emily boiled milk on the little electric hot plate they kept in their room, Gloria lay flat on her back, glumly surveying her huge stomach.

'I look like a barrage balloon,' she groaned. 'I swear to God I was never as big as this the first time round,' she whispered, so as not to disturb Robin.

'It'll soon be over,' Emily assured her. 'And then you'll be back to your former slender self,' she teased.

Gloria smiled gratefully at her friend as Emily handed her a steaming mug of cocoa.

'Oh, Em, promise you won't leave the Home until I've had the baby?' she begged. 'I know I've got lovely Ada and sweet little Shirley, but I'd be lost without you, Em,' she admitted with tears in her eyes.

'Don't worry: I'll stay until they kick me out,' Emily joked. 'Though, to be honest, Gloria, I'm getting worried about where I actually will go next. I'll have to make some sort of arrangements soon; I can't stay at Mary Vale forever.'

'Unlike me,' Gloria pointed out. 'We'll be here until it's safe to return to London – the last of our gang: you, me, Isla, Nancy, Daphne,' she murmured as she sipped her cocoa. 'I read in the paper that a lot of evacuees have already returned to London; they say they can't see the point of being in somebody else's home when they could be in their own. Some are calling it a Phoney War – I must say, I'm tempted myself, though Stan would have a fit.'

Emily didn't look convinced. 'Lovie, don't do anything rash,' she warned. 'It might seem quiet but that doesn't mean Hitler and his armies have downed tools.'

'God! How I wish that carpenter had succeeded in killing Hitler a few months ago,' Gloria said with a heavy sigh. 'Without him and his crazy rhetoric, people might begin to see sense.'

Emily shook her head. 'I don't think so: if it wasn't Hitler, it would be some other crazy man; now that the wheels of war have been set in motion, there'll be no easy way of stopping it.' Determined to change the subject to something more light-hearted, she looked up with a grin. 'Come on, cheer up, tell me what your New Year's resolution is?'

'To have this baby as soon as possible!' Gloria laughed.

'Seriously, what else?' Emily persisted.

'To write to Stan more often, to knit him more socks and send him tins of spam and bars of soap.' Her eyes swam with tears. 'I can't think of him without wanting to cry these days. It's only been just over two months since he went off to war, but it feels like an eternity.' Reaching out, she stroked Emily's hand. 'Your turn, missis: what's your resolution for 1940?'

'To get a job and be a good mother and pray every day, twice a day, for George to come home and marry me.'

At which point she burst into tears.

'Oh, heck, what a pair we are,' Emily cried. 'Is it my hormones that're making me so weepy and emotional?'

'No, sweetheart,' Gloria replied. 'It's just love.'

On New Year's Day, Mary Vale went about its business as usual, though Sister Mary Paul tried to make it a bit special by baking scones and a custard tart, which she served to the residents in the dining room after their meal of Lancashire hotpot and baked beans.

'There's talk of food rationing starting soon,' she said gloomily.

'You'll manage, Sister!' Sister Ann exclaimed. 'You're an absolute miracle worker, coming up with delicious meals the way you do.'

Sister Mary Paul gave a little shrug. 'Not as good as what Jesus did with his five loaves and two fishes!' she chuckled.

In the afternoon, before tea was served, Emily took advantage of the last of the daylight, and, after wrapping Noel up warmly and popping him into a big Silver Cross pram, she set off for a walk around Mary Vale's pretty grounds.

'Won't be long,' she told Ada. 'Just in need of some good fresh air.'

Ada gazed longingly out of the wide bay window. 'Wish I could come with you,' she said, her eyes drifting towards the fells. 'I'd love to be on the tops on a day like today.'

'Well, I can promise you I won't be pushing a pram up Hamps Fell,' Emily joked. 'Not all of us are intrepid mountaineers!'

It was good to be outside with Noel tucked up warm and cosy, fast asleep in his pram. Humming softly to herself, Emily strolled along the pathway, gently bouncing the pram, slowing down when she saw a car in the distance turning into the driveway. When she came to the bench positioned at a high point of the garden, giving views of the vast sweep of Morecambe Bay and the tide that was roaring in sparkling silver-grey waves across the marsh, Emily sat down to admire the view, and it was there that the visitors from the car found her.

Recognizing the smartly dressed, middle-aged man and woman who were approaching her, Emily sprang to her feet. 'Mr and Mrs Holden!' she cried in complete amazement.

'I hope you don't mind, dear,' Mrs Holden quickly apologized. 'The nice ward sister said we'd find you out here.'

Emily's heart began to beat rapidly; turning to Mr Holden, who was tall and broad across the shoulders, just like his son, she suddenly felt dizzy and light-headed; swaying, she grabbed hold of the bench to support herself.

'Please,' Mr Holden cried, as he rushed forwards to help her. 'Please, sit.'

'We shouldn't have come like this; we should have warned you, dear,' Mrs Holden said, sitting down beside Emily. 'But we just couldn't stop ourselves,' she blurted out. 'After we got your phone call, we were anxious to see you . . . both.'

Mrs Holden's eyes strayed longingly towards the pram.

Finding her voice, which was squeaky with shock, Emily gasped, 'How nice of you to come all this way.'

'May we see Noel?' Mrs Holden asked softly.

'Of course,' Emily cried.

Getting to her feet, she gently lifted the soft, woolly blanket that was keeping Noel snug and warm. 'He's just dozed off,' she whispered.

When she handed the baby to his grandparents, they were both visibly overcome. Dabbing tell-tale tears from his eyes, Mr Holden said gruffly, 'My God! He's the spit of our George.'

'He's perfect,' Mrs Holden sighed, as she cradled him in her arms.

Grouped around Noel, they stared, transfixed, into his sweet, perfect baby face.

'My dear,' Mrs Holden said, as she laid her hand on Emily's. 'You have no idea how very happy you have made us.'

Ada discreetly left the visitors alone with Emily for a short time, but, as rain clouds gathered, she invited the

Holdens into the Home for tea, which was made even grander by Mrs Holden's unexpected, luxurious gift: a box of chocolates. Robin's eyes all but popped out of his head when he saw the layers of chocolates nestled in tissue paper.

'Are they really real?' he gasped.

'Try one,' Mr Holden urged. 'Try two, in fact,' he laughed.

When Robin bit into a coffee cream, followed by a strawberry fondant, his green eyes grew round in wonder. 'Thank you!' he declared. 'They're even better than Merry Paul's jam tarts.'

While Noel slept, Emily sat in the sitting room drinking tea with (now on first-name terms) Reggie and Margaret.

'We have no further news of George, I'm afraid,' Reggie said before Emily could ask. 'I wish I could say otherwise.'

For the second time in an hour Margaret's eyes filled with tears, 'The silence is just killing us!' she exclaimed. 'Not knowing is simply unbearable.'

Readjusting the weight of sleeping Noel in the crook of her arm, Emily's voice was heated. 'WHY can't somebody somewhere tell us something? Did George and his squadron just disappear into thin air when they were transferred overseas? Were they shot down? Captured? Are they all dead?' she choked.

Seeing her tearful, Margaret said apologetically, 'We shouldn't be talking like this; it's too upsetting for you and the baby.'

'To be honest, it's a relief to be able to speak freely to somebody who feels the same pain and fear,' Emily confessed.

'We just miss our lad so very much,' Reggie said with a

crack in his voice. 'He's a wonderful young man,' he added proudly.

Emily smiled at the couple before her; she had been so worried they would disapprove of her and judge her harshly, but now she could see they were only eager to get to know her, and baby Noel too. After talking about the Home and Noel's birth (Emily left out all the drama that accompanied the delivery!), Margaret looked a little nervous as she prepared to say something.

'Emily, my dear. We were wondering if you had made any progress on your plans after you leave Mary Vale?'

Not wanting them to feel sorry for her, Emily skirted round the hard truth. 'I've been looking at residential positions, places where I could work and live in. That way I'd be able to look after Noel . . .'

Margaret turned to her husband.

'You see, Emily, we've been thinking,' he started rather shyly. 'It's just, well, Margaret and I would like you to consider the possibility of you and Noel coming to live with us, for a while, until you get yourselves settled, in Chester? That's if it suits you, of course?' he added with a nervous smile.

Seeing the blush deepen on Emily's face, Margaret was quick to add, 'We don't want to rush you; take your time, dear.'

Holding back the tears that threatened to engulf her again, Emily struggled to find the words she needed. 'But what about, you know, what people might say if I turn up at your house, an unmarried woman with a new-born baby?'

'That's their business, not ours,' Reggie replied firmly.

'We have no doubts about our offer, Emily. After losing touch with George, we couldn't bear to lose touch with our precious grandson too – nor you, George's beloved,' he concluded.

Emily smiled at him gratefully. 'I cannot thank you enough,' she said in an emotional rush. 'I am so very grateful to you both. I'd love to accept your very kind offer.'

Later, after she'd changed Noel's nappy, Emily laid him in his grandmother's arms. 'Have a cuddle before you leave,' she urged.

Leaving the new grandparents to enjoy a few moments' privacy with their grandson, Emily sought out Ada on the ward to tell her the good news.

'I know!' Ada cried. 'Before they came looking for you, they asked me for advice on the matter; they were worried they might come across as too pushy. I hope you don't mind, Em? I said I thought you'd appreciate their offer.'

'Of course I don't mind!' Emily cried. 'I'm so relieved. Imagine having a safe and secure home to go to after I leave here. It's wonderful! And to be with George's parents – it's the closest Noel and I are going to get to being with him.'

When she returned to her visitors, Reggie was now holding Noel in his arms, and, after staring rapturously for several seconds into his grandson's now wide-open eyes, he looked up and smiled warmly at Emily.

'We'll look after you both,' he promised. 'You're part of our family now.'

39. The Visit

Though Isla longed to see her friends, she wrote a letter instead to beg their forgiveness for not coming to Mary Vale to visit them.

I just can't bring Heather to Mary Vale. Even though I know Matron's been sacked and Percival is banished, it doesn't make any difference to me: the thought of what might have happened to little Heather in their 'care' simply frightens me to death. Is there any way you can visit me here in Windermere before Gloria gives birth? Jeannie said she'd pick you up and drive you both over here, and Ada too if she's off-duty. Please come soon and forgive my nervousness.

Lots of love
Isla xx

Both women completely understood Isla's fears.

'I would feel the same way,' Gloria admitted.

'But are you fit to travel?' Emily inquired, as her eyes swept over Gloria's vast tummy.

'Of course! Anyway, it's only Windermere, not Land's End! We needn't trouble Jeannie: we can take the train,' she suggested. 'It's not far.'

But when Ada heard of their plans, she insisted on driving them over to Windermere in the same garden van that had been used to rescue Heather from the Grange. 'It'll be a squash,' she laughed. 'But we can all squeeze up on the front seat and sing "One Man Went to Mow" all the way over the tops! I've a day off due, and I could certainly do with a change of scene,' she said with a grin. 'Plus, I'm longing to see how Heather is progressing.'

Robin stayed behind to help Sister Mary Paul muck out Big Ears's stable, but Noel accompanied the girls, his carry-cot safely lodged in the back of the van while all the girls sat on the front seat.

The journey over the fell roads on a cold, bright January morning was fun – the three of them never stopped laughing and chatting – but when the steep road dipped down into Windermere and Bowness came into view, they all caught their breath at the sight of the sun glinting on the lake where little boats skimmed across the tranquil water.

'It's hard to believe there's a war on when you see beauty such as this,' Gloria gasped.

'How lucky are we?' Emily murmured, as she watched puffy, white clouds drift across the mountains that tumbled down to surround the beautiful lake.

'Yes,' Ada agreed, as she slowed the car in order to take in the spectacular views. 'Days like this are simply a gift from God.'

Isla was delighted to see her friends.

'I haven't seen you two since I left Mary Vale,' she cried, hugging Gloria and Emily. 'Though I have seen Ada more recently, of course,' she added with a smile, hugging Ada too.

In the cosy sitting room, where Jeannie greeted them

with coffee and home-made orange-rind-and-oatmeal biscuits, they gathered around the babies, whom Emily and
Isla had laid side by side on a rug before the fire.

'Heather's grown!' Ada exclaimed in delight. 'She's
twice the size she was.'

'She never stops feeding,' Isla said proudly. 'And look
how strong Noel is,' she cried, as she smiled at the little
boy who, after Emily had changed his nappy, was happily
wriggling his fat little legs.

'How marvellous to see them both together,' Jeannie
said. 'Only one more to make the picture complete,' she
added, smiling at Gloria's bump. 'Not long now, dear.'

'And I know I'll be in the safest pair of hands – Ada's
the best midwife in the whole of the North of England!'
Gloria enthused.

'Get away with you!' Ada laughed. 'I'm second best
after Sister Ann.'

'So, come on, girls, tell me all your news – how's
Shirley? Robin? Sister Mary Paul? Sister Ann?' Isla
inquired excitedly.

After Isla and Jeannie had been brought up to date with
all the Mary Vale news, Emily told her own special news.

Isla whooped in delight. 'Wonderful!' she cried, over
the moon for her friend, who had been so worried about
where she would go when she left Mary Vale.

'What are George's parents like?' Jeannie asked curiously.

Emily cocked her head sideways as she considered the
question. 'Bear in mind I've only met them twice,' she
started. 'They seem kind and generous – not like my rotten family, who would kick me out, and Noel too. They
don't even know I've had a baby!' she admitted. 'I'll have

to tell them soon, before somebody else does, but, quite honestly, I don't think it will be worth the effort; they won't want to know,' she concluded realistically.

Isla gripped Emily's hand. 'Concentrate on the good news, lovie. George's parents have given you and your baby a home, just like Jeannie did for me! We're lucky,' she added gratefully. 'Now,' she said with a nervous smile, 'I've got some news too.'

Her friends looked at her expectantly.

'I'm keeping Heather,' Isla announced.

As a body, the three girls moved in to hug her.

'I knew you would!' Ada cried. 'But you had to come to that decision in your own time.'

'It didn't take long,' Jeannie chuckled. 'I could see the bonding going on before my very eyes.'

Isla gazed at her little daughter in adoration. 'It was an agony parting with her, but I was sure it was the right thing to do, for her sake especially, but once I got home to Windermere all I could think of was Heather. Where was she? What was she doing? Who was feeding her? Who was rocking her to sleep? Then, when Ada came knocking on my door, just like Santa, she had a present for me.' After laying a gentle kiss on Heather's perfect cupid-bow lips, she continued. 'She's mine now, my perfect little treasure.'

'I'm delighted for you, but I do have a question,' Ada said with a smile. 'You're a clever girl, and you mustn't forget your studies. Please don't tell me you're going to give them up, Isla?'

'Not at all,' Isla replied staunchly. 'I've been looking into part-time courses close by.'

'And I'm happy to babysit my granddaughter for as many hours as there are in the day,' Jeannie told Isla's friends. 'Between us three strong women, we'll get there!' she said confidently.

After a delicious lunch of rabbit pie, mashed potatoes and cabbage, the girls dragged themselves away from Isla, who stood in the doorway with Heather in her arms to wave them goodbye.

'See you at the trial,' she said a little anxiously.

'If not before,' Ada added, as she kissed Heather for the third time.

'I'm quite looking forward to seeing those two wretches in the dock,' Jeannie added with undisguised pleasure. 'God knows, they deserve a severe judgement after what they've been up to.'

Holding Heather in one arm, Isla put her free arm about Jeannie's shoulder. 'I'm going to have to keep my wild grandmother well away from Matron; otherwise she might be arrested too!'

In the car going home, with the winter sun starting to sink low over the western fells, everybody agreed that Isla had made the right decision.

'With a woman like Jeannie behind them, Isla will be fine – and so will Heather,' Ada laughed.

Thinking of George's parents' recent visit and the joy they had shared together that very special afternoon, Emily sighed. 'It's sad that Isla's mother and father have turned their back on her.'

'Their loss,' said Ada. 'I feel sorry for them, actually: they're the ones who'll live to regret their decision.'

*

Not long after their visit to Isla, it was Gloria's turn to go into labour, and it happened in the schoolroom. Mercifully, Shirley was there reading a story book about King Arthur and the Knights of the Round Table to Robin, who was sitting on her knee, pretending to be a knight riding his horse.

'Gee up, horsy!' he laughed.

When Shirley looked up, she saw Gloria's face suddenly twist in pain.

'Gloria! What's the matter?'

Gloria shook her head, then nodded towards Robin.

'Excuse me, I'll just pop out for a minute or two.'

Leaving Robin in Shirley's good care, she hurried towards the ward, but had to stop on the way because of further pains shooting up her back. When she caught her breath, she located Ada, who was making notes in her office.

'Morning, sunshine!' Ada called as she walked in.

'I think it's started,' Gloria announced. 'Back pains and twinges down below, quite strong too.'

Slipping into her relaxed professional mode, Ada gently guided her out of the office and on to the ward. 'Let's get you into bed, then I can see what's happening myself,' she said calmly.

A few hours later, after a speedy but extremely painful delivery, Ada brought Gloria's baby daughter into the world. And the first person to visit her (after Gloria had been tidied up and given a much-needed cup of tea) was of course Robin, who – escorted by Shirley – gazed in enchantment at the little baby in the cot beside his mother's bed.

'She's pink!' he announced. 'And she's got no hair.'

Gloria held out her arms to her son. 'She's only just been born, sweetheart; she'll change as she grows up.'

'Can we call her Pinky?' Robin asked in all seriousness.

Seeing Ada and Shirley, at the end of the bed, struggling not to laugh, Gloria started to giggle. 'I don't think so, lovie. We'll think of another name, I'm sure.'

Gloria's joy at the birth of her daughter was slightly marred in the days that followed her delivery when she simply couldn't stop crying. 'I feel so guilty loving her so much when her father's not even seen her,' she wept in Ada's strong arms. 'Oh, I wish he was here, I miss him so much.'

Ada let her patient cry herself out, then spoke to her calmly and with complete professional confidence. 'You know, lovie, this feeling of anticlimax is not uncommon in newly delivered mothers.'

'I remember feeling a bit blue after Robin was born,' Gloria admitted. 'But Stan was there to pull me through. Now I feel so lonely and overwhelmed.'

'We're here, lovie, your friends in Mary Vale – all of us – we will help you through,' Ada assured her. 'Your body has had a huge upheaval – think about all the changes it's gone through in the last nine months – and now you've produced a fine, healthy daughter. Give your body time to get back to normal,' she advised. 'Be patient with yourself.'

Gloria nodded. 'You're wonderful, Ada, you make me feel calmer already,' she whispered gratefully.

'And I'm sure you'll hear from Stan soon,' Ada said with a hopeful smile.

By sheer good luck, Ada turned out to be right: a letter

arrived for Gloria while she was still on the post-natal ward. Ada couldn't believe the timing of its arrival – God did indeed move in mysterious ways. Ada took the baby from her arms and handed her the letter.

'We'll leave you in peace for a few minutes,' she said with an understanding smile.

My darling wife,

I think about you every hour, in fact, there's hardly any time of the day and night when I'm not thinking of you! Your time must be coming by now, I do hope so for your sake, my darling. Oh, if only I knew how you were, my love! I feel so useless, so helpless, so far away and worried. The good news is, when I asked my senior officer for a short leave of absence to visit you, he agreed! So I'll be coming home soon! Only for forty-eight hours, but that should give me enough time to get to Grange. I'll walk there if I have to! Oh, my darling, write to me and tell me your news, give my love to Robin and the new baby – if he or she has arrived.

Your loving husband,
Stan

When Ada returned to Gloria's bedside, she found her patient lying back on her pillows with the most radiant smile on her glowing face.

'He's coming home,' she cried, as she threw her arms high in the air. 'My Stan's coming to Mary Vale!'

40. Tears and Joy

When Robin found out that his daddy was coming home, he went wild with joy.

'DADDY! DADDY!' he cried, as he ran round the garden, where Shirley, who was taking his little sister for a walk in a pram, smiled in pleasure to see the boy so happy.

'He's obviously been missing his dad but kept it to himself, and now he can let it all out, brave little boy,' she thought fondly.

She herself had something to delight in too: that very morning, after the nuns had completed their morning office, Shirley (and her mentor, Sister Ann) had been called into the Reverend Mother's office, where she had been told that her postulancy would officially begin.

'You'll be given a novice's habit and a postulant's veil – which is different to the ones worn by the community of nuns – when you join us in the convent,' the Reverend Mother announced to Shirley, who had to stop herself from jumping up and down in gratitude. 'At a later date, if you get through your postulancy, you'll take your temporary vows of poverty, chastity and obedience.'

With stars in her eyes, Shirley turned to the Reverend Mother. 'Thank you for accepting me – God's showing me the way,' she said with an odd mixture of humility and supreme confidence. 'I feel his love all around me every day.'

After enjoying her walk with Robin and his sister, Shirley went in search of Emily, who was sorting out her belongings prior to leaving Mary Vale. Shirley's little bubble of joy slightly deflated at the thought of saying goodbye to Emily, whom she loved like a sister. She was glad Emily and Noel had a comfortable home to go to, but she would miss her friend so much. When Shirley arrived in the bedroom, she found her friend lying on her bed with a letter in her hand. Seeing her, Emily leapt to her feet.

'It's from George!' she cried, as she literally spun round the room like a dancer. 'Can you believe it, I've finally heard from George! And he's alive, he's alive, he's alive!' she laughed joyfully. 'Come on – let's find Ada and Gloria,' she cried, as she snatched up Shirley's hand and ran out of the room.

Once Emily had assembled all her friends in the empty dining room, Ada insisted that she sit down in one of the big old armchairs,

'Rest, young lady,' she said firmly. 'You've only recently given birth.'

Flopping down, Emily handed the letter to Ada. 'Please read it: I'm completely out of breath.'

My dearest darling sweetest Emily,

I have only just received your many precious letters and my heart is bursting with love for you, and guilt too, that I left you alone for so long. God only knows how much you must have suffered – and my poor parents too.

'But you weren't alone,' Shirley said sweetly. 'You had us!'
'Shhh!' Gloria flapped. 'Go on!'

*How are you, my darling girl, and how is my son, Noel? I love
him so very much already — my parents tell me he is the image of
me, but I want him to have your beautiful face and laughing eyes
and your cute dimples too!*

*I can tell you only a little of what's been going on. The fact is
my squadron have been involved in a top-secret mission for months
now, hence all the secrecy about my whereabouts. It's still ongoing
but nothing like as perilous as it was when we were first posted
overseas. I'm sorry, my dearest, I can't divulge any more
information than that, but rest assured that if I had got your
letters sooner, I would have moved heaven and earth to write back
to you. I'm so sorry that I couldn't.*

*In our present posting we've finally been allowed to receive mail;
I have a large pile from you, and some from my parents too. I
don't think I will ever forgive myself for putting you all through
such anguish but, really, we had no choice. Now, while the
situation is a bit less tense, we're allowed to write home, and we
can receive letters too. Write to me, my darling, and I beg you to
send a photograph of you and my baby boy.*

*Blast! The hooters just sounded out, duty calls.
I love you more than words can say . . .*

Ada stopped there and discreetly handed the letter
back to Emily. 'The rest is private,' she giggled.

Emily clutched the letter, which she kissed over and
over again. 'Ada,' she begged, 'please may I use your office
phone to call George's parents? I want to tell them the
good news right away! They've probably had a letter too,
but just in case . . .' she cried.

'Of course I'll come with you,' Ada immediately agreed.

Skipping out of the room like a child, Emily all but ran on to the ward and into Ada's office, where she talked for half an hour to George's parents.

'Oh, thank God,' Mrs Holden said, and, relieved beyond words that her son was well, she burst into tears.

'You're bound to get a letter soon,' Emily assured them; then, after all the wild, joyful excitement, she burst into floods of tears too.

'I'm so, so, so happy,' she sobbed.

'Come to us soon,' Mrs Holden implored. 'You make us so happy, Emily.'

'And we miss little Noel too,' Mr Holden admitted.

'I promise we'll both be with you very soon,' Emily vowed.

After finishing the conversation, a beaming Emily turned to Ada. 'You know what?' she said with tears of happiness brimming in her big blues eyes, 'Noel and I are needed elsewhere – the time has come to say goodbye.'

When Reggie and Margaret arrived at Mary Vale a few days later, a great many tears were shed. As Reggie and Margaret packed Emily's luggage and popped Noel in a new carry-cot into their car, Emily turned to her friends, who had gathered to say their goodbyes. Seeing the smiling, familiar faces of Ada, Shirley, Gloria, Robin, Mary Paul and Sister Ann, Emily almost broke down.

'Oh, God, I'll miss you!' she cried, as she buried her face against Ada's shoulder.

Determined not to get over-emotional (though, in truth, she felt it), Ada answered in a clear firm voice. 'We'll miss you too, lovie, but we won't lose touch – we'll write, and you'll visit us. Tell us you will.'

'Oh, I will!' Emily replied. 'Goodbye,' she cried, as she clung to each of her friends in turn, but when she reached Gloria her resolve broke down completely.

Taking her cue from Ada, Gloria did her best to stay strong too. 'I'll come and see you just as soon as I can,' she assured weeping Emily.

'And me too,' a little voice at her side chipped in. 'And Merry Paul and Big Ears if you like?'

'Heavens above!' the nun joked. 'The little lad will have the lot of us in the car if you're not careful.'

As laughter spread among the group, Emily cuddled sweet little Robin, then climbed into the back seat. Waving and blowing kisses to her friends, she was driven away by Reggie and Margaret to a new life with her son in Chester.

In truth, Mary Vale felt empty without Emily – her larger-than-life personality, her ready laugh, her strong opinions and her straight talking were much missed by her friends – but, as ever, life at Mary Vale continued at its own hectic pace, which was heightened considerably only a few days later by Stan's arrival. Walking up the leafy path from Kents Bank Station with his rucksack slung over his shoulder, the first thing he heard was a high-pitched, squeaky voice.

'Bomber attack!' followed by the improvised sound of an engine. 'Brrrrrrrrrrr!'

Hiding behind a tree trunk, Stan waited for his son to flash by, then he joined in the game too.

'Enemy fire – brrrrrrrr!' he went, but in a deep, growly voice.

Startled, Robin whirled around then – saw his dad – and ran straight into his wide-open arms.

'Daddy! Daddy!' he cried rapturously.

'Robin, my boy,' Stan murmured as he pressed his son's warm little body close to his heart.

Clutching each other, they savoured the moment before Robin, with his characteristic joie de vivre, spoke again. 'Come and see Big Ears?'

Stan burst out laughing. 'I'm assuming that's not Mummy!' he joked.

'No, silly! Mummy's asleep with the baby; Big Ears is my donkey.'

'I think I really need to see Mummy first, and then your sister,' Stan said softly. 'Will you show me the way, son?'

Robin very self-importantly marched his father upstairs to the bedroom he shared with his mother and baby sister, and, pressing a finger to his lips, he softly opened the door and pointed to the bed on which Gloria had dozed off with her baby in her arms. Holding his breath, Stan crept forward and gazed in wonder at his beautiful wife and daughter sleeping peacefully side by side. With her long, dark hair lying in a cloud about her face, Gloria looked tired but more lovely than Stan had ever seen her before. Unable to stop himself, he bent down and softly kissed her full, pouting lips. Gloria opened her eyes and blinked, and, gazing into her husband's rugged, unshaven face, she really thought she was dreaming until Robin spoke up. 'Mummy, Daddy's come home!'

After holding on to her husband like she'd never let him go, Gloria presented him with his daughter, who, now wide awake, gazed at him with eyes as dark as his wife's.

'Hello, my darling girl,' Stan said, fighting back tears that he thought might well engulf him. 'I'm your daddy and I love you, very, very much, my sweetheart.'

'She's still not got a name,' Robin bluntly announced. 'Mummy won't let me call her Pinky; she said you might have a name for her.'

Stan looked at Gloria, who couldn't take her eyes off her husband, cradling his precious daughter. 'Robin's right: I thought you might like to name your little girl.'

'Well, then,' said Stan, and, still holding the baby close, he strolled towards the big bay window that gave views of the garden and the wild, windy marsh and the churning Irish Sea. 'This has been a very special home for both of you; it's kept you safe while I was away, so I think we should name our daughter after the place where you've both been happy.' Turning to Gloria, he added, 'Can we call her Mary?'

Gloria nodded. 'I knew you'd come up with the perfect name,' she said happily. 'Mary.' She savoured the sound of her daughter's lovely new name. 'Our own sweet, little Mary.'

Epilogue

In March of 1940, on the day that the Germans bombed Scarpa Flow, Sir Percival and Matron were sentenced to prison, while Dr Jones was struck off the medical register. Ada, Shirley, Gloria, Emily and Olive were called to give evidence at Lancaster Assizes. When the hideous truth was revealed – that Bertie had died in his sleep on Matron's watch and that Tom had been falsely diagnosed with measles and declared dead – the courtroom was in profound shock. When they heard that the babies had been swapped, and that Bertie was, in fact, buried in Tom's grave in the convent cemetery, heartbroken Daphne completely broke down and wailed like an animal in pain.

'Oh, my God!' she sobbed in Ada's strong arms. 'I left Mary Vale hoping my son was heading for a new and better life . . . such a sweet little life gone.'

The Bennetts were also called to give evidence. Nancy, terrified that they might not want her son any more, refused to meet them until they convinced her that they had no intention of abandoning their adored Rupert, who, Nancy told her friends in private, still looked the image of the spotty lad who'd seduced her! When the Bennetts were informed of the true facts – that they had been handed a substitute baby – they indignantly told the judge that, though Percival was a cad who'd wickedly deceived them, under no circumstances would they ever give up their adored son and heir. Nancy and the Bennetts parted on the most amicable of terms, and for years afterwards Nancy and her mother (living happily by themselves in a terraced house in Bolton) were sent a photograph of Rupert every Christmas, along with a Harrods food hamper and a generous cheque.

Putting the horrors of the past behind them a month later, on a warm April day with birdsong ringing out in every lane and leafy garden, three young and beautiful mothers wheeled their babies in big old Silver Cross prams borrowed from Mary Vale nursery along Grange's wide and sunny promenade.

'When I think of what I was planning this time last year,' Isla laughed as she rearranged Heather on her bank of soft pillows. 'Everything's changed so much – I feel like another woman, an entirely different person.'

'I know what you mean,' Gloria laughed too. 'Mary's stolen my heart away – though I wouldn't go as far as telling Robin that!'

Emily gazed adoringly at her son, who was now nearly three months old. 'I can't imagine life without Noel, and his astonishing grandparents. I talk to him every day about his daddy.' With her characteristic strength of will and sheer determination, she continued, 'I'll keep George's baby safe until God sends his daddy safely home to us.'

Sitting on a bench, with the sun on their faces, the three women gazed across the marsh, which was presently bright with spring flowers and loud with the sound of new-born lambs.

Gloria's expression grew soft as she gazed out over the vast sweep of the bay. 'I love this place,' she said with a happy sigh. 'You've no idea how I dragged my feet about leaving London,' she smiled, as she recalled how stubborn she'd been when Stan had suggested that she and Robin left the city for a safer place. 'Now I can't imagine ever leaving here.'

'If you did leave, you'd have to take Merry Paul with you or Robin would have a fit,' Emily joked.

'Seriously, though,' Gloria continued, 'I have a purpose at Mary Vale these days. Now that so many evacuees are arriving, my schoolroom is packed with noisy children every morning. Luckily, Shirley – or should I say Sister Shirley?' she added with a big warm smile, 'occasionally has time to help me.'

'Sister Shirley in her sweet blue novice's dress and white veil,' Isla said fondly. 'Who would believe she's the same girl we rescued from the marsh?'

'She looks a picture until she gets her bucket out and starts mopping round the toilets,' Gloria chuckled. 'She says it's the best way of communing with God!'

Isla shook her head. 'Shirley's the same all the way through,' she smiled. 'Just like a stick of Morecambe rock!'

Later, in Mary Vale's garden, the girls were joined by Ada, Sister Ann, grinning Sister Shirley, Father Ben (restored to favour), the Reverend Mother, Robin, Jeannie and Mary Paul, who'd miraculously put together a picnic to celebrate the happy occasion. Knowing how frugal Mary Paul was with their now daily rationed food, Ada smiled at the feast laid out before them: egg-and-cress sandwiches, cheese scones and jam-sponge slices.

'My word, Merry Paul, you've done us proud!'

The nun blushed. 'As it's such a special occasion, I had a word with the Mary Vale farmer, who slipped me a few little extras,' she answered self-consciously.

Cheeky Robin burst out laughing. 'The farmer wants to marry Merry Paul!'

Pretending to scold the naughty boy, Sister Mary Paul flapped a tea towel in his face. 'Get away with you, child!' she giggled.

After the delicious picnic had been consumed and the late-afternoon sun slowly started to slide over the sparkling Irish Sea, where seagulls swooped and called, Isla asked, 'Is it wrong to feel so contented?'

Sister Shirley shook her head. 'Everybody deserves a little happiness now and again,' she said with a knowing smile. 'Especially you wonderful brave women! Where would I be without you three?'

Father Ben held up a warning finger. 'Though be warned: the way Hitler's carrying on, tougher times are coming.'

Isla stuck out her chin as she declared proudly, 'Hitler might think he can beat us down, but he forgets we're a nation that never surrenders.'

'Amen to that,' murmured the Reverend Mother.

Ada smiled at the women she'd grown to love so much. 'When the war is over, maybe you'll speak of the things you fought for and achieved here at Mary Vale.'

'How we came in shame to a home for women and babies, to give birth hidden away from society,' Emily recalled.

Watching Robin cuddle up to Sister Mary Paul, Gloria smiled fondly. 'How we made life-long friends.'

'How you stopped a terrible crime and saved lives too,' Ada reminded them.

'How brave you all are!' Sister Shirley exclaimed.

With tears brimming in her dreamy blue eyes, Emily said yearningly, 'Perhaps one day, when our boys come home and the war is over . . .'

Acknowledgements

I'm grateful to Karin Briden, who suggested I paid a visit to the Cartmel Peninsula, a wonderful, fascinating area between Morecambe Bay and the edge of the Lake District National Park. It was the perfect location for Mary Vale Mother and Baby Home. Thanks also to Dr Clive Glazebrook and Midwife Patsy Glazebrook for their advice on childbirth past and present. Special thanks to all the cheerful volunteers at Grange-over-Sands Tourist Office and Carnforth Station Heritage Centre (home of *Brief Encounter*), who provided me with lots of local history, and to Jon Styles, who helped me map routes over the fells. A special thanks to my enthusiastic editors at Penguin, Clare Bowron, Rebecca Hilsdon and Donna Poppy. Finally, thank you to all my readers. On days when I sit staring blankly at my computer screen I recall your enthusiastic comments on my Facebook page and they urge me on – so please don't stop!

Also by
Daisy Styles...

Out Now

Also by
Daisy Styles...

Out Now

Also by
Daisy Styles...

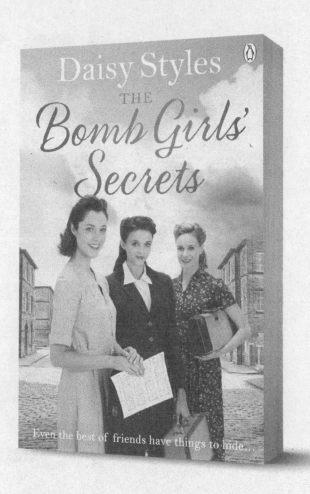

Out Now

Also by

Daisy Styles…

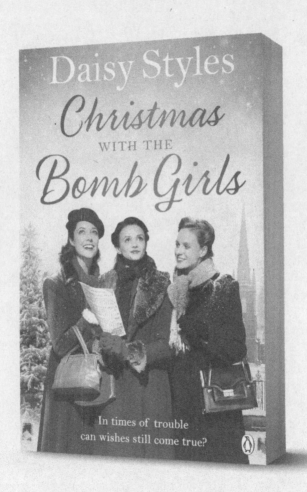

Out Now

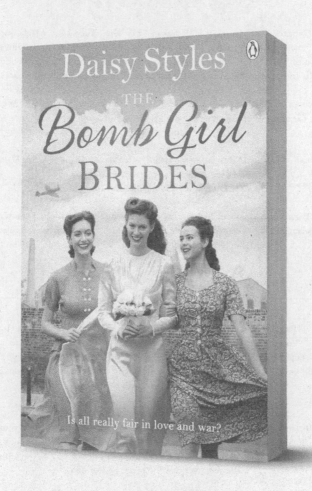

He just wanted a decent book to read ...

Not too much to ask, is it? It was in 1935 when Allen Lane, Managing Director of Bodley Head Publishers, stood on a platform at Exeter railway station looking for something good to read on his journey back to London. His choice was limited to popular magazines and poor-quality paperbacks – the same choice faced every day by the vast majority of readers, few of whom could afford hardbacks. Lane's disappointment and subsequent anger at the range of books generally available led him to found a company – and change the world.

'We believed in the existence in this country of a vast reading public for intelligent books at a low price, and staked everything on it'
Sir Allen Lane, 1902–1970, founder of Penguin Books

The quality paperback had arrived – and not just in bookshops. Lane was adamant that his Penguins should appear in chain stores and tobacconists, and should cost no more than a packet of cigarettes.

Reading habits (and cigarette prices) have changed since 1935, but Penguin still believes in publishing the best books for everybody to enjoy. We still believe that good design costs no more than bad design, and we still believe that quality books published passionately and responsibly make the world a better place.

So wherever you see the little bird – whether it's on a piece of prize-winning literary fiction or a celebrity autobiography, political tour de force or historical masterpiece, a serial-killer thriller, reference book, world classic or a piece of pure escapism – you can bet that it represents the very best that the genre has to offer.

Whatever you like to read – trust Penguin.